UNMANNED

DAN FESPERMAN

CORVUS

First published in the United States in 2014 by Alfred A. Knopf, a division of Random House LLC, New York, and in Canada by Random House of Canada Limited, Toronto, Penguin Random House companies.

Published in trade paperback in Great Britain in 2014 by Corvus, an imprint of Atlantic Books Ltd.

10 9 8 7 6 5 4 3 2 1

A CIP catalogue record for this book is available from the British Library.

Trade paperback ISBN: 978 0 85789 342 0
E-book ISBN: 978 0 85789 343 7

Printed and bound in Great Britain by TJ International Ltd., Padstow, Cornwall.

Corvus
An imprint of Atlantic Books Ltd
Ormond House
26–27 Boswell Street
London
WC1N 3JZ

www.corvus-books.co.uk

For all men and women who serve –
whether with the pen or the sword

UNMANNED

CHAPTER ONE

THIRTY SECONDS TO IMPACT.

On the video display, Captain Darwin Cole watches black cross-hairs quiver on a mud rooftop. He doesn't budge the stick and rudder. No piloting needed now. All that matters is the missile, which Airman Zach Lewis guides by laser from a seat to Cole's immediate right.

Ten seconds pass while Cole wiggles his toes, numb from the air-conditioning. No one speaks into their headsets. Even the chatter screen is calm, as if everyone in their viewing audience was holding his breath. It is 3:50 a.m., and Cole's sense of detachment is so profound that he has to remind himself this is not a game, not a drill. It is death in motion, as real as it gets, and for the moment he is reality's instrument of choice, the one whose name will go on the dotted line now and forevermore. His kill.

A sobering thought anytime, but especially when you're sitting in a trailer on the floor of the Nevada desert, drowsy from breathing air that smells like warm electronics. Cole is a grounded fighter jock, as wingless as a plucked housefly, yet here he is about to zap a roomful of bad guys on the other side of the world. The upholstery creaks as he shifts in his seat. Nearly four hours in the saddle. Numb butt, numb toes, numb brain. Zach begins the countdown in a voice edgy with youthful eagerness.

"Ten, nine, eight, seven, six, five, four . . ."

On the screen, sudden movement.

The door of the house opens and a girl appears at the threshold. On Cole's eighteen-inch monitor she is only three inches high, but the afternoon sunlight paints her vividly—red shawl, white pants, blue scarf. She looks young, ten or eleven, and for a disastrous second she gazes straight at the lens before she darts left, disappearing from the screen just as two small boys run out the door behind her, sandals flopping.

"What the fuck!" Cole says. "Can you—?"

"Too late."

Zach shoves the joystick anyway, but it will take two seconds for his command to reach the missile across seven thousand miles of space and wiring, and by then the whole thing will be over.

Cole is wide awake now, and in the panic flash of this final moment before the explosion he is reminded that all his commands tonight have passed above the schools, rivers, farms, houses, malls, and highways of a sleeping America. Each twitch of his hand flings a signal of war across the nation's night owls as they make love, make a sandwich, make a mess of things, or click the remote. The signal then hurdles the Atlantic, Europe, and the Middle East before finally reaching the bright blue afternoon of eastern Afghanistan, nine hours into the future, where at this moment his MQ-1 Predator drone gazes down from ten thousand feet upon the stony valley and mud homes of Sandar Khosh, a remote village of farmers and herdsmen.

Cole hopes the girl is running fast. The boys, too.

"Zero," Zach announces.

The main screen erupts silently in a boiling cloud of fire and dust.

Cole gawks. The job does not allow him to turn away. No one says a word.

Already he feels the moment taking root in a fallow corner of his imagination—a seed of torment, a nascent preoccupation. From experience he knows that during the next few hours, word of this event will filter from the trailer like a noxious gas. By the end of his shift the chaplain will be waiting, along with the shrink who insists on calling himself a medic, as if they were right there on the battlefield with the dead and wounded. As always, Cole will politely decline their offers of counsel, although doom seems to follow him everywhere lately, closing in like a posse that rides only by night.

For the moment there is pressing business to attend to. He speaks into his headset.

"Zoom out, Zach. Where'd those kids go?"

Cole's mind wants to shriek, but his voice remains calm, a cool Virginia baritone in the reassuring timbre of pilots the world over. It is an intelligent voice of great utility, patient and searching. Only seven hours earlier it was reading a bedtime story to Danny, his youngest, employing the soft cadences needed to make a restless five-year-old fall asleep. Somewhere toward the back of Cole's brain the book's rhythmic words still tumble as gently as socks in a dryer:

In the great green room
There was a telephone
And a red balloon . . .

The lens draws back. The wider view reveals three small bodies just to the left of the ruined house. The worst part is that Cole believes he knows these children. Not personally, but in the way of all watchers who grow familiar with their subjects. He has seen them playing cricket in the rocky field by the old shepherd's house, digging onions with their mother, hauling firewood from the grove of poplars by the stream. He knows these homes and this village, although it is little more than a smudge on their tactical map. How can this be possible? Then he remembers. Zach and he snooped around here only a month ago with their Predator, first by day and then after dark, switching the camera to infrared so they could lurk like an owl in a high pine while, far below, cook fires burned, animals lay down in their stables, and children—*these* children, he is sure of it now—played in the open air of an October evening. And with that memory comes the realization that those three kids should not have been in that house, not the one that Zach and he have been watching so intently for four hours. He is not sure how he knows this. Something he noticed earlier, perhaps, or during tonight's stream of chatter, the ongoing cyber-conversation between all the usual interested parties.

Cole sometimes has to remind himself of what part of the world he's watching. It might be any dry and rocky valley here in Nevada. It could be the vacant lot behind his daughter's school. The picture is unaccompanied by smell or soundtrack. When characters move their mouths, it seems almost possible that they're speaking his language, and when he departs at the end of the day their images accompany him home, a silent movie unspooling in his head during the long drive to the 'burbs of Vegas—shot after shot of hobbled lives in their slow progress, with Cole as the omnipotent eye above; a kindly uncle with a camera, perhaps, making home movies for the world at large. Until you fired a missile.

"We've got activity," Zach says.

On the screen, two adults emerge from a neighboring house, where the door has been blown off its hinges. They stagger as if dazed or wounded, Chaplinesque in their movements.

A fresh line of dialogue pops up on Cole's chat's screen, gold letters on a black background:

(FORT1) Nice shooting. Check the truck.

The truck, a white Toyota, is a key piece of the scene. Its arrival moments earlier was their cue for action, the agreed-upon signal that the targeted bad guys had moved into place and were now present and accounted for.

Fort1 is the mission's J-TAC, or joint terminal attack controller. He has directed much of the action tonight, the stage manager of this drama. Cole knows him only from his call sign, assuming Fort1 is even a he. Cole's CO, Lieutenant Colonel Scott Sturdivant, mentioned Fort1 only cursorily during the pre-mission briefing, a tipoff that Fort1 is from the intelligence side. He could be in Washington—the Pentagon, the CIA, even the White House—or he could be on the ground at the scene, posted on a nearby hill. Theoretically he could even be here at Creech Air Force Base, a bustling little place tucked against barren mountains, a mere forty miles from Vegas. He could be anywhere his laptop will travel, as long as he has the correct passwords and encryptions.

Wherever he is, Fort1 seems unduly satisfied with what they've just accomplished. Cole restrains himself from typing a snarky reply. Everything he says and does tonight will become part of the official record. His "What the fuck!" from a moment ago already weighs against him, so now he must be doubly careful. Swallowing hard, he masters his tone, and then says to Zach without turning his head, "Our J-TAC wants a look at the truck."

Zach eases the camera right. A white shape emerges from the smoke and dust.

"Here it comes," Zach says, a slight tremor in his voice. "I'll zoom it."

Zach Lewis is only twenty-two. A year ago he was an image analyst, examining satellite photos in quiet rooms. After six months here he still seems to be acclimating to this life on a battlefront where the aftermath must always be studied, evaluated, autopsied.

The truck's crumpled roof is visible beneath a collapsed wall. Little else of it is recognizable except some orange markings on the hood and a Toyota logo on the tailgate.

(FORT1) Now the house.

So far, not a peep from Colonel Sturdivant. Cole wonders if Sturdy and Fort1 have ever met, or spoken by phone. The ways of such relationships are a mystery to him. By design, of course. For his protection, they tell him.

Cole relays the request. Zach shifts the camera.

Sometimes Cole is overwhelmed by all there is to keep track of at his cramped workstation. He has two keyboards—one for typing flight commands, the other for chat. Occasionally he reaches for the wrong one. Apart from the screens for video and chat, four others display maps, flight telemetry, and masses of other information that change by the second—readouts for velocity, altitude, fuel levels, oil pressure, wind speed and direction, missile paths, air traffic, weather conditions, terrain. It is a neural nightmare, a bit like trying to conduct five trains at once as they careen toward the same station.

The ruins of the house swing into view.

"Holy shit," Zach mutters.

"Easy as she goes," Cole says, hoping to soothe him.

The damage is complete. Roof collapsed, everything in a heap. The floor plan, roughly thirty by forty feet, was big enough to hold a lot of people, and here and there Cole spots arms and legs, bright clothing, smears of blood, the fleshy blur of faces with fixed and open eyes. In the calamitous jumble it is impossible to say whether the bodies are male or female, adult or child.

From an operational point of view he supposes that the most important consideration, perhaps the only one, is that their HVT—high-value target—is now dead, along with whoever came to meet him. A nasty gathering, according to Colonel Sturdivant at the briefing. A worthy target. But that's what they always said, or why bother to shoot?

(FORT1) Move closer.

What could Fort1 be searching for in this mess? Lewis zooms to the camera's limit, but there is little more to see. Cole finds himself scanning for toys. Seeing none, he is relieved, until he recalls that these children almost never possess anything beyond a slingshot, a cricket bat, and the clothes on their backs. During their earlier reconnaissance of Sandar Khosh his overriding impression was that of a quiet hamlet of farmers, armed only with the occasional stray Kalashnikov, which are as common as pitchforks in these hills. No one even carried a grenade launcher. By local standards the village is as quaintly pacifist as an Amish homestead. Dirt farmers, in other words—their slang for the jetsam of the countryside. Sandar Khosh, the land that both time and terrorism forgot, no American soldiers within miles.

Yet here they were with their Predator for the second time in a month.

Why?

Not his job to ask, nor Sturdy's to answer.

One of Cole's occupational hazards is that he has begun to wonder what it would be like to lead a life in which every action was observed from on high for hours at a time. How would he function under those conditions? What must it be like to become an image lodged in the memory of some secret database, your digital signature retrievable by anyone with the proper clearance? More than ever before in his life, Cole now notices all the cameras that seem to be mounted almost everywhere he looks—at stoplights and in convenience stores, in school hallways and Walmarts, shopping malls and parking decks. At toll plazas, the ATM, the branch library. In elevators and hotel lobbies. There is even one installed in the top rim of the screen of his wife's laptop, right there on the kitchen table, open to the world. Here at Creech, cameras are everywhere. No escape except the desert, and even there you're an easy mark for the satellites, especially at night, when a man shows up as a throb of thermal brightness marooned on an empty cooling sea. Zach told him all about it.

The chat screen blips.

(FORT1) Any squirters?

Escapees, he means. So called because on infrared they display as squibs of light, streaming from the action like raindrops across a windshield. Before Cole can respond, the screen flashes again.

(FORT1) Check out back. Someone couldve gone out window.

Cole counts to three, then relays the order in his steadiest bedtime story voice. . . . *And a quiet old lady who was whispering hush* . . . Zach moves the camera. No one is behind the house, but a pair of legs in green pants protrudes from beneath the fallen rear wall.

(FORT1) Hold her there.

Why does this body interest him more than the others? Is this the HVT? Zach holds the close-up for several seconds, then, on his own initiative, pans back toward the front of the house. Cole braces himself as the three small bodies slide back into view. His eyes are drawn to the girl.

Incredibly, her body twitches.

She is alive.

(FORT1) Check the house again.

Fuck that. Did Cole say that or just think it? Zach stays on the girl. Her right arm is severed and lies a foot from her shoulder, with blood pooling in the gap. She struggles to rise, trying to prop herself on her left elbow. Cole watches but says nothing. Zach is also silent. The girl slowly raises her head.

(FORT1) I said the house.

The man is obsessed, either with death or with rubble. Cole opts for life and continues to ignore him, despite a growing sense that there will be consequences—for himself, for Zach, for everyone involved.

An old woman crosses onto the screen from the left. Reaching the girl she bends stiffly to the ground. Her mouth opens wide, and so does the girl's. Cole's imagination supplies the soundtrack—two voices in awful harmony, a cry that is keening and forlorn, as if someone had torn open a tender and damaged part of the earth and this is the unbearable sound that issues from within.

The time signature at the bottom of the screen flashes to 04:00, but his mind is still lodged at 3:50, the moment of impact.

Cole blinks. In four hours his shift will end. He will exit the trailer, dodge the chaplain, brush aside the shrink. Then he will drive home on an empty highway with only these images for company. After thirty miles or so he will ease into the dense weave of Vegas traffic and take the exit for his suburban refuge. He will click the remote to open the garage and enter the kitchen door with a smile for his wife. Then, while cartoons blare and the neighbor starts his mower, he will eat Saturday pancakes with his children.

No one but him will know what has happened.

(FORT1) *Still need more from the house.*

Don't we all, thinks Cole, mesmerized.

CHAPTER TWO

Fourteen months later

A CONTRAIL OF DUST marked the car's progress, undulating like a brown caterpillar across the wide expanse of the desert floor. The car was a mile away, maybe two, but there was no mistaking its destination. The only person up here was Darwin Cole, seated on a lawn chair at the door of a sagging trailer in the shade of a sandstone bluff.

Now he could hear the laboring engine, the ping of gravel in the wheel wells. Silver Chevy, practically brand-new. Meaning it was either a rental or government issue. The latter prospect made Cole reach inside the trailer for the loaded 12-gauge he always kept handy. He sat back down and laid the shotgun across his lap like a hunter in a blind, waiting. Then he squinted into the morning sky to check the position of the December sun. Almost nine. Early for company. Early for bourbon, too, but he took another warm swallow from his tumbler of Jeremiah Weed.

The Chevy disappeared into a dip, then reemerged before stopping a hundred yards out, engine idling. The chrome grille smiled up at him like a salesman. Somebody wanted something, but Cole wasn't in a giving mood. Nothing to give, anyway, except flies, scorpions, a few cans of stew. Plus all those memories, circling like buzzards.

The engine stopped. Everything was silent as the last of the contrail silted to the ground. A door clicked open and a woman got out from the driver's side. That surprised him. Roughly his age, but not his wife. White blouse, pressed black slacks, brown hair, windblown. She walked around to the passenger side, facing him. Sunglasses hid her eyes, although just as he was thinking that, she took them off.

Her face was vaguely familiar, stirring a warmth that was only skin deep and faded within seconds. He opened his mouth to speak, then thought better of it. Let her go first. Besides, he was unsure of his voice. He'd stopped talking months ago, even to himself, which at the time he'd regarded as a sign of progress.

"You're not going to shoot me, I hope." She smiled uncertainly. Cole cleared his throat and reached back for something extra, not wanting to croak.

"Depends on who you are, what you're here for." The old baritone seemed fine. Nice to know some things were still in working order.

"That would be easier to explain face-to-face. Then, if you still don't like me, I'll go, easy as I came, and nobody will be the wiser. The Air Force doesn't seem to know you're up here, if that's what's bothering you."

"Oh, they know where to find me."

Cole nodded at the sky, as if that explained everything. Instead of answering, she watched, hesitant, while the silence grew between them.

"I've got news of your family," she said. Her voice was a little timid. Cole got the impression she'd been hoping to hold that item in reserve but now had nothing left. "They don't know where you are, either. I wasn't planning on telling them unless you want me to."

Was there a threat in that statement? Or maybe in the one about the Air Force?

"State your business. I'll decide if it's worth your while to come any closer."

"Fort1 is my business. Mine and two other people's. It's kind of a club—people who want to know all about Fort1 and everything he's done. We heard about what happened to you, so we figured you were a prime candidate for membership."

Cole took a deep breath and stood slowly, still holding the shotgun. Then he remembered her face. A journalist. He'd met her during a deployment, years ago. Aviano Air Base, in Italy, a reporter from Boston back during the air war over Kosovo. She'd interviewed him in the canteen while a PAO hovered nearby, making sure Cole didn't misbehave. She'd charmed him for an hour, then written a puff piece that made all the generals happy.

"You're the reporter, aren't you? Keira something?"

"Keira Lyttle, yeah. Thought you'd remember." She sounded relieved, her shoulders relaxing. "So what do you say?"

In the car, something moved behind the smoked glass, which reminded him why he didn't trust reporters. They hid things—motives, opinions, the stuff they already knew. And, like the brass, they were always eager to either piggyback on your success or hang you for your mistakes.

"Who's in the car?"

"A colleague. His name's Steve."

"I don't want him taking my picture. Does he have a camera?"

She shook her head.

"I want to see him."

Lyttle knocked on the passenger window. "Steve, roll it down."

The window hummed open. He was about the same age as Lyttle, hair clipped short. He nodded but didn't speak. No sign of a lens, but that didn't mean anything.

"Steve Merritt," the man offered. "Pleased to meet you."

"He's part of the club," Lyttle said. "He didn't feel comfortable letting me come up here alone."

Cole looked down at the gun in his hands. Feeling a little foolish, he propped it against the trailer. The standoff was making him weary. His inclination was to send them away, tell them to forget it. But the mention of Fort1 had hooked him somewhere deep and painful, so he stepped forward, feeling older than his years and wondering if he was ready for this. Shifting his weight from his right foot to his left, he announced his decision.

"Just you. He stays in the car. No cameras, no tape recorders, and no laptops."

"How 'bout this?"

She held up a small notebook.

"Fine. Long as you got your own pencil."

She held that up, too, then started climbing the rise toward the trailer. A shadow crossed between them and they flinched, but when Cole looked up he saw it was only a hawk hunting its breakfast. His memories began descending from their holding pattern, and in the vanguard as always was the girl in the red shawl, white pants, and blue scarf, with two boys edging forward from the shadows behind her. Just above them was the black vector of the crosshairs, emblazoned on the mud rooftop like the mark of Cain: *Strike here and incur the wrath of God.*

"Ready?" Lyttle asked.

She'd materialized in front of him, notebook in hand.

"Not out here." He nodded at the sky. "They'll see us. Inside."

Lyttle turned and waved toward the car, as if to signal the all-clear, although to Cole her smile looked forced.

"You first," he said, nodding toward the door.

Her lips tightened, but she did as he asked.

They disappeared into the trailer.

CHAPTER THREE

STEVE MERRITT WATCHED the door shut, then checked his phone for a signal. Three bars, even way out here. Barb Holtzman was a late sleeper, but back in Baltimore it would be almost eleven, and she'd want to know. He punched in the number.

"Hi. We made it."

"You found him?"

"Keira's in the house as we speak."

"He has a house?"

"A dump. Trailer in the middle of fucking nowhere. Broken windows, bottles in the yard. If you can call the desert a yard."

"Charming. Is he lucid?"

Lucid. Another of Barb's words that worked better in print than in conversation.

"Hard to say. He looks like a horror show."

Steve glanced at Keira's newspaper clipping on the front seat, with its old photo of a young Darwin Cole. He'd been a fighter pilot then. Flew F-16s, hottest bird in the sky. Switching to drones must have been like going from a Maserati on the Autostrada to a stationary bike in a mildewed basement. The picture showed a clean-shaven young man in a flight suit, clear-eyed and handsome, a soldier who wasn't too macho to smile. Maybe Keira had been the reason. She still tended to have that effect on men of a certain age. Steve wasn't immune, but he kept it under wraps for the sake of teamwork. Most of the time, anyway.

The story itself was a blow job, the kind of piece he would've written only if he wanted something in return. Keira said she'd been angling for better access to Air Force intelligence sources, but it hadn't worked out. Today maybe she'd finally collect on her investment. He hoped so. Come up empty on Cole and they might soon reach a dead end.

"Isn't that how we expected him to look?" Barb said. "His antisocial tendencies are well documented."

The stuff from Cole's court-martial, she meant. A source had sent them a transcript, and the details were ugly. Not long after blowing up a house in the middle of nowhere, Cole and his wingman had nearly botched a recon mission, endangering an American platoon. A day after that, Cole went AWOL in a stolen Cessna Skylane, flying his kids out to Death Valley, where he made camp and proceeded to drink himself into a stupor. A park ranger found them early the next morning, the kids huddled in a tent with Cole outside, passed out in a circle of vomit, flies everywhere. The next night he was caught breaking into his CO's office at Creech Air Force Base at three in the morning, which landed him in the stockade. He was damn lucky to have made it out after six months with a dishonorable discharge and credit for time served. He'd been released nearly eight months ago, and by that time his wife had hired a lawyer and skipped town, taking the children to her parents' place in Saginaw, Michigan.

"It doesn't even look like he's got electricity," Steve said. "He greeted us with a shotgun."

"And you let Keira go in alone?"

"Relax, he left the gun outside. I'm here if anything happens."

"That's not what I meant. What if he opens up, tells her everything? You really think she'll share?"

"We've been over this, Barb. Trust. Remember?"

"Trust but verify. Like those treaties with the Russians."

"You're comparing Keira to the Soviet Union?"

"No, but you're too nice."

"And you're too mean."

"Just saying. Ask Nick Garmon's wife if you don't believe me."

"Love's different."

"Love had nothing to do with it."

"Whatever. We're in this together, and we all agreed."

"*I'm* fully aboard. I just wonder sometimes if Keira is."

"Says the woman who hid her General Dynamics source for a month."

"That's how *he* wanted it."

Steve smiled and lightened his tone. Teamwork had its limits for all three of them.

"Whatever you say, Barb."

They moved to safer topics, discussing what the Ravens had done the day before, the shitty weather in Baltimore, the beauty of the high desert, the weirdness of Vegas. Although maybe they should've stuck to love and trust. Steve would be the first to admit they were a pretty needful bunch when it came to such things. Barb and he were both divorced, and from the way they sometimes argued you might have thought it was from each other. Keira's most recent boyfriend, the aforementioned Nick Garmon, was a married wire service photographer who'd been killed in a plane crash the year before while flying to see Keira in Paris. All three of them were reasonably fit and attractive, but their once powerful newspapers had crumbled around them just as they'd entered that range of ages—thirty-six to thirty-nine—that seemed especially calibrated for loneliness among the unattached. It hardly helped that they were consumed by their work, and by this story in particular, each for his or her own reason.

Barb asked something about "the fauna on an arid landscape." Steve made a crack about snakes and coyotes. Then he looked up in surprise.

"The door's opening. I think she's done."

"That was fast."

"Holy shit."

"What?"

"He's coming with her. And he's got a suitcase."

"I'm sure love has nothing to do with this, either."

"Gotta go, Barb. We'll keep you posted."

Truth was, Keira's appeal had barely registered on Cole. The mere presence of another human being was overwhelming enough, and the moment she entered the trailer he realized what a wreck he must look like. He hadn't shaved or cut his hair in months. The only bathing he did was from a bucket beside the trailer. Water from the cistern, a wafer of soap. A white washcloth hung from a sagebrush like a flag of surrender, dried stiff by the desert sun.

The trailer's linoleum floor was scuffed raw and creaked with every step. Dirty dishes filled the kitchen sink, where a leaky faucet dripped away the supply from the cistern, every drop precious, but still he let it go. At least he'd finally burned the pile of garbage out back. But the coyotes had kept coming, scavenging among the chicken bones and charred cans. Every night he heard their snuffling through the thin walls as he lay in bed beneath wool blankets, oddly comforted by the presence of his only visitors. He was like Romulus and Remus up here, suckled by the wild on a barren hill. Now that he actually had company he was uncertain how to proceed. *God, look at this place.*

"You want coffee? It's instant, but . . ."

She was already shaking her head. Who could blame her? He lit the burner anyway, to show this was nothing out of the ordinary.

Cole hadn't come here intending to drink his life away. Not at first. He came for privacy, seclusion, even introspection. Zach had found the trailer for him, through some dubious connection at his apartment complex. An easy agreement with a single key and no lease. Straight-up cash, good for a year. No utilities to connect, and no official address.

In the beginning Cole lived like a biblical ascetic. Lean and sober, reading paperbacks and basking in the sun. Long walks up into the hills without compass or canteen. Every meal from a can or a box. He drank only water, supplied by the cistern. Metallic on the tongue, but it never made him sick. He slept well, and for ten hours at a stretch.

After a few weeks he began jolting awake in the middle of the night with an eerie exactitude—always at or about 3:50 a.m., the very minute when Zach and he had fired their missile. He began checking his watch as soon as he would sit up in bed, and the news was always the same: 3:50, 3:50, 3:50, with the girl's face flashing in his memory as she ran for her life, the boys right behind her. Three fifty. The hour of death, a wake-up call for the rest of his days. An unbearable prospect.

So one morning he walked out to the highway, hitchhiked to the nearest town, and bought his first case of Jeremiah Weed. Even on his worst days he was not a binge drinker. It was a matter of slow mood maintenance. Sips and occasional swallows, paced evenly throughout the day, an IV drip of erasure and negation designed solely to ease him past his personal witching hour for as many nights running as possible.

And this was where he had landed, less a drunk than an overmedicated hermit, a tipsy slob completely unmanned by his first visitor in ages. How long since anybody had come up here? Zach was the last, and that had been months ago, a courtesy call to make sure Cole hadn't gone and done something tragically stupid.

Cole walked past the small window over the sink and couldn't resist another glance at the morning sky. Bright blue. Empty. Then a distant glint, a fleeting pinprick of reflected sunlight—or maybe he'd imagined it. He popped open the window and tilted his head, listening for the faint lawnmower buzz of the four-stroke engine, the same as in a snowmobile. All he heard was the tinnitus whine that had lately set up shop between his ears.

"You okay?" she asked.

"Yeah. Fine."

Fuck the coffee. He switched off the flame, watched it gutter. Then he turned to face her.

"Have a seat."

At least there was a couch. Nothing fancy, but clean enough. She sat primly at one end in case he wanted to join her, but he pulled up a rickety barstool from the kitchen and sat astride it. He wondered how they'd found him. Through Zach, maybe, the kid talking out of school in one of those pilot bars near Nellis where he liked to pretend he was part of the brethren, just another jock.

But at least Zach had held it together. Only twenty-two then, twenty-three by now, and he rode out the storm. Probably still pulling six-day shifts in the box, switching hours in that Predator rota that seemed especially designed to deprive you of sleep and sanity—midnight to eight a.m. for three weeks running, followed by eight a.m. to four p.m. for three more, and then four p.m. to midnight. Round and round until you'd awaken from some bad dream without knowing if it was night or day. He tried to picture Zach still seated before the godawful pileup of ten-inch screens, scanning for bogeys, squinting in concentration like a kid at a spelling bee.

"How'd you find me?"

"We asked around. Got a lead on an address."

Sounded like she was protecting somebody, which was probably a good thing. Maybe she'd do the same for him. Although the way things were now, only a fool would believe in that brand of protection. Giving your word meant nothing when there were a hundred other ways to find out where you were, what you were doing, who you'd been talking to. Nothing was protected anymore. Nothing was unseen, even out here.

"Didn't know this place had an address. So I guess you know about what happened at Sandar Khosh."

She nodded. "Thirteen people, wasn't it? Mostly women and children?"

The totals still made him wince. He saw the girl as clearly as if she were seated at the other end of the couch, still dressed in the colors of the flag, one arm missing. Today, at least, she was alone. Often she was accompanied by his own kids, Danny and Karen, plus the two boys who had probably been her brothers. A playgroup of the lost and the damned, frolicking in his head.

"That's what the Red Cross said, anyway," she continued. He snapped back to the present.

"I'm sorry. What was that?"

"The Red Cross. They said it was thirteen."

"It was Fort1's call. The mission, the target, all of it. Other than that I can't tell you a hell of a lot."

"You never met him?"

"Doesn't work that way. We almost never see the J-TACs."

"Jay whats?"

"Joint terminal attack controller. They run the show on Predator missions. Usually from a forward position, in theater. But not always. Standard procedure." Listen to him, talking like a pilot again. The buzzwords returned so fast, like lyrics to a familiar old song.

"No one ever mentioned his name?"

"That kind of stuff was above my pay grade. But . . ." He paused, wondering whether to continue.

"But what?"

She slipped out her notebook. It reminded him of their earlier interview, years ago, and the memory almost overwhelmed him. He'd been gung-ho then, full of himself, ready for anything. Good husband, newly married to Carol, no kids yet to take their minds off each other. What was he now? Certainly none of those things. He looked away from the reporter and again glanced at the patch of sky in the kitchen window, seemingly benign. If people only knew.

"I saw something."

"Just now?"

"Back then, in my CO's office. A file."

"About Fort1?"

He nodded.

"Was this during the break-in?"

He turned abruptly.

"You know about the fucking break-in?"

"It was mentioned in some documents. What did you see?"

He eyed her carefully, suspicious now.

"You sure you're not with them?"

"Them?"

"The Air Force. The powers that be. Everybody who fucked me over. This could be a security check, an excuse to haul me in."

"I'm a reporter, that's all."

"For the Boston paper, right?"

"The *Globe*, yes, but not anymore. They closed my bureau, so I took a buyout. I'm freelance now. We all are, so we've pooled our resources. We've got maybe three months before we start running out of money. We're hoping this story will be our ticket."

"Fort1? Is he really that big of a deal?"

"Maybe. We think he's part of something larger. You said you saw a file?"

"That's right."

A pause, then nothing.

Cole was again lost in thought. Something had just occurred to him—a possible means of escape from the trailer, from these surroundings that suddenly felt so desolate. There was a huge, empty landscape waiting beyond the closed door, endlessly patient, one that was swallowing him whole, cell by cell. Unless he took action to stop it, he would soon disappear. A set of dry bones in the sand, left to be scattered by birds and coyotes, then covered forever. At that moment a notion flitted across his brain that startled him as much as the hawk had a few moments ago: If this woman hadn't come here today, or at all, would he ever have seen another living soul? He wasn't sure of the answer, which told him all he needed to know about what to do next.

"Well?" she prompted again.

"I can help you. But I need to know more about what you're doing, what you're after."

Now it was her turn to pause. Cole couldn't blame her. He probably didn't look very reliable.

"Hey," he said, spreading his hands wide. "Who the hell would I tell, way out here? I don't own a car, or even a cell phone. It's a three-mile hike to the nearest pavement."

"Well, for starters, Fort1 is CIA."

"That much I figured."

"We think he's gone off the reservation. Some kind of rogue operation."

"Over there, you mean?"

"We're not sure where he is anymore. The working theory is that he built a private network of his own clients on the government's dime. For his own benefit, of course."

"Clients? Like who?"

"Warlords and tribal chiefs, private security firms wanting a piece of the action. Anybody who'd pay him, including black hats of all kinds. Meaning that every operation he was involved with—Sandar Khosh, for one—is now suspect."

"Then why haven't they shut him down? Brought him in?"

"Maybe they have. At this point all we know for sure is that everybody who's ever been officially involved with him, public or private, at home or abroad, has gone into cleanup mode, trying to erase all his little messes from the record. Which is why we have to move fast. Pick up as many pieces as we can before everything gets swept away."

"Like I said, I can help."

"Great." She flipped a page in her notebook, pencil poised. "No rush. Take all the time you need. If you want, we can take you into town for supplies afterward."

"No. That's not how it's going to work."

"Okay. You tell me, then."

"Where are you based? You said there were three of you?"

"Baltimore for now. Barb's house. She's the third one. She and Steve both worked for *The Sun*."

"Then I'm coming with you. I want to be a part of this."

"Whoa now." Keira held up the notebook like a stop sign. "I can understand why you'd want to get out of here. Maybe we can help you. But you can't be part of this the way we are. The three of us have the same goals, the same way of doing things."

"Fine. Then I'm out. Nice talking to you." He slid off the stool and stepped toward the door.

"Wait." He kept going, turning the doorknob while she talked. "Maybe there's some kind of middle ground. But you can't expect us to just take you on as a partner."

He stopped and pivoted smartly, a parade ground move that, thanks to the bourbon, started to come apart toward the end. He steadied himself and wet his lips to speak.

"Why not? I know these ops firsthand. The procedures, the pecking order, the in-house politics. I've got names and contacts, and, like I said, stuff from the file."

"Just tell me, then. New sources are what we need most right now. Believe me, we'll know what to do with them. You won't."

He shook his head.

"Only if you take me with you. A trial period, one week. If it doesn't work out, then I'm history. I won't even ask for bus fare back."

"You know, you're acting kind of like I did when I wanted all that access at Aviano, just for writing that profile. Your people said no, and they were right. It was their business, their war. Well, this is ours, and you don't know the first thing about the way we do our work."

"It's my war, too. You know that or you wouldn't be here. Thirteen people. Ever make a mistake that big?"

She looked down at her feet.

"Well?"

"No. I haven't."

"One week. That's all I'm asking."

"It's not my decision."

"Then ask your friends. I know names, ops, other guys who got burned the same way. Just think of me as one of those embedded correspondents, tagging along with a combat unit. I play by your rules and do as I'm told."

Cole was speaking with passion now, hands in motion. He felt more clear-headed than he had in ages, although he craved another sip of Jeremiah Weed.

She stood.

"I have to talk to Steve first. Give me five minutes."

"Not till I've packed a bag. I'm not letting you guys ditch me that easy. You sit tight till I'm ready."

He went to the bedroom and started throwing clothes into an Air Force duffel. The whole time he listened carefully for Keira's footsteps, the slam of the door, the spin of car wheels in the dirt. But when he came out into the hall she was still on the couch, notebook in her lap, pencil in hand.

He looked around at the mess. It was time to leave. Time to go to war against somebody other than himself. He hefted the duffel, his stomach fluttering just the way it used to at the beginning of a deployment.

"Ready," he said. "Lead the way."

CHAPTER FOUR

STEVE THOUGHT IT WAS a bad idea from the moment Darwin Cole climbed into the backseat. The smell alone raised doubts. Body odor and bourbon, the trailer's rank essence of stale food, kerosene, and warm vinyl.

He looked over at Keira but she wouldn't meet his gaze. She'd stated her case a few minutes earlier with the windows rolled up, while Cole stood outside, bag in hand, like a kid waiting for a ride to a sleepover.

"You want to bring him *with* us?"

"One week is all he's asking. I think he means well."

"It's not even our house. What's Barb going to say?"

Steve kept his hands on the wheel, ready at a moment's notice to pop the locks, turn the key, and floor it out of there. Thank God the guy was no longer holding a shotgun.

"I'll handle Barb."

"That'll be fun to watch. What makes you think he's worth it?"

"He's connected in a way we'll never be. The operational side. Failed missions, stuff Fort1 was doing on the ground."

"So I take it he doesn't even know Fort1's name?"

"I think he's seen his file." Steve raised his eyebrows. "Or *a* file, anyway. Something the Air Force had."

"And?"

"That's what he's holding back. That's his ticket to Baltimore."

"Not worth it."

"How do you know? I'm not saying it'll be easy, but my vote should count for something."

"Look at him."

"I know. He's definitely still affected by what happened. He's sort of . . ."

"Disturbed? Deranged?"

"No. I don't think so."

"Well he's a drunk, that's for sure. Look at all the empties."

"Yeah, he may have a problem with that."

"Great. So you've invited a drunken, unstable fighter jock back to Baltimore with us."

"He invited himself. I'm just asking you to take him on the first leg."

"You're thinking we can ditch him in Vegas?"

"If we have to. Once we get a better idea of what he knows. Or if, well . . ."

"What?"

"If he becomes a problem first."

"Wonderful. Maybe we can get the cops involved, or the U.S. Air Force. Where do we put him in the meantime?"

"Our hotel room?"

"Jesus, Keira."

"Just for a night."

"He could kill us in our sleep. I mean, *look* at him."

"Careful, he's probably reading our lips."

"Like Hal in *Space Odyssey*."

They laughed uncomfortably and watched him for a second. Same pose as before, still holding his bag and looking up at the sky. He hadn't moved an inch. Steve sighed loudly and finally took his hands off the steering wheel.

"Okay, then. Let him in." She reached for the door handle. "But promise me one thing." She paused, waiting. "If we have to unplug him, you're the one who does it. Deal?"

Keira swallowed hard, then nodded.

"Deal."

No one said much during the ride back to Vegas. Every time Steve stole a glance in the mirror, Cole was searching the sky out his window.

Bat shit crazy, probably. Who wouldn't be after eight months out here all by yourself? But maybe Cole would get sick of this before they did. They'd clean him up, buy him a meal, take him out on the Strip, and after a day or two of fresh sheets and hot food the novelty would wear off. He'd grow weary of their questions, their persistence. Or maybe he'd run out of information, make himself obsolete. He'd realize his mistake and they'd return him to the trailer, or to some friend's house in the 'burbs. Surely somebody from his old circle of friends would take him in, wouldn't they?

Steve felt a stab of pity for the man. He'd been in need himself from time to time since making the decision to go it alone professionally. Self-sufficiency was a risky business nowadays, unless you had money to burn, and neither Cole nor he enjoyed that kind of advantage.

It was only when Cole emerged from the hotel bathroom, showered and shaved, that Steve saw the potential for more complex problems than he'd first bargained for in this arrangement. The man he saw now was a craggier, more intense version of the one from the newspaper photo. He looked refreshed and reconnected, his movements crisp and athletic, the zeal coming off him like steam. It reminded him that Keira's profile—blow job or not—had portrayed Cole as an intelligent and even thoughtful young man. A bit of a thrill seeker, too—a hotrodder and pole vaulter in high school, but with grades good enough for the Air Force Academy. The star of his class at pilot school. High marks from his officers. In action over Kosovo in '99 he'd shot down a Yugoslav MiG, one of the few air-to-air kills by an American pilot since the Korean War. His quotes were long and contemplative, which also said something, unless Keira was the kind of reporter who dressed them up. Steve had heard stories but had never known for sure.

Looking closer, Steve saw that the pilot's pleading blue eyes, lively and eager back then, were now haunted and needful. Just the sort of face that Keira and Barb would want to nurture or, worse, would compete for. Or maybe Steve was feeling jealous, a little threatened, one repressed alpha male detecting the scent and hunger of another. Although if anyone had a right to feel proprietary about their current arrangement it was Steve, who'd put the group together three months earlier. He'd been working the Fort1 story for *Esquire*—on spec, but working it nonetheless—when he started coming across enough of Keira's and Barb's footprints to realize they were stalking the same quarry, albeit from different angles. So he'd called a summit.

As luck would have it, both women had just been offered buyouts by newspapers desperate to slash payrolls. Steve knew all about the joys and limitations of a buyout. He had taken one from *The Sun* in an earlier round of cuts two years ago. That money was long gone, and carving out a living as a freelancer hadn't been easy. Stories like this one were especially trying, because they took time to develop.

They compared notes, grudgingly at first, and soon discovered that between them they already had the basis for a story that, with a little care and watering, might grow into something altogether more satisfying and lucrative. If they were lucky they might even land a book deal.

They decided to move in together to economize. From the beginning Steve had been the resident counselor and peacemaker, the soother of bruised egos, and from that perspective he sensed that Darwin Cole would be a risky ingredient to pour into their sometimes volatile mix.

"Where's Keira?" Cole asked, looking around the room. He was wrapped in a towel.

"Down at the front desk, getting another room."

"You guys are sharing?" He scanned the two double beds as if trying to figure out which ones had been slept in the night before.

"We *were* sharing, but not like you think. You're my roomie now. For tonight, anyway."

"What are the sleeping arrangements in Baltimore?"

Christ, this guy really believed he was in it for the long haul.

"We'll figure that out later. But it's strictly platonic. You're not joining some sort of hippie commune."

"That wasn't what I meant."

Cole threw on a pair of jeans and was buttoning up a flannel shirt when the door opened with a click and in walked Keira.

"They put me next door." She looked at Cole and stopped short. "Wow. A new man."

Steve watched her carefully, then took charge.

"It's almost lunchtime," he said. "Should we talk or eat?"

Keira looked to Cole for his preference.

"Whatever you two want. Some food might be good."

"Room service okay?" Steve asked. "That way we can get started while we wait."

"Oh, c'mon, Steve. He needs a real meal, a chance to stretch his legs."

Coddling him, although Steve had already been thinking the same thing. He smiled ruefully and looked at the pilot.

"What do you say, then, Captain? Looks like you're the boss on this one."

"Sure. Going out's fine. Whatever you guys want."

Cole went to fetch a clean pair of socks from his duffel by the window. Then, just as he'd done in the car, he looked up at the sky, long and hard, as if he were searching for something. Steve couldn't let it go a moment longer.

"See anything?"

"No. Doesn't mean nothing's there."

"What is it you're looking for?" Keira frowned, but Steve kept going. "Not Predators, I hope."

"You'd be surprised what they do with those things. What they look at."

"The ones flying out of Creech are just for training, right? The only real action is in the trailers, where they pilot the ones overseas."

"Even the training flights have to look at something."

"Nothing but mountains and desert out that way. Plus the old test range, farther west."

"The old nuke site, yeah. Bunch of A-bomb craters from the fifties and sixties. All the new stuff's underground, but, still, they don't like us poking around."

"Sounds like Area Fifty-One."

"Stop it, Steve." Keira shook her head.

"No, I want to hear. What do they look at, then?"

"Some other time," Cole said it abruptly, as if he'd realized how he was sounding. Or maybe he was trying to head off an argument. The silence afterward was strained until Keira changed the subject.

"How'd you end up flying Predators? You volunteer?"

"Nobody volunteers for Preds. Except those video gamers the Air Force is signing up."

"Video gamers? Really?"

Cole shrugged.

"Might as well, since they grew up with a joystick in their hands."

"So they shanghaied you?" Steve asked.

Cole nodded.

"Christmas weekend 2008. I'm still at Aviano. My CO calls me in, says, 'Monkey, I got a shitty deal for you.'"

"Monkey?"

"My radio call sign. Monkey Man. 'Cause of my first name, the whole Darwin thing. He says, 'There's this new program out in Nevada threatening this entire unit, and you're victim one.' I asked if he meant that Xbox shit, the fucking drones. Yep, that was it."

"Bad, huh?"

"You gotta realize, Vipers were the top of the food chain. Slide into the cockpit and you're wired in straight to God, every system integrated. Tilt your helmet to aim a missile, that kind of thing. You can practically think a thought and make it happen . . ." His voice trailed off. "When you arrive at Creech they take you inside a GCS for a Predator and you want to throw up."

"GCS?"

"Ground control station. Some geek's idea of a cockpit. Video monitors stacked up like junked TVs in the window of a pawnshop. Shit piled on shit. The stick and rudder are an afterthought."

"Isn't somebody else in there with you?" Keira said. "A copilot or something?"

"Your sensor sits to your right. Same array, pretty much. But, hell, you're glad for the company and he does half the scut work—operating the camera, handling the maps, keeping the audience happy."

"Audience? Sounds crowded in there."

"Not in the trailer. They're watching on their own screens, from a bunch of different places."

"Like the J-TAC?" Keira offered.

"Plus your CO, or whoever the MIC happens to be. Sorry. Mission intelligence coordinator. Then there's an image analyst, at Langley AFB in Virginia, plus some desk jockey at Al Udeid."

"Al Udeid in *Qatar*?" Steve asked.

Cole nodded. Keira had started taking notes, but the pilot didn't seem to mind.

"The Combined Air and Space Ops Center," Cole said. "Went there once for a dog and pony show. Big-ass warehouse. Industrial strength air conditioners going full blast. Hundreds of people at monitors, with headsets on. When both wars were going, everything that was airborne was displayed up on wall-sized maps of Iraq and Afghanistan, like movie screens. The Preds showed up as little blue dots, barely moving. Slowest damn dots on the board."

"So, at least four people are looking over your shoulder?" Keira asked.

"And all of them think they know better than you what to do next. You have to just sit and take it, when what you really want is to say, 'Hey, I know this is neat and new to you, but I'm not just driving a bus to take pictures for you guys on the ground.'"

"What a cluster fuck," Steve said.

"Sometimes."

"How much can you see from that high up?" Keira asked. "Somebody told me once you can even recognize faces."

That stopped him for a second. He turned away toward the window.

"Not really. But if it's some village you've been to before, you do start to recognize people. From the way they move, the clothes they wear, the things they carry. You end up feeling almost . . . like you know them."

"That's kind of horrible."

"It can be. Especially when you start to like it. Not really *like* it, I mean, but, I dunno, it gets into your head. You hate it one minute, get off on it the next. It's their little world, but in some ways you know more about it than they do. If bogeys are over the next hill coming for 'em, you know about it hours before they do."

Keira, who couldn't see his expression, seemed eager for more, but Steve was troubled by Cole's fixed stare. He could easily picture Cole the way he must have looked the day of the disaster at Sandar Khosh, surveying the wreckage on video screens while everyone told him what to do next. Drone pilots were often burnouts, he knew that as well, from a Pentagon study he'd sourced on the Internet. Thirty percent or something, with almost a fifth suffering from clinical depression. And now, after just a few minutes of pointed conversation, Cole looked like he was at the end of his rope, cornered and hopeless. They were opening up this poor guy like a lab animal. When Keira started to ask another question, Steve cut her off.

"Hey, he must be getting hungry. I know I am. Why don't we go?"

"I'm fine with room service," Cole said. His voice was drained of energy.

"No, Keira's right. Let's get some air. Take in the freak show out on the Strip."

"One other thing," Cole said, turning back toward Keira. "You said you had news of my family."

She smiled uncomfortably. "What is it you want to know?"

"Anything, really. I haven't exactly been in touch. Not for a while."

"Well, let's see. There's your boy."

"Danny."

"Yeah, Danny. He's eight now, going to a private school in Saginaw. Third grade. Seems to be doing great."

"Private school? Carol's dad must be paying. How's Karen? She'd be twelve. Probably boy crazy by now. Did you see them?"

"No. But I, uh, went up there. Asked around. At first we thought that, well . . ."

"That *I* might be up there?"

"Yeah."

Cole snorted.

"Carol would call the cops if I ever showed my face. Besides. The Air Force, well . . ."

"What?" Steve asked.

"I'm supposed to stay close to home, meaning right around Creech. Keep them apprised of my whereabouts." He nodded toward a sheaf of folded printouts on the bedside table, page after page, with lots of lines of print blacked out. "Part of my plea agreement. It's all in there. I see you've got the transcript from my court-martial. They told me it was going to be sealed."

"It was," Steve said. Then he shrugged, as if to apologize. "Sources. Don't worry, we won't spread it around."

"Most of it's bullshit. The Cessna wasn't stolen. The owner's another pilot, a friend of mine. We had an understanding. I could use it on weekends and pay him later. And the whole Death Valley thing." He shook his head. "They made it sound like I kidnapped my kids and dumped them in the wild. It was a trip we'd made before, the whole family. They were all for it. There's a landing strip there, a Park Service campground with picnic tables and everything. They were loving it. I just had a little too much to drink after they went to bed. Carol overreacted."

Steve and Keira said nothing.

Cole couldn't blame them. Even if he was right, what more was there to say? Besides, Carol *hadn't* overreacted. Cole had shut her out during those final weeks together. He'd never even asked for help as he drifted beyond reach. And she had tried. Tried hard. It was like he was locked inside a cockpit, with Carol banging on the glass. Strapped in for the duration, mute and unreachable, while telling himself the isolation was for security reasons. *Can't talk about our missions, it's classified. You wouldn't understand anyway.*

And maybe she wouldn't have, but he'd never given her the chance, and now he missed her, the kids too. During his desert exile the idea of his family had seemed as remote as the moon. A blank landscape in a blank mind. Now, stirred to life by this conversation, Carol and the kids were a ready presence, their voices alive in his mind. Danny with his picture books, Karen with her soccer ball, Cole slicing a banana onto their Cheerios at the breakfast table while Carol cooked him an egg. A household at peace.

He looked up to see Steve and Keira staring at him. He blushed and took a deep breath.

"Okay, then." he said. "Let's go eat."

Keira headed for the door.

Cole took a last glance out the window, craning his neck to look higher into the empty sky. When he turned he saw Steve watching closely. *The nutty pilot, seeing things in the sky*—that's what they were probably thinking. Fine. Let them. Three years ago he probably would've felt the same. But he'd learned. They would, too.

They filed out of the room without a word.

CHAPTER FIVE

THREE YEARS AGO, before Cole knew the truth of things, he was living in the 'burbs of Vegas, out in Summerlin, believing that all was well, all was secure. Freshly arrived from overseas, he had just begun learning to fly Predators out at Creech. Karen was in grade school, Danny in diapers. Compared to a deployment it was a soft life, although he'd never tried to hide his disappointment. He sulked through the first weeks of classroom work, and in the mock-up trailers where they piloted simulators he was listless, robotic. He never joined the others afterward for a beer.

After a month of this behavior the captain running the show took Cole aside for a chat. His name was Lodge, a relaxed fellow who grinned in dopey gratitude whenever a student contributed. Cole thought of him as Mister Rogers in a flight suit.

"Hey, Captain Cole. Got a second?"

Cole shrugged gloomily.

"Great. Come on back."

They walked to a green cubicle where Lodge shut the door and pulled up a chair.

"Well, Captain Cole, I've tried my damnedest. But you're just not a happy camper."

"I guess." He folded his arms.

"What do you suggest we do about that?"

"You offering an exit strategy?"

"Oh, goodness no!" Lodge's grin widened. "And frankly the reason why is that you are *exactly* the kind of soldier we need most in this program. Top pilot. High marks all around." Lodge moved his hands as if checking items off a list. "Smart. Attentive. Good attitude. Well, until you got here, anyway. Most important of all, you're a natural leader. Your colleagues take cues from you, Cole. Always have, I'll bet. You just never had a chance to show it up there alone in your Viper. And, well, it doesn't exactly hurt that you're a family man, someone who might value the virtues of settling down for a while. The beauty of this program is that you can be in the thick of the action without the hassles of a deployment."

"I'm not sure I'd call this 'action.'"

"That's because you aren't yet sold on the value, the *power* even, of what a UAV can accomplish with the right man at the controls. That's why you need to see this." He picked up a remote control for a DVD player, which sat atop a television in the corner. The recording must have been ready to roll, because a picture appeared instantly.

Great, Cole thought. Yet another orientation session. He'd rather suffer through an Amway presentation—Carol and he had already attended two, both hosted by cash-strapped neighbors facing foreclosure—than endure another stilted Air Force video, leaden with acronyms and fake team spirit.

But he could already see that this was something else. It was an aerial shot with a time signature from the day before. Cole recognized the main gate at Creech.

"We shot this around fourteen hundred hours yesterday, just as you guys were getting out of class. The cam is on a Predator, of course. Flew it myself. Your other instructor, Captain Gravely, was the sensor. I guess it occurred to both of us as we watched you frown and shake your head these last three weeks—and let me tell you, that kind of behavior is contagious—that maybe we'd short-changed you guys in conveying, well, exactly how *effective* these things can be. And in ways you'd never imagine."

Lodge was still grinning amiably, but his eyes gleamed with the promise of something harder.

"We're at about 12,000 feet. Pretty normal resolution, as you can see. So I had Gravely zoom her down a bit. Here we go."

There was Cole, walking toward his car.

"Nice trick."

Hardly surprising, although he couldn't deny it was a little unsettling, if only because he hadn't heard the Predator or even known it was up there. Most of the training flights stayed at fairly low altitudes, buzzing like weed whackers. His recollection of the sky from the day before was of a clear and silent blue, empty and unthreatening.

The camera followed his car's progress out the main gate and onto Highway 95. Cole was a little annoyed, wondering how long this object lesson would last.

"I can see you're restless, so we'll skip ahead."

They jumped forward twenty minutes, toward the halfway mark of the drive home. In those first weeks at Creech the family had lived in an apartment complex only a few blocks from where they eventually bought a house. The camera showed Cole's car parked on the shoulder of an empty Highway 95. The door was open and Cole was walking away from the road.

"Forgot to take a leak at the base, huh?"

The shot zoomed closer, and even though Cole had shielded himself from the road by standing behind a shoulder-high sagebrush, you could see his stream sparkle in the sunlight. This was stupid, juvenile. The Cole on the screen yawned. So did the one in the room.

"See what I mean?" Lodge said. "Contagious behavior."

In watching himself he remembered exactly what he'd been thinking at the moment, and the memory worried him. He'd been running well ahead of schedule, with nearly half an hour to kill before picking up Karen from school. So he had decided then and there to drop by an old jock bar near Nellis AFB in Vegas, where he'd once been based long ago, a place where fighter pilots still ruled the flight line. Surely the Predator hadn't followed him all the way there? Doing so would have violated all kinds of rules.

"We'll skip ahead again."

Lodge's voice had an edge now. On the screen, there was his car parked outside the Kicking Mule, and there was Cole coming out the door of the bar. You could tell right away that his walk was different. Part swagger, part bourbon. For old time's sake he had ordered a shot of Jeremiah Weed, the hundred-proof bourbon liqueur favored in pilot hangouts the world over. He had intended to drink only one, but just as he sat down some drunken jocks from Nellis had begun singing "The Predator Eulogy," a ditty about a drone that went haywire and had to be shot down. It was an anthem of derision, brutal but bearable—at least until the last verse, which had punched him in the gut:

They shot down the Predator
I wonder how that feels
For that drone operator
Who lost his set of wheels
It must feel so defenseless
Like clubbing baby seals

After that he needed two more shots, and now Lodge and he were watching the predictable results. Lodge grinned in his dopy Mister Rogers way. Can you say "inebriated"? Cole wanted to punch him.

"Don't worry, Captain. I'm not here to make a citation. That's the Highway Patrol's job. But by being there twenty-six minutes I figure you had time for, what, maybe three, four shots of the hard stuff? And that paper bag under your arm. Took the rest of the bottle home, didn't you? Good old Weed."

They watched him drive toward Karen's school, not a pretty sight. He supposed next Lodge would try to make him feel like a bad dad. It was pissing him off.

"Isn't this breaking about a thousand rules?" Cole said. "You must've been way out into civilian air space."

"This show is strictly between you and me, soldier. Besides, we're not even to the good part."

Lodge skipped ahead six minutes, not nearly long enough for Cole to have reached Karen's school. Yet, there was the school, flag flying out front. How had they known where he was heading? Cole was liking this less every second. No kids were yet emerging from the doors. The time signature told him it was a minute before the final bell, and he remembered having been a good seven or eight minutes late.

"How'd you know that I was—?"

"Keep watching, soldier!" Lodge's tone was angry. "You're seeing this country's newest and greatest weapon in the Global War on Terror, working hand in glove with good intelligence from an experienced forward operator, so you'd better pay attention."

Forward operator? Had someone been posted at the school? Exactly how had they learned so much about his daily routines? Kids began streaming from the school. Cole spotted Karen right away from the clothes she wore and the distinctive red twisty in her hair, plus the little skip in her walk. Something cold gripped his stomach as the camera followed her progress. How had the sensor known who to look for?

"I've seen enough," Cole said.

Lodge didn't answer. The camera followed Karen to the curb. She looked up the street in both directions while other kids jostled past her on their way to cars with moms positioned by the doors. Hadn't *any* of them noticed a lurking observer, or the buzz of a funny-looking plane high overhead? Look at them, oblivious.

A few more agonizing minutes passed until Cole's car weaved into view. To his shock, you could easily sense the signs of disapproval in the body language of the remaining moms. They folded their arms as he walked past after parking crookedly up the street. He must have smelled like a distillery, and he was still carrying the paper bag by the neck of the bottle. Lodge froze the shot just as his mouth opened to call out to Karen.

"There's more if you want to keep skipping ahead. Of course when the day got on toward dusk we switched to infrared. If I was you, I'd think about closing those curtains on the sliding glass doors next time you're feeling frisky."

Cole actually blushed, even as he told himself that what he was thinking wasn't possible. Carol had been angry with him when he got home, smelling the bourbon and laying into him about driving drunk. They'd sent Karen and Danny out to play with the neighbor's kids, and proceeded to have a full-blown shouting match, which ended with hugs, a few awkward laughs and a vigorous round of makeup sex, so spontaneous that they had done it right there on the family room couch, which faced out toward the sliding glass doors. The wooden back fence was enough to prevent any curious neighbors from watching. But from a vantage point high in the sky, well . . .

Lodge was grinning, hand poised on the remote. If they'd been in a bar, Cole would have busted him up, a fist to the chin—jock tactics, officially frowned upon but unofficially tolerated, at least in some places he'd served. But this was a different Air Force out here at Creech, so he swallowed hard and kept his seat. As he mastered his anger another emotion rose up to replace it—a grudging respect. Not for this smug asshole Lodge, but for that damned thing up in the sky, trained to his every move, spotting things that even a nosy neighbor would miss. He would never view the sky the same way again.

Much later, after his hitch in the stockade, he'd moved to the trailer, taking it mostly because the price was right and he didn't want neighbors. Under the terms of his release he was supposed to keep the Air Force posted on his movements, and for three weeks running an official car had driven out to check on him. The first time the car came all the way up to his front door. An MP with a sidearm hopped out for a quick look without saying a word. A power play. By the second week the MP was stopping a half mile out, rolling down a window to check with a pair of binoculars, the lenses gleaming in the sun. Then the visits stopped.

Cole first noticed a Predator a few days later, first from the faint buzzing which never would have been audible over the background hubbub of a city or even a suburb. He learned to look for the telltale glint as the Predator circled, and from then on he noticed at least one every week—or thought he did. With all the drinking, Cole would be the first to admit that his powers of observation hadn't exactly been razor sharp.

Annoyed, he made it a point to stay inside the trailer whenever he heard one, although once he snapped and pulled his trousers down to his knees, bending over to moon the bastards while shouting curses at the sky. Then, like pretty much everything in life once it's repeated enough, he got used to the damn things and went about his business as if nothing was out of the ordinary. Although he never stopped looking.

So, yes, go ahead and laugh, he thought, watching the two reporters as they waded through the noise and jumble of the casino on the hotel's ground floor. They were clueless about what was possible, or about how the so-called rules no longer applied. But they would learn soon enough.

CHAPTER SIX

"SO TELL ME SOMETHING," Cole said.

He ate as he spoke, wiping the plate clean with the last shred of pancake from their moo shu pork. They'd picked a Chinese place, not a takeout but a real restaurant with a hostess, a wine list, and white tablecloths. A little touch of civilization that Steve hoped would continue Cole's process of normalization. Judging by the man's appetite, it seemed to be working.

"Tell you what?" Keira asked.

"Why Baltimore? I mean, I know that's where your friend lives. Steve, too. But is there some other reason you guys decided to bunk there, maybe even having to do with the story?"

Steve was impressed, although he was still a little worried about the double shot of Jack Daniels that Cole had downed with his meal.

"Go ahead," he said to Keira. "You tell him."

"There's a security company based out in Baltimore County. Intel-Pro. One of those Blackwater-type outfits. Steve and I were both working stories related to them, independent of each other, when we started picking up traces of Fort1's misadventures. He's blown some of their ops, too."

"Burned a few of their field men," Steve added.

"Or so they say."

"I've pretty much verified it."

"Barb was working another angle, but she ended up on some of the same trails, and we all kind of bumped into each other through IntelPro. And, well, since they're right in Steve and Barb's backyard, it seemed like the best place to hole up, at least for a while. Not that we've been able to take the IntelPro connection much further."

"Okay." Cole nodded. "IntelPro. That makes sense. What about the ground rules?"

"That's Barb's department," Steve said. "Her house, her rules."

"Not sleeping arrangements. Rules of the road, expenses, that kind of thing. I'm done with charge cards, too easy to track. Cash only. And before I travel I'll need a fake ID, something to keep the Air Force off my trail. You can buy 'em in the pawn district out by Nellis for about a hundred fifty. You guys are probably flying, but I'll go by bus. Airports are just about the worst possible places for showing up on security cams."

Already setting down rules before he even knew Barb's address. The man certainly had his nerve. And, frankly, some of the rules were pretty wacky. A bus? To Baltimore? More evidence of paranoia.

"You sound like you've been reading too many spy novels," Steve said.

"This is stuff from training."

"The Air Force teaches countersurveillance techniques?"

"Sort of. Infowar training, part of some war gaming we did at Nellis."

"I thought war games were for fake combat," Keira said.

"That's the fun part. We'd go up against 'aggressor' units that flew MiGs, or other foreign birds. But they do a lot of situational stuff on the ground. Testing your security awareness, seeing how leaky everybody was."

"And?"

"We were like a beer can with a hole in the bottom."

"Loose lips sink *air*ships?"

"Loose lips weren't the problem. A lot of it was paper stuff—credit card receipts, postcards home, or dumb shit people did online. Turned out there was a special unit dogging us the whole time, hacking our PC accounts, even dumpster diving outside our barracks, the PX, everywhere we went. On our last day they ambushed us with the results. Some obnoxious techie laid out everything they'd learned, all our fuck-ups. Pretty mind-blowing. Then he tipped us on how to avoid it next time, stuff we could use in the field to disguise our movements, our intentions. So those are my conditions: cash only, fake ID, a bus ticket to Baltimore."

"You seem to be forgetting the price of admission. Keira said you got a look at a file?"

"I did. But if I tell you now what I saw, what's to stop you from ditching me?"

Steve looked to Keira for help.

"Our word of honor?" she said.

Cole snorted. Steve tried again.

"Give us nothing and we'll ditch you for sure. Right now all we have is *your* word of honor that you've got anything we can use."

"Fine. Then leave without me. I'll hitch back to the trailer."

Steve looked again at Keira, who touched Cole's hand so quickly that he almost missed it.

"Look," she said, "this isn't easy for us, either. We're all in favor of making you feel safe and secure, and we'll buy you an ID if you're strapped for cash. But you have to give us some kind of an idea of whether you're worth the investment. We've got sources to protect, proprietary information. Things that took us months to find out. And we're not used to letting just anybody into the club, especially people we don't know."

"Okay. I get that. Where would you like me to start?"

"How about the op at Sandar Khosh?" Steve said. "Who were you really looking for that day? What was your objective?"

Cole took the request like a blow, then stared down at his empty plate.

Keira threw Steve a look, like he'd moved in the wrong direction. She again touched Cole's hand, more noticeably this time.

"Only if you don't mind talking about it," she said.

Steve held his tongue and watched them. This was Keira's strength, getting people to talk when they didn't want to, drawing information out of them like poison. Afterward you could almost see the relief in their faces, as if she'd done them a favor. And maybe she had.

"It was a hit job, plain and simple," Cole said. "One HVT and his entourage."

"High-value target?"

"Yeah. But I don't have a name. They never tell us, and we didn't hear it later."

"Meaning you missed him?"

"Probably. The trigger cue for the mission was a white Toyota truck with orange markings on the hood. It was supposed to be bringing the HVT to some kind of meeting. All the other bad dudes were supposedly already inside, waiting."

"Why not just shoot the truck?"

"We discussed that. Vehicles are a more reliable kill as long as you can land the dart right on the roof. It's laser-guided, so as long as you keep the crosshairs in the right place you're golden. But it can get tricky. From ten thousand feet a Hellfire takes about a minute to reach the target. At the last second the vehicle might move behind a building, or into the trees. A flock of sheep might come along, or a bunch of kids. Then what? So we decided to stake out the house, wait for the truck, get 'em all."

"What went wrong?"

"You tell me. Three seconds before impact, three kids come running out the front door. The first was a girl, same age as my daughter. I still dream about her."

"Jesus," Steve said.

Keira put her hand on Cole's forearm and left it there. "How did Fort1 react?"

"Hard to say. We were only in contact by chat. But he kept asking to see the wreckage."

"Looking for the HVT, maybe?" Steve asked. "For a positive ID?"

"Maybe. There was a body toward the back that he seemed interested in, but mostly he wanted to scan the rubble, the ruins. We must have spent half an hour going back and forth. Not a pretty sight, let me tell you."

Then a long pause before Steve broke the silence.

"Well, that's good stuff. But what can you give us from the file?"

"How 'bout a name? Fort1's."

Steve sat up straighter.

"You saw it? You saw his *name*?"

"Not just saw it. Recognized it. I can even describe him for you. I'd helped train him, earlier that year."

Blood rushed to the end of Steve's fingertips, the same way it did whenever he was about to do something momentous.

"Wade Castle," Cole said. "An Agency guy."

"And you *trained* him?"

"On Predator stuff. He came to Creech with two other CIA guys. They were setting up their own drone program out of some base across the Pak border, down in Baluchistan. I was supposed to show them the ropes, let them sit in on a few of our missions."

"And they told you their names?" Steve asked.

"No. They didn't even say they were CIA. OGA was all we knew— other government agency—not that everybody didn't know what that meant. The names thing was a fuckup. The asshole in charge, a guy named Lodge, gave them a welcoming gift of Air Force flight suits. Somehow he'd gotten a look at the paperwork, which was a screwup right there, way above his clearance, and he had the suits personalized with their last names printed on the ID patch. I was there when he presented them. They took the things out of the box, laughed kind of nervous and folded everything back up as fast as they could, but everybody saw the names. All three of them. Castle, Bickell, Orlinksy. Later we went strictly by first names, and his was Wade. Then when I saw the file and the same name popped up, everything clicked. It was him."

"Does the Air Force know you saw it?"

Cole shook his head, then glanced around to make sure no one was eavesdropping.

"I didn't even tell my sensor, Zach. My attorney, either. Didn't want to give them any excuse to stick me in some hole in the ground for the rest of my life. You're the only ones I've told."

"What else did you see?"

"Sorry. That was my admission ticket. The rest comes later."

Steve looked at Keira, who nodded. Cole was in, at least for now.

"We better get over to the pawn district, start working on that fake ID," Steve said. "Keira and I are flying back tomorrow. The sooner we get you on a bus, the better."

But Keira had a question first.

"Those other two agency guys you trained, Bickell and Orlinsky—you remember their first names?"

"Sure. Owen Bickell, Wally Orlinsky."

She wrote them down and looked at Steve.

"You're thinking they might be sources?" he asked.

"If we can find 'em. It's doubtful they'd talk."

"Unless . . ." Cole said. "Bickell was near retirement age. He said something once about quitting to go fishing. He'd brought a fly rod and was hoping to get over to Utah, to fish the Sevier River. Said something about a summer place of his, out on some lake back east."

"Where?" Keira asked.

"New Hampshire, I think."

"Well, if he *is* retired . . ." Steve said.

"Barb's ex-Agency source?"

"Yeah. I think he could find us an address."

Steve got out his cell phone and punched in a text.

"I'm betting we'll have an address quicker than that fake ID. And if that happens, maybe you and I can stop off to see him on the way to Baltimore."

"You want *me* to approach him?" Cole asked.

"He knows you, maybe even trusts you. Better than having some scribbler show up on his doorstep. He'd tell us to fuck off. Don't worry, I'll draw up a list of questions. All you'll have to do is ask 'em."

Cole nodded uncertainly, then looked at Keira, as if seeking verification.

"Look at it this way," Steve said. "You're getting a week's room and board, minimum, plus travel expenses. This way you can start earning your keep, right?"

"I guess so."

Steve slapped a wad of cash atop the check, then pushed back his chair.

"Time to get moving."

Everybody stood and turned to go.

"Wait," Keira said. "He never opened his fortune."

Steve rolled his eyes, but waited. When Cole hesitated, Keira went back to the table for the cookie. She tore open the plastic, snapped the cookie in half, and fished out the white slip of paper. Then she frowned and dropped it back onto the table.

"Well?" Steve asked.

"You were right. Stupid idea."

Cole went over and snatched up the sliver of paper. He scanned it and nodded grimly, as though he'd expected nothing less. Then he read the message aloud: *"Important people follow your progress with interest."*

Steve again rolled his eyes. They left without another word.

Four hours later Cole boarded a bus with his fake Nevada driver's license and a pocketful of cash. Keira and Steve waved like a mom and dad sending their son off to college, then watched until the bus disappeared around a turn.

"Think we'll see him again?" Keira asked.

"Do we really want to?"

"I do. I like his vibe."

"His *vibe*?"

She nodded. "He'll be good for Barb. For me, too, maybe. That house needs some balance."

Steve figured she was referring to gender until she elaborated further.

"It'll be good for all of us. He comes from a different narrative, a fresh point of view. He's part of the system we're always butting heads with, the whole warrior mentality."

"Yeah, and look what it did for him."

"So maybe we'll convert him, turn him into an anarchist." She smiled, then softly punched Steve on the shoulder to make him smile back.

It would definitely be interesting, Steve supposed, the four of them holed up together in a house built for two. Like an experiment in social dynamics, or, if things went wrong, one of those reality TV shows where it was every man for himself.

"C'mon," he said. "We've got planes to catch."

CHAPTER SEVEN

OWEN BICKELL PULLED BACK the curtain and watched the visitor approach through the trees. Even if he hadn't recognized the face, the walk would have told him it was a pilot. More swagger than stroll, like they were God's gift to the heavens. Bickell had seen them strut their stuff on landing strips from Vietnam to Iraq, a high priesthood of arrogance and physicality. And now the defrocked Captain Cole of Nevada was heading up his gravel driveway as assertively as a cop serving a warrant.

Bickell's security alarm had signaled the arrival. Cole must have tripped the motion sensor at the head of the drive. If he'd parked a car out there, Bickell would be able to get a tag number from the digitally archived images captured by the surveillance camera that he'd installed in a tall pine. Maybe Cole was smarter than that, but Bickell had his doubts. He'd given a great deal of thought to the various approaches an intruder might take to reach his house, and he'd concluded that the best one involved beaching a boat at the end of the peninsula and working your way down the shoreline on foot. But only someone with good tradecraft would try that. Cole looked like an amateur.

Whatever the case, score one for Bickell's former employers, who had predicted this event only two days earlier. *Expect a possible visitation from out of the blue*, they said, *by that pilot who trained you at Creech. He'll have lots of questions. Stall him, stonewall him, feed him a line if you want. But follow our instructions to the letter.*

The glitch was that Bickell didn't know what to make of his old employers anymore. They were barely on speaking terms. Not at all like the mutual trust that prevailed when he joined the Agency, way back in '68. Arriving in Saigon for his first posting only a month after the Tet offensive, Bickell believed everything the old hands told him down at the Duc Hotel, and the wartime routines suited him. Poker and bourbon after dark, maybe a hooker and a toke at bedtime, then a Bloody Mary with your scrambled eggs. Everyone talked a good game, same as now, but it turned out that none of them knew shit, and he had never forgotten the lesson.

In those days management had been a cabal of aging Ivy Leaguers. Tweeds and weekend duck hunts. Pack-a-day smokers who drank themselves silly at each other's town houses in Georgetown—not that Bickell was ever invited. Card-carrying liberals, to hear the way they trashed the ghost of Joe McCarthy. Yet whenever they cast their eyes abroad, they, too, saw a commie behind every bush. And why not? Back then, the enemy *was* everywhere.

Later Bickell was posted to other wars, other countries. His operations often stalled, throttled by Agency lawyers or, later, by congressional busybodies, nobody wanting another Vietnam, or another leak in the press. The bureaucratic death spiral continued right up to 9/11, when suddenly it was back to bags of cash and anything goes, except by then the ideology of the crowd upstairs had shifted rightward. No longer so big on tweeds or Ivies, but the same preponderance as ever of blowhards and careerist know-it-alls.

These were the people Bickell had eventually run afoul of in a far corner of Pakistan, his final posting. He went to help run the Agency's new Predator program, three of its very own birds parked at the Shamsi airstrip, deep in the desert of Baluchistan, the dark side of a lost planet. At first he enjoyed it. The novelty was appealing. So was the spic-and-span way of killing bogeys without bloodying your hands. Ops that the Soviets would once have called "wet jobs" had turned into something dry and tidy, at least for those watching on a video screen. Gradually he grew uneasy, disillusioned by doubt before he could even say why. Make your living from a technological shortcut and pretty soon other shortcuts looked equally tempting, no matter how reckless. Bickell had spotted their mistakes coming from a mile away. Unfortunately he said so, meaning that once things began to go wrong he was automatically part of the problem, another messy element that needed sweeping aside. So they rewarded him with a medal for distinguished service—pinned in secret, of course, in some windowless room at Langley. Then they cut him loose a year ahead of his scheduled retirement.

Now, judging by this flyboy headed up his driveway, they were still in cleanup mode. Two days ago they had telephoned to prep him, giving him a role, a script, and detailed instructions for afterward. He was ambivalent about the whole business. For one thing, his old employer no longer seemed to be speaking with one voice. Inquiries to his old boss had gone unanswered. When they contacted him, they no longer seemed to use the usual channels. This suggested a rift, an ongoing competition between rival factions, and with Agency rivalries you inevitably got crossfire. Once that started, even outsiders like him needed to take cover. For all Bickell knew, Cole and he might even be on the same side. Or maybe the pilot was yet another bumbler with a gas can and a lighted match and should be left to burn on his own.

The first knock at the door came as Bickell reached the hallway closet where the new equipment was installed. Agency techs had turned up yesterday morning in a Verizon van with forms to sign and promises to keep. *Easy to operate*, they said. *All digital, so pay attention.* Like he was some sort of relic who could only work a reel-to-reel. He pressed the button for Record just as Cole knocked again.

"Keep your shirt on," Bickell called out, watching the needles jump. "I'm coming."

Act like you know what you're doing. That was the thought Cole had clung to all morning as Steve Merritt and he crossed into New Hampshire toward Lake Winnipesaukee with the driving directions spread on the seat between them. They drove a new Toyota Corolla, a rental Steve had picked up at Boston Logan the day before Cole's arrival at the Trailways terminal on Atlantic Avenue. Cole's journey east had been a nonstop blur of rest stops and fast food joints, filled by a thousand nervous glances out the bus window as big rigs rumbled past on empty stretches of highway. Nothing in the sky but commercial jets, as far as he could tell. He'd nursed a fifth of Jeremiah Weed most of the way, then picked up a new bottle on the last stop before Boston. He'd already cut his consumption to half a bottle a day. Still too much, and he was feeling a little shaky, but it was a start. Strength, patience, vigilance. The watchwords for making good with the journalists. Not that they seemed very disciplined themselves, except about making sure they stayed caffeinated throughout the day.

Steve was proving to be an unexpectedly agreeable traveling companion, generous with his encouragement, not to mention his dollars, and minimally intrusive with questions about Cole's personal life, and his ordeal of the past fourteen months. He prepped Cole for the Bickell interview by going over a list of possible questions, and offered a few reporter's tips on how to break the ice. The success or failure of the encounter would come down to a single conversation, perhaps a single turn of phrase, and Cole figured he had better arrive looking confident, even if he didn't feel that way.

A few miles before reaching their destination they stopped in Moultonborough to pick up a local map. Then they double-checked the directions and plotted their approach. Bickell lived on a small cove on a remote neck, way up a dirt road. As a precaution they parked well short of the driveway to let Cole cover the final stretch on foot, a decision he was grateful for as soon as he spotted the security camera peering down from a tree by the mailbox.

Just like an old spy to guard the perimeter, Cole supposed. It creeped him out the way these intrusive little eyes kept watching him at every step along the way. He had noticed surveillance cameras at virtually every stop along the bus route—at service stations, convenience stores, fast food joints, even inside the men's room. Grounded little Predators, from sea to shining sea.

He knocked, paused, then knocked again until a voice called out impatiently from inside. When Bickell opened the door, Cole was reminded of why the man had once struck him as a perfect choice for a posting to the Muslim world. Olive skin, brushy mustache, brown eyes. With the right clothes he could have passed for a falafel vendor in a Middle Eastern souk, or a hack in Kabul. Cole cleared his throat and began his pitch.

"Mr. Bickell? I'm Captain Darwin Cole. I'm not sure if you remember me, but—"

"Sure I do. From Creech. You're a long way from home."

"I was hoping for a few minutes of your time, and maybe some advice."

"I didn't figure you'd come for a cup of sugar. Is this official?"

"No."

"Well, I'm not either. Not anymore. Come on in, I guess. Coffee? An hour old but still hot."

"Sure. I've been traveling pretty hard." Then wishing he hadn't said it, because Bickell seized on it right away.

"You drove the whole way?"

"The last leg, anyway." He didn't want to mention Boston, and certainly not Steve.

Bickell nodded, face unreadable. From the threshold Cole saw a sun porch at the back of the house—louvered windows, a panoramic view of the lake, the eaves dripped melting snow. Bickell steered him instead to a darkened living room up front, then motioned him toward a brown couch by a cold and empty hearth. The coffee had yet to materialize, which didn't bode well.

"Still flying Preds?" Bickell continued to stand.

"I'm out of that now. Out of the Air Force. Maybe you heard."

"Maybe. Fascinating machines. Amazing what they've been able to accomplish."

"Hope we were able to help you. Have any luck with them?"

Bickell shrugged. "What's this advice you're after?"

"About one of your colleagues. Wade Castle."

"Last I heard, he's still employed by the Agency. You'll have to ask them."

"Well, this is kind of delicate."

"It usually is when it's unofficial. All the more reason for you to go through channels. I've got a number in Langley that will put you straight through to his desk officer. Fellow named Bishop."

Cole shifted in his seat, beginning to feel he had come a long way for nothing.

"You said something about coffee?"

That at least drew a smile. Bickell grunted and headed for the kitchen. By the time he returned—full mug, no steam—Cole had retooled his approach.

"What happened to you over there? You retire on schedule, or did they send you home early?"

Bickell's eyes flared, but he didn't answer right away.

"You don't exactly seem gainfully employed yourself, Captain."

Cole shrugged.

"This and that. So you're out for good?"

"You see me complaining?" Bickell spread his arms to encompass the room. Vintage fly rods were mounted on the knotty pine paneling behind him. On the opposite wall was a crossed set of varnished wooden skis. No sign of a feminine touch. No household noises that a wife might make. Cole was guessing he lived alone. He prodded again.

"Castle fucked up big-time, but I guess you knew that. He was my J-TAC on a flyover at Sandar Khosh. Called in a dart that killed thirteen civvies. The whole thing felt wrong from the get-go. From what I hear, it wasn't the only time."

"What does any of this have to do with me?"

Why had he come? What could have made them think this visit would be worth the trouble? He pictured Steve's disappointed reaction when Cole delivered the news that he'd struck out—a big fat zero on his first mission, the long journey wasted. At this rate he wouldn't last a week. They might not even bother to pick him up at the bus station in Baltimore.

"Well, I thought you guys trained together because you were going to serve together. Am I wrong?"

Bickell shrugged and shifted his weight to his other foot.

"Look, if you really have nothing to say—"

"After you came all this way, you mean?" Bickell frowned. "I'm sure it wasn't that hard to tell that I'm not exactly fond of Castle. Nobody likes the prick, if you really want to know, so I don't give a rat's ass what happens to him. But he's not a fuckup. He's one of the few people over there who knew his ass from a hole in the ground."

"That's a start, I guess."

"It's also an end."

Bickell gestured toward the door. Just like that, without even a scrap of useful information. Cole's desperation surged toward anger. He stood, face flushed, and stepped within inches of Bickell, who didn't budge.

"So you're good with all this, then? The fuckups and the mistakes? All those dead kids, that's okay by you?"

Bickell came right back at him, and for a moment it felt like being back in basic, or his first year at the Academy, getting reamed out nose to nose by some screaming asshole on a parade ground.

"Did I *say* I'm good with it? Fuck, no! But I'm not risking my ass for some weak vessel who's going to leak secrets all the way back to Vegas. And please tell me you didn't fly commercial, with a ticket on plastic and two forms of ID. Please tell me you're not that much of a fuckup."

"None of your business."

"It's *completely* my business. I might be more pissed off than you are about the state of play, but I'll be damned if I sweep any dirt toward some stupid bastard who might as well be posting this conversation on Facebook. So, to repeat, how did you get here? By what means?"

"Not by plane."

Bickell backed off an inch.

"Using any plastic?"

Cole shook his head.

"Cash only, and a fake ID."

"Cover name?"

"None of your business."

"Good answer. Next time don't volunteer all that other shit, even if somebody asks." Cole reddened in embarrassment. "And you can consider this a favor, Captain Cole, like a free security evaluation. But maybe I underestimated you. Or maybe I just wanted to. Always hated all you cocky bastards on the flight line." This finally coaxed a smile out of Cole. "Before you say another word I want to show you something. Then we're going to start over, beginning with your knock at the door."

Cole followed him to a hall closet, which Bickell opened onto a recorder, red light on, needles jumping with every sound. Cole blanched, then looked around, as if expecting a team of operatives to emerge from behind the furniture. When nothing happened he drew a deep breath.

"You tape all your guests?"

"Only when some Agency geek drops by to set up the equipment. This is their stuff. They were here yesterday." He let that sink in.

"You were expecting me?"

"Everybody was, apparently, to hear my people tell it. Tell me something . . ." The needles kept jumping. Bickell paused, annoyed, then punched the Off switch. "If you were to find out what actually went wrong, and why—which I don't know myself, by the way—what would you do with that kind of information? Who's your client?"

"Client?"

"Who's paying the freight?"

"Nobody." He didn't dare mention the journalists.

"For the sake of argument, let's say I believe that. Where do you go next, then? Where do you take this kind of material?"

"I guess that depends on who I thought would be in the best position to make sure these things don't keep happening. At least not with our birds."

Bickell shook his head.

"Don't duck the question. This isn't Amnesty International and you're not working for some war crimes tribunal. Where do you see yourself going with this? To a desk jockey in the Pentagon? To goddamn CNN, even? Or maybe back up the chain of command, to whoever the hell didn't officially send you here and didn't officially give you any marching orders? I know about your court-martial. Was this part of your plea agreement, maybe? Some sort of undercover arrangement?"

It was an odd but appealing theory, which made Cole wonder what other forces might be in play. It also offered an easy way out.

"Something like that."

"And this superior of yours, who's he reporting to?"

"I don't know."

Bickell smiled.

"Well, if my people knew you might be coming, that tells me your sugar daddy is compromised, no matter how high up the chain of command. So act accordingly. And wherever you go next, it better not be Creech. Once you've started something like this there's no reset button, no reboot. It's shop till you drop, understand?"

"Then where should I go next?"

"I've got a few ideas. But first, a little housekeeping."

CHAPTER EIGHT

BICKELL ERASED THE RECORDING and told Cole what to do next. Cole left the house through the front door and waited on the porch until Bickell called out from inside. "Okay. Silent five count, then let 'er rip."

Cole counted slowly to five, then knocked. Twice, like before.

"Keep your shirt on," Bickell said again. "I'm coming."

This time Cole refused the invitation to step inside. He tried to sound natural as he repeated the lines Bickell had fed him.

"No offense, but I'd be more comfortable doing this outside. We can walk while we talk."

Bickell hemmed and hawed, playing the spider to the fly. But Cole didn't give in, so Bickell finally came out onto the porch. Having concluded their performance for the recorder, they headed toward the lakeshore, where even on a chilly winter day distant motorboats were plowing the main channel, throwing plumes like snowmobiles. Once they were a safe distance from the house, Bickell got down to business.

"Let me ask you something. What makes you so sure this is all about the Agency?"

"It was Castle's op."

"He might have ordered up the bird, but there are plenty of people with wish lists in that part of the world. Privateers and fly-by-nighters. Sheep-dipped Special Forces platoons, green badgers with their own outfits, you name it. Down on the ground it's a regular fucking carnival."

"Whoa, whoa. Sheep-dipped?"

"Active military, but with a special security clearance so they can work directly for the Agency, or maybe for some green badger with his head up his ass."

"And a green badger is . . . ?"

"Cleared by the Agency, but not an Agency employee. A green badge gets you into the building at Langley. A blue badge means you work there."

"Are you talking about contractors? Like Blackwater, or IntelPro?" Cole watched for a reaction, but Bickell was poker-faced.

"This is even murkier and more incestuous. Maybe it's an ex-employee doing a contract job. And maybe he's working with a contractor, or maybe he isn't. Either way, green badgers can do shit that blue badgers can't. If they're caught on the wrong side of the border, well, hell, they're not government employees, are they?"

"Plausible deniability."

"They can also operate domestically. Right here at home. Places that are no-go for the Agency are always open season for them. Same with the contractors—the Blackwaters and IntelPros—except they operate out in the next orbit where things are even loopier. Not just different rules of engagement, *no* rules of engagement. The Wild West, Fort Apache, take your pick. The new frontier of covert warfare."

"With the drones?"

"With everything. Firefights by proxy. Security checks on the home front. In some ops, half the guts get farmed out to some hireling, or to a bunch of converted nut jobs with M-16s. It's a damn good business to be in, that's for sure. When the Agency got rid of me, who do you think my first visitor was, one day after I got here?"

Cole shook his head.

"An international security consultant with two slots to fill. Offering triple what the Agency pays and twice the freedom. Before I even had time to say no, two more called. It's great for the job market—No Spook Left Behind—but down on the ground?" He shook his head.

"A mess?"

"We had an op going last July, sheep-dipped unit near the border pulling an all-nighter on the prairie. They staked out the house of some former source who'd been tipping off our targets. Our Pred is at twelve thousand and I'm in the trailer, watching. Two hours before go time, eight bogeys show up in the opposite quadrant, moving in on the same party. Who are they? Fuck if we know, but before we can lift a finger they storm the house, clear every room, then leave our bad boy dead on his doorstep. Mission accomplished, but by who? Blue badgers? Green badgers? Contractors? We never did find out. They're all out there, and every damn one of 'em has his own list of HVTs."

"Who's keeping tabs on them?"

"I asked that question a month before they sent me home. Took it all the way to the desk chief in Washington. Nobody would give me a straight answer. At first I thought they were stonewalling. Now I'm convinced they just didn't know, which frankly kinda blows my mind. They've got a rough idea for numbers, maybe even names. But ops and targets? Spheres of influence? Or who's shooting at who? Good luck with all that. So naturally you end up with competition—for sources, clients, results. And competition breeds mistakes."

"Who's making them?"

"Who isn't?"

"And that's what happened with my missile strike?"

"I'm not the one who can answer that. I just know it's more complicated than Wade fucking Castle going rogue, or getting his coordinates wrong. He's king of the hill for this kind of shit, the Agency's tech guru on both sides of the water. No way it's just a matter of him being duped by a single source."

"Or maybe that's what you've been told to say."

"What I was *told* to say was absolutely nothing. I erased the goddamn tape to cover my own ass as much as yours."

"It's not like you've given me much."

"I'm getting to that. The name of an op, for starters. Wade Castle's baby from day one. Magic Dimes. As in dropping the dime. You watch cop shows, right?"

"Ratting somebody out, you mean? Like a drug dealer snitching to the feds?"

"Except these dimes do the snitching for you. That's what gives them their mojo."

"Are you talking about tracking beacons?"

"No bigger than a silver dollar, even though they're called dimes. Slide one under somebody's couch and he'll get a rocket down his chimney faster than you can say Osama bin Laden."

"That was how Castle marked his targets, by getting his sources to drop the dimes?"

"Some of them, anyway."

"There was no beacon signal of any kind coming from the place we hit."

"Not that you knew. When an Agency bird did the shooting, he let the Pred crews in on the signal telemetry. Whenever the Air Force was involved he kept it all to himself, to protect his sources. His only contact with the flight crews was by chat."

"That's how it was with me."

Bickell nodded. "Castle likes to play things neat and simple, with minimal interference."

"Then how'd things get so fucked up?"

"Partly because the beacon program grew faster than he wanted. Even before he could set up the first shot, somebody upstairs decided to make it a sort of pilot project, a trial run for interagency use. And not just for overseas use."

"For using it here, you mean? Homing beacons for Predators?"

"Or for any other piece of hardware you might use to carry out remote surveillance on a suspect."

"So, for the FBI, too, then."

"Plus any of our so-called trusted partners in the private sector. Because if you're not acting officially, then who needs a warrant?"

"Sounds sketchy."

"If you want sketchy, read the PATRIOT Act. Enough loopholes to fly a whole squadron of Predators through. Castle was pissed when he saw where this was headed. And he only got more bent out of shape once he saw how wonderful everything was going with the Magic Dimes."

"Like with my op."

"Him and me both. I started asking myself what went wrong as soon as I saw the casualty report. Castle dropped off the radar shortly after that. I never did get his take on it. They sequestered him somewhere.

Days of debriefing. All I ever heard before they canned me was a name. Castle's source, the guy he chose to place his beacons."

"And?"

Bickell eyed him closely, as if still weighing whether to take the plunge.

"Mansur Amir Khan. A little shit Pashtun smuggler, everything from soup to nuts. Back and forth across the border with pack mules and bodyguards, maybe a dozen fighters on his payroll. Not a hell of a lot going on upstairs, but apparently he knew where a lot of the Indian chiefs liked to hide out. Maybe 'cause he was supplying them with something, I don't know. Ammo, meds, gasoline. He was a conduit for everybody."

"So he was the problem?"

"This is where it gets complicated." *Great*, thought Cole, already overstuffed with information. He was the one who needed a recorder, not the Agency. "Not long after Castle starts dealing with him, Mansur becomes a very popular fellow in certain circles. By then of course he's got a handful of Castle's magic dimes jingling in his pocket. Somebody else got wind of it and wanted in on the action, and they had the money to outbid us."

"The other side?"

"It's not that simple. Could have been anyone from an al Qaeda groupie to some wild-ass green badger looking to make his name with a big hit. Or maybe just a local warlord looking to rub out a rival. Whoever it was, Castle's dimes started rolling all over the floor, meaning he had to either track them down or shut down Mansur."

"If he thought the targets were iffy, why keep calling in strikes?"

"Castle's the only one who can answer that. But first you'd have to find him. And when you do, my old station chief would be much obliged if you'd let him in on the secret."

"He's *missing*? Even to the CIA?"

"Only for guys at my level. This kind of info gets compartmentalized beyond belief once a fuckup occurs. Especially when somebody's name starts showing up on consultants' enemies lists. Because you weren't the only one who got burned by these mistakes."

"IntelPro, you mean."

"They're one possibility. Tricorn Associates. Overton Security. Those are two more. Plus any sheep-dipped outfit of mercenaries you care to name. Just about any of them might have been hung out to dry if a beacon got misused."

"So what's the Agency saying—that he's gone?"

"What, admit they've lost the handle on one of their top-level experts?" Bickell shook his head. "Besides, someone inside is bound to know where he is. Someone always does. You know anything about that fucked-up game they play over there, bushkazi?"

"The one on horseback, yeah."

"Like polo for barbarians, except instead of a ball they've got a dead goat, with both sides trying to keep it. Sometimes the goat gets torn to shreds before either side wins. Well, right now, from what I hear, Castle's the dead goat in a big game of Agency bushkazi. So good luck if you think you're going to find him. The way this one's going, you'll be more likely to bump into Mullah Omar."

"I wasn't exactly expecting to run him down."

"No, but you might find Mansur. A year ago, when things started to get a little hot for his family, he supposedly used some of his Agency winnings and consular contacts to buy his way out of Dodge. Got a one-way ticket to Europe and a Canadian visa."

"So he's in Canada now?"

"Was. Disappeared about a day after the Agency went looking for him. No trace for months, then he supposedly turned up down in Baltimore."

Jesus, Cole thought. Was everyone in Baltimore?

"So they found him?"

"Tried to. Or had the Bureau try for them, jurisdictional rules and all that. No luck."

"Well, if the FBI couldn't find him—"

"Maybe they weren't looking very hard."

"Why, 'cause they hate the Agency? The whole rivalry thing?"

Bickell shook his head. "Cooperation's better than ever on stuff like this. I'm betting my people made a decision at some point that they didn't *want* to look very hard. Far better to hear that a cursory check showed no sign of him, so thanks for trying and call off the dogs until further notice, pretty please. Or maybe they found him but hushed it up. Put him under surveillance. By request, of course. Either way, it's more cover-up, more stuff no one would talk about. Not when I asked, anyway."

"Is that why they pushed you out? For asking about Mansur and Magic Dimes?"

"Plus some other shit. Even when Wade was still active there was all kinds of noise around the Agency's Predator program, so I'd already been asking questions."

"Noise?"

"Funny stuff nobody could or would explain. Not even Castle, and he was supposed to be running the show."

"Like what?"

"People coming in and out of our ops center who I'd never seen before. They'd nod at Wade like they were buddies and he'd nod back."

"Green badgers? Blue badgers?"

"No badgers. And no names, far as I could tell. I'd ask Wade and he'd say something about it being strictly need-to-know, so butt out, but I could tell he didn't like 'em, either. So I averted my eyes, at least for a while. Then I asked the station chief. He told me to drop it, let Wade handle it. So I let Wade handle it, and Wade disappeared." He shook his head, gazing out across the lake. "Tell me something, in all your ops did you ever get any unexplained visitors to your chat group?"

"You mean besides you guys?"

"Hell, we were OGA. Duly announced and reporting for duty. Might as well have been displaying an Agency icon every time we posted. No, I mean true interlopers, guys who might ask a question out of nowhere, with a handle you'd never seen before, then slink off into the ether."

Cole thought about it. Drew a blank.

"Don't recall any. Nobody beyond the usual crowd, from Al Udeid on down."

"Nobody with the handle Lancer?"

The name stopped him, literally. He stood still on the path. A bird called out from overhead, and a droplet of melted snow smacked his forehead just as he locked on to a memory.

"Yeah, there was a Lancer. Just once. Or once that I can remember." Bickell was intense now, staring straight at him. "It was during our recon at Sandar Khosh, the month before the missile strike."

"Remember what he asked?"

"No. But I remember wondering who the hell it was, just for a second. His handle popped up, he asked one or two questions, then he vanished, just like you said. It happened so fast I didn't think about it again. Until now."

"I got him pretty regular. So did everybody in our shop. I asked Wade who the hell he was."

"And?"

"Told me he was a privileged guest, nothing more. After that I always wondered if he was bird-dogging you guys as well. Your CO never mentioned him?"

"Nothing. Before or after."

"Curious."

"You think it's related to all this stuff?"

"Hell, everything's related. But how? No idea. Just another part of the noise."

They walked on, footsteps crunching frosted mud in the shadows along the shoreline before they turned back into sunlight. Bickell looked up at the sky. A small private plane, a Cessna or a Piper, soared across the far side of the lake. They watched for a few seconds before it veered through a notch in the gray hills, leaving behind only the faint drone of its engine as it disappeared over the horizon.

During the pause another possibility occurred to Cole: Maybe this whole conversation was part of a setup, and the whole scene with the tape recorder had been for show. Bickell could be wired, transmitting the conversation to some guy in a van a few hundred yards away. Steve and he would then be intercepted before they could even make it to the end of the dirt road. But to what purpose? He couldn't think of one, so he kept asking questions.

"This guy Mansur—why Baltimore?"

Bickell shrugged.

"I wondered, too. It's not like there's any Little Kabul down there, someplace where he might blend in. Only a handful of Afghans in the city, although one of them *is* a brother of Hamid Karzai, president of the fucking country. Owns a bunch of restaurants there." Cole raised an eyebrow, but Bickell waved him off. "It was checked. No connection. Besides, that's not exactly the low profile they wanted for Mansur. All I can figure is that there must be a sponsor nearby, somebody who helps keep an eye on him."

"Like IntelPro?"

Bickell narrowed his eyes.

"What makes you keep mentioning them?"

"They're located down there, aren't they?"

"Maybe you're more on the ball than I thought. But the only thing the Bureau dug up locally was the name of a Mexican takeout where Mansur was stuffing burritos for a while. Taco Rojo."

"The Red Taco?"

"All I got. It's all the Bureau had, too, if that's any comfort, and he no longer works there."

"Why would they ever put him out in public like that?"

"No idea. Unless he was being used as some kind of bait. Which could also explain why the Bureau would back off—to keep from fucking up somebody else's mousetrap."

"Then who's the mouse?"

"Good question. But it tells me that Mansur is findable for anyone with the means, motive, and opportunity."

They continued walking in silence until they reached the edge of the property. Bickell stopped, stuffed his hands in his pockets, and looked straight at Cole.

"If you do happen to find him, don't waste your breath asking about Wade Castle. He was using a cryptonym over there. Hector. Like the Greek warrior."

"The *dead* Greek warrior. I saw the movie."

"And Castle read the book. But I guess he doesn't believe in jinxes. Another word of advice. The moment you hit the trail I'm supposed to give the Agency a heads-up. They want a fix on your departure time, a starting point for further tracking. I can fudge it by maybe twenty minutes to give you a head start, but anything more and I'm playing with fire. So don't stop for lunch, don't stop for gas, and by all means avoid the toll roads. Too many cameras rolling at the collection booths."

More little Predators, Cole thought, *parked and waiting.*

"Thanks."

"Obviously I won't tell them I mentioned Mansur, much less Hector. But if you head down to Baltimore, watch yourself. Just because the Bureau says they never found him doesn't mean they don't know where he is. For all I know they've staked him out with another goddamn beacon in his pocket, trolling him in the water to see who comes sneaking up from behind. Turn up on their radar and you'll be seen as a potential member of the competition, and you don't want the Agency *or* the Bureau thinking of you that way."

"Now if I just knew one other thing."

"What's that?"

"Whether you're really trying to help me, or baiting a trap."

Bickell smiled. "Welcome to my world, Captain Cole. The way things work in this business, I could sincerely be intending to do you a favor while really doing the opposite, and neither of us would be the wiser."

"Great."

"You get used to it, believe it or not. If you're good at it."

"And how do you get good at it?"

"By keeping your own counsel, trusting only yourself. A cliché, yes, but only because it's good advice. The moment somebody tells you he's on your side, you better start looking for reasons he'd want to do you in."

"Sounds like a recipe for ending up alone."

"Guilty as charged." Bickell spread his arms to encompass the empty lawn. "My wife moved out seven years ago." He walked a few more feet in silence, a crust of ice crunching beneath his feet. "Back when I bought this place I figured someday all I'd be doing is hunting, fishing, tooling around on the water. But look at that boat of mine—falling apart, stem to stern. I haven't taken it out since August. Still, the life has its rewards. You'll see."

"I'll keep that in mind when they take me in for questioning."

Bickell chuckled, but Cole didn't join in. Bickell turned back toward the house, signaling that he was ready to bring this to a close. Cole had one more question.

"So what's your theory on Castle, then? You lived and breathed this stuff right there with him. Where do you think he's gone?"

Bickell stopped. He stroked his chin and looked hard at Cole, as if mulling whether to say anything more.

"Knowing him, and knowing how many players eventually dipped their fingers into this pie at one time or another, I'd say he's here."

"Back in the States?"

Bickell nodded grimly.

"Why?"

"Because this isn't about what happened over there anymore. It's about what's happening here. Right now. And he's determined to be part of it."

"For which side?"

"His own."

"Is that the same as the Agency's?"

"You tell me. No one in Langley will. Why the hell else would I be talking to you?" He looked down at his watch. "I'd say it's time you got moving. And seeing as how the clock just started, you'd be best advised to walk straight around the house. Stay as far to the right of the drive as you can so you won't trip the sensor. The alarm will show up on the recording, and the next sound I want them to hear is me coming back through the front door, twenty minutes from now."

"Much obliged to you."

"Hey. I never said shit. That's your version to anyone who asks. And the clock is ticking, Captain Cole."

Cole nodded and left at double time. By the time he reached the front yard he was sprinting.

CHAPTER NINE

COLE SLID ONTO the passenger seat, out of breath.

"Well?" Steve asked.

"We need to get moving."

"What did he say?"

"It can wait. We need to go *now*, and stay off the toll roads."

"Never should've let you read that fortune cookie. You have any idea how long that'll take?"

"Bickell's advice. He was expecting me, okay? He had a whole taping system. The Agency set it up for him yesterday on the off chance I'd show up."

"Holy shit. *Yesterday?*"

"Said he's giving me a twenty-minute head start, then he's phoning in to report my departure."

"Fuck!" Steve cranked the engine and threw it into gear, spraying gravel from the shoulder. "Why didn't you just say so?"

"Go easy," Cole said. "Last thing we need is to get pulled over by some local cop."

"But he's phoning this in? To the CIA?"

"That's what he said."

"Sorry, I'll risk the ticket, at least till we're back to civilization."

Steve floored it up the dirt road, raising a dust cloud you could've seen for miles. Cole checked the map.

"How much gas we got?" Cole asked.

"Enough for a couple hundred miles."

"Enough to reach Logan, then. And the bus station for me."

"Was he any help?"

"He thinks this all started with homing beacons, for targeting Predator strikes. Castle paid some guy named Mansur to place them, then got outbid by black hats or privateers, which led to a bunch of fuckups. Like Sandar Khosh, probably. Now everybody's looking for Castle and Mansur."

"Castle's *missing*?"

"Bickell's heard he's back in the States. Thinks he's caught in the middle of some Agency power struggle."

"But he's still official? Still employed?"

"Maybe. Just not at any level he knows of."

"What about this guy Mansur?"

"You'll like his last known whereabouts. Baltimore."

"You're shittin' me."

"Bickell seems to think there's an IntelPro connection, although he never actually said so."

Steve furrowed his brow.

"Doubtful, from what they've been telling me." He shook his head. "But they could be lying. Or Bickell could be full of it. Maybe neither of them knows what the fuck they're talking about. What a mess."

"Why else would Mansur be in Baltimore?"

"Family, maybe? Or a Washington connection, somebody who wants to keep him stashed forty miles down the road. Close, but not too close. Where in Baltimore?"

"Some taco shop. The FBI went looking for him at the Agency's request. No luck, but Bickell thinks they weren't trying too hard, and maybe that's the way the Agency wanted it. Or that they found him but agreed to keep it under wraps."

"The Bureau's in on this, too?" Steve grinned, and shook his head in appreciation. "Good stuff. Really good. You did well."

"Thanks. It was mostly him doing the talking."

"You ask about any other ops?"

"I, uh, didn't get to some of the stuff on the list."

"What about Castle's job description, the Agency's chain of command over there?"

"No. Sorry. He was off and running with this beacon stuff. I never got back to some of the other things."

"It's okay. You're new to this. You did well."

But Steve couldn't mask a note of disappointment. It was clear that he felt Cole could have gotten more, and maybe he was right. Probably was.

Steve sat up straighter behind the wheel.

"Whoa. What's that up ahead?"

A black SUV had just crested the horizon, barreling toward them in the oncoming lane. Smoked windows made a head count impossible. They tensed as it approached, and exhaled as it whizzed by with a huge snatching sound.

"Not hitting their brake lights, thank God," Steve said, checking the mirror. "Massachusetts tags."

"Better than government tags. The Agency or the Bureau would be looking for a car with one guy. Bickell thinks I'm traveling alone. Besides, it's only been fifteen minutes."

"You actually believed that shit about a twenty-minute head start? Jesus, listen to me. I'm as paranoid as you."

"Good. Stay that way."

From force of habit, Cole craned his neck to check the skies overhead. This time Steve was too busy checking the mirrors to notice.

They drove on in silence.

CHAPTER TEN

ANY WORRIES THAT the journalists would abandon him disappeared when he saw Keira waiting at the downtown bus station. A bottle clanked as he put his bag on the backseat of her Datsun. He winced in embarrassment, but Keira either didn't notice or had the tact to pretend not to. He'd limited himself to only two swallows in the past three hours. Getting there.

From all he'd heard about Barb's place, Cole had assumed it was a cramped row house in the heart of the city, a bohemian roach trap with on-street parking and a nightly din of sirens and car alarms. Then Keira told him to strap in for a half-hour ride.

"Barb's way out in Middle River," she explained.

"On the Bay?" Now he envisioned a yuppified community of waterfront condos, with docked sailboats and European sedans.

"Kinda sorta." Keira laughed. "Wilson Point Road is sort of a Redneck Riviera. Just down the street from Martin State Airport, so you should feel right at home."

"Seriously? Do you know what unit's based there?"

"Some Air National Guard outfit. Mostly it's a bunch of old planes."

That certainly ruled out the prospect of gentrification. In Cole's experience, neighborhoods next to air bases were always a little rough around the edges.

They passed the airstrip shortly after turning off Eastern Boulevard. A chain-link fence topped by barbed wire offered a view of a tarmac with tubby C-130 transports parked wing to wing next to a column of aging A-10 Warthogs, slow and ugly fighter-bombers. Ungainly, but right then Cole would have given anything to take one up for a spin, especially in the coppery light of dusk.

He missed flying. He'd missed it even more when he was piloting Predators. It was one reason he took his kids out in the Cessna, to give them a taste. A few hours in the sky always worked wonders on his state of mind. By taking off from here you could make a long, low run along the jagged shoreline of the Chesapeake, heading south toward the city center or east across the main channel toward the farmlands and marshes of the Eastern Shore. You'd be right up there with the V formations of geese, the setting sun at your back. Turn south and in less than an hour you'd reach the sawgrass flats of his boyhood in Tidewater Virginia. No one down there worth seeing anymore, not since his parents died. But he could buzz his old high school, or the rooftops of his friends' old houses. He saw it all in his head now, the bird's-eye view: duck blinds and fishing holes peeping from between bare trees, reflected sunlight flashing up from the rippled water.

Barb's street had a similar feel, a jumble of modest frame houses on compact lots. Boat trailers sat in driveways with massive pickups, clunky American sedans, the occasional Harley. It was only the first week of December, but most houses were decorated for Christmas, which made Cole think of his kids, already putting together their lists for Santa. Although not Karen, who'd be too old for that by now. He wondered if either of them ever asked to see Daddy. Maybe not.

It was chilly out, but Cole rolled down his window to inhale the familiar bouquet of brine, boat fuel, and wet leaves. Not at all like the lay of the land at Bickell's place, where the lake was hemmed in by hills. This was tidewater country, with an open horizon and a lunar cycle. Mudflats at low tide, shallows at high tide, with the baitfish jumping. A long way from the desert.

He spotted Barb's place from a block away, pegging it by the lack of decorations and the make of the cars in the drive—a Toyota Prius and a Honda Civic. The house was a funky little cottage with whitewashed cedar shakes and a single gabled window on the second floor. The lot, out toward the end of the point, backed up to Stansbury Creek, with a view of a grassy marsh, a stand of pines, and a marina with bobbing boats.

Steve was waiting for them just inside the front door.

"Good timing," he said. "Five minutes later and you would've missed me. I'm headed off to an interview, but I'll help you get squared away. Let me take your bag."

He turned and called toward the back.

"They're here!"

A petite redhead in jeans and a white peasant blouse emerged from the kitchen with a wooden spoon in her right hand.

"So you're Darwin Cole." She held aloft the spoon, coated with red sauce. "My night to make dinner, so I hope you're not too hungry."

"You must be Barb."

"Holtzman. Couch or cot?"

"Excuse me?"

"Your choice of sleeping accommodations. Crash on a cot in Steve's room, or take the couch down here."

She was certainly direct.

"Couch, I guess."

Steve nodded, looking relieved. Cole surveyed the room, barely decorated apart from a threadbare oriental rug and a brass Middle Eastern coffee set on an end table. The furniture looked straight out of an IKEA showroom, lending the place a faintly nomadic air, as if to convey that she could pick up and go at a moment's notice.

Barb, brandishing the spoon like a bloodied swagger stick, pointed toward an alcove in the back.

"The dining room is where we work." Three laptops were open on a small table.

"The nerve center," Steve said, sounding a bit self-conscious. For all his initial reluctance about Cole at the beginning, he now seemed determined to make the arrangement work smoothly, the obliging host who only wanted everyone to get along. Barb led Cole to the couch, where she cleared away a pile of newspapers and shooed a fat orange cat from the cushions.

"Scoot, Cheryl, you've got company."

The cat bared its teeth, but jumped to the floor and trotted off toward the kitchen.

"Sorry, Kitty," Cole said.

"It's all right. Cheryl's the neighborhood slut. I just happen to be her pimp for the week."

Cole wondered if that's how everything was in Barb's life—stray animals and sublet friends, coming and going like the tide but not nearly as reliable.

"Keira, why don't you make him a drink while I finish up. Make me one, too. Gin and tonic. Although I hear you're a bourbon man, Captain Cole."

Fair enough, he supposed.

"I've been cutting back."

"Don't mind Barb," Keira whispered, touching his shoulder in passing. "She's just nervous. We all are, I guess. Who knows how this will work out?"

Steve, watching from the doorway, wondered what Cole must make of their odd little household, and of Barb in particular. She was one of those rare redheads without freckles, deeply appealing when she bothered to smile, although that wasn't often. Journalistically she was easily the best digger of the threesome, a Jack Russell terrier for whom no hole in the ground was too narrow or deep for her to tunnel to the end, or at least until she sank her teeth into the flanks of her quarry. Their skills were fairly complementary. Keira's greatest asset was her personal touch, a gentle schmoozability, not in the unctuous way of a lobbyist or a salesman, but out of a natural ease and curiosity. Plenty of reporters only pretended to be interested in their interview subjects. Keira really wanted to know what made them tick, a quality that had helped pry loose secrets from distraught refugees, suspicious bureaucrats, and soldiers of all nations. Steve ranked himself somewhere in the middle on the scales of both doggedness and empathy, which probably explained why he often ended up the designated peacemaker. If the chemistry ever failed, he'd blame himself.

Yet, being a fairly typical male, he occasionally found himself contemplating the group's sexual possibilities, speculating on what circumstances might be required to turn their arrangement into a complicated but gratifying—for him, at least—lust triangle. He always came to his senses. Each of them knew firsthand the hazards of sex in the workplace. And when the workplace was also your home, well . . .

"Back shortly," he said, twirling the car keys. Then, calling out to Barb, "Save me some chow."

"No guarantees!" Barb shouted from the kitchen. "Yon pilot hath a lean and hungry look."

Steve thought so, too, but not necessarily from an appetite for food, and for a fleeting moment Steve felt more concerned for Barb and Keira than for Cole. How well did they really know this man, after all? He hoped they were doing the right thing.

Cole sipped his bourbon and settled onto the couch, avoiding the furry spot the cat had left behind.

"I've got some work to do upstairs," Keira said. "But welcome to our zoo." She pulled the ever-present notebook from her hip pocket and disappeared up the stairway with an appealing little wave.

The only noise then was the banging of pots and pans from the kitchen, where it sounded like Barb was at war with their dinner. Cole reached into the pile of newspapers for the sports section of *The Sun*, hoping for news of any off-season transactions by the Orioles, the team he'd rooted for as a boy. Finding only Ravens coverage, he tossed it back on the pile, then stood. After the long bus ride his legs needed stretching. Maybe he'd go look at the Warthogs. Or maybe not, since there were probably cameras mounted along the base perimeter. He wandered back to the cluttered dining room, their de facto office, where the last light of dusk illuminated a pair of framed photographs hanging from the wall. They were easily the most striking items in the house.

The first one showed two boys, roughly the same age as Karen and Danny. They were all smiles, natural charmers. Afghan, probably, judging by their clothes and skin tone. In the second, which seemed to have been snapped only moments later, the same two boys were wide-eyed and wailing, terrified by something that must have just happened. The focus was slightly blurred, as if the photographer, too, had been taken by surprise. The effect was stunning, a yin-yang pairing that seemed to perfectly sum up the chaotic and unpredictable way of life in that part of the world. Leaning closer, he noticed that in the second photo the boys' clothes were spattered with dark droplets. He reached up to touch them, as if they might still be wet.

"Blood."

Barb's voice made him jump.

"Sorry," she said. "Didn't mean to sneak up on you."

"They're amazing," he said.

"Fort1's handiwork."

"*He* took them?"

"I took them. He provided the backdrop, so to speak. The motivating drama. Or so I found out later. It's why I'm on this story. Eight killed. And two of them were standing ten feet away, right next to where I was taking those pictures. I turned around and there they were, an old man and his wife, bleeding out at my feet. I never could get the stains out of that pair of shoes. Blood and viscera. Brain matter, probably. The shoes are upstairs in my closet if you want a look."

"No thanks."

"I hung up those photos the day we set up shop. For motivation."

"I keep mine up here." He tapped a finger to his forehead.

"So I've heard. Sounds like Owen Bickell was worth the journey."

Presumably Steve had told them all about the meeting in New Hampshire, which was a little unnerving. Cole wasn't accustomed to a culture where people played so fast and loose with privileged information. The Air Force always kept things within the tightest possible circle. Op-sec, compartmentalization, need-to-know. Tough habits to break.

"Yeah, he was. I probably could've gotten more. First-timer. I was kind of fumbling around."

"Sounds like Steve got after you," she said.

"Not really. Or nothing he said, anyway."

"Oh, he'd never say it. It's that look he gives you. All of us do. All of us like to think we could've squeezed more juice from the fruit than the next guy. Most of the time we're full of it. The point is, this guy Bickell knew you, trusted you. He wouldn't have said shit to any of us. Besides, you'll have another chance to prove yourself soon enough. Steve's got a little mission planned. A recon of that taco joint where Mansur was last seen."

"Great. Might as well get to it."

She smiled for the first time since he'd arrived, then turned back toward the kitchen.

"Soup's on in ten minutes."

From upstairs he heard the soft burble of Keira's voice, filtering down the stairwell as she laughed with some source on the phone, or maybe just a friend. Charming his socks off, no doubt. For some reason, Cole was almost certain it was a he.

CHAPTER ELEVEN

IN THE DESKBOUND WORLD of Captain Trip Riggleman there was a time, not so long ago, when the opportunity to bring down a target like Darwin Cole would have been the best possible motivation for getting up in the morning. Being an Air Force man, Riggleman would have preferred to go after Cole the old-fashioned way—by shooting him out of the sky. A fireball in the clouds, the enemy vanquished in an instant. Now *that* would have been perfect, not to mention cathartic.

Alas, any chances for that brand of satisfaction had gone by the board years ago, when Riggleman washed out of flight school. Poor vision and vertigo. He remained in the Air Force, but forever after was marked as a penguin among eagles, a mortal among gods.

Yet even within the cumbersome workings of military bureaucracy, the oddest cogs sometimes tumble into exactly the right openings, snug fittings where they not only mesh but function at the highest possible efficiency. And that is what happened to Riggleman, mostly because his mind was as quick and agile as those sleek jets he had once hoped to pilot.

He first showed promise as an Infowar "aggressors" trainer, by thoroughly disrobing the operational secrets of visiting units in war game after war game. From there he worked his way into the good graces of self-interested brass, up-and-coming generals forever hoping to pry loose their rivals' deeper secrets. Although his current title didn't sound like much—special assistant for logistics to the commander, 57th Wing—his duties had evolved to the point that he was now a sort of informational sniper on call, an ace handler of assignments both on and off the books. His particular specialty: Sniffing out any sort of trail—paper, telephonic, or virtual—that even a government auditor or trained investigator might not find.

Riggleman looked perfectly engineered for such duties. He was built low to the ground, a hard man to budge. Having wrestled in college, he was well versed in takedowns and escapes, the best ways to leverage bigger opponents to the mat. He knew never to loosen his grip until he was ready to employ the next move. He also knew to keep his mouth shut, especially when carrying out special assignments for his boss and wing commander, Brigadier General Mitchell Hagan.

That was the relationship that gave his talents their special potency. Hagan, a power in his own right, had a direct pipeline to Major General Salvador Shorter, whose command of the U.S. Air Force Warfare Center made him king of the mountain at Nellis Air Force Base.

Moments ago, Hagan had called Riggleman into his office. The general closed the door, shut the blinds, and instructed his secretary to hold all calls. Riggleman found it a bit theatrical, but also thrilling. Like some old scene out of film noir, he thought—Sam Spade preparing to deliver the goods to his top client. He sensed he was about to be asked to do something marginal, which meant something interesting. All that was missing was cigarette smoke, although Hagan reputedly kept a bottle of bourbon stashed in a drawer. Riggleman, wanting to maintain a military bearing, had to fight off an urge to lean forward in his chair.

"Captain," Hagan began, "I want you to drop whatever you're working on in order to give your full attention to a matter of the highest urgency."

"Absolutely, sir."

Hagan nodded, a barely perceptible gesture for a man whose head sat so low on his shoulders that it looked as if it had been mashed into place by a hydraulic press. Riggleman had always wondered what sort of opponent the general would have been on a wrestling mat. The kind who might bite in a clinch, perhaps, especially if he thought the referee wasn't looking.

"We have a pilot who's gone missing," Hagan said. "We'd like you to locate him for us."

"AWOL, sir?"

"Ex-pilot, actually. Ex–Air Force, when you get right down to it. So, not AWOL in the technical sense. But one of ours, all the same. A dishonorable discharge who was under orders, per his plea agreement, to keep us apprised of his movements. Given the sensitive nature of his previous duties, as well as his access to certain other information, we'd like to know his whereabouts as soon as possible."

Hagan slapped onto the desk a glossy photo of a clean-shaven man in his mid-thirties with the hint of a smirk hiding just beneath a casual smile.

"Darwin Cole. You may have crossed paths when he did his Infowar training."

"I don't recall the name, sir."

Hagan launched into a brief bio and slid forward a file folder. The moment Riggleman heard that Cole used to fly F-16s, his interest was piqued further. Cole was the very sort of fellow who had once lorded it over him on the flight line, back when Riggleman was a mere wash-out grunt. In those days, jocks ruled the clouds and everyone else got rained on. Especially the unfortunates who wore eyeglasses and carried clipboards. Yes, this was the sort of target Cole liked best. Or so he thought until he heard the rest.

"His final posting was right down the road at Creech."

"Creech, sir?" Riggleman was stunned. "He made a combat kill in a Viper, and they assigned him to a Predator wing?"

"Yes, soldier, he was flying Predators. If that Xbox bullshit can really be called flying."

Now the man had his pity.

When Riggleman had first heard about the drone program, he'd loved everything about it. Part of the appeal was plain old schadenfreude. It was deeply satisfying to see jocks stripped of their dreams just as abruptly as he had been stripped of his. He also appreciated the way drone technology represented the triumph of brains over reflexes, cunning over muscle. The very people who the frontline showboats had always derided as REMFs—rear echelon motherfuckers—were now the very people who were winning the war.

But the longer it went on, and the bigger it grew, the less he liked it.

The pilot talent pool was being drained into banks of windowless trailers. The very thing that had once attracted him to the United States Air Force—the dash, the glamour, the whole edgy idea that every time you went up you might not come back—was being bled from the skies, pilot by pilot, and it felt like each of them was a lesser man for it.

"Creech was where Cole crashed and burned," Hagan continued. "Figuratively speaking, of course. Little more than a year ago." The general skimmed the particulars of Cole's court-martial. "The full transcript is available, but it's under lock and key, so you'll have to file an official request. All you need to know for the moment is that, following his discharge, Cole moved to a trailer in a uninhabited sector about halfway between here and Creech. Goddamn road isn't even marked on a map."

He slid a glossy photo across the desktop, a shot of Cole's trailer taken from ground level with a long lens. It looked like something from an old black-and-white film about a down-and-outer who'd turned to crime.

"No car, as you can see. No electricity, no cell phone. Not much of anything out there but empty bottles of Jeremiah Weed. Maybe that explains why they took their eyes off him. In any case, sometime before last weekend, the former Captain Cole seems to have up and disappeared. At first there was speculation he might have just wandered off into the desert to die, but a thorough search of the area has dispelled those hopes."

Hopes? They *wanted* that to happen?

"Then this image turned up from last Thursday."

He tossed another photo Riggleman's way. It was also a shot of the trailer, but taken from high above. A dark compact sedan was parked nearby.

"The tags aren't legible, but we suspect it's a rental, so I suppose that's a sort of lead already."

"Is this from satellite surveillance, sir?"

"No. We used our own hardware."

"A Predator? But wouldn't that site be outside of—?"

"Draw your own conclusions, soldier."

Riggleman already had. Someone was flying a drone beyond the proscribed limits, and they'd compounded the crime by taking photos. He knew better than to ask what sort of secrets Cole was harboring. Besides, he had his own ways of checking on such things. He would put in a few calls—discreetly, of course—then cover his tracks. That's one thing people like General Hagan always failed to realize about people like Riggleman. Tell them to find out one thing and they were almost certainly going to find out other things as well, including stuff you didn't want them to know. Given Cole's key role in classified ops abroad, the possibilities seemed limitless, all the way up to espionage. A little spot on Riggleman's spine began to tingle. He picked up the surveillance photo.

"May I keep this, sir?"

"You can keep the whole damn dossier once we're done here, soldier."

"Thank you, sir."

"During his posting to Creech, Cole lived in Summerlin with his wife and two children." Hagan tossed out yet another photo. Nice house in the 'burbs, nothing spectacular. The wife must have been a gardener, judging by all the flowers. "His wife is estranged. Two months before his release she took both their children to her parents' house in Saginaw, Michigan." Three more photos hit the desktop in succession, like cards in a hand of draw poker.

Cute children. Attractive woman. Riggleman's hopes went into a nosedive. Maybe this was nothing but a domestic incident that had gotten out of hand, and Hagan was only worried about bad PR. There had been some recent stories in the media about burnout among Predator pilots. Low-key coverage, but it had stirred enough grumbling upstairs that Air Force shrinks and chaplains had been ordered to put a lid on the topic. Maybe that was their worry with Cole. If so, then Riggleman's job would be easy but boring.

"However," Hagan said, "we currently do not believe that Cole intends to go anywhere near Saginaw. His interests appear to be elsewhere, and we suspect they are directly related to his previous work as a Predator pilot."

Riggleman pulled neatly out of his tailspin. Hagan's next comments soon had him soaring.

"His last known whereabouts were in the vicinity of Moultonborough, New Hampshire, two days ago, at a waterfront home at Lake Winnipesaukee, where he attempted to establish an unauthorized contact with a recently retired employee of the Central Intelligence Agency. We'll of course supply you with the operative's name, address, and phone number. As of yet, we're not certain what means of transportation Captain Cole is using. Of the two personal vehicles registered in his name, one is now in Saginaw and the other was sold more than a year ago. It is suspected but not confirmed that he traveled to Moultonborough by rental car, although it's not known how he reached the Northeast. A cursory check of security footage from Las Vegas International produced no matches. Ditto for the cameras at the likeliest airports near Moultonborough, which would have been Boston Logan and the Portland Jetport, in Maine."

Damn. They'd already done a lot of legwork. This was urgent. And how juicy was it that the CIA might be involved? Hagan dropped more papers onto the pile.

"Here are summaries of the most recent activity on his wife's home and cell phones, and for all of her credit cards. As you'll see, nothing suggests any contact with Cole. As you'll also see here"—yet another sheet—"Cole hasn't used any of his own credit cards for more than a year. Apparently he's been living by cash only."

"If I can take the liberty, sir . . ."

"Please do."

"He would appear to be using classic espionage tradecraft."

"Let's not overstate things just yet, Captain Riggleman."

"Yes, sir."

But Riggleman could tell by the look in Hagan's eyes that the general hadn't dismissed the idea, and there was an edge to the general's voice, an undertone of aggrievement and anger that usually didn't accompany these sessions. He wondered whether, just maybe, this matter might have a personal dimension.

"Permission to ask a nosy question, sir."

"Seeing as how that's your specialty, permission granted."

"Has Captain Cole ever been under your command?"

Hagan hesitated, and looked him over carefully before answering.

"The answer is in his dossier, but your suspicions are correct. What made you ask?"

"Just a hunch, sir. Something about your intensity, I guess."

A look of grudging admiration gave way to one of mild concern. Hagan shook his head and smiled tightly.

"Captain Cole served under me in Afghanistan. A good man. In those days, anyway. Solid pilot, spectacular at times. Followed orders to the letter." Hagan paused, as if he wasn't quite sure how to word his next comments. "But he did show an occasional tendency toward . . . unwarranted independence. And I suppose that under the wrong influence, that might turn into a point of vulnerability."

"Well, he *was* a Viper pilot, sir. Doesn't that go with the territory?"

Riggleman realized by the look on Hagan's face that his remark had crossed the line. The general, too, had once been a fighter jock. The same was true of most Air Force brass. It was part of the built-in bias of the Air Force pecking order—an automatic advantage for those who got to have all the fun.

"No disrespect intended, sir."

"None taken, Captain. I flew Eagles, not Vipers. And your point is valid, although I do think at times you might be a little quick to find fault with skills you might also envy."

"Yes, sir." And there was no "might" about it. But that didn't mean he was wrong.

"You'll have every resource at your disposal, of course," Hagan said. "And I say that with full awareness that those of us in the public sector don't always have the best possible access to certain cutting-edge technology. Sometimes for budgetary reasons, sometimes due to, well, legal technicalities. So I'm authorizing you to be as, ah, flexible as you deem necessary. Understood?"

"Understood, sir."

In other words, he was free to use better software than the official stuff, for things like data mining, facial recognition, or even outright hacking, if it came to that.

"One other item, which I'd appreciate if you didn't mention outside these walls."

Hagan produced a small key and proceeded to unlock a desk drawer.

He reached inside and pulled out a black business card and slid it across the desk, carefully, as if a chip of plutonium might be encased within. Riggleman picked it up and saw that it contained only a name in white lettering—Harry Walsh—along with a cell phone number with an area code Riggleman didn't recognize. Nothing else.

"Take a good, long look, Captain. Commit the name and number to memory. When you've finished, hand it back. And don't write anything down, please."

"Yes, sir."

Riggleman studied it. The name was easy enough to remember. So was the number. But he wanted to put on a convincing show, so he waited an extra beat or two before placing the card on the desk and sliding it back, just as carefully as the general had done.

Hagan locked the card back in his desk and cleared his throat.

"Should your labors in this case ever reach a dead end, Captain, or should you ever find yourself in need of any, ah, tactic or consideration or *methodology* that is beyond your reach, then I suggest you contact this individual. With all due discretion, of course."

"What's his affiliation, sir?"

"I'm not in a position to answer that. But, as I said, if a need arises . . ."

"Of course, sir."

Now he was almost as curious about Walsh as he was about Cole. He also felt a stirring of self-interest. Walsh was probably some sort of security privateer, and not for the first time Riggleman wondered whether his own talents might be more gainfully employed out in the world at large as a specialist in "information pursuit," as he liked to call it. This gun for hire. A sort of ground-bound air ace with unerring aim. At the very least, this Walsh fellow might have a few insights on the going rate for his brand of skills.

Then again, help from people like Walsh tended to come with certain risks attached. Riggleman had always been wary of seeking aid from the shadows, so to speak, and unless he could find out more about Harry Walsh's bona fides—his employer or sponsor, his usual clientele—then he would contact the man only as a last resort. Fortunately, that also seemed to be the approach Hagan preferred.

"To be perfectly blunt, Captain, I suppose what I'm really trying to say is that while I expect you to keep this clean, don't be overly concerned with playing by the rules. As long as your work remains neat and compartmentalized, do whatever needs to be done. Just find him."

"And when I do?"

"The exact parameters of any follow-up have yet to be determined. The loop is very tight on this one. But, rest assured, when the time comes you'll be fully involved in whatever sort of wrap-up is deemed necessary."

The general's wording was a jolt. Riggleman had only heard General Hagan use the term "wrap-up" in the context of war gaming, when it had always been slang for "the kill." Did the general mean it literally this time?

Riggleman swallowed. Then he nodded.

"Yes, sir. I'll do my best."

CHAPTER TWELVE

TACO ROJO WAS a tidy establishment with chrome tables and a scrubbed tile floor. It was on O'Donnell Square, a half-gentrified block of restaurants, cafés, and taverns along a village green that managed to look pleasant even under the streetlamp glow of a gloomy December evening. They parked around the corner on a cramped street of form-stone row houses.

"It's after the dinner rush, so it ought to be pretty quiet," Steve said.

"How do we want to do this?"

"Why don't I go in first? You can come in a few minutes later, maybe ask whoever's working the counter whatever happened to that guy Mansur."

"Isn't that kind of obvious?"

"Completely. And I'm open to any better ideas. Got any?"

He didn't.

So Steve went in while Cole made another circuit of the block. The square's more rough-and-tumble past showed itself here and there, but some of the newer proprietors seemed determined to resist any backsliding. A sign in a pub doorway forbade entry to anyone wearing "urban wear, baggy clothing, large chains, skullies, wife beaters, doo-rags, long shorts, etc."

Yeah, Cole thought, *I get it.*

By the time he entered Taco Rojo, Steve was seated at a table to the left, already eating a burrito. Barb's spaghetti sauce was decent enough, but the noodles had been a pasty mess, glued together like the pages of a wet phone book, and both men were still pretty hungry. As the door closed behind him, Cole spotted the requisite security camera just as its red light came on, activated by a motion sensor. The counterman was a hulking fellow with a trimmed mustache. A clock in the back showed 8:09. Steve was the only other customer.

"Can I help you?"

Cole scanned the menu on the wall.

"Beef burrito with black beans and pico de gallo. And a large iced tea."

"For here or to go?"

"I'll eat here."

"Eight forty-eight."

He gave the man a ten as he pondered what to say next.

"Utensils are along the wall. It'll be a few minutes."

"Thanks. How long you guys been here now?"

The counterman impaled the order on a spike and shrugged, looking bored.

"Few years."

"Whatever happened to that guy who worked here a while back? Mansur, I think it was. We used to talk when I came in."

The counterman snapped to attention and narrowed his eyes. He tilted his head and gave Cole a long, quizzical stare.

"I doubt that. His English sucked, and he worked in the back. Who are you?"

"Hey, no big deal. It's just he was a nice guy and I hadn't seen him in a while."

The man's voice slammed down like a cleaver. "Who *are* you? What do you want?"

"Skip it, okay? Maybe I'll take that burrito to go."

But by then the counterman had snatched the wall phone from its cradle and was punching in a number, like one he'd memorized. Following orders? A prearranged alert? Cole glanced at Steve, who shrugged, chewing. He backed away from the counter toward the door. The red light on the camera was still shining as he turned the knob.

"Don't forget your food, sir!" More demand than plea. "Only a minute more!"

Cole stepped outside into a gust of sleet, an icy blast that seemed determined to scour the block of all newcomers. He flipped up the collar on his jacket and set off toward the car, not daring to look back even as he heard Steve coming through the door in his wake. He had asked a very simple question, really. A small, tentative step. Yet it had set off some sort of alarm.

"Shit," Steve said, trotting up beside him. "That was weird. What do you think it was all about?"

"No idea. When the Bureau came poking around earlier it must have freaked them out. Maybe now they think Mansur's some kind of terrorist. Who do you think he called?"

"The Bureau?"

"Maybe. Jesus, what's happened to the weather?"

Another blast of sleet raked them like birdshot. They crossed the square and walked around the corner to take shelter in Steve's Honda. Cole was glad they hadn't parked on the square, where some camera might have picked up their tags. Sleet bounced crazily off the windshield. The sidewalks were empty. People on the block had started turning on their Christmas lights—blue-clad plastic Madonnas face-to-face with faded Santas, flanked by three-foot candy canes on marble stoops.

"Maybe I should have taken it slower," Cole said.

"It wasn't you. It was him. Like he was expecting it. The minute he heard the name Mansur he was reaching for the phone. And he didn't look happy about it. Shoulda seen his face when you were leaving. Pissed, but also scared, like he knew he'd fucked up."

"What do we do now?"

"Not sure there *is* a next move. Not with that guy."

"We could check their dumpster, look for old paperwork. It's probably out back."

"Like from your Infowar training? I guess. But isn't that kind of risky?"

"How much worse can it get? We're already on camera. And I doubt he'll be looking for us out back."

Steve thought about it.

"Why not? Won't be the first time I've gone through somebody's garbage."

They got out of the car, checked their flanks, and doubled back to O'Donnell Square, giving the storefront a wide berth before heading up a side street to an alley running behind Taco Rojo. It was dimly lit and lined with small green dumpsters. Cole heard the skitter of rats, assembling for their own dinnertime rush. One panicked at their approach, nearly running over his feet.

Each dumpster was marked with the name of its owner. Steve had just thrown open the lid for Taco Rojo's when Cole spotted a pair of blue recycling bins—one for glass, the other for paper—just down the way. These seemed to be shared by the whole block.

"Let's try those first." Steve, already recoiling from the stench of the dumpster, nodded and let the lid slam shut.

The paper bin was about a quarter full. Cole leaned inside until his feet left the ground and grabbed an empty cardboard box. He handed it to Steve, then pulled out a second.

"Hold these," he said. "I'll grab the loose papers and pile them in."

It was mostly unopened junk mail, empty cups, old newspapers. But there were also torn envelopes and loose papers, some stacked, some crumpled. He took it all, eventually filling both boxes and then a third while Steve kept watch over the alley. No cops, thank goodness, although they'd both spotted a camera mounted at the end of the alley. Their only live audience was a young couple who passed up the side street, a man and woman in black leather who paused at the mouth of the alley just long enough to shake their heads in either pity or disgust.

They carried the boxes to Steve's Honda.

"Back to the house?" Cole asked.

"Somewhere closer. Where we can ditch this stuff once we're through with it. Some parking lot, where we won't stand out as much."

They drove northeast a few miles, crossing beneath the Beltway before pulling into the vast lot of a Walmart. Steve switched on the dome light and starting sorting through items from the first box. Cole climbed into the backseat and started in on the second one. They proceeded carefully, tossing loose newspapers aside to focus on mail and crumpled papers. Most of it was bills, receipts, or sales pitches from vendors of restaurant equipment. There was an unintentionally hilarious letter from a customer, complaining that a take-out meal had poisoned her pet hamster. Form letters from the block's landlord warned three different tenants about overdue rent.

Twenty minutes into their search, Cole struck gold—a stack of printouts from Taco Rojo payroll records for September and October. Eleven employees were on the report for September, ten for October. The extra name in September was Mansur Amir Khan. His last day on the job was September 6, probably about the time the FBI came looking for him. The Social Security number was probably bogus, but Steve wrote it down. There was no phone number, but there was a Baltimore address on Gough Street, in care of a Consuelo Reyes.

"Whaddya think?" Steve asked. "Strike while the iron is hot?"

"Sure. But maybe this time we should try a different approach."

"Keep that sheet handy, with his name and address. I've got an idea."

CHAPTER THIRTEEN

STEVE WENT INTO the Walmart and bought a business envelope with a plastic window. He folded the payroll report inside it so that Mansur's name and address showed through the window. Then they headed for Gough Street.

No gentrification there. There were more boarded-up windows than Christmas lights. So many houses were empty that there was plenty of on-street parking. To be on the safe side Steve pulled into a space around the corner. He rubbed his hands together in the cold, then held aloft the envelope as if it was their ticket to the Promised Land.

"This time I'll do the talking. You watch our backs."

The sky was clearing, the temperature dropping. Fallen sleet filled sidewalk cracks in glowing white seams. At the address on Gough Street the outside door was unlocked. A mailbox in the foyer showed a Reyes on the second floor. The door to the stairwell was ajar, so they went on up. Reyes was the middle apartment. A television blared from the place on the left, shouts and laughter from the one on the right. Steve's knock was answered by the bark of a dog—it sounded big— followed by shuffling footsteps. A deadbolt shot back and the door opened to the limit of a security chain, spilling a yellow band of light onto the landing. A middle-aged woman in a bathrobe eyed him suspiciously. A cigarette smoldered in her right hand.

"*Qué?*"

Steve showed her the envelope just long enough for her to read the name and address.

"I have a check for Mansur Amir Khan. Does he still live here?"

A thin arm darted through the opening like a striking cobra. Steve barely kept her from snatching the envelope.

"The check is mine!" she said. She unleashed an agitated burst of Spanish.

"Does Mansur still live here?" Steve asked again.

"Who are you?" she asked in English. Same question as at Taco Rojo. Same narrowed eyes and tilted head.

"Unless I see Mansur, I can't leave this."

She switched back to Spanish and pulled a cell phone from the pocket of her robe. Another trip wire, another alarm.

"Let's get out of here," Cole whispered. Steve nodded, and they took the stairs two at a time, pursued by shouts all the way to the ground floor, where an arriving tenant stood by an open mailbox.

"She's nuts," he said, circling a finger by his ear.

"You got that right." They brushed past him toward the door.

"Did I hear you say you were looking for Mansur?"

Steve turned in the open doorway. The guy was mid-twenties, T-shirt and jeans, a white hard hat tucked under his right arm.

"We've got a check for him," Cole said. Steve showed the envelope. "She wanted us to leave it with her, but, well, like you said. Nuts."

"Never knew why he put up with her. Screaming, taking his money. I saw him over on Broadway a few days ago." He shook his head. "Clueless as ever."

"Mansur?" Steve said. "Where?"

"One of those Latino bodegas, buying a candy bar. Almost jumped out of his skin when I called his name. Like somebody was after him. Of course, maybe somebody *was*." He nodded upstairs, where the woman was still muttering on the landing. Then he paused, as if he'd already said too much, and eyed them with renewed scrutiny.

"Maybe you could find a way to get this check to him?" Cole said, hoping to establish some trust. The man's expression softened.

"No need. He's living on Pickard now, not far from here. Being Mansur, he didn't remember the address—you know how he is, and his English still sucks. But he said you couldn't miss it. Called it the tall house, whatever that means."

"Pickard?"

"Right off Fayette."

"Thanks," Steve said. "The tall house?"

"That's what he said."

The woman upstairs was still making noise, speaking into her phone now. Her enforcers might be only minutes from arrival. Steve and Cole shoved through the door and ran toward the Honda.

Pickard was less than a mile away, and even drearier than Gough. It ended at Fayette, which made hunting for Mansur's house easier. It was immediately apparent what he must have meant by "the tall house." Just down the block was a three-story row house that towered over its two-story neighbors.

Steve parked at a metered spot on Fayette that offered a view of the front door around the corner. It was almost ten. He got on his cell phone. Cole heard Barb pick up.

"We're outside what we think is Mansur's new address. We've already raised alarms at two other locations, so we'll probably sit tight awhile." He looked questioningly at Cole, who nodded in approval. "Anyhow, this could take some time, so don't wait up for us."

"We'll leave a light on," Barb said. "Call if you need reinforcements. Where are you, exactly?"

"Pickard Street, at East Fayette."

"Quaint digs in a salubrious location. If you're not back by sundown I'll alert the desk sergeant for the Eastern district. Don't step on any needles."

They decided to stake out the house until midnight. If no one came or went by then, they'd return in the morning. They were both a little puzzled by the tenant's description of Mansur. Cole had expected to find a rough-and-ready tribal type, not easily intimidated. He instead sounded like an object of pity. Bickell had implied Mansur wasn't exactly a bright light. So had this guy. Maybe here he was at an even greater disadvantage. But hadn't he brought his family with him? That's certainly what Bickell had implied.

Steve and Cole had little to keep them busy, and almost no one was out on the sidewalks in the bitter cold. By ten thirty they were stamping their feet to stay warm and wishing they had coffee.

"You do a lot of this kind of stuff?" Cole asked.

"Stakeouts? Almost never. Last time was years ago, down in Arnold, waiting to see if a governor would show up at his mistress's apartment. Which, come to think of it, was also the last time I went through any-body's garbage."

"Find anything?"

"The gov was a no-show. But there were some pretty good credit card receipts. That was the story that was supposed to get me a foreign bureau. Barb got it instead."

"Hard feelings?"

He shook his head.

"I was slated for the next opening. Then they closed all the bureaus, hers included. All those jobs are gone now. Newspapers. Equal oppor-tunity unemployers."

"So that would've been you instead of her with those two kids, get-ting brains all over your shoes?"

"Yeah, there's that, too. Barb doesn't always sleep so well."

"Firsthand knowledge?"

Steve smiled and shook his head.

"Our lives are already too complicated. But you've seen the house. Not much happens that the other two don't know about. Barb can get pretty restless late at night, moving around in the dark. Her and the cat. So what about you? No stakeouts in your Infowar training?"

"Not much call for that in a fighter wing."

"I never did ask what your fake name was. The one on your ID?"

"Oh." He smiled. "Floyd Rayford."

"Wasn't he—?"

"Orioles third baseman, back in the eighties. Four errors in one game, but I liked him. Sugar Bear. Had some pop in his bat."

"The Wally Pipp of the Orioles. Ripken replaced him at third in game two of a doubleheader. That's when the Ironman streak started."

"You're shittin' me. How did I not know that?"

"How'd I not know you're an O's fan?"

"Listened to 'em on the radio when I was a kid. Virginia Eastern Shore is O's country. Or used to be. So when I was thinking up a name I figured why not?"

"Hey, what's this?"

A black SUV was pulling up in front of the house, brake lights shining. It was shortly after eleven. Two men in dark warm-ups hopped out from either side and scanned the block in both directions while Cole and Steve slid down in their seats. The man on the right opened a rear passenger door and hauled out a much shorter fellow in light clothing. Cole was reminded of Bickell's description of Mansur as a "little shit Pashtun."

"Think it's him?" he asked.

"If so, not exactly a happy homecoming."

The two big fellows escorted the smaller one toward the house. If this was an FBI operation, activated by the alarms they'd tripped, Cole doubted they'd be delivering Mansur back so soon, if at all. These men were acting more like jailers than protectors, with hands clamped on either arm. Hardly the sort of arrangement you'd have expected Mansur to cook up for himself.

"He must have *some* freedom of movement if he's got his own apartment," Steve said. "I mean, if he's hanging out at some bodega when that other guy saw him. Maybe they just keep him on a short leash."

"Well, they're yanking it tight now."

The three men disappeared into the house while the SUV idled out front. Ten minutes later the big guys returned, doors slamming. The SUV made a U-turn back toward Fayette, Steve and Cole sinking below the dashboard as the headlights swept the Honda. They popped up just in time to see it flash past them toward downtown. A GMC Yukon Denali, Maryland tags. Steve wrote down the numbers and phoned Barb.

"Got a tag for you to run with your guy at DMV." He read her the number. "We may be a while longer, but I'm shutting down the phone for now. We're gonna do some poking around."

"Be careful."

"You bet." He switched off the phone and turned to Cole. "Let's go see Mansur. Only this time, not through the front door."

They walked up the alley behind Pickard toward the back of the house, where a fire escape stairway was bolted to the bricks. To foil burglars, the iron ladder hanging from the bottom was folded up just out of reach, held in place by a counterweight on a steel cable. Steve and Cole jumped for the lower rung but came up short. Steve got an aluminum garbage can from next door and rolled it into position beneath the ladder. He climbed shakily atop it and steadied for a leap. A dog began barking from a fenced lot across the alley. If Steve missed, the racket would be even worse. Cole readied himself to act as spotter.

Steve's first try was awkward, and if not for Cole he would have landed in a heap. The barking dog was in a frenzy now.

"Christ, what am I thinking," Steve said. "You're the fucking pole vaulter, right?"

"In high school, but yeah."

They traded places. Cole crouched carefully and pushed off, achieving just enough lift to grab the lowest rung with both hands. It was rough with rust, and for a moment he dangled like a trapeze artist while the can rattled back into place. The dog was still going nuts, and a light flashed on in one of the opposite windows just as the ladder began easing lower from the weight of his body. As soon as his feet touched the ground he started climbing. Steve followed him up, and they quickly reached the latticed platform outside the second-floor windows.

No lights were on. They paused to wait for the dog to quiet down, which took another five minutes. By then the light had gone back out in the window of the house across the alley. There were no curtains in either second-floor window of Mansur's house, and both were dark. A streetlamp at the end of the alley offered just enough light for them to see that the rooms were empty and unfurnished. They crept slowly up to the top floor, where a window spilled light between the crumpled slats of an aluminum blind. They heard a voice from inside, a woman speaking Spanish. Cole moved close enough to peek through a slit and saw her facing into a dingy room from an open doorway. Like Consuelo Reyes, she, too, was shouting angrily, gesturing emphatically with her right hand. Crouching lower, Cole now saw that she was speaking to a man seated on a narrow bed against the far wall. He was short and sallow, with a scanty beard and the weathered, old-before-his-time look of a tribal Pashtun, although instead of a billowy *shalwar kameez* he wore baggy jeans and a white T-shirt. It had to be Mansur.

He looked cowed, submissive, and when he opened his mouth, his voice was so meek and muffled that Cole couldn't even make out what language he was speaking.

The woman left, shutting the door behind her. A lock snapped with a click. Mansur rose to turn out the light. His footsteps approached the darkened window, so Cole shrank out of sight, bumping into Steve, who steadied them on the landing. Then, in a stroke of luck, Mansur shoved aside the blinds and unlocked the window. The lower sash groaned as it rose an inch or two. He slid a shoe into the opening to keep the window from shutting, its scuffed leather toe poking into the frigid night. The old blinds settled back into place with a noise like a Slinky, and they heard Mansur's receding footsteps. There was a creak of bedsprings, then silence.

Steve checked his watch: 11:24. They whispered in consultation, and decided to wait another twenty minutes to give Mansur time to fall asleep. They settled their rumps onto the cold steel slats, hoping no one was looking out from the back of any houses across the alley. Even in the darkness they probably showed up like a pair of giant spiders.

When the twenty minutes were up, Cole stood quietly and tugged at the sash. It was stiff and swollen from years of repainting, so he pulled harder, knees bent. When the window finally came free it shrieked loudly.

They paused to listen for any signs they'd awakened Mansur. His breathing was slow, regular, so Cole pulled aside the blinds and slid feetfirst into the room while holding back the blinds for Steve, who also dropped quietly to the floor. No wonder Mansur had opened it. An old steam radiator hissed in a corner, and the heat was stifling.

As Cole lowered the blinds back into place they came free from their wobbly brackets and clattered loudly to the floor. Mansur sat up in alarm as Steve crossed the room in two big steps to clamp a hand on the small man's mouth just as he was about to shout. Mansur thrashed and squirmed as Cole grabbed him from the other side. The little man felt brittle, his bones like sticks you could snap with your hands, and his eyes were wild with fear. Cole whispered into his ear.

"We are here to help you, Mansur." Then he took a gamble. "We are here about your family."

Mansur relaxed only slightly, but Cole was heartened enough to ease his grip. When Mansur didn't try to break free he took it as a sign of progress and nodded to Steve, who gently let go.

Cole whispered again. "I am going to take my hand off your mouth, but do not cry out. Do not call for anyone. Do you understand?"

Mansur nodded, his eyes still wide.

Cole let go. Mansur sagged in apparent relief. When he finally spoke, his voice was a soft rasp.

"Who are you?"

Third time today for that question.

"We're friends. But for security reasons we can't give you our names."

Mansur nodded resignedly, as if he'd grown accustomed to that kind of dodge. Cole leaned closer and kept his voice low.

"Those men who brought you here tonight, in the black SUV, the black truck. Who are they?"

"The angry people."

"Angry why?"

"Angry for Mansur, angry for me."

"Angry *at* Mansur?"

He shook his head in apparent irritation, as if he'd been over this a thousand times. It reminded Cole of his son, Danny, the way he got frustrated when he couldn't explain something.

"The angry people, who do they work for?"

"Not know," he said, shaking his head again. "Bring here. I sleep home, then I bring here, the angry people. Now *all* places, the angry people."

He looked at Steve as they tried to piece together Mansur's fractured English.

"They came for you, in Afghanistan?" Steve asked.

"Yes. Sandar Khosh."

The effect on Cole was electric.

"Sandar Khosh? That's your home village?"

"No, no. Mandi Bahar. Mansur home." He tapped his chest, placed a hand over his heart. "Mandi Bahar."

The name stirred a memory, hazy and remote, another of those forlorn dots on the tactical map, one of hundreds. Surely he'd seen it.

"Sandar Khosh," Mansur continued. "Very kilometers."

"Very *many* kilometers?" Cole offered. "Far from Mandi Bahar, is that what you mean?"

"Yes. Far."

"I know Sandar Khosh," Cole said. "I've . . . been there."

"Yes?" Mansur looked straight into Cole's eyes, and for the first time he seemed pleased, almost hopeful. Cole wondered if Zach and he had ever seen Mansur during their recon of Sandar Khosh. Surely he must have been one of those robed men on the ground, moving like ghosts among their neighbors.

"In Sandar Khosh, did you drive a white truck?"

"Yes. No. He does, but . . ." His voice trailed off.

"Who does?"

"Truck gone. No truck." Mansur shook his head, no longer smiling.

"Whose truck, Mansur?"

"Men's truck."

"The angry men?" Steve asked. "The ones who brought you here?"

"No!" He was irritated again. "First men."

"From earlier?"

"Yes. From here."

"Americans?"

"Yes."

Had Cole's missile strike killed Americans, then, along with the women and children? If so, then why had Castle wanted them killed? Or maybe that, too, had been a colossal mistake, a gross error of faulty intelligence. Unless they were talking about a different truck altogether. The way Mansur spoke English, he supposed that almost any interpretation might fit.

"The Americans," Steve asked. "What were their names?"

"Not know." Mansur shook his head again. "Not know. From Lancer."

Lancer again, the handle Bickell had mentioned, that had popped up on Cole's chat screen, whereabouts unknown. A name with no face, no affiliation.

"Lancer," Cole said. "He's American?"

"Yes, yes."

"Working for who?"

"For who?"

"Who does Lancer work for?"

Mansur frowned and again shook his head, exasperated.

"Not know. Not know. He is *American*!"

As if that explained everything, all those Americans working for the same side. That's probably how Mansur saw it, which would certainly explain how he could have been manipulated so easily by one faction or another. If one American offered to pay you more than another, what was the harm in switching if they were working for the same side?

"What about Hector?" Steve offered, trying out Castle's code name.

"*No*," Mansur said, his voice rising. "I say everything. I say everything and *no more*!"

Now he was downright angry. Cole worried the landlady would hear.

"Do you know about Magic Dimes?" Steve asked. "Did Hector or Lancer ever talk about that?"

"Magic? No magic. No one." He was drifting away from them, on a cloud of either weariness or indifference.

"Shit, this is useless," Steve said. "His English sucks."

Cole tried another tack.

"Your family. Where is your family, Mansur?"

"Family?" His eyes brightened again.

"Yes. Your wife and children. Where are they?"

"Children, no." He went glum, shook his head. "My children make toy. They make toy and it is ruin! *Ruin!*"

"Easy, Mansur," Steve said. "Shit, he'll wake up the whole house."

Cole, utterly baffled now, was about to try another question when a woman called out in Spanish from down the hall. Mansur went rigid.

"Great," Steve muttered. "The bitch is back."

"What is she saying?" Cole asked.

"The angry men. Here."

"The ones in the black truck?"

"Yes. Here now."

They heard the sound of car doors slamming from out front, an engine revving. Probably the same SUV as before.

"She say they bring movie."

"A movie?" Steve whispered.

Mansur nodded. "Movie from taco."

"What the hell?"

With a sinking feeling, Cole realized what Mansur must be talking about.

"From the security cam at Taco Rojo." They heard the slam of a downstairs door, footsteps coming up the stairway. "They want to show him, see if he knows us. Or me, anyway."

"He will now. Let's go!" Steve said.

He and Cole moved to the window. Cole decided he had better do something about the fallen blinds, lest they rouse unwanted suspicion, so he hastily slid them beneath Mansur's bed while Steve heaved up the sash. Cold air poured in. Cole half expected Mansur to try to come with them, but the young man sat impassively on the bed, rubbing his arms against the chill. He felt a stab of pity for the man, stranded alone and obviously lacking the means to help himself. And who knew what he'd say about this visit?

"Mansur," Cole whispered, getting his attention one last time. "This is our secret, okay? Our secret from the angry men, or we will never be able to help you. You and your family. Okay?"

Mansur shook his head.

"My family. It is away."

"Away where?"

"You not know? Then how you help?"

He was growing agitated again, so Cole moved to calm him.

"We will help them, Mansur. We will help them. But you must help us. You must keep our secret."

Mansur nodded solemnly, then flinched as the footsteps pounded closer and stopped on the third-floor landing. The landlady called out. Cole followed Steve onto the fire escape, pulling down the sash behind him as he heard the snap of a deadbolt lock. He stepped away from the window just as they heard the door to Mansur's room rattle open. A pool of light appeared at the spot where Cole had just been standing. He backed away slowly and followed Steve down the metal stairs. They heard the muffled voices of men in consultation, but no one was shouting in anger or alarm. Still, Mansur might tell them anything in his current state of mind, so they moved fast.

Steve clambered onto the ladder at the bottom. It sank toward the ground, the steel cable groaning as it raised the counterweight. Cole followed him down, dropping lightly to the ground. Figuring that it wasn't yet safe to return to Steve's Honda, they headed down the alley in the opposite direction from the way they'd come. It was nearly midnight, and the empty streets made them feel hunted and exposed. With the video from the security camera, these men would now know what Steve and he looked like. With good enough connections, the men might soon even learn their names.

Cole felt they'd gotten precious little information in exchange for their trouble. A location for Mansur, yes, and another tantalizing trace of the mysterious Lancer, whoever he was, plus some sort of link between the villages of Sandar Khosh, which he knew all too well, and Mandi Bahar, which was familiar, but he couldn't recall why. But where was Mansur's family now? Who was holding him here, and why? Steve and he were leaving with more questions than they'd brought.

They trotted across Fayette and disappeared up another alley. Checking over their shoulders for pursuers, they picked up the pace and headed deeper into the city.

CHAPTER FOURTEEN

THEY FINALLY MADE IT back to Barb's at one in the morning. Every light was on. Steve recounted their adventures, with Cole chiming in here and there. But mostly he watched Barb, intrigued by her still and watchful silence, lips compressed. She reminded him of a card player careful to conceal a winning hand, and he wondered what she was holding in reserve.

"Nice work," Keira said after Steve finished. "Between that and Bickell, we've got plenty to keep us busy."

"First we need to find out who's holding Mansur, and why," Steve said. "Maybe property records will help."

Barb played her hand.

"My guy at DMV ran the tags. That SUV is registered to Intel-Pro. Your guy's been lying to you, Steve. They're involved in this way deeper than we thought."

"*My* guy? I'm not the only one with an IntelPro source."

"Okay, then. All our guys. But yours is supposedly the most plugged in, the closest to the top."

Steve kept a game face, but his earlobes reddened. Cole sensed that something more than a professional disagreement was at stake. Up to now, Steve had been the closest thing to a chief executive in their tenuous little democracy. Barb was challenging the pecking order.

"Maybe Steve's guy is also in the dark," Keira said, trying to mediate. "We don't really know how high up the ladder he is."

"Steve knows, he just won't tell us. Maybe his guy is just covering his ass."

Steve frowned and shook his head, but his earlobes had faded to pink. Then he sighed deeply and gave in. Sort of.

"Entirely possible," he said. "I guess he could be using me for just about anything. I'll certainly ask him about this. But none of it explains why Castle's missing, or where he's gone, or whether he's working for himself or for the Agency."

The concession blunted the force of Barb's attack, and for the next few minutes they kicked around other possible motives and scenarios. Most involved names Cole hadn't yet heard of. It was obvious he had a lot to learn about IntelPro, the role of the Agency, and the state of their reporting if he was going to stay abreast of them. He wondered how much they would be willing to educate him.

"Your corneas are glazing over, Captain Cole," Barb observed. "Are we boring you, or are you just craving a drink?"

Baiting him, so he held his tongue. Intemperate remarks would become part of the record against him, just as on Predator missions.

"You guys are talking about a lot of people I know nothing about. Maybe you could bring me up to speed."

"How 'bout tomorrow?" Keira said, drawing sharp looks from the other two. "After we've all had some sleep."

"Sure. Thanks."

"We could all use some shut-eye," Steve said.

Barb seemed about to object. Then, as if thinking better of it, she nodded, and soon afterward the three reporters were heading upstairs to bed. Keira, leading the way, paused halfway up.

"I'll check the deeds for the Pickard Street house first thing tomorrow," she said.

"You're the morning person," Barb answered.

"Just be careful," Steve said. "Keep it as quiet as you can."

Alone downstairs, Cole took stock of his new billet. Barb had made up the couch with fresh linens and a spare duvet. The cat was gone, presumably out on a prowl. His only company was the pair of boys on the photos, facing him from the shadows of the dining room. He thought back to his trailer in the desert, wondering whether the coyotes were still visiting nightly. That monastic existence felt like the distant past. His only connection now was a mild urge for a drink. He turned out the lights before it had a chance to sharpen, not even bothering to brush his teeth. Then he settled beneath the sheets and drifted off to the pinging of halyards against masts on the sailboats docked across Stansbury Creek.

For the first time in months he dreamed of his wife, Carol. She was smiling. They were here, the whole family, seated on their couch four abreast in the house on Wilson Point Road, alone downstairs with the TV on. All the furniture and photos were from their old place in Summerlin. Or, no, now the room looked like the vacation home they'd rented at Lake Tahoe a few months before they split up, with the kids asleep in a loft upstairs and Carol and he in bed, no television. A half-empty bottle of wine stood on the bedside table. Cole raised a glass to his lips, swallowed greedily, then tasted it on Carol's lips as they kissed, a wonderfully familiar sensation, although the touch of her hands on his arm, his back, his face, was somehow Keira's—feathery and thrilling, her short fingernails brushing like a caress. When he looked up into Carol's face he was shocked to see she had red hair, uncombed, like Barb's. Now they were half undressed, unbuttoning and unzipping, everything moving fast, their clothes shedding as easily as bath towels. Carol lay back against the bed, eyes closed, but it was still Barb's hair fanned against the pillow. She smiled slyly as Cole entered her, as if harboring a secret, which only thrilled him more. The body beneath him was warm and sinuous, but indeterminate now, belonging to no woman he had ever made love to before. It left him feeling strange but no less passionate as he rocked and bucked with abandon, then release.

Cole jolted awake in a silent room. The air outside was still, the masts no longer pinging. His surroundings were barely visible in the pale glow of a streetlamp seeping through the blinds. His boxers were wet with semen.

"Shit!" he whispered.

He threw back the top sheet. The air smelled like baked mushrooms, a simmer of sex.

"Shit!"

The bottom sheet was damp. He groped his way into the kitchen, where he tore off a paper towel and ran it under the tap before dabbing it to the wet spot, hoping the couch wouldn't be stained in the morning. His first night as a houseguest and he was ruining the furniture, exactly the sort of animalistic influence they probably feared most. And now he truly craved a drink, preferably two fingers of bourbon in a glass tumbler.

He returned to the kitchen to throw away the paper towel, taking pains to stuff it out of sight beneath the garbage on top. Then he opened the fridge. Maybe a beer would tide him over. He grabbed a cold bottle, unscrewed the cap, and drank half of it while standing in the light of the open door. He carried the rest into the dining room, where the reporters' laptops were all open, like place settings for a party of three. He touched a key on one and the screen lit up, a phalanx of icons on a field of blue. They weren't exactly security conscious among themselves, which he supposed was a good sign. With his left hand he pressed the beaded bottle to his forehead. With his right he moved the cursor to the icon for Internet Explorer and clicked. The Google homepage came up.

Might as well begin his education.

He eased into a chair and typed in a search for IntelPro. The company website was the first hit. A sober home page, even dignified, with the company slogan—"Protection Is Our Watchword"—splashed atop an impressive slide show depicting IntelPro employees in action around the world. Things loosened up a bit once you started clicking on the links.

A page headlined "A Company of Global Reach" displayed an interactive map of the world with IntelPro logos marking every country where they were doing business. Cole clicked on Kabul. Up popped a summary of local manpower and a brief description of duties. An IntelPro security detail guarded the presidential palace. There was a reference to support units based in various provinces, but no mention of any work in the tribal borderlands out where Mansur had lived and worked. No mention of either Mandi Bahar or Sandar Khosh.

Cole clicked on another page and activated a video. It opened with a shot of a dozen or so muscular, heavily armed fellows in skintight T-shirts advancing across a swampy field at the company's two-thousand-acre training facility on the Maryland Eastern Shore. Gunfire erupted, loud enough to awaken half the household. Cole quickly shut it down.

He returned to the map and clicked on the logo just north of Baltimore. A photo of corporate headquarters popped up, a gleaming three-story building in Hunt Valley. Close enough to Washington to keep a hand in, but not so close as to appear to be breathing down the neck of the Pentagon, or the CIA. And it was certainly convenient for keeping tabs on Mansur.

He searched the site for any reference to "Lancer," just in case, but came up empty.

The deeper he explored, the wackier things got. Embedded in the section for prospective employees was a page offering company logo products like T-shirts and caps, so you could dress like a mercenary in your own backyard. At the bottom, in a deft bit of cross-marketing, you could click a link to join the National Rifle Association, a paid advertiser.

He navigated to the description of IntelPro's corporate structure.

The founder and chairman was Michael "Mike" Boardman. Former U.S. Army Ranger. West Point, class of '87, meaning he'd be in his mid-forties. Decorated during the Persian Gulf War in '91. Family man. Self-made millionaire. In his picture his hair was clipped as short as on the first day of basic. Not even a hint of a smile. Charcoal gray suit, white shirt, red tie. Just another uniform, in other words. Below the photo were links to profiles in the news media, plus a *Wall Street Journal* editorial that praised him as a "visionary entrepreneur" and concluded, "While some misguided souls inevitably label him a mercenary, Boardman has found a creative and muscular way to serve his country even as he serves his company's impressive bottom line."

A blow job. That's what Steve would've said, and Cole found himself agreeing. He doubted he shared many political viewpoints with the journalists, but in some ways he was already seeing things from their point of view. Stockholm syndrome, which made him chuckle.

His laughter caught in his throat when he saw the next name in the IntelPro hierarchy:

Phil Bradsher, Chief of Operations.

Or, as the web bio helpfully pointed out, "Major General Phil Bradsher, recently retired from the U.S. Air Force." He'd come aboard almost two years ago. A quote from CEO Mike Boardman summed up the rationale behind the hire: "With Phil in the cockpit, IntelPro hopes to motivate its associates to ever bolder and more decisive action. While we believe we have already made an impressive mark on a brave new frontier of private endeavor, with Phil's guidance and counsel the value of our mission will become ever more apparent, perhaps even to those who tend to question our raison d'être."

A bullshit way of saying it was time to take no prisoners, or so it sounded to Cole. The same boilerplate the brass used to imply that they were men of action in a passive world. On paper, anyway.

The most intriguing thing about Bradsher was his former spot in the Air Force chain of command. He had led the U.S. Air Force Warfare Center at Nellis, a plum posting reporting directly to Combat Command. Just below Bradsher at Nellis—and presumably still just below Bradsher's successor—was Brigadier General Mitchell Hagan, commander of the 57th Wing, with jurisdiction over Colonel Archer Milroy, head of the 432nd Air Expeditionary Wing at Creech, with all its Predator crews, including the ones commanded by Cole's CO, Lieutenant Colonel Scott "Sturdy" Sturdivant.

He studied the photo and thought about the timing. By the time the shit hit the fan for Cole, Bradsher had been out of the Air Force several months. But Cole was guessing he stayed in close touch with all his old buddies, and he probably knew exactly what was going on inside the Predator program—its successes, its fuckups, its booming budget appropriations, and the growing chatter about pilot burnout. Cole recalled Bickell's complaints about green badgers and blue badgers and all the incestuous relationships out in the field. If IntelPro's people ever needed help from a Predator crew, they certainly had the right man to ensure their request would be heard at the highest levels. He was pondering the implications of that when a voice made him jump.

"Next time, ask first."

Barb stood in the kitchen doorway, hands on hips. Cole exed out the page and sat up straight.

"Sorry. Couldn't sleep, figured I'd look some stuff up."

"Like my emails, maybe?"

"No. Web stuff. Didn't even know this was your machine."

She crossed her arms, the same pose his mom had used whenever

Cole missed curfew. She wore a white flannel nightgown, decidedly unsexy, although her hair looked disturbingly the way it had in his dream. He shifted self-consciously.

"Maybe you should have a password for your log-on," he said.

"Up to now I've never needed one. We're a team here. Or were. We trust each other not to go snooping around on each other's laptops."

"Even team members need to keep some stuff to themselves."

"Tell me about it. I'm having a drink. Want one? And no, this isn't a test of your sobriety."

She turned back into the kitchen. He heard the clink of bottles, the gurgle of a pour.

"Maybe just a touch."

She emerged with two glasses, no ice. He could already smell the bourbon.

"What were you perusing so intently?" She handed him the glass.

"IntelPro website. Trying to get up to speed."

"Learn anything?"

He told her about Bradsher. She raised an eyebrow and swallowed without a shudder, an old pro. Then she leaned over his shoulder and tapped the keyboard until the general's bio popped back up. Her flannel sleeve brushed Cole's cheek. It smelled like her skin, like the warmed sheets of a slept-in bed.

She nodded, reading.

"Good stuff." She sounded pleased. "That chain of command you mentioned, write it down. You said the line goes straight to your unit?"

"Like an arrow."

"And you think Bradsher would be able to exploit those connections?"

"Absolutely."

"At what price?"

"He wouldn't need a price. It's an old boy network."

She smiled and lowered her head, as if embarrassed for him.

"There's always a price, *especially* in old boy networks. But that's a good thing. Gives me more trails to follow. Deeds, stock transactions, any sign that your old chain of command is living beyond its means." She sipped more bourbon. "You always keep these hours?"

He shrugged. In the desert he'd never been conscious of time, apart from what the sun told him. Earlier, when he flew Preds, the shifts had changed so often that his inner clock had been constantly out of balance. She shook her head.

"Just what this crowded little house needs. Another insomniac."

"You, too?"

"Only since that." She nodded toward the photos.

"How long ago?"

"Year and a half. But at this time of night it always feels like about an hour ago."

"I know the feeling."

"I suppose you do."

"Where'd it happen?"

"The back of beyond. Little tribal village, Tangora, in Nangahar Province."

The name was vaguely familiar.

"Were you embedded?"

"No. Hated that shit. Went on my own. Stupidest thing I've ever done, but I was going stir crazy in the hotel. Pounding drinks every night at Bistro and L'Atmosphere. Telling war stories with other hacks like we knew what it was all about. Same sources, day after day."

"Nangahar's out in Indian country. How'd you get there?"

"There's an old Swede, runs an NGO that trains midwives. Been there since the nineties, contacts out the wazoo, friends on all sides. He put me on to a fixer, Mohammed, supposedly connected to a mid-level Taliban, an old thug named Engineer Haider who sent word he'd talk to me. I paid Mohammed a hundred fifty a day, plus two hundred to set up the meet. We took a taxi for the first leg, out past Gardez. Stupid as hell, begging to be kidnapped. Later we switched to a Nissan pickup that couldn't shift into fourth. I was covered head to toe like a local and sat in the back. Mohammed was pretending to be my husband and liking it a little too much. But he got us there."

"Was Haider really Taliban?"

"When it suited his needs. He had other constituencies, too. Said he even ran a few errands for an American contractor, when they paid him enough."

"IntelPro?"

"Overton Security, a competitor."

"You believe him?"

"No reason not to. Guys like Haider are fucking gangsters. At the end of the day it's only about the money. All that tribal bullshit about the enemy of my brother, the wisdom of the elders, it's been completely crushed by the weight of greed."

"Sounds like a line from a story."

She smiled, tilted her glass as though making a toast.

"More or less." She nodded toward the photos. "Haider had a walled compound, but because I was a woman he would only meet me outside, in a stable where the boys brought in the sheep every night. We'd been talking for about an hour when some older kid runs in, all excited, saying somebody had spotted a white swallow."

"Swallow?"

"Like the bird. His name for Predators. Haider had posted two of his sons up on the walls with binoculars. Their only job was to look for drones. He *liked* having drones around. Said that meant they were hunting his rivals. Said his work for Overton meant he had an understanding with the Agency, protection. So he leaves Mohammed and me to cool our heels while he goes up to the roof for a look. His house was inside the compound, maybe forty yards off. I went outside to watch for him. That's when those boys showed up." She nodded at the photos. "They wanted cigarettes, but I don't smoke. Then they wanted money, but Mohammed said not to encourage them. I took out my camera and they lit up, mugging and laughing. That was the first shot, the one where they're smiling. I took two more before the missile hit."

"Haider's house?"

"Dead center. Blew him to pieces. There was a torso, other things I never want to see again. Inside the compound it was like a butcher shop, half his family. Blood and stuff flew clear over the wall, like somebody had tossed it in water balloons. Then those two old people, ten feet away. I guess shrapnel got them."

She swallowed the last of the bourbon, then hugged herself. Cole studied the second photo—the wild eyes, the dark flecks on white garments.

"The official count was eight dead," she said. "Somebody high up must have decided it was a fuckup, because they went into the books as civilians. Three men, three women, two children."

The totals alighted in Cole's memory in the same place where the name of the village, Tangora, had come to rest. Now he knew where he'd heard it.

"When was this again? Exactly."

"August 2010. The fourteenth, a Saturday. I filed a piece in time for all the Sunday editions and they put it on page three. Got bumped off the front by a piece about a bear cub in Florida with its head stuck in a jar."

But Cole was no longer listening. The date fit perfectly.

"I know the crew, the one that fired the dart."

Barb uncrossed her arms. Outside, a heron squawked in the gloom.

"Captain Rod Newell. Sensor Billy Flagg. Everybody was talking about Rod and Billy. It kinda blew 'em away, like what happened to Zach and me. But I never heard anything about Fort1, I would've remembered. You sure this was his doing?"

Barb nodded. She told him how Fort1 had arrived on the scene an hour later, hopping off a Pave Hawk chopper with a handheld radio and an armed escort of three green badgers with no official markings on their uniforms. She heard Fort1 speak his call name into the radio just after landing.

"A real asshole. They all were, but he was the worst. Shoved one of those boys right to the ground. 'Get these little fuckers out of my hair!' That kind of shit. When he saw me with my notebook I thought for a second he was going to kill Mohammed and me both."

"Why was he pissed?"

"He wasn't happy with the results. Maybe he'd been after somebody else. When he searched the compound he was cursing everything in sight."

"How'd you get out of there?"

"One of his guys escorted us back. So I owe him for that, I guess."

She stared off into space. Cole knew the look. But just as he'd concluded she was lost in her memories, she asked a question indicating that her brain was still fully engaged.

"What kind of records do they keep for those Predator raids?"

"There's a full written transcript, with all the chatter and commands, plus the entire video record of whatever the camera shot."

"With the view from the Predator?"

"Yeah. The whole op. They use 'em for training sometimes."

"Where do they keep that stuff?"

"On base, digitally stored. There might be copies at Langley and Al Udeid, but that's above my pay grade."

"Could you get access?"

"Me? I can't even get through the main gate. Besides, that shit's classified."

"But you've still got friends there, right?"

Cole shrugged. "My old wingman, my sensor, Zach."

"Zach Lewis. Age twenty-three. Born McKeesport, P.A. Used to spend all day looking at satellite imagery until he volunteered for the Predator program. A bit of a drinker. A month or two behind on his rent."

"Impressive."

"It was in your court-martial papers. I've got a phone number for his apartment, a personal email address. You could phone him in the morning."

Cole shook his head.

"They'd trace it. Or get a record for the call. They'd know where I was."

"Then send him an email. I'll set up a Gmail account, route it through another server so they won't even know where it came from."

"Everything can be traced."

"Okay. So it won't be *easy* to trace, and it might take a while. And he can erase it right after reading it."

"I thought erasure was impossible, too?"

"Off his hard drive, I mean. I'll send him instructions."

"Even if he got access, how would he send us a copy?"

"With digital records there would be about a thousand ways."

She pulled up a chair and set up an address. Even then Cole was reluctant to send a message, and wasn't sure what to say. Barb offered to help him write it. She asked him which archives to request, and he named the dates and places. Their wish list grew to include not only the video for Tangora but both missions that Zach and he flew over Sandar Khosh, plus any missions flown by any crew over Mansur's home village of Mandi Bahar.

Barb composed the whole thing in a flash. He marveled at how quickly and clearly she marshaled their thoughts, and by the time she finished, even Cole believed that the request sounded earnest and innocent, like a well-intentioned man searching only for the truth. And that's just what they were doing, wasn't it?

"Anything else before I push the button?"

"*If* you push it."

"Oh, I'm pushing it. Because you want me to."

True enough.

"Ask him if he remembers any missions where a guy named Lancer popped up in the chat audience. And if he does, then send those, too."

The keyboard clattered.

"Done."

For all their precautions, it took his breath away when she clicked Send. He was already in trouble for disappearing. In the hands of a military prosecutor, his request to Zach might look like attempted espionage. The instructions telling Zach how to cover his tracks, while sensible, would look even worse.

He sipped the bourbon while his thoughts wandered farther afield. If he could risk a message to Zach, why not one to his kids, or to Carol? If only to let her know that he was sober, and as stable and safe as he'd been in ages.

The look on his face must have given him away.

"You miss them, don't you."

"My family?"

She nodded.

"I do now. Out in the desert it got to where the only kids I ever thought about were the ones we killed. I'd kind of blank out for days at a time. Then, almost the second Keira came into the trailer, I knew I had to get out, get away. She looked up at me and all I could think about was the total emptiness of everything out there."

"Keira has that gift, making people see themselves more clearly. People want to open up, tell her what they've just seen."

"What about you, what's your gift?"

"Wasting time and spinning my wheels, apparently. That's how it feels lately. My specialty is supposedly public records and FOIAs. Freedom of Information Act requests. Paperwork safaris. But I've been stuck on zero for about a month now. We all have. That's why we went looking for you after I dug up those court-martial papers. And maybe it's working. You gave us Fort1's name, for one thing. We need to spread that around. Being free and easy with a protected identity is always good for shaking the trees, seeing what falls out. Plus this stuff with Mansur, and now Tangora." She shook her head, marveling. "Rod and Billy. Pretty amazing you know who did that."

"Who's this IntelPro source of Steve's?"

"He won't say. I wouldn't either, if it was me. They meet at some bar out in Baltimore County. Usually on Fridays, so I guess he's due. But I don't trust the guy."

"How can you not trust someone when you don't even know who he is?"

"Because they're all part of the same crowd. Castle, Bickell, Steve's source. All of them are trained to lie when necessary, and to give only one version of the truth. Maybe he's got good stuff, but we only get part of it, and without the context how do we know it's leading us in the right direction? But Steve's solid, Steve's good. He'll pin him down on Mansur. For better or worse he'll come back with another piece of the puzzle. Maybe this will even convince him it's time for us to move."

"Move where?"

"Over to the Eastern Shore. Keira's parents have a summer home near Easton. Rent free, utilities paid. She's been offering it for weeks and I could rent out this place. We'd save a bundle, enough to buy an extra four months, minimum."

"Sounds like the middle of nowhere."

"We're doing most of our reporting by phone and Internet anyway at this point. And IntelPro's training facility is practically next door. Two of Castle's old Agency buddies work there, and the only way we'll ever have a chance of talking to them is in person. They're Bickell's old buddies, too, but I'll bet he didn't mention that, did he?"

"No."

"Like I said. None of these guys ever gives you the whole story. It's one big process of triangulation."

There was a footfall above, then a heavy tread moving toward the stairs.

"Steve's up," Barb said. "My God, it's six twenty."

Seconds later Steve appeared in the dining room, surveying the scene.

"Big doings?" he asked.

"Pull up a chair," Barb said. "I'll fill you in."

Then Keira came down. The cat rubbed against her leg. It was still more than an hour before sunrise. Cole marveled at the hours that this crew seemed to keep. Pilots were often nocturnal, on the job and in the barroom. But that was usually due to the demands of warfare, shift schedules, or orders from on high. The journalists took to it naturally, like vampires, coming alive in the darkness before the glow of their laptops.

"Looks like we have a quorum," Barb said. "I better make coffee."

CHAPTER FIFTEEN

BARB SUMMARIZED WHAT they'd just done. Steve and Keira seemed impressed, and Steve promised to follow up with his source. Cole was more intrigued by what Barb chose *not* to mention. When she summarized General Bradsher's place in Cole's former chain of command, she didn't cite any of the other links by name. Maybe she wanted to keep them to herself a while longer, so she could start tracking their financial records. Cole considered volunteering the names in the interest of full disclosure, but before he could make up his mind, Barb ambushed him with a fresh demand.

"So, Captain Cole, looks like you're off to a good start. But as we always say in this business, what can do you do for me now?"

"'Scuse me?"

"That file you saw," Steve said. "That would be a good place to start. You saw Fort1's name, but what else?"

"Not much of anything really. I was just getting a look at everything when the SPs came through the door, pulled a gun on me."

"But you said—"

"I know. I lied. Sorry. But I did give you Castle's name. And I just gave Barb the tip on Tangora."

"Relax, Steve," Keira said. "He's contributing."

"Then how 'bout some sources," Barb said. "That's the one place you could help us most. Now that you've got a secure email address you could start reaching out to other colleagues, anybody who might have worked these Fort1 missions."

"I haven't seen most of these guys for more than a year. And I'm not likely to get a warm welcome if—"

"C'mon," Steve said. "You can at least *try*."

"Maybe it's better if he eases back into things," Keira said, "instead of cold-calling like a salesman, especially with people who outranked him."

"I'm with Steve," Barb said. "We're not asking for some Deep Throat with all the secrets. We'll take anybody, at any level. Preferably reprobates and malcontents, or anybody else who might have thought this wasn't such a great setup, letting these IntelPro guys run the show."

Her description immediately brought to mind a likely candidate.

"Well, there was this one Pentagon guy," Cole said. "Came and spoke to us at Creech. Pretty plugged in, but he was based in Washington."

"Air Force?" Steve asked.

"Civilian. Some kind of design guru, not just for the Predator, but for all the integrated systems. Worked a lot with outsiders, too. That was one of the things that was pissing him off."

"Name?" Barb asked.

"Sharpe. Nelson Hayley Sharpe."

"Three names. Sure sign of a huge ego."

"The brass kinda thought he was a loose cannon."

"And you met him?" Steve said.

"He spoke to our attack group. It was supposed to be a pep talk on how we were riding the wave of the future, trailblazers, all sorts of feel-good bullshit. But at the end there was a Q and A, and he sorta ran off the rails. Somebody asked him how much longer before the other side started getting this kind of capability, and what that would mean. He said it had already happened. Not al Qaeda or anything, but the world at large. Friends, enemies, public, private, you name it. He said some of the best tech was being fed straight from the Pentagon to the street, and that as much as we all loved this shit now, in five or ten years we'd be scared to death of it because everybody would have it."

"And he was civilian?"

"I think that was part of the problem. 'Not from our culture.' That's what our COs were saying afterward. One of them called him a hippie bastard."

They had a good laugh over that while Barb topped up his coffee.

"So he was what, Pentagon staff?" Steve asked.

"I think so. Some special R and D group."

Keira, who'd been quiet awhile, was now busy on her laptop, the keys moving in a flurry.

"They fired him," she announced. "Or he retired, take your pick. Three months ago, it says."

"Perfect," Barb said. "No flacks to head us off at the pass. Where's he now?"

"Doesn't say. I'll keep checking."

"Think he'd remember you?" Steve asked

"Probably. Before his talk he spent an hour inside our GCS, watching Zach and me on a recon. We were showing him how we used all the shit he'd developed, but he knew some of the apps better than we did. Plus, I was the guy who asked the question that set him off."

"You hippie bastard!" Barb said.

More laughs. More coffee. As if, with enough caffeine, she might jazz out every last drop of his memory.

"Here we go," Keira said. "Looks like he's set up a little consultancy. Eclectic mix of services, everything from security software to aerodynamics. There's a photo. What a face!"

Everybody leaned in for a look.

"Yul Brynner with a hangover," Steve said.

"Or on quaaludes," Barb said.

"His website says he's based in an old farmhouse," Keira said. "Loudoun County, Virginia."

"Easy driving distance," Steve nodded at Cole.

Another clatter on the keyboard while the rest of them watched.

"There's an email address." She turned the laptop around, facing Cole. "Sign on to your account, if you want. You can message him right away."

"Okay," he said uncertainly, looking at the others. "What should I ask for?"

"A personal audience," Steve said. "Set that up and we'll help with the rest."

"Maybe throw him a hint that you've taken his advice to heart, and now you're trying to do something about it," Barb said.

Keira frowned.

"Don't lay it on too thick. If he's fresh out of the pipeline they'll still be keeping tabs on him. It might make him wary."

"Good point," Steve said. Barb shrugged.

"Whatever. But send it now."

Cole felt their eyes on him as he began typing. He pecked in Sharpe's address, paused, then . . . nothing. Where to begin?

"Want me to write it?" Keira asked gently.

"Sure."

He turned the laptop around, and for the second time that morning he submitted to the authority of a ghostwriter, marveling again at their ease with language, their ability to move to the heart of things in a few quick sentences. Keira's message was a model of clarity and humility, asking for assistance and advice even as it seemed to offer the promise of a sympathetic ear.

"Look okay?" she asked.

Her question was for Cole, but Steve and Barb also wanted to see. After a few tweaks and tugs, the request to Nelson Hayley Sharpe for a meeting at his earliest convenience was soon hurtling into the ether.

By then it was nearly eight o'clock.

Soon afterward, Keira left for downtown to check property records at the courthouse for the row house on Pickard, and Steve set off for points unknown. Barb refilled her mug and went back to her laptop.

Cole watched her from the couch. After a few clicks she entered an almost trancelike state. From the flashing of the screen he could tell she was surfing through a wide array of archival sites.

A community of loners, Cole thought. Even when everyone was here, the house felt strangely hollow, emptied of almost everything but secrets—their own, and whichever ones they'd pried loose from others. Or maybe he was just tired and out of sorts. He missed his children, his home, his old life back in the 'burbs of Vegas. He missed flying, too, the feeling you got when you were up there alone, soaring above everything.

Feeling drained, he rinsed out his mug at the sink while looking out the window at the gulls circling above Stansbury Creek in the morning light. He set the mug on the draining board and returned to the couch. With a stab of shame he briefly inspected the stained sheets. Then he pitch-poled onto the cushions and pulled up the blanket, hoping to steal a few more hours of sleep. Barb's keyboard clattered on.

This time he slept without dreaming.

CHAPTER SIXTEEN

NELSON HAYLEY SHARPE RUBBED the bumps on his shaved head and considered his options.

He could shut the gate and activate the lock, so they'd have to get out of their car and walk the last half mile. Or, as always, he could let them drive straight to his door, clomping into the house with their lawyerly warnings and institutional arrogance, hiding behind aviator shades as they pawed through his papers and clicked at his mouse, searching for God knows what sort of bullshit.

Choosing the former would make them more ornery than usual, but he'd at least have the satisfaction of watching them stumble and swear as they worked their way uphill through the stubble and cow patties. Because lately they were really pissing him off. They'd even started poking around among his clients, issuing vague warnings and generally endangering his ability to make a living. Three customers had already cancelled. Even Stu over at Whitethorn, who never let anything rattle him, had begged off.

"Nothing personal, Nellie. Ingenious stuff, as always, but I can't have the feds breathing down our necks, know what I mean? Maybe later, when you're not such a hot commodity."

And so on, until the flow of checks dwindled to almost nothing and the bills began to pile up.

His finger hovered above the mouse as he continued to deliberate while watching their progress on the desktop screen. The government-issue car bounced slowly in the ruts, field sparrows fluttering from its path. A few seconds later they passed through the open gate, deciding the issue for him.

"Fuck," he said to himself. "This is getting really old."

He knew what had brought them here—a statement he'd made yesterday to CNN. The reporter had interviewed him for twenty minutes. The irony was that he'd talked mostly about how the drones were a *good* thing. Compared to the so-called surgical bombings of the past, drone combat was far more efficient, and despite the occasional mistake, it killed far fewer civilians, largely because it allowed you to be more deliberate and precise in your targeting. He was proud of that. But those weren't the quotes they used. They seized on his final comments, when he sermonized briefly about how recklessly we were forging ahead with drone technology, making up the rules as we went along—if indeed there *were* any rules—heedless of the toll on our privacy, not only in war zones but potentially in every nook and cranny of our own country. Except that he forgot to say "potentially." The quote the Pentagon probably would have hated most had, of course, been the one CNN liked best, and the reporter used it not only in the news segment but also in the promotional tease at the top of the hour: "What should really scare you is that right now they're employing only a fraction of their capabilities. Soon they won't just be looking down your chimney. They'll be flying down it, too, with aircraft the size of hummingbirds, or smaller. I know, I helped develop them, at a testing ground right around the corner from where the Wright Brothers used to work."

So here they came, to tell him yet again in their own by-the-book fashion to please shut the fuck up, as specified in his severance agreement. Or else he'd pay a price. As if he wasn't already.

He stood, waiting for the door to open. He was a craggy monolith of a man whose angular peaks and hollows had grown more pronounced with age. Shaving his head had only made his big brown eyes look bigger. He could've passed as a distant cousin to those bug-eyed space aliens depicted in so many wacko fantasies.

They knocked. Progress of a sort. Then they opened the door before he crossed the room. No matter. He had already taken the usual precautions. It's why he had posted so many sensors and security cams outside, a whole alarm network monitoring every approach to his house. Advance warning gave him time to activate the software he had designed himself. Within seconds it cloaked, and in some cases erased, whatever work was likeliest to draw their unwanted scrutiny, while simultaneously disabling the passwords for his desktop, his notebook, and his smart phone. They hadn't yet wised up to the trick, which told him once again that the Pentagon's security experts weren't half as skilled as the ones earning the big bucks in the private sector. To his mind, that illustrated one of DOD's biggest blind spots: If they thought their new technology was devastating in their own hands, just wait until they started sharing it on the outside, with people who in some ways were far better equipped to exploit it.

"Welcome, gentlemen, as always."

He stood with his arms crossed. The two men, familiar by now, actually seemed a bit sheepish this time. The first one, taller and older, always did the talking.

"Should I read you the usual warning, Mr. Sharpe?"

"I'm aware of my obligations. Tea? The kettle's still warm."

"No, sir. We should only be a minute."

Maybe they, too, were tiring of the charade. Probably acting under orders issued more out of pique than practicality. And they hadn't yet come up with a damn thing. He looked around the place with a hint of embarrassment. His house had always been a bit of a dump, ever since his last daughter moved out in '91. But this morning it was particularly messy. Books and magazines everywhere, empty Chinese takeout boxes still on the coffee table, dishes stacked in the kitchen, clothes strewn on chairs and doorknobs, outdated and oversized stereo components coated with dust, cables everywhere. Was he becoming a hoarder, one of those lonely old misfits you always saw on TV? At least he didn't own any cats. No smell of urine or stale beer. Just garlic from the Chinese, the herbal rot of wet tea leaves, the ticklish funk of dust, the leaden silence of too many hours alone. The shorter fellow sneezed as he began sorting through a stack of papers.

"You went through those last week. Not that it makes any difference."

The man didn't even look up.

"Got any more interviews scheduled?" the taller one asked. Sharpe didn't even know their names, their ranks, anything about them.

"None presently. They're good marketing tools for my business, that's why I keep doing them. I'm entitled to promote my business, you know."

"And we're entitled to keep letting your clients know of the restrictions you've agreed to operate under."

So they weren't even going to try to hide their recent meddling.

"I really don't want to get lawyers involved."

The shorter one spoke up for the first time ever, stopping what he was doing and looking Sharpe right in the eye.

"Then don't."

Sharpe took a step toward him, caught himself, and silently counted to ten. They'd be gone soon, back out on the highway and headed for the Capital Beltway. And he still had other ways of fighting back, ways that would piss them off even more if they ever found out. Foolhardy, probably, to try such things, but maybe it was inevitable once you got your back up.

"Okay, then." The taller one again. "I'll leave the paperwork."

"Don't forget to check the mailbox on the way out."

"Already did. Publisher's Clearinghouse thinks you may be their next lucky winner."

This drew a smarmy grin from the shorter one. Sharpe held his tongue, barely.

Within seconds they were out the door, shuffling off like a pair of missionaries who'd failed to win a convert. He listened to the engine turn over, and then the creaking of the car as it bounded down the drive toward the bypass. Then he got to work.

First he pulled his keys from his pocket. Attached to the key chain was a cigarette lighter, or so it appeared. It had taken him an entire Saturday afternoon to produce the likeness. It was actually a flash drive, containing the software he always used to protect his data during these inspections and, just as important, to restore it once the coast was clear.

He plugged it in to let it work its magic, which included the random selection of a dozen new passwords for various accounts that he used. Then he pocketed the flash drive, printed out the list of the new passwords, examined it just long enough to commit the list to memory—which for him took only about twenty seconds—and then incinerated the printout in his pellet-burning woodstove.

Sitting back down at his desk, he used one of the new passwords to sign on to his email account, which he'd been using just before the alarms went off a few minutes ago, alerting him to the arrival of his visitors. Now a new message was waiting for him, from someone he'd never heard from before, although he recognized the name of the sender. One of the pilots at Creech. A bit of a malcontent, he remembered now. Or at least he hadn't been afraid to ask a provocative question. And now he wanted to meet.

But Sharpe also remembered hearing that this fellow had gotten himself into trouble, after a raid that ended badly. Just the sort of fellow, in other words, who might get him into even deeper trouble than he was already in.

Sharpe sighed and typed a curt reply, feeling a bit cowardly as he did so.

Yes, I remember you, and wish you good luck with whatever you're pursuing. But meeting with you wouldn't be in my best interests right now.

He was about to send it when the alarm sounded. He clicked to his security camera, and there they were again, coming right back up the driveway, this time at twice the speed, and having already cleared the gate, as if they'd finally figured out how he was outsmarting them and were trying to return before he did it again.

He slipped the flash drive back into the slot and activated another shutdown. To buy a few extra seconds he ran to the door and slammed home the deadbolt and security chain. No sooner had he finished than they were turning the knob, then pounding their fists. He slowly backed up, all the way to the kitchen door.

"On my way!" he sang out, with one eye on his computer screen as it worked through the final stages of the shutdown.

"Open *now* or we're breaking in!"

He grabbed clumsily for the flash drive disguised as a lighter as the screen went dark, then shoved it into his pants pocket just as the door crunched open, the frame splintering against the lock.

"What the fuck! Forced entry now? I was two steps away, assholes!"

The shorter man pinned him against the wall and pulled back his arms, binding his wrists with a plastic restraint. The taller one scanned his desktop, feeling the console for warmth as he scowled at the darkened screen.

"Where is it?" he shouted.

"Where's what?"

"Whatever piece of shit software you're using to shut this thing down."

"Hell, I didn't even have time to log back on!"

"Check his pockets! Check up his ass for all I care!"

The shorter one emptied his pockets. The key chain with the lighter fell out along with some loose change, a handkerchief, and a stubby pencil.

"Nothing!" the shorter guy said. "Maybe he really didn't have time."

"You saw the signal. He's lying his ass off."

"Maybe the signal was bad. You know sometimes in the tests—"

"Shut the fuck up!"

So they had a new weapon now, some sort of sensor that showed when he was online, although Mutt didn't seem to trust it, and now it looked like Jeff wasn't so sure.

"You bring my Publisher's Clearinghouse entry?" Sharpe asked. "It's the only shot I've got at any income if you guys keep this shit up."

"You know where the mailbox is," the taller one answered. He sounded discouraged, the zeal gone out of his voice. Without a further word the men left, climbed back into their car, and drove slowly down the driveway. Sharpe tried closing the door, but it wouldn't latch on the shattered jamb. The strike plate was dangling by a single screw, and there was a pile of splinters on the floor.

"Shit! There goes another fifty bucks."

He went out to his workshop to see what he could find for repairs.

Two hours later, after a half-assed fix, a long walk to cool his temper, and a cup of tea to clear his head, Sharpe logged back on to his computer, re-upped his passwords and regular software, and then checked the view on his security cams to make sure no one was lurking within immediate range of the house or driveway.

Finally satisfied that, at worst, he had a few minutes to work with, he went back into his email account. There was one new message. Yet another client, one of his best, was asking for a meeting at his earliest convenience "in order to re-assess our current working arrangement."

Another one bites the dust. At this rate he'd be out of business by the new year. Fortunately, he had another iron in the fire that even the Pentagon didn't yet know about.

Sharpe noticed the email from the pilot again, and reconsidered his answer. Yet another lonely rebel, discarded by the powers that be. Well, fuck it. How much more trouble could he get into than he was already in? This fellow at least deserved the courtesy of a sympathetic ear. If he'd make the effort to visit, then Sharpe would make the effort to hear him out. If he turned out to be a plant from those assholes at the Pentagon, Sharpe would know soon enough. And if he was legit? Who knew? He might even be useful, a valuable tool for one of his new ventures. He typed a reply that was even briefer and more cryptic than before.

8 a.m. tomorrow, McDonald's, Bingham Ferry Road, Leesburg. Use the drive-through window.

He had some valuable allies, but it was time to start recruiting a few more, and maybe this fellow was a good place to start. If his enemies wanted to up the ante, so would he. Maybe, as the Mafia liked to say, it was time to hit the mattresses.

He sent the message. Then he retrieved the flash drive from his pocket, shut everything down, and went upstairs to pack a bag.

CHAPTER SEVENTEEN

TRIP RIGGLEMAN DROVE SLOWLY down the lonely dirt road leading to Darwin Cole's abandoned trailer, raising a contrail of dust that must have been visible for miles. He glanced over his shoulder to behold the bleak beauty of it—sort of like a vapor trail from one of those muscular fighter-bombers, a thought that made him wistful.

He was in a hunting mood, airborne or not, and this was his initial sortie. Before he began his online pursuit in earnest he wanted to try to take the measure of the man with a firsthand inspection of his recent home ground.

Riggleman felt strangely vulnerable out here in the open, as if a missile might zoom in from above at any moment, slamming into the modest Ford sedan from the base motor pool and blowing it right off the road, a blackened smudge on the prairie. Those unauthorized Predator photos had spooked him even as they excited him. Someone had already strayed out of bounds in this case, and Riggleman figured that before long he would probably do the same.

But did the earlier interest mean that someone would be snooping over his shoulder as he proceeded? This was certainly the kind of countryside that made you wonder—empty from horizon to horizon, with every glint from above winking like a potential eye in the sky. The feeling of being watched grew so strong in him that at one point, just after Cole's trailer came into view at the base of a distant bluff, Riggleman braked to a halt and cut the engine. Silence. Nothing moved except the dust in his wake, which settled to the ground like a long brown serpent coiling itself to sleep—or maybe to strike.

He reached down to restart the engine, then hesitated and got out of the car. He walked around to the front, where he sat on the warm hood and peered off toward Cole's saggy trailer. From here it looked like an encampment for some kind of survivalist cult. Between him and the trailer, not a single sign of life. Looking back in the direction he'd come from, he saw the long line of tire tracks left by the Ford. Over to his left, his own footprints, preserved for anyone who came later. Now he was feeling eerier than ever, so he hopped down and got back under way. He turned on the radio for company but got only static on AM, and nothing at all on FM. Some sort of dead zone, maybe. Nothing to beam your signal to out here anyway.

The trailer sat deep in the shadow of the bluff. The damn door was wide open, swaying in a fresh breeze. An unpleasant smell wafted from the opening like bad breath. Just inside was a pile of animal shit, probably coyote, still fresh enough to have attracted a squadron of green flies, which buzzed in protest as Riggleman stepped across.

A shotgun was propped against the wall near the door. He picked it up. Well maintained. He levered it open. Still loaded. Now that was odd. He propped it carefully back against the wall, wondering how long it would stand there, loaded and ready, until someone else came along. Years, maybe.

The kitchen sink was full of dishes and more flies. Coyotes had torn apart much of the furniture and bedding, leaving claw marks on the upholstery and dusty paw prints across the floor. Unwashed clothes were piled by the bed. The scene emanated an air of a life suddenly interrupted, so much so that he wondered for a moment if Cole might have been abducted.

It was an alarming thought. For one thing, it would cast Cole's visit to the ex-CIA man in New Hampshire in an entirely different light. Had he been accompanied by others? Was he a hostage to a foreign government, perhaps? A dupe doing someone else's bidding? Maybe his kidnappers had threatened to harm his family unless he cooperated.

But apart from the coyote damage there was no sign of a fight or struggle. No bloodstains, or broken glass, or clumps of human hair. And there was also the loaded gun, unfired and neatly set aside.

He went back outside. He'd checked the recent meteorological data for the location, and it hadn't rained out here since Cole's disappearance. Yet there were no marks on the ground to suggest a scuffle, or the dragging of a body. Just footprints—two sets besides his own. One was man-sized, probably Cole's. The other was almost dainty, probably a woman. Both led to a second set of tire tracks that presumably had been left by the sedan in the surveillance photo. Riggleman got out his smart phone and took shots of the tread pattern and the footprints. Then he went back inside for a more systematic search.

On a closet shelf, well beyond the reach of the coyotes, was a cardboard box stuffed with transcripts of depositions and courtroom proceedings from Cole's court-martial. It felt providential, his first stroke of luck. Already, the long trip was worthwhile.

Earlier that morning, just before leaving Nellis in the Ford, Riggleman had fired off his first piece of paperwork, an official request to the USAF legal eagles who'd prosecuted Cole, asking for copies of everything they had on the case. But he knew from experience that even in high-priority investigations, these kinds of requests routinely took days, even weeks, to achieve a result. This trove in the trailer, provided it was complete, would save lots of time and bureaucratic aggravation.

Finding nothing more of value inside, Riggleman hauled the box out to the Ford and began scouting the perimeter for a radius of roughly two hundred yards. It was hot, dry work, and the only signs of life were more coyote prints, which seemed to be everywhere, plus some empty cans that they must have carried off from a charred garbage pit behind the trailer. What a way to live.

By the time Riggleman got back to Nellis there was a box sitting on his desk that looked a lot like the one from Cole's closet. It was the complete record of the court-martial. And when he signed on to his desktop computer there was an email from the legal office, which, based on the time signature, indicated that they'd sent over the box by courier within two hours of receiving his request.

Well, that was certainly a pleasant surprise, enough so to make him slightly uncomfortable. Once again he wondered how many people above him knew what he was up to.

He took the two sets of documents out of their boxes and stacked them side by side, then methodically arranged each set in chronological order. Each stack contained the same number of documents. He then compared the two versions of every document. Everything matched up there as well until he got to the depositions. The official version of the one taken from Cole's commanding officer, Lieutenant Colonel Scott Sturdivant, was lighter and thinner than the copy from the trailer.

Riggleman counted the pages. Twenty-two were missing from the official copy. As if to hide this, whoever had made the duplicates for the legal office had placed the originals in the copying machine in a way that cut off the page numbers from the top. The gap was further disguised by the way one of Sturdivant's answers ended at the bottom of the last page before the gap, and then a question from a lawyer led off the first page afterward. If he hadn't known about the missing pages, the document would have appeared to be seamless.

But when he checked those twenty-two pages in Cole's set, nothing leaped out at him as something the Air Force would want to keep secret. Part of it was a dry discussion of Cole and Sturdivant's chain of command. Part was a section in which Sturdivant read into the record a chat exchange from one of Cole's recent Predator missions, in which the only two participants apart from the ones you'd normally expect were two code-name handles—Fort1 and Lancer.

The names were meaningless to him, but he filed them away for possible further consideration. More disturbing was the way in which the missing pages reinforced his nascent sense that there was something eerily different about this case. Enough so that he began to view the subject—Captain Darwin Cole—in a different light.

On the surface Cole was a drunk, a loser, a hermited fuckup in the desert who, by all appearances, had lived in barely human conditions and had disappeared with little regard to the mess he was leaving behind, literally and figuratively. Yet his first moves once he was beyond the squalor of the trailer had left virtually no trace. None that Riggleman had yet found, anyway. That suggested a deceptively careful man, a challenging quarry.

It brought to mind one of Riggleman's opponents from a wrestling match long ago, a big-eyed boy from the Corn Belt who'd stepped onto the mat looking decidedly flabby for his weight class. Ponderously slow in his movements, too, the kind of slack-jawed victim that

Riggleman usually made short work of by employing a few deft moves. A feint, a pivot, and a leveraged throw, leading to a takedown and then a pin as he slapped the poor fellow onto his back like some bug for a specimen jar. Match over.

But from the moment the match commenced this boy had proven to be almost impossible to budge from any angle, no matter how easily Riggleman was able to outmanuever him. It was as if his feet were welded to the mat, and by late in the second round, Riggleman grew so exasperated that he let down his guard for the briefest of moments to rethink his position. The flabby boy responded in a flash, and within seconds had achieved a takedown. Riggleman avoided being pinned, but lost the match on points, and he still remembered the boy's eyes as the final whistle blew—a fleeting flash of triumphant intelligence, a mild taunt that challenged anyone to ever underestimate him again.

Maybe Cole was that kind of adversary. Deceptively dangerous. A shrewd opportunist.

Riggleman picked up the shortchanged deposition from the pile on his desk. He picked up his phone and began punching in the number for the legal eagle who'd sent him the copy. Time to ask a few delicate questions.

Then he stopped and hung up. It was too soon to be setting off any alarms in high places.

He swiveled back toward his computer, interlocked the fingers of both hands, and stretched them until his knuckles cracked, making a noise like a string of firecrackers. Then he got down to business, already determined not to underestimate anyone from here on out.

He would work fast, work late, and leave no avenue unexplored.

He would get his man, come what may.

CHAPTER EIGHTEEN

STEVE'S INTELPRO SOURCE always insisted on meeting at Tark's Grill, a watering hole where the happy hour crowd made enough noise to cloak any conversation. He demanded that Steve wear a jacket and tie so they wouldn't look like such an unlikely pairing. Steve, who'd made the mistake of revealing this detail to Barb and Keira, now kept a blazer and tie in his car rather than tip them off every time he had a rendezvous.

The ground rules for these meetings were simple. Steve could use the Source's information however he pleased, but it could never be attributed in any way, shape, or form to IntelPro. In other words, under the journalistic rules Steve and his colleagues played by, it was fit to print only if they verified it elsewhere. In addition, whenever possible in these public conversations they avoided using each other's names, or those of their colleagues, favoring instead a rough code of initials and euphemisms.

Tark's was just north of the Baltimore Beltway, a long drive from Middle River and a short one from Hunt Valley. Yet it was Steve who was always punctual, while the Source invariably arrived exactly five minutes late, as if he'd been sitting in the parking lot eyeing his Bremont chronometer until just the right moment.

On entry he never failed to convey an air of having reached the southernmost limit of his tolerance for all things urban, as if this was as close to the city center as he ever cared to travel. That was the vibe Steve got from most of Tark's clientele—old-line locals who had grown up in Baltimore's best neighborhoods, then migrated to the 'burbs to raise families in exile, comforted by the county's lower taxes, safer streets, and neighbors who looked just like them. He guessed that at least half the males present had once played lacrosse for a local private school.

This time Steve was running late. He pulled up the parking brake and rummaged in the glove compartment for his tie among maps and repair invoices. Some of the paperwork was from more than a decade ago, when the car was new and so was his marriage. Jill, his ex, lived in Takoma Park with a new husband. Steve sort of kept up with her on Facebook, while wondering if she did the same. Not that he ever posted anything.

The hostess took him to a pedestal table near the bar, where a "Reserved" placard staked out their usual spot in the middle of a yammering mob. The music was deafening. The Source always made a reservation under the name Langley, his idea of a joke. And there he was now, coming through the door with a smile for the hostess, greeting her by name, the amiable and silver-maned Mr. Langley, in a pressed gray suit, white shirt, and red tie, shooting his cuffs as he approached the table. He slid onto the facing chair, ordered an outrageously expensive single malt Scotch—which Steve would have to pay for from his meager budget—and got down to business.

"I take it your natives are restless, Old Pro."

Steve, unable to hear him over the din, leaned closer.

"What's that?"

"I said, *I take it your natives are restless.*" He was practically shouting.

"Why shouldn't they be?" Steve shouted back. "You fucked us over in not telling us about Mansur."

His use of Mansur's name was an intentional breach of protocol, for shock value, although the Source took it in stride.

"Did *what* about Mansur?"

"*Fucked us over!*"

The Source smiled and leaned back, mouthing "Moi?" as he spread his arms wide. Steve was about to answer when the waitress arrived with the Scotch and a bowl of nuts. She disappeared before taking Steve's order.

"Yes, you," Steve prodded. "How 'bout an explanation?"

"A what?"

"You heard me."

The Source leaned across the table.

"You know how it works between us, Old Pro. Give some to get some. A two-way street."

This was another ground rule, one that Steve had never dared mention to Barb and Keira. As part of the arrangement, Steve provided updates on the progress of their investigation, including a summary of what his colleagues were up to. It made him uneasy, but it was the only way the Source would agree to keep talking.

"Not much to report, other than the arrival of the pilot," Steve said. "B ran the tags on your vehicle. That's how we learned it was your guys holding Mansur."

"We were transporting him, not holding him. Important distinction."

"And now you've moved him. K checked this morning and the whole place was cleared out, furniture and everything. They even left the door ajar."

"Of course we moved him. You'd compromised his safety."

"So a reporter can scare him away, but not the FBI?"

"They know where to find him."

"That's not what we heard."

"Use your head, Old Pro. It would hardly be a secure arrangement if the Bureau wasn't in on it."

"Secure from what?"

"From whom would be the better question."

"Our main man?"

"It's all right. These drunks will never notice if you use his name." He grinned smugly. "Even his real one. Wade Castle."

So the Source had known the name all along. It rankled, but it would be useless to complain, so Steve instead pushed for more.

"An Agency source of ours doesn't seem to think Mansur is being held for his own protection. And he's pretty certain the Bureau doesn't know about it."

The reference to Bickell's information was also supposed to raise an eyebrow, but the Source again took it in stride.

"What makes you so sure the Agency really wants to find Mansur, much less old Wade Castle? Tell me, on your little visit to Lake Woggawogga, or whatever they call it up in New Hampshire, did your friend with the dirty fishing boat surprise you by being more helpful than expected?"

Who had told him all this? Somewhere there was a leak, either among themselves or among their sources.

"How do you know about that?"

"I know all sorts of things. The hidden ball trick. How to smash a trachea with a rolled-up newspaper."

"Then why should I tell you anything?"

"Because that's our arrangement. You haven't answered my question."

"Yes, he was helpful."

"Which should tell you what?"

"Disinformation?"

"Eureka. You begin to see the light. People like him are very squeamish and virginal about people like me. He probably ranted on and on about green badgers and blue badgers, didn't he?"

True enough. But Bickell's info on Mansur had certainly been more helpful than any recent offerings from the Source. The problem, Steve supposed, was that both men might have good reason to lead a trio of journalists astray. The Source leaned forward again, this time until their foreheads were almost touching. The music rose to a throb, and there was an explosion of laughter from the bar.

"I can see that you're conflicted, Old Pro. Totally at sea. Let me clarify the situation. The story is the same as it's been from the beginning. Wade Castle has gone rogue, and his employers are still covering for him. So please get your partners—carnal or not—into line on that as soon as possible."

"My colleagues will pursue any line of inquiry they choose, and we're not fucking."

"You should freshen your drink, Old Pro. You get testy when you fall behind."

"Stop calling me Old Pro. And the waitress never took my order."

The Source frowned.

"My goodness. You're absolutely right."

He held aloft his right hand and nodded.

"It's not important," Steve said, but she was already on her way.

"A beer for this gentleman, please. Something worthy and on tap."
She smiled and disappeared.

"Bickell said Castle's in-country," Steve said.

"So even they're admitting it, now? Interesting."

"You knew that?"

The Source shrugged.

"We hear things. Sometimes it's hard to know what to believe."

"He seems to think Castle's been misunderstood, that he's a whistle-blower on a crusade."

"More damage control."

"Bickell didn't seem like the type to spout the company line."

"It's part of his charm. The wronged man, so therefore he must be telling the truth. And to his mind I'm sure it feels that way."

"A lot of it adds up."

"Cover stories usually do. Tell me, when's the last time you heard of an Agency asset—a legitimate one—working a domestic operation?"

"Point taken."

"Point taken? I believe that's what is commonly known as news. You should be doing backflips of joy. It's illegal as hell, what he's up to. The fucking cherry on top of your story, unless you wait so long that someone else eats it, or the whole thing melts away. Which is what will happen if you let those two women lead you down a false trail. What's the matter—worried that if you don't play along they'll fuck the pilot first?"

"Go to hell."

The waitress arrived with his beer. Steve slid it away, sloshing foam down the sides of the glass.

"Calm yourself, Old Pro. Your instincts are sound, always have been. Look, does my shop stand to make a tidier sum if certain people who don't like us dirty their reputations? Well of course. But that doesn't change the basic facts."

"Give me something fresh, then. Something we can use."

"How 'bout asking a question first?"

"All right. What do you know about other ops he screwed up, yours included?"

"What's the matter, thirteen lives aren't enough for you? Plus those other bodies your friend B says she saw?"

"Why hold out on me unless he interfered with something you weren't supposed to be doing?"

"Sounds like a Bickell theory. Muddying the water again."

"Then clear it up for me, starting with who his handlers were, who's covering for him, and why. Names, dates, and places, the more the better. Proof. Proof and verification. Because we can't just go with a hunch like you guys."

The Source looked thrown off his stride for the first time, and he sipped his Scotch before answering.

"I can't do your job for you."

"Then what about those ex-Agency jocks working at your training facility? B says there are two of them, and they were both connected to Castle."

"And she wants access?"

"Of course."

He gave it some thought. Nodded.

"I'll do what I can. But it can't be by phone."

"She'll go wherever she has to. In fact, we may be moving soon. To a place on the Eastern Shore, not too far from your facility. I'm fighting it, but it's rent free, so don't get bent out of shape if it comes to pass."

The Source narrowed his eyes but didn't raise an objection. Steve, who'd been worried about how he might react, was relieved to get that revelation out of the way.

"As long as that's all there is to it. I can even arrange a tour of our entire training complex if it will cool any unwarranted curiosity. But the minute your people start trying to sneak a peek behind my back, our whole arrangement's off. Understand, Old Pro?"

"Yes."

"What else?"

"Tell me about this new executive of yours, the one you hired right out of the Air Force."

"Boardman? You're losing focus again. What about him?"

"The pilot says Boardman was wired in directly to the Predator program."

"Meaning?"

"That's what we'd like to know."

The Source shook his head. "Look, does your friend B want access to those contacts or not?"

"Sure she does."

"Then stay on topic."

"Fine. What can you tell me about the name Lancer?"

The Source frowned.

"As in Prancer and Dancer? You chasing magic reindeer now?"

"It's a code name."

"I gathered as much, but not one I'm familiar with. Where'd you hear it, in what context?"

"What does it matter, if you've never heard it?"

"Give some to get some, Old Pro."

"I just gave you Lancer."

"Worthless without context."

Steve sighed, looked at his beer. He pulled it toward him, then pushed it away. He sensed that the Source had already given out all he was likely to offer today, and Steve wasn't in the mood for chitchat, or for any further lectures on where they should direct their energies.

"So is that all for now?" he asked.

"Not from your end, I hope. What is the lovely K up to?"

Steve stood to go.

"The beer's all yours. So is the tab."

"Fine, Old Pro. But if you think I'm a bit of a bastard for trying to keep your colleagues on the straight and narrow, try to imagine how insistent your friend in New Hampshire might become. Or his friends. Trust me, if their ilk ever starts shouting 'Stop the presses!' they won't do it nicely."

Steve edged around the table, leaning closer to hear better.

"What's that supposed to mean?"

"Don't worry, I'm sure they know the unbreakable rule."

"What rule?"

"The one the Mob always talks about. Kill a cop if necessary, but never a reporter. The problem for you is that one of their people has stopped playing by the rules, and they're apparently fine with that. Which reminds me, you haven't asked the one question you always bring to this table. Aren't you interested in the latest whereabouts of Fort1?"

"Back in the country, we covered that."

"A little vague, don't you think?"

"You know more?"

"Like I said, we hear things. But only if you're interested." The Source gestured toward the empty chair. Steve stepped around the table and sat back down. "There's a trail of sorts. Traces, here and there. The last one we picked up was right down I-95, Northern Virginia, practically in Langley's back yard. Little more than an hour's drive from your place, if you're not fool enough to try it at rush hour. And if he's been tasked to clean up after himself, his laundry list is going to include you and everyone else in your little love shack. I'd like to help you avoid any calamity, of course. But only if the arrangement continues to be reciprocal."

"You're getting all I can give you in good conscience."

"Yes, I thought you'd say something like that. I wonder what your conscience will say if one of your colleagues drives her car off the Bay Bridge. Not that I won't still be available to you. It's not my choice for you to go it alone." He stood, gave a farewell nod to the waitress, and began edging away from the table. "Oh, and leave her a nice tip, Old Pro. She's been very attentive."

Then he strolled away, pausing only to say good-bye to the hostess as he pushed through the crowd and out the door. Steve, furious and troubled, wanted to chase him down, follow him all the way to the parking lot if necessary to demand more answers, more information. But that would probably end the relationship. So he kept his seat and tried to calm down, his mind racing in a dozen different directions.

Was Castle a genuine threat, or was the Source just trying to keep them in line? And if the former was true, was there a damn thing they could do about it, short of asking IntelPro to post a sentry?

He looked at his beer glass. Bubbles were rising to the top, but the head was gone. What he really needed now was something stronger, but this would have to do. He sipped, then swallowed. Then he drained half the glass in one long pull before setting it back down, wondering what the hell was he going to tell the others.

CHAPTER NINETEEN

COLE PULLED INTO the McDonald's parking lot fifteen minutes before the appointed hour. He took a space in the back and waited, searching in vain for Sharpe's bony, bald head behind the wheel of each arrival. He'd allowed two hours for the trip down. It was partly to be punctual, partly to escape the turmoil of the little house on Wilson Point Road. An argument from the night before about the move to the Eastern Shore had spilled over into breakfast.

Steve was against it. "It's the middle of fucking nowhere."

Barb was for it. "Nowhere? It's practically next door to IntelPro."

"Great, so we can spook them into clamming up."

"You said your source would arrange face-to-face access to the ex-Agency guys. He even offered us a tour. That doesn't sound spooked to me. And you've seen the numbers. The rent, the utilities, everything's paid for over there. It's a helluva lot cheaper for us. So what's a little extra driving if we can buy another four months, maybe more?"

Steve sighed, shook his head. "It's too vulnerable."

"Vulnerable to what?"

That's when he told them about the Source's warning, and how IntelPro had already known about their visit with Bickell in New Hampshire. Cole was shocked. Barb was unmoved.

"Is that really so surprising? All these guys talk to each other. Maybe it's a *good* thing. If they're all leaking to each other about us, maybe they'll start leaking to us about each other."

"It's vulnerable. It's fucking wide-open spaces over there. How many acres did you say, Keira?"

"Two hundred."

"And backed up against the water. Nowhere to run but up a single dirt driveway."

"You think we're any safer here?" Barb said. "They could come up the creek, or straight down the road. Nobody would know a thing. If they want us that bad, location won't mean a damn thing."

"But why make it easier for them?"

"Don't you know a bluff when you see one? He's scaring us to keep us on the straight and narrow. As if he'd lift a finger to protect us. Besides, Keira's got sources out there, too."

"Since when?"

"Since always. She told me the other day."

"Barb's right," Keira said. "Not that she was supposed to spread it around. But, yeah, a government type who lives down there."

"Doesn't your agent also have a place down there, Keira? Sure would make a book deal easier to come by if you ever kick us out."

Barb turned toward Keira. "Your agent lives out there? You never mentioned that."

"What's to mention?" Keira said. "It's her vacation house, way over in Dorchester County. If it makes you feel better, Steve, there's a gate to the driveway. We'll lock it at night. Anyone who wants us will have to come a mile on foot, and anybody that determined is going to get us no matter where we sleep. Okay?"

"Says the woman who already got one man killed," Steve said.

Keira reacted as if he had slapped her, and Steve already looked as if he wished he could take it back. Cole wondered what the details behind the remark must be. Barb looked away and shook her head.

"Why are you shaking your head?" Steve said. "You're the one who put the idea in my head."

"Fuck off, Steve."

He was blushing even before the rebuke, the peacemaker caught red-handed being warlike.

"Sorry. Heat of battle. A stupid thing to say."

Keira said nothing, her lips drawn tight. That ended the wrangling, at least until morning, when they rehashed the same arguments in gentler and more civil terms. When it came time to vote, Barb sided with

Keira. Cole didn't raise his hand for either option, and no one seemed to expect him to. Steve accepted defeat with a measure of grace, as if already preparing to make the best of it.

Keira departed just before Cole, having packed her bags the night before. She was on her way to the Eastern Shore to open up the house, air out the rooms, clean the linens, turn on the heat, and otherwise prepare for their arrival. She left behind directions and a spare key. The cat leaped into Keira's car just before the door closed, and Barb glared as if Cheryl had committed the ultimate betrayal. The plan was for the rest of them to head across the Bay Bridge that evening.

Steve then handed Cole the keys to his Honda and, when Barb wasn't looking, a pair of twenties.

"Gas it up if you need to, and get yourself something to eat. You're still looking a little worn around the edges."

"Thanks."

"Oh, and that Van Morrison CD you like. It's still in the player. Good luck, and keep us posted."

On the way to Northern Virginia, Cole bought a disposable cell phone, paying with some of his own cash. He'd already texted his number to the others in case of emergency.

It was now five minutes before the scheduled time for the rendezvous. Cars continued to come and go from the McDonald's, but none was carrying anyone who looked like Nelson Hayley Sharpe. Cole waited, listening to Steve's CD for the second time through. A song came and went and he again checked his watch. It was a minute before eight. He started the Honda and eased into the line for the drive-through window, feeling a bit ridiculous about the whole arrangement. Cole wasn't sure which prospect worried him more: being stood up, or actually having Sharpe arrive.

During his appearance at Creech, Sharpe had come across as a strong but manageable personality, although Barb's online research had turned up further info that, if anything, had made the man seem potentially unstable.

Sharpe had risen rapidly through the ranks of civilian designers while working with some of the pioneers of his trade, such as a personal hero of Cole's, John Boyd, the peerless fighter pilot who helped design the F-16, and his civilian sidekick, Pierre Sprey, another brilliant maverick who helped revolutionize the way combat aircraft were designed and tested. Along with Sprey and others, Sharpe also made noise as part of the Pentagon reform movement in the 1970s and '80s, attacking the defense department for the needless complexity of its weapons systems and its bloated costs, such as the outrage of the "$300 hammer."

None of this endeared him to the brass, and they probably would have gotten rid of him far sooner if his design work, particularly with the Predator program, hadn't made him indispensable. But in recent years critics, as well as a few friends, had expressed worries that he was becoming too headstrong, too outspoken. There were even mutterings that, for all his brilliance, he'd become vulnerable to conspiracy theories and had strayed too far toward the fringe. Others said that kind of talk was nonsense, the smear tactic of generals and contractors who were fed up with his griping.

At exactly eight a.m. Cole rolled up to the speaker by the red and yellow menu board. He half expected Sharpe to step out from behind it like a magician, or to announce his presence over the squawk box.

Instead, the voice of a teenage girl crackled, "Welcome to McDonald's, may I take your order?"

"Sausage biscuit and a small coffee, black."

"You want juice or hash browns with that?"

"No."

"Your total is two ninety. Please drive forward."

He rolled around the bend toward the pay window, glancing to either side and at both mirrors. Nothing. The only people getting out of their cars were members of an overweight family of four, spilling from a massive SUV with Ohio tags. Cole pulled up the hand brake and reached awkwardly for his wallet as the window slid open. He paid the girl, who handed over a warm bag and counted out his change. The moment he rolled up the window, the Honda's passenger door swung open, startling Cole so much that he dropped the coins. A big man with a shaved head slid onto the seat.

"Drive," Sharpe said, nodding and looking straight ahead.

Cole glanced back at the pay window, but the girl was already speaking into the mike, oblivious.

"Did you—?"

"Don't talk. Drive. Take a right out of the lot and do as I tell you."

Cole put the car in gear. The bag sat in his lap and the loose change rolled onto the floor. He turned right as directed, while wondering if Sharpe had come by car, by bus, or on foot. Was he accompanied? Cole checked the mirrors and nearly ran a red light.

"Are you armed?" he asked.

"This isn't a kidnapping, for God's sake. But how 'bout we go a while longer before we talk."

"Sure."

The light turned green. Glancing to his right, he saw that Sharpe's hands were folded in his lap. No weapon, unless it was in his pocket. Cole relaxed a bit and eased into the flow of traffic.

"Up ahead, the turnoff to the right. Take it."

It was a two-lane road, practically empty, and it ran through farm fields with widely scattered houses. They were at the outer reaches of D.C. suburbia, and this road headed straight into open country. Cole wasn't sure he liked that. Checking the mirrors again he saw that no one was behind them, which began to feel like a mixed blessing.

Sharpe glanced backward, also checking the road.

"Good," he said, seeming pleased. Then he lapsed into silence.

They crested a hill, corn stubble in a red clay field to their left. To the right, a weathered empty barn, no doors.

"There's a turnout up ahead on the right, another two hundred yards. Pull over."

Cole bumped off the pavement, braking to a stop on gravel. He put the Honda into neutral and pulled up the handbrake, then put his hand on the keys before glancing at Sharpe, who nodded. He shut off the engine. Not a sound, then, except the wind against the windows, whistling at the seams.

"Let's take a walk up the lane here."

A narrow gravel road led away from the road at a ninety-degree angle. There was a row of old mailboxes tilted at various angles.

"Okay."

Cole pocketed the keys and got out. They slammed their doors shut—the only noise for miles, or so it seemed. The icy wind stung his cheeks where he'd shaved that morning. Sharpe gestured up the lane.

"Shall we?"

"Sure."

They walked, crunching gravel. Sharpe wore rubber-soled black leather shoes, that ugly brand with sunken heels and a fat instep that was supposed to be good for your leg muscles. He needed a shave. His coat, unbuttoned, was a knee-length duster of waxed canvas with a leather collar, as if he was dressed to herd cattle. The bumps on his skull were pronounced in the low-angle sunlight. His mouth was creased into a scowl, but his deep-socketed eyes were in shadow, making it impossible to read his mood with any certainty. He might have been angry, he might have been deep in thought.

Cole, figuring that Sharpe would get down to business when he was good and ready, said nothing. After they'd covered maybe twenty yards, Sharpe stopped and pivoted so they were face-to-face, only a few feet apart. Anyone driving past might have guessed they were either old friends or old adversaries, but they definitely looked like two men with a history.

"Apologies for the dramatics," Sharpe said gruffly. "The car could be miked, for all I know."

He reached into a big pocket of his overcoat and drew out one of those metal detector wands like the ones at airport security checkpoints.

"This will only take a second. Arms up."

Cole, figuring what the hell, obliged him as the wand whooped and wailed, making zipper sounds as it passed up and down his arms, legs, and crotch.

"Turn around."

Cole did.

"Excellent."

He dropped the wand back into the pocket.

"You do this to everyone you meet?"

"Can't be too careful. Not in my shoes."

"Or in mine."

"Duly acknowledged."

He paused, as if to allow Cole a chance for further comment. Then he proceeded.

"So, what does a court-martialed fighter jock want with a pariah like me? More to the point, what reason could I possibly have for wanting to talk to you, other than to suit my own spiteful urge to bite the hand that feeds me? I suppose that's the only reason I showed up. Your email was perfectly timed, catching me as it did at a moment of absolute pique."

"Pique?" He'd get along great with Barb.

"Vexation. Animosity. The Pentagon has decided that my days as a productive citizen are over, so they've gone about industriously obstructing my ability to make a living. What is it you're up to, exactly?"

"I'm collaborating with some journalists. Three of them. We're all in the same house, literally, working a story on Wade Castle."

"Collaborating with journalists. Now there's a certain path to mutually assured destruction."

"It's pretty much the only path I had."

"And you've concluded that somehow I can be of assistance?"

"Castle was the Agency's top drone guy. You must have worked with him at some point."

"Oh, he was much more than 'a drone guy.' He was their guru at large for all things technical."

"See, that's the kind of information we need."

"'We.' That's your first mistake. Thinking you're one of them."

"You sure seemed to like the press back in the days of the three-hundred-dollar hammer."

"I liked *using* them, that's true. It's half their problem. They're too easily managed and manipulated. Who do you think led us into Iraq? They rise up in dissent when it humors them, but mostly they're just another tool of the system."

"These guys seem different."

"Stockholm syndrome. You've been around them awhile and you've already bought into their myth—a crusade for the truth with a capital T."

Cole had to smile, since he'd already been thinking the same thing. Sharpe eyed him closely.

"You were in on that fuckup at Sandar Khosh, weren't you? That's your beef with Wade."

"If you know that, you probably know other stuff that could help."

Sharpe looked down at his feet. His right toe scraped a furrow in the dirt, then crossed it, an X to mark the spot.

"Let me tell you what I'd like out of this arrangement. Assuming there *is* one."

"Okay."

Sharpe resumed walking, heading further down the lane, so Cole kept pace. Out on the paved road, a car rushed by. Cole glanced back, but Sharpe seemed lost in thought.

"I will become a party to this only if I can hit those bastards where it hurts. Only if I can create a little anarchy in their ranks. Inside that whole public-private nexus—or *axis*, that's a far better word for it. What Ike used to call the military-industrial complex."

"We're kind of focusing on just Castle for now. Him and his field-work."

"But he's their creation, don't you see? Wade wasn't just the Agency point man on drones, or technology. He was at the center of the frame—still is, as far as I know—for all the sharing and distribution of data, of specs, of, hell, you name it. He was involved with my work, the Air Force's work, everybody's damn work, from R and D to application. And no doubt he saw what I saw—that everybody's stuff, from the absolute shit to the absolute gold, was running in one great big pipeline to all the customers. Or at least to every customer with enough juice to tap in."

"Contractors?"

"In Afghanistan, Iraq. Those aren't just theaters of war for these people. They're glorified test labs, proving grounds, marketplaces for the barter of influence and, most important of all, for state-of-the-art technology. Those women and children at Sandar Khosh were guinea pigs in somebody's ill-advised experiment, and Castle was at Ground Zero for all of it."

"What kind of experiment?"

"Ask Wade. If you can find him."

"He's on the lam. Somewhere not far from here, we're told."

Sharpe looked up abruptly. It was clear the revelation had caught him off guard. He wrinkled his brow, then again looked down at his feet.

"Is he back at Langley?"

"Apparently not. He's at large. Operating on his own. Possibly no longer officially."

Sharpe thought about this for several seconds. "That's hard to process. Hard to say what it means."

"Join the club."

"Maybe I will. If only so I can shout it from the rooftops once you find the answer."

"So you'll help us?"

"I'll help *you*. If you choose to share with the infidels, so be it. You say you're living with these people now?" Sharpe made it sound as if Cole had moved into a colony of religious cultists.

"In Middle River, outside Baltimore, but we're about to move to the Maryland Eastern Shore. One of them has a summer home, some family estate."

Sharpe's eyes lit up.

"How many acres?"

"Two hundred."

He smiled, mulling it over. "Give me a day to do some thinking, some planning. I'll be back in touch. When are you moving?"

"Later today. Soon as I get back."

Sharpe smiled again. "Even better."

He said nothing more as they walked back to where the car was parked. Cole popped the locks but Sharpe made no move to get in.

"Ready to roll?"

Sharpe shook his head. "Go ahead. I've made arrangements."

"Way out here?"

Sharpe waved dismissively, as if the details were of no importance.

Cole had half a mind to stick around long enough to find out if Sharpe was just blowing smoke. But he didn't seem like the kind of guy who'd see much humor in that, so Cole climbed into the car and started the engine. He was about to pull out when Sharpe knocked on the window. Cole rolled it down.

"How 'bout we take a little field trip tomorrow, just you and me on the far side of the Bay?"

"Doing what?"

"There's something I want to show you. It's not for the others to see. Not yet, anyway. Where's this farm where you're staying?"

"Talbot County. Near Oxford."

He nodded, seemingly pleased. "The place I've got in mind is about forty clicks away. We'll meet halfway, just past Easton on Route 50. Let's say morning, nine thirty. We'll make a day of it. Box lunch and a blanket, if you want. Sit down and watch some geeks take this shit to the next level. And with the government's blessing, my friend. Its complete and benevolent blessing. Then you'll see how this battle has to be fought. Not with notebooks and quotation marks, the way the scribblers do it."

"Okay. But what's—?"

"Great. I'll email you the rendezvous point. Nine thirty it is."

He slapped the roof of the Honda and began walking away. Cole wondered what sort of weirdness he'd just committed to, but Sharpe had already reached the shoulder and was headed in the opposite direction from the way they'd come.

Cole eased the car onto the pavement. Checking the mirror, he saw Sharpe raise a hand in farewell without turning around. As he accelerated, Sharpe grew smaller in the mirror. He looked like a hitchhiker on a lonely road, a drifter with no destination.

He looked like trouble.

CHAPTER TWENTY

MOVING DAY.

At dusk they drove east, joining a caravan of headlights streaming across the Bay Bridge. Cole gazed down through the trusswork at container ships, gliding beneath them like sparkling cakes on inky water flecked by whitecaps. He was riding with Barb in her Prius, the radio tuned to NPR. Steve followed closely in his Honda, a two-car convoy. A team, however fractious.

Cole was reminded of how he used to feel heading out on a deployment—excited, a little daunted, but comforted by the shared sense of mission, the knowledge that everyone around him was going through exactly the same thing. He missed that. It wasn't that he enjoyed going off to war, or leaving his family behind. But there was something to be said for the isolation of a foreign posting, the hermetic life among fellow warriors who were cleared to hear your stories, your operational secrets, just as you were cleared to hear theirs. You ate and slept with the same problems, obsessions, and insecurities.

The Predator assignment at Creech had lacked all that. You came and went from drone warfare the way you would with any other job, commuting home to ball games and cookouts, to bill paying and homework questions, the nightly debate about what to watch on TV. A quiet dinner with Carol was always a nice break in the routine—sex, even better—as long as she wasn't preoccupied with the children, or chores, or talking on her cell to her family in Saginaw. Not that you could ever say much about your job even when she had time to listen. Events at Creech stayed locked up, bubbling inside your brain until it was time to return, back to that pixelated world where ghostly characters lived on silent screens, awaiting the verdict of your fingertips.

"You okay?"

It was Barb. She'd turned off the radio and they were across the bridge, less than an hour from their destination.

"Just thinking about the job. The old one."

"Flying drones?"

"We never called 'em that. Preds. UAVs. Whatever."

"Some of the stuff I've read makes it sound pretty terrible."

Was it? The job itself? Or was it the back-and-forth that he'd hated more? Entry and reentry, with never enough time for proper decompression. A mental case of the bends that had eventually doubled him over in pain. And with no real flying, which would have at least offered some release. No flying at all. Just a seat in a trailer, rump to vinyl to floor.

Still. The job had its charms, he could still recall them, even in his current detachment. Having had more than a year to think about it he now realized that, yes, there were parts of it that he'd liked, that had even been a little addictive.

"Not always," he said.

"No? How so?"

"It was important. It wasn't fun, and it sure as hell was no thrill a minute. But you were up there seeing shit that nobody else saw."

"Godlike?"

He smiled.

"A little. But it's more complicated than that."

She drove on, waiting for more. If it had been Keira, he probably would have continued. But this felt more like an interview than a conversation, so he stared at the road and held his silence. To their right, a strip mall. To their left, a marsh. A vee formation of geese passed overhead.

"Speed trap," he said, spotting a patrol car parked on the grassy median dead ahead. A state trooper stood by the car, aiming his radar gun. Yet another camera, relentless.

"Shit." Barb slowed down, glancing nervously at the speedometer. "I was only doing sixty, we should be okay. Maybe he'll ticket that rube in the monster pickup that blew by us a second ago."

"Saw him. Reminded me of my dad."

She didn't answer that. Her dad probably never drove a pickup. A few seconds later she turned the radio back on, but the public station had faded. She pressed search and landed on hip-hop, then country-western, then a glitzy pop star screeching her lungs out. She turned it off.

A horn tooted. It was Steve, pulling up on their left. He made an eating motion with his right hand and mouthed the words, "I'm hungry."

"Damn, Steve, just call me on the cell, you Luddite."

But she played along, tucking in behind as Steve zoomed ahead, then signaled for a turnoff at the next interchange. They looped back across an overpass to an old-style restaurant next to a motor hotel, with a long counter like in a diner, and a menu to match—meat loaf, crab cakes, club sandwiches, fried chicken. They dug in, seated three in a row along the counter, which wasn't conducive to talking. Cole overstuffed himself on grease and a milkshake, and within minutes of pulling back onto the highway he sank drowsily into his seat and nodded off.

He didn't awaken until the tires were bouncing off the pavement onto a narrow gravel lane. Steve was still in front, the Honda throwing a dust cloud into the beams of their headlights. Cedars hugged the lane from either side, brushing the doors like a car wash. Steve's brake lights flashed.

"This must be the gate," Barb said. "Not even closed, much less locked."

"Maybe she wanted us to be able to get in."

"Still." They rolled through. "Doesn't even look like there *is* a lock."

"That's what hardware stores are for."

"If she's even been to one. You like her, don't you? I can tell by the way you always defend her."

"I don't know about *always*. Don't you like her?"

"Sure. But you know what I mean. You should be careful. Her track record with men is not the greatest. Certain men have been known to die for her sins."

So there it was again.

"What's the story behind that?"

"It's a long one. Maybe she should be the one to tell you."

"Then maybe you and Steve should stop bringing it up."

"Point taken. But there you go again."

He was glad she couldn't see him blush in the dark.

They emerged from the cedars into open country. The moon was up, and even at night the view was impressive. Fields stretched off into the distance on either side. Long rows of corn stubble, no houses in sight. Out toward the horizon were lines of bare trees. Dead ahead, a forest and another field, with the roofline of a large house and a couple of outbuildings looming against a distant sparkle of water. Lights were on in a few of the windows, but it was still quite a way off. The driveway seemed to roll on forever. They'd already gone half a mile and didn't seem a whole lot closer.

"Oh. My. God. *Look* at this place," Barb said. The glow of the dashboard light gave her eyes a fierceness Cole had never noticed by day. "Now *this* is money. Big money."

"Looks like land to me."

"Same thing down here, especially if it's waterfront. Cheney and Rumsfeld both have places near here, you know."

"That ought to keep the goblins away."

"Or attract a whole new breed of 'em."

"Whoa! Speaking of goblins—"

A huge owl flapped across the driveway just ahead, caught momentarily in their beams as it pursued a mouse or mole, or maybe they'd startled it from its perch.

"Double, double, toil and trouble," Barb said. She laughed, giddy. "So I guess this is what's it like to really have it."

"You sound resentful."

"Not at all. Envious? You bet. But not resentful. Not as long as I get to stay awhile. I've decided to pretend I'm attending a writers' retreat. Cocktails before dinner. Therapy runs before breakfast. Bonbons and soap operas for lunch. Maybe we can hire a masseuse."

Cole smiled, and noticed that the fierceness was gone from her eyes. Every time he started to dislike Barb, she won him back, usually by not trying so hard to have an edge.

They parked and unloaded in the dark until a porch light flashed on. Steve was about to knock on the door when Keira opened it.

"Welcome!" she said, as they filed in past her. She carried a stack of folded linens that smelled fresh from the dryer, and she was flushed.

"Beautiful spread, Keira." Barb sounded like she meant it. She leaned over and gave Keira a peck on the cheek. "Thanks for having us."

"Did I see a boathouse on the way in, with a couple of kayaks?" Steve sounded as excited as a kid at summer camp.

"There's a day sailer, too, if you want to launch it. Although the sail hasn't been out of the bag in years, so I have no idea what kind of shape it's in."

Cole stayed quiet, but he couldn't help feeling caught up in the excitement. It was like arriving at a resort, even though they had plenty of work to do. The house was newer than he'd expected. Twenty years old, if he had to guess. He wondered if her parents had torn down some older farmhouse to build it. It was a solid colonial, two stories, with three upstairs gables along a slate roof, and working shutters on mullioned windows. Conventional, but seemingly solid. It would have to be to withstand some of the storms that blew in off the Bay. The back wall was no more than twenty yards from the shoreline, and he'd noticed that out by the water most of trees were stunted on the windward side, just like on mountaintops and blustery capes. Even now there was a stiff breeze, with a raw brackish tang.

The view from the foyer was of the living room and a den off to the left, with a hallway beyond. The furnishings were neither showy nor garish, but to Cole's untrained eye everything from the light fixtures to the curtains looked like top quality, if a bit bland. Off-white walls, oriental rugs, silky upholstery. There was a big fireplace with a grand oaken mantelpiece in a natural finish, which faced a massive earth-tone couch. Oil landscapes, mostly tidewater scenes, hung from the walls.

"Wow," Steve said. "Do we get a tour?"

"If you want. I thought you might want to get your bags squared away first."

"Sure. How many bedrooms?"

"Four. Not counting the one out in the pool house."

"There's a pool house?" Barb asked.

"It's the de facto guest house. For longer-term visitors."

Steve hefted up his bag. "Where do you want us?"

"Upstairs. I thought I'd put Cole and you on the west side, Barb and me on the east."

"And Colonel Mustard in the study with a candlestick," Barb said.

Steve gave her a look. She made a face at him. "Sorry. This is fun. The whole idea of being here is fun."

"You know," Steve said, "maybe Captain Cole would like some extra privacy. Would it be okay if he bunked in the pool house?"

The suggestion caught Cole off guard. He immediately took it as a snub, and he knew that reacting against it would make it seem like more of one. He'd already picked up his duffel and taken a step toward the stairs, but now he reversed course, stepping toward the door.

"I'll be comfortable anywhere you want me."

Keira seemed taken aback, but she didn't challenge it. Maybe after getting her way on the move she felt she owed Steve a few smaller victories. So it was left to Barb to speak up, and as usual she wasn't shy.

"Getting a little prickly about living with the help, Steve?" It wasn't clear from her tone whether she was joking.

"Hey, I just thought that he might like—"

"It's no problem," Cole said, wanting to head off any further disagreement. "I'm fine with it."

Steve had sounded sincere. Maybe he was. But their arguments were becoming too much like the ones his parents used to have, which made him feel about fifteen. He continued toward the door to signal that the matter was settled.

"I'll get you the key," Keira said meekly.

He looked over at Steve, who seemed crestfallen, embarrassed by his faux pas. But the deed was done, so Cole hefted his bag and headed back out the door. The pool house was flush against the woods, some forty yards from the left side of the house. The pool itself was covered by a tarpaulin stretched as tight as a trampoline, with fallen leaves on top. The furnishings inside were comparable to what he'd already seen, and if anything, the pool house was probably a few years newer, although the air was musty and the heat was off. Keira brought along linens and a pair of towels.

"The thermostat's here, by the door," she said. "It shouldn't take long to heat up. Let me make the bed for you."

"I can do that."

"You sure?"

"Really. It's okay. I'm fine with it."

Her shoulders sagged.

"Here." She handed him a pair of keys. "If it's privacy he wants for you, then you're the only one who gets a key for this place. Plus one for the main house, of course. I hope we'll be seeing you at breakfast."

The key for the main house looked brand-new.

"You get these today?"

She nodded.

"Four copies."

"Did you get a lock for the gate? Barb was already wondering."

"Shit. Knew I was forgetting something."

"I can take care of it tomorrow, if I can borrow a car. I'm meeting Sharpe up on Route 50, out past Easton."

"Steve told me. Sharpe sounds like a piece of work. But I guess we should be glad he's being careful. Any idea what he's cooked up for tomorrow?"

"None. A bunch of geeks doing weird stuff together, by the sound of it. Probably worthless, but if I humor him maybe it'll pay off."

She touched his arm, her fingers warmer than anything in the room.

"See? You're contributing, and you'll keep contributing. It's why you don't really belong out here, so don't feel like a stranger, and don't act like one. Breakfast, okay? Don't drift away on us."

"Sure."

Maybe she was worried he would drink out here, or maybe she just liked him. It was also possible that she would say such things to any guest, simply because it was in her nature to do so. Whatever the reason, she was right on point. It would be a bad idea to drift. He had purposely left behind his last bottle of Weed, still a quarter full. The craving lost a little more of its edge every day, although it was usually sharpest around this time of day, a few hours after nightfall. Backsliding would be an easy choice out here, so he would need to be doubly careful. Tomorrow he would probably drive past several liquor stores, just as he had on the trip to see Sharpe. Each was a temptation, but he'd resisted. He must maintain discipline. Pit stops only for the hardware store, to buy a lock, and for lunch. Maybe he'd be better off packing a sandwich.

Cole showered, which calmed him. Later, after a walk, he thought of Keira as he climbed beneath the crisp new sheets, which didn't exactly help him settle down. He tried another tack, thinking about Carol, his children, but that was even worse. He got out of bed. What the hell, it was still pretty early. There were some books on a shelf, cheap paperbacks mostly, but none captured his interest. It was damn quiet out here, with only the wind in the trees for company. He opened the curtains on the bedroom window, with a view of the moonlit woods. Bare limbs and underbrush, the icy pinprick of winter constellations. At ten o'clock he climbed back into bed.

He wondered whether he should set the alarm on his watch, but the peace of repose was beginning to get the better of him, so he stayed put, watching the night. There was life out there in the trees, he knew, restless and prowling but posing no threat to him. Footfall of deer and fox. Wing beat of owl and hawk. The forest primeval. Those were the thoughts that finally dragged him under.

Three hours later he sat up in bed, wide awake. He had a vague impression that something had bumped against a wall, but soon realized that everything was still. Maybe a limb had blown off a tree. But now he was restless. He remembered seeing an entire library of books in some built-in shelves in the main house, so he decided to go look for something to read. In the back of his mind was also the knowledge that somewhere over in the house there was probably a liquor cabinet. And if everyone had already gone upstairs to bed, well . . .

No, don't even think about it.

He pulled on his clothes and picked his way across the dark lawn, negotiating a winding path between boxwoods and juniper bushes. The door was locked but he had the new key from Keira. He made as little noise as possible, figuring they'd all be jumpy on their first night. Easing the door shut behind him, he heard a murmur of voices from the back. Dim light spilled from a doorway. It sounded like Barb and Steve. He moved toward them, stopping just out of view. They were in the very room where he'd seen the books and, he now admitted to himself, a cabinet that had seemed the likeliest home for any alcohol. There'd been a tray on top with a set of glasses and an ice bucket.

Out of the question now, although he supposed it would still be okay to interrupt long enough to grab a book. He was close enough to make out some of their words, and just as he was about to step into the open he heard his own name, then Keira's, which stopped him.

He could only decipher enough for a vague sense of the conversation, but their tone wasn't happy. The word "smitten" jumped out at him from Barb, and he supposed it was true enough, if a little embarrassing. What was more disturbing was the idea of factions forming and hardening, rifts and wrinkles that could create bigger problems later on.

Cole sensed that he had altered their chemistry for the worse, and it dismayed him. He had seen these dynamics before—in poorly managed fighter squadrons, and in flight school, closed societies where everyone was hyperconscious of the pecking order and someone was always scheming to change it. The results were never favorable. He caught a whiff of Scotch, which only sharpened his craving.

Steve said something about Keira's book agent, another topic that didn't bode well. An interval of dark laughter followed, like the kind you'd hear after a joke told at someone else's expense. Then the clink of ice as someone set down a tumbler on a tabletop.

"Good night," Steve announced clearly.

Cole quickly backed into the deeper darkness of the foyer, where he remained while Steve's footsteps headed up the stairway toward the bedrooms. Barb, the night owl, had presumably remained behind.

He wondered if she was thinking of those photos she'd left behind, the terrified boys in their bloodstained clothes. If his own experience was any guide, she didn't really need the pictures to remind her. Those images would never disappear, or even fade. The photos, he knew, were only her way of telling others what she'd endured, and was enduring.

He heard another tumbler being set down on a table, and the sound of liquid gurgling from a bottle, the rattle of ice, and then a deep, mournful sigh.

Cole departed the house as quietly as possible and threaded his way back to his room.

It was another two hours before he was able to sleep.

CHAPTER TWENTY-ONE

SOMEONE WAS RAPPING LIKE a woodpecker on the passenger window of Steve's Honda.

"Open up, flyboy!"

It was Sharpe, who once again had materialized out of nowhere just as Cole was dozing off. Cole was parked outside a convenience store on eastbound Route 50, their designated rendezvous point. He checked his watch and rolled down the window. Cold out there. Sharpe smiled craggily, but Cole wasn't in the mood for it.

"You're half an hour late."

"I'm right on time, Captain Cole. *You* were half an hour *early*."

"You said nine thirty."

"I know what I said. I was giving you enough extra time to lower your guard. Which is exactly what happened, sleepyhead. Now unlock the doors so I can load the freight."

"Freight?"

"You'll see."

Cole popped the locks. Sharpe opened the rear door and hefted a black hard-shell suitcase that looked big enough to hold a bass drum. He tried awkwardly to wedge the case onto the backseat, bumping and scraping against the door frame.

"No damn way, not with this Jap go-kart of yours. Unlatch the trunk."

"What the hell's in there?"

"*Unlatch the trunk!*"

Cole did as he was told. He watched Sharpe in the mirror, the bald head barely visible above the raised lid. There was some jostling and swearing, a lot of bumping around, then a slam. Sharpe walked around to the front and climbed in, his scalp beaded with sweat. There were only two other cars in the parking lot, and both had been there when Cole arrived.

"Where's your car?" he asked.

"How do you know I came by car? You need coffee?"

"No."

"Then let's get moving. East on 50. I'll direct you from there."

"I'm sure you will." Now he was wishing he'd grabbed a coffee, although the blast of cold air had braced him up.

They pulled onto the highway. It was midmorning on a Saturday. Waves of Christmas shoppers would soon be heading for the nearest malls and big box discounters, but for now traffic was light. Cole figured Sharpe would tell him what was up soon enough. Instead he pulled out a smart phone and began tapping commands onto the touch screen. Five minutes of this was all Cole could stand.

"Mind telling me where we're going?"

"I'm going to show you that rare phenomenon: a genie escaping his bottle."

"Then what, you put him back in?"

"Nobody puts him back. Once he's out, it's all about who owns the bottle, who rubs the lamp."

"What's this have to do with Wade Castle?"

"Wade is the Agency's keeper of the lamp. Or was. For all I know, he might be the genie by now. If you want to find him, or know what he's been doing, then you better get a good look at the lamp, don't you think?"

Cole waited for more of this cryptic bullshit, but Sharpe went back to work on his phone, as intently oblivious to their surroundings as a teenager texting his friends. Or so it seemed until ten minutes later, when, without looking up, Sharpe announced, "Take a right up ahead, by that old farm stand. Three more miles and we're there."

"Okay."

"You're going to need a name to use this morning. An alias. So think of one. I'm known to this crowd as Len Baker. They like calling me Lenny. So try for something a little different."

"There's a crowd?"

"Not a big one. Select company. Invited guests only. C'mon, pick something. We haven't got that much time. And don't use the names of any of your Air Force buddies. Too risky. Might be a way of tracking you."

The name on his fake ID, Floyd Rayford, probably wasn't a good idea. Too many Orioles fans around here. So, Cole thought back to his high school days, maybe because they were driving through similar country—the straight tree lines, the plowed flatness, the shimmer of creeks and inlets, peeping from the margins.

"Joe Cooley. How's that?"

"Another pole vaulter?"

"No, but he was on the track team. How'd you know?"

"I never go into a job unprepared. By the way, for our purposes this morning I'm a retired engineer from Black and Decker. I live in Delaware."

"Is that how you normally get here? In a car with Delaware tags?"

Sharpe ignored the question.

"For the past couple years I've been raising chickens for Perdue. I thought it would be a good way to ease into retirement, but instead it's been a shit sandwich. I also hate the government."

"Well, at least half of it's true. Does everybody else lie about their identity?"

"Probably nobody who'll be there today."

"So the Grand Dragon is a no-show?"

This at least drew a smile.

"These people are more interesting than a bunch of racist clowns in bedsheets. More dangerous, too. They just don't know it yet. Turn in to that school up ahead, Joe. Then pull around back, toward the baseball field. Joe. Joe Cooley from Baltimore. You need an occupation."

"Schoolteacher. Ninth grade algebra."

"That'll work."

"What if they ask for more?"

"Then keep it vague. But they won't. It's not what they're here for."

They drove around to the back. Five other vehicles were already there—two massive pickups, a couple of SUVs, and a minivan with a dented fender. Five men stood on the diamond, leaving footprints on a dirt infield that was the color of putty. Each carried a laptop or a tablet, and each had some sort of toy aircraft, like oversized model planes, although three of the toys were equipped with multiple over-head propellers.

"What the hell is this?"

"The Delmarva Cyclops Command. One of probably at least a hundred worldwide chapters of a bunch of tinkerers and geeks known as DIY Drones."

"Do It Yourself Drones?"

"With cameras, in-flight computers, sensor chips, and a whole lot more. All of it state of the art."

"Is that what's in the drum case?"

"A quadcopter of my very own. I'm the only one who doesn't use a laptop."

"Then how do you—?"

Sharpe brandished his smart phone.

"It's really all you need anymore to control one of these things. Comforting to know, isn't it?"

He opened the door and stepped outside. One of the men on the field immediately called to him.

"Lenny! Get a move on, you old chicken plucker, we've got birds to fly. Paul's gonna do his maiden!"

"That's Stan," Sharpe said to Cole through the open door. "The mouth of the bunch, but you'll like him. He's got a fixed-wing X8 with enough battery power to stay aloft for three hours. He once covered ninety miles, and he's got a sweet little GoPro high-res camera on board. If he wanted, he could've tracked you all the way out here from the moment you left your country estate. Hell, maybe he did. C'mon, I'll introduce you."

Everybody shook Joe Cooley's hand. Sharpe, or Lenny, explained that Cole, or Joe, was a newbie who wanted to see what all the fuss was about. They were cool with it, not the least bit worried. Besides, most of the day's attention was already focused on Paul, a potbellied day trader from Salisbury, Maryland, who looked as excited as a kid on his birthday. He was gearing up for the maiden voyage of his very own X8, and at the moment he was down on his hands and knees, getting his pants muddy out past the pitcher's mound as he tweaked and tightened with a mini-screwdriver and a tube of epoxy.

Three other members of the group faced him in a tight semicircle, hands gesturing as everybody talked at once. Paul kept nodding as if to say *yeah, yeah, I get it,* but he said little. Between adjustments to his aircraft he ran his fingers through his hair and frowned, like he was worried about screwing up.

Cole edged closer, listening to their patter. He picked out a few aviation terms, but the rest was geekspeak.

"Hey, man, did you check your APM settings to see how the elevons respond?"

"Dude, you know you're gonna crash your maiden, so maybe you should offload some of that high-end gear."

"Does that software overlay a 3-D HUD on the video when the plane's flying Gmaps?"

"Paul, what's your SVGA output?"

Sharpe sidled up to Cole.

"So what do you think, Joe?"

"What the fuck are they talking about?"

"You could learn most of it in about ten minutes."

"Do these things really do the job?"

"Once you get the hang of 'em. And it's pretty cheap. Ten times better and cheaper than when people started in on this stuff a few years back."

"What's it take to get started, about a thou?"

"A few hundred, as long as you've got a laptop or a smart phone. The aircraft's the big expense, but it's the chip package that does all the work, and you can buy a pretty kick-ass autopilot for about the cost of two double cappuccinos and the Sunday *New York Times.*"

"What's in the package?"

"Oh, nothing but a gyroscope, a magnetometer, an accelerometer, a processor, a pressure sensor, and a temperature gauge."

"Damn. That's pretty much everything."

"Except the camera."

"I remember hearing about this shit a few years ago. You'd see message boards with all the hobbyists. But it was nothing like this."

"Smart phones. That exploded it. The same tech that puts all those apps in your pocket helps fit all these controls and capabilities into your very own private spy drone. Not that any of these fine fellows is up to no good."

"Except Joe and Lenny, the two guys using fake names."

"Only two? You sure about that?"

"Do you know something?"

"Later. On the drive back."

Cole reassessed the crowd, trying to pick out who Sharpe might be referring to. Chattery Stan was now busy with his own X8, preparing for takeoff about thirty feet away. The three guys watching Paul—Bert, Wallace, and Leo—all had different models of quadcopters, like small helicopters but with four overhead rotors. Everyone looked harmless enough. Jeans and khakis, down jackets with a comfortable Saturday rumple. Nobody had shaved. A few had coffee in travel mugs. But how else would he expect them to look?

Bert was talking up the idea of payloads. "I figure she can carry maybe three pounds the way she's rigged now. A few modifications, maybe a little more horsepower, and I'm thinking I can ramp it up to eight, maybe even ten."

Ten pounds of what? Cole wondered. Anthrax spores? A pipe bomb? A Glock 19, mounted on a swivel with some whiz-bang chip to activate firing? You could fly these things just about anyplace, right past security checkpoints and every metal detector known to man. It would have to be outdoors, of course, but it still seemed like a nightmare waiting to happen. Or maybe Sharpe's paranoia was rubbing off on him. And maybe that was foolishness. Because out here in the fresh air, with a touch of brine on the breeze and the sound of easy laughter among friends, the whole idea of anyone trying something terrible seemed remote, even laughable.

"Look out!"

He turned just in time. A gust of wind had gotten a hold of Leo's quadcopter, a metallic green model that veered toward him like a wayward June bug. It buzzed past him, about eight feet to the left of his head, then caught itself in a hover and adjusted, rising twenty feet into the sky.

"Sorry, man."

"No harm, no foul."

Leo nodded, smiling appreciatively. Cole already felt accepted, a part of the club, and he might have been anyone, seeking to learn this technology for any purpose. Just like those quiet young men who had enrolled in flight schools in the months before 9/11. He wondered how they would've received him if his name was Hassan, or Mohammed. "Hi, guys, I'm Osama and I want to build a drone for my friends."

Sharpe walked over to the huddle around Paul's X8. Cole headed back over to see what was up.

"Paul, the time has come." Sharpe said gruffly. "It's put up or shut up."

Paul evidently agreed. Only seconds later he stood and stepped out toward second base, holding the slender body of his drone just behind the wings. Everyone gave him room. He set the engine running and buzzing, then extended his arm, posed like a kid with one of those rubber-band balsa gliders that Cole used to buy in dime stores, with wings that fell off every time it landed.

Paul flung it forward. The X8 rose sharply without stalling, just as it was supposed to.

"How's he flying it?" Cole asked. "He's not even at his laptop."

"The autopilot takes over," Sharpe explained. "The damn chips. He programmed in a flight path. If he wants to change it, fine, he can do it with a few clicks. All he really has to do manually is land her, so it's a pretty easy guess where he's going to screw up."

Cole walked over to check the image on Paul's laptop. It was alarmingly good. Brown fields, a tree line, all of it crystal clear, an HD display as good as an NFL broadcast. Then, as the plane banked, there they were, all seven of them below, gazing up at the X8.

"Can you zoom it?"

"Sure," Paul answered. "I can change the view, too."

The plane kept circling, widening its arc, but Paul pointed the camera out toward the road, then zeroed in on a red sedan cruising past the school. You could see the driver's face through the window, completely unaware. *Just like those Afghan dirt farmers, oblivious.*

Paul punched in some commands and his drone soared higher, zooming off toward the open skies of the eastern horizon.

Over at the edge of the field Cole saw a silver BMW sedan pull into the school parking lot and come to a stop among the other vehicles. It sat for a minute or two with no sign of movement behind the smoked glass. Then a door opened and a silver-haired guy, maybe in his fifties, got out. He wore a shiny cordovan leather jacket, unzipped, and a blue oxford shirt with the top buttons undone. He nodded toward the group, and several of them nodded back. He went around to the trunk and unloaded a drum case a lot like Sharpe's, then wrestled it awkwardly across the grass to the edge of the dirt infield, where he set it down. He made no move to open it. Instead, he eased back a few steps, as if to say that was enough activity for now. Then he folded his arms and started watching the others.

Cole would've guessed he was a stranger to the group if not for the reactions of the others, who seemed perfectly comfortable with his presence. After five minutes or so, he began to find the man a little unnerving.

"Who's the guy in the Beemer?" he asked Bert.

"Oh, that's Derek." He smiled, like it was some sort of inside joke.

"Man of mystery," Stan chimed in, making Bert giggle.

"He never does much flying," Bert said. "I think he's too worried he'll screw up. So he mostly just soaks up the atmosphere, watching the rest of us crash and burn."

"But he's got some pretty hot birds," Stan said. "On occasion."

"When he actually gets 'em out of the box. How many do you figure he's actually flown down here with us?"

"Five?" Stan guessed. "Maybe six. But never for long. Hot stuff, though, like I said."

"Payload obsessed."

"That's for sure." Stan laughed.

"Payload?" Cole asked.

"Always wants to know what your stuff's capable of carrying—weight and volume, the impact on the aerodynamics, all kinds of related shit."

"Do his birds ever carry anything?"

Bert and Stan exchanged questioning glances.

"Not that I've ever noticed," Stan said.

"Leo says he's seen him load up some stuff. Dummy weights, I think he said."

Stan laughed again. "Typical Derek. Hey, Paul's doing okay!"

He was indeed. Cole watched the X8 do some fairly nimble maneuvers off in the distance, out over a bare lot. Five minutes later Paul brought it back toward the baseball field. A low trajectory carried it across the chain-link fence in left field, and it zoomed down the foul line like a throw to the plate. It bounced once on its plastic wheels, then a second time, before planting nose-down in a sudden blat of prop and wing that stopped the engine and tumbled the plane onto its back about halfway between third and home.

"Out by a mile!" Stan yelled.

"Shit." Paul trotted over, brow furrowed, expecting the worst.

"Yep. That's a maiden," Bert said, which triggered muffled laughter and a few gentle words of condolence.

"She'll fly again, Paulie."

"Duct tape, baby. Duct tape and epoxy and she's good as new."

Nice guys, he thought again. Fun to be around. And he could tell Sharpe liked them, too.

But something about the setup kept him off balance, and as he looked around at the barren expanse of the dirt infield he felt almost wobbly, as if he was back in the desert, gazing up past his trailer into a threatening sky as he listening for the telltale buzz. At that moment it was easy to imagine this same crew milling around on some postapocalyptic dreamscape, scalded and empty, yet they were still chattering, pointing, playing with their winged tools of intrusion. Watching all their fellow survivors from afar.

"Wanna try 'er, Joe?"

It was Bert, snapping Cole out of his morose reverie with a welcoming grin. Cole blinked and looked around. It was a baseball field, nothing more. Fresh footprints and the chatter of humans.

"You okay, man?"

"Yeah, sure. What was your question again?"

Bert held aloft his quadcopter.

"Was wondering if you wanted to try 'er. You looked like you were feeling a little left out. And she's practically indestructible. Has to be, the way I fly 'er."

Cole smiled.

"Then I guess she's the perfect one for me to try out. What's the drill?"

In addition to an iPad, Bert had rigged up a headset control with goggles that offered a bird's-eye view from the camera, and an optional function that let you control the flight by tilting your head. Otherwise, the autopilot did most of the work. It took Bert only a few minutes to explain it, and Cole was up and running in almost no time. He marveled at the smoothness of the setup. For probably no more than a few hundred bucks, Bert had developed a ground control station miles better than anything Cole had ever used in piloting a Predator.

"Jesus," he exclaimed, "your GCS is better than—" He stopped himself.

"Better than what?"

"Better than, well, just about anything I've seen."

"I'm still working out some bugs, but, yeah, it's not bad."

Cole was transfixed by the images on the goggles, which made him feel he was up there with the machine, an illusion of flight that lifted his spirits and made his stomach do little bounces and flutters with every movement of the aircraft. It felt great. He was out there over the edge of a marsh, then speeding along above farmland, the sun to starboard as he soared toward points unknown.

"Looks like there might be some sort of power plant coming up. Down by a river."

"Oh. Better steer clear. They might not like us buzzing their stuff."

Cole did as Bert asked, veering gracefully away from the sun toward the open water of the Bay. Bert was monitoring his progress via the display on his iPad.

"You're good at this," Bert said. "Instinctive. Ever done any real flying?"

"Oh . . ." What would Sharpe want him to say? "Just simulator stuff. I've thought about taking lessons."

"You should do it. Looks like you're a natural. Not that this is all that tough, once you've got the right components."

"Do you fly?"

"Nah. Took some lessons, but it was costing a bundle and my wife hated it. Kept thinking I was going to crack up, come home in a box.

So I do this now. Gets me up in the air and I survive all the crashes. Hey, look at that guy. You see him?"

He did. Cole was back over dry land, above a fallow field. Below was a hunter carrying a shotgun, marching across the mud toward a distant blind tucked at the edge of a tree line.

"Think he'll take a shot at us?" Cole asked.

"Hey, it happens. In Texas, anyway. But I doubt this guy can even hear us. I just installed some noise suppression gear. Plus, you're up pretty high."

"How high?"

"Maybe six hundred feet. That camera's on full zoom, pretty much."

"Oh, sorry. Isn't there some kind of altitude limit for this stuff?"

"The FAA says four hundred feet, unless you've got a permit. But why bother? And way out here who's gonna give a shit? Especially if they don't know."

Cole switched back to autopilot and took off the goggles, handing them back to Bert, who then took command via the iPad.

"Thanks. I enjoyed that."

"Looked like it. So, Lenny says you're thinking of getting into this?"

Who was Lenny? Oh, right. Sharpe.

"Maybe. Looks pretty cool."

"As long as you don't mind a lot of crack-ups and false starts."

Cole glanced over to see what the others were up to, and saw Derek in his ugly leather jacket. The drum case was still locked up tight, but Derek held out a smart phone and seemed to be shooting video of Cole and Bert. Cole quickly turned away. He felt foolish for doing so, but he didn't turn back around. No sense ending up with his face on somebody's footage that might go up on Facebook within the hour.

When he glanced back over a few minutes later, Derek had put away his phone and was chatting amiably with Leo, both of them with their hands on their hips, at ease with each other, which made Cole feel better.

After another ten minutes, Bert brought his drone in for a smooth landing near home plate.

Sharpe walked over. "Joe? Time we got moving. We're on a schedule today, Bert. Just wanted to give him a taste of it."

They said their good-byes. Everyone invited him back. Under other circumstances he might even have accepted. In some ways it was the same dynamic as in the fraternity of pilots. A similar kinship, albeit without the dangers. And at least they were out in the open air, not in some damn trailer, running other people's missions while people barked at them on a chat screen. He would have enjoyed sticking around for a beer or a bourbon afterward, although he doubted their drink of choice was Jeremiah Weed.

Sharpe loaded his gear. He had made only the most cursory of flights with his quadcopter, just enough of an exercise, perhaps, to show that they weren't there only to gawk. Maybe he'd been too intent on watching Cole to indulge in his usual level of play. They drove out of the parking lot. Cole was about to speak when Sharpe held up a hand to silence him and said brusquely, "Open your window."

"What?"

"Roll it down. Stick your head out and tell me what you see."

Cole eased off on the gas and lowered the window. Glancing back, he saw one of the fixed-wing X8s buzzing angrily in their wake, maybe thirty feet overhead.

"Jesus. Who's doing that?"

Sharpe laughed uproariously.

"Fucking Stan. Always follows the first one to leave, then stalks him back to Route 50."

"Why?"

"To show that he can. Flip him the bird for us, they'll enjoy it. Go on."

Cole held out his left hand for a good five seconds while steering with his right. They heard a faint outburst of good-natured cheering. Then he shut the window. Stan's X8 zoomed out in front of them and veered west, waggling its wings good-bye while Sharpe bent over the dash for a better view.

"Well, if you were trying to freak me out, it worked."

"Good. Your former employers fully support this kind of thing, you know."

"The Air Force?"

"DARPA. The Defense Advanced Research Projects Agency. The brain bin Ike created after everybody freaked out over Sputnik."

"Shoulda known."

"Drones are their pet project these days. A couple years ago they posted a public challenge, with a hundred-thousand-dollar reward. Lots of specs and guidelines, but basically they were asking the DIY crowd to build the world's perfect little spy drone. Crowd sourcing. Smart move. Their way of tapping in to the wisdom of the mob, all those armchair geniuses. A thousand bad ideas for every good one, but still. Nobody met the specs by the deadline, but they picked up some good stuff along the way."

"Like what?"

"Oh, that's classified, of course. You wouldn't understand half of it anyway."

"You would."

"Would and do. Give enough free time and resources to enough quick, creative minds and they'll always solve some problems for you. Most of the really hot shit DIY chapters are out west or overseas—Australia, Indonesia, you name it. But this little bunch of ours has been identified as a group that can hold its own. Once that happens, you'd be surprised how many interested parties will want to tap into the brain pool."

"Like who?"

"We had a newcomer a while back. Nice guy, kind of like you. Came for a few weekends, asked a zillion questions. Everybody liked him. I ran the tags on his car, made a few checks, but never told anybody what I found out. Turns out he was some kind of engineering supervisor with Aerostar Dynamics. And I know firsthand that other defense contractors have seeded some of the other groups. Quite openly, in some cases. Let's face it, it can be a helluva lot of fun. And perfectly legal, of course. But you can see why I like to be careful with my name and all that."

"What's the story with Derek?"

"Piece of work, isn't he? Always brings shit—good stuff, too—but hardly ever flies it."

"He was taking video of me."

"He seems to do that a lot."

"Maybe you should run his tags."

"Maybe I have."

"And?"

Cole waited. Got nothing.

"Is Derek even his real name?"

"Yes."

"What else?"

"Maybe you don't need to know everything I know."

"So what was this little excursion really about, then? I get the whole 'genie out of the bottle' shit, but why did I need to see this?"

"Because another interested party who showed up in mufti a while back was a hired gun from IntelPro. Claimed he was an insurance salesman from Kent County. Ran his tags, too. And this is the kind of thing, really, that goes straight to the heart of what Wade Castle is up to. In my humble opinion"

"Drones and IntelPro?"

"Something like that."

"But they're not an aerospace contractor. They're security. All they build is private armies."

"True. But commercially speaking, this field is about to explode. Right now the FAA is choosing six nationwide test sites. Places to try out every sort of drone application you could imagine. By the end of 2015 they'll be coming up with a whole new set of rules for what drones can and can't be used for. IntelPro, like plenty of other kids on the block, is positioning itself to cash in. Thanks to their many friends in government they're in great shape to do so, and Wade Castle has been one of their best friends of all."

"But—"

"Let me finish. All that tech that's out there on the cutting edge— the secret stuff from my shop, and yours? It's all been thoroughly field-tested on those foreign battlefields where you used to operate, and in the nation's best-secured laboratories. And all of that—*all* of it—has been handed to IntelPro and a handful of other firms like pieces of candy, candy they've quietly begun to resell, still in its wrappers, to their new friends in aerospace. So that's one part. Down at the other end of the food chain, they're preparing to employ every possible application for domestic surveillance and security. They want to become as big on the home market as they are abroad. Why do you think they've tied themselves so closely to all the people flying Predators and Reapers overseas? Because they'd like to use the same shit here."

"In U.S. air space? Even I don't think they'll get approval for that."

"Who needs approval when you've got the PATRIOT Act? And they've definitely got the juice in Washington to influence those new FAA rules. Add it up, and you've got a pretty damn lucrative business model, plus the power to look inside every window in America. And if nobody can hear it or see it up there at twelve thousand feet—well, I don't need to tell you what that means."

No, he didn't. Especially considering what Cole already knew about certain parties who were already willing to cheat beyond the supposed limits.

"How is Castle part of this?"

"From what I always heard he was one of the people pushing the envelope overseas on IntelPro's behalf. A great advocate of sharing—sources, flight access, chat access, and just about any and all the tech they want to load up on. The way he saw it, the more people looking for bad guys, the better."

"Do you think they were in it together on the fuckups, too? Like mine?"

"One way or another."

"Then why would they be trying to ruin him now?"

"Maybe he spoke up. Maybe he's just a scapegoat. Or maybe they realize he's already a known quantity, so why not use him to divert a little attention, a little misery. To clear their own path to a more prosperous future. They also know the Agency won't ever talk about anything, except for the cryptic stuff Bickell's peddling. That makes Castle the perfect foil, and it would explain why they're feeding your friends all that bullshit about how he's back in the neighborhood. A means of scaring you, to throw you off the real story. Or this whole smear campaign could be cover, to help keep the Agency off their backs while they keep Castle under wraps."

"In other words, you really have no fucking idea."

"Which is another reason for bringing you here. To show you how we might find the answer. Because I'm convinced that Ground Zero of IntelPro's drone program is out in those woods in the middle of their training acreage. And your reporter friends, with their new waterfront location, offer the perfect vantage point for taking a peek from above. That farm can be our passport into IntelPro's great unknown."

"You want to launch a drone from there? A spy drone?"

Sharpe smiled.

"Keira's place must be thirty miles from the training center."

"By road, yes. All those twists and turns, the bridges, a ferry, up one peninsula and down the next. But as the crow flies? Or a drone? Seven miles, tops."

"What's the range of your quadcopter?"

"Oh, hell, that thing? That's a toy, and a damned noisy one. I'm way beyond that."

"So you've got another one."

"Of course. Too big to fit in any damn Jap car, even when I break it down. But I'll bring her tomorrow, you'll see. A range of fifty, sixty miles, air speed about seventy-five, max, with state-of-the-art noise reduction and stabilization. And it's got two cameras. One mounted where the cockpit would be, so the pilot can see where he's going, what's ahead, with a one-hundred-eighty-degree range of visibility side to side. Pretty much what you'd see if you were flying it yourself, right up there in the sky. The other one's below the nose cone, just like with a Predator. Full turret action and a complete field of vision, and it displays on my iPad. The pilot camera displays in a pair of goggles, sort of like the ones you were using to fly Bert's quadcopter, only better."

"Two sets of eyes."

"It's the way I wanted to configure the Predator. But I was over-ruled, of course. I've only got one problem, but it's a big one."

"What's that?"

"The autopilot's fine, as far as it goes. But without knowing the lay of the land over at IntelPro I'll have to do most of the flying myself, and, well, I'm pretty damn awful at it. This thing needs a professional hand."

"So you want me to do it."

"It's what you're trained for. Hell, you even flew Bert's wobbly little copter right off the bat, no problem at all. He was impressed, I could tell. So what do you say, Captain Cole? Ready to get back in the saddle?

And believe me, this will be ergonomically better than any damn setup the Air Force ever built for you, and that's the gospel. When they put together that shitpile of a GCS you ended up with out at Creech they ignored every last one of my recommendations. But what else is new."

"You're serious about this."

"Hell, yes, I'm serious. I'm bringing it over tomorrow for a test flight, so you'd better prepare your friends for my arrival. While you're at it, have someone make a bed for me at that country estate. My own house is going to be out of the question for a while. Too risky to go home now."

"Oh, they'll love that."

Sharpe laughed.

"They'll tolerate me, once they see what I can give them. A bird's-eye view of forbidden territory. A reporter's dream come true. No more public relations gatekeepers to bar the door."

"And if they don't go for it?"

A smile spread across Sharpe's face and stayed there.

"What? What are you thinking?"

"Maybe your friends need to have the fear of God put in them to make them go for it."

"What the hell's that mean?"

"All in good time, Captain Cole. All in good time."

Sharpe's smile widened, as if the film version of whatever he was thinking was playing out across the windshield.

Whether the journalists would welcome the idea or not, Cole wasn't sure he was ready for this. The old emotions from his Predator days were already stirring. Anxiety and edginess, the pressure to not fuck up, the long and lonely aftermath when you couldn't tell anyone what you'd seen, what you'd done, what it felt like. The dying girl, propped on an elbow, mourning the loss of her arm. A scream emanating from the center of the earth.

"Pull over up here," Sharpe said.

"Where?" They were back on Route 50, ripping along through farm country at sixty-plus, but they were nowhere near the convenience store that had served as their rendezvous point.

"*Anywhere*, goddammit!"

Cole looked in the mirror, wondering if Sharpe might be responding to someone in pursuit. Maybe Stan's X8 was out there, buzzing along in their wake. But the sky was empty, the traffic routine. He braked and pulled onto the shoulder.

"Here?"

"As good a place as any. I've made arrangements."

Just like before.

"Tomorrow you won't have to ferry me around anymore. I'll be driving a van, someone else's. And I sure as hell won't be using E-ZPass." Sharpe gestured toward the white plastic transponder stuck to the windshield of Steve's Honda. "They don't call it a transponder for nothing, you know. If they ever connect you to the journalists, which I'm betting they've already done, it will only be a matter of days before they track you down."

"Shit." Cole stared at the device, wishing he'd thought of that himself.

"All the more reason for us to act quickly. Unlatch the trunk."

Sharpe went to the back and hauled out his big drum case. Then he slammed the lid shut and began lumbering down the highway with his quadcopter, like an overage member of some washed-up rock band, hitching his way to a concert.

Cole pulled back onto the highway and slowly accelerated. He watched Sharpe recede in the mirror until he was no more than a dot. Then he floored it for home. Okay, so "home" wasn't the right word. But for now it was all he had. And tomorrow it would become his new place of work, his own little air force base with its own mini-Predator. Back in the saddle, indeed. He took a deep breath and drove on.

CHAPTER TWENTY-TWO

TRIP RIGGLEMAN CHECKED his notes a final time, stacked them neatly, and slid them into the folder. There were two copies—one for him, one for General Hagan. He was always a little tense before these review sessions, especially the first one, when it was paramount to show signs of progress.

Today there were additional grounds for concern, including some items that he could mention only with the greatest care and delicacy, if at all. His earlier uneasiness over the unusual nature of this case, which he hoped would disperse as he dug deeper, had only intensified and grown more complex. Something was in the air with this one.

"General Hagan will see you now."

It was Hagan's secretary, standing in the open doorway, hair pinned up in a 'do straight out of a 1960s sitcom.

"Thanks."

Riggleman stood, checked the creases of his trousers, the neatness of his shirttail, the position of his spectacles on the bridge of his nose. Everything in place, everything ready. Except for his stomach, which grumbled in warning, a product of nerves and three cups of coffee.

As he entered the office, a squadron of jets roared over the building. The floor trembled, the windowpanes buzzed in their frames. It had been going on all morning at Nellis, and the whole base reeked of jet fuel. Even in here, with the air-conditioning tuned to a crisp 68 on an unseasonably warm morning, there was the slightest whiff of the runway.

"Sir."

He snapped off a salute, which Hagan returned from behind the desk. The general broke into a slow smile of anticipation as Riggleman placed a copy of his notes on the corner of the desk and slid into a facing chair.

From experience, Riggleman knew there would be no small talk, not for a while yet. Nor would the general offer food or drink. Hagan's style was to get right down to business. They waited for his secretary to shut the door, then the general cleared his throat.

"What do you have for me, Captain?"

Riggleman knew better than to offer the most important material first. Hagan liked him to save the best for last, and, like any armchair detective, he relished a blow-by-blow of how his favorite sleuth was proceeding.

There was an art to Riggleman's spiel. A smattering of geekspeak, a few of his own terms. It never hurt to show off a little, and it gave him license to resort to bullshit at points where the material was thin—and there were certainly a few of those points this time.

Cole was proving to be an elusive quarry, a complicated man. A fuckup, yes, or he wouldn't have washed out to begin with, but a fellow who seemed to be proceeding with caution and deliberation. Not that Riggleman wouldn't eventually find him, as long as General Hagan gave him the necessary time and resources. And that was part of his job today, to convince the general that he'd earned the chance to finish. That made it all the more necessary for Riggleman to present his findings professionally, smartly, in a manner that would hold Hagan's attention to the end. He drew a deep breath and began.

"First I took a fresh look at the preliminary findings—credit records, phone records, airport security footage," he told Hagan. "The legwork was solid but incomplete. I expanded the credit search to include his in-laws and anything under his children's names. His parents are deceased, but I checked their names as well in case he might have used an older identity. Nothing. He was an only child, so there were no siblings. I did the same sort of sweep for phone records or any other sort of activity that might have raised a red flag. Still nothing.

"I took the available security footage from Vegas International Airport and from Logan and the Portland Jetport and ran it with some video enhancement software and a few facial recognition tools, using images from two fairly recent photos of Cole that were on file with the DOD.

"When that came up empty, I used the same tools to analyze video footage from the identical time period for four additional regional airports here and in the Northeast, plus three Amtrak stations, two local bus stations, and multiple toll facilities on all major highways leading out of Vegas and in the corridor between Boston and Moultonborough, New Hampshire.

"There is very little facial capture at the tollbooths, although sometimes people without E-ZPass capability will lean out their windows enough for a pickup. Admittedly a long shot, but no luck. Most of the footage from the train and bus stations was of such poor quality that it was virtually useless. I did sample a few random public rest stop facilities on theoretical eastward routes for the days in question, but at some point you're dealing with the law of diminishing returns."

"Understood. Continue."

He could tell that Hagan was loving it—the thoroughness, the tech at Riggleman's fingertips, his ease in employing it. In a weird way, the general also seemed to be enjoying the apparent elusiveness of their quarry. Or maybe Riggleman was projecting his own admiration. However Cole had proceeded, he seemed to have shrunk his footprint to the bare minimum. Not off the grid, perhaps, but close to it.

"All of Cole's current and past email addresses have been inactive for more than a year. Complete radio silence under all known cyberidentities. So I used data mining software to forage all recently created accounts for Gmail, Hotmail, AOL, and other major servers. I swept that material searching for anything that might allude to his own name, his children's names, or any of his known Air Force nicknames, such as Monkey Man."

"His Viper call sign," Hagan said with a hint of fondness. "Remember it well."

"I focused especially on Internet signatures from Nevada. Again, nothing. I augmented this with a data sweep of message boards, chat rooms, and discussion forums with any topics related to DOD policy on UAVs, Afghanistan, Air Force issues, you name it. A few suspicious entries turned up, but all of them were accounted for."

Hagan nodded, still a captive audience. But Riggleman had arrived at the delicate portion of his presentation, material that was tricky not so much because of what he'd discovered—precious little—but because of how the process had unfolded.

"Personal interviews were next," he said. "I began with Owen Bickell, the former CIA man. He declined to be interviewed in person but agreed to speak over a secure line, which I arranged."

"He was cooperative, I hope?"

Riggleman paused, weighing his words.

"Yes and no."

"No?"

Hagan had nearly come up out of his chair.

"He was cordial and pleasant. He fully acknowledged Cole's visit, and he candidly discussed their previous relationship of a few years ago, when Captain Cole trained him and two other Agency officers in UAV operations and techniques, out at Creech."

"Which we already knew."

"Yes, sir. But when I asked about the nature of their recent conversation, he referred me to his superiors."

"Superiors? Hell, he's *retired*. He has no superiors."

"Yes, sir. Nonetheless."

"Do you think this was some kind of legal precaution, a way to cover his ass until you produced the necessary paperwork to authorize him to speak?"

"No, sir. He made it clear he has no intention of discussing this matter with us under any circumstances. He said any sort of comment would be up to the Agency."

"Well, hell, did he at least offer an Agency contact?"

"No, sir."

"*No?*"

"No name. No number. He didn't even advise me as to which department or desk to contact."

"Well, hell's bells. What in the blue fucking blazes kind of help was that?"

"I posed a similar question, sir. No less forcefully, but in less colorful vernacular."

"And?"

Riggleman consulted his notes.

"He responded that this was, quote, 'an Agency matter currently subject to internal review, involving matters of a highly sensitive nature with regard to current and continuing operations, as well as confidential sources and methods.' Unquote."

"Do you think that was his way of saying they think Cole's a spy?"

"That's one interpretation. It could also mean they still consider him a reliable source and want to keep him that way. For all we know, they've reached some sort of working agreement with him, which could also help explain why his movements have been so hard to track."

"Hell's fucking bells. That's all we need." Hagan ran his hands through his hair.

"In any event, sir, Bickell maintained that the entirety of their conversation would remain classified."

"Of course it's classified. *All* this shit is classified. But you're cleared. I'm cleared."

"I reminded him of that. Nonetheless."

"Goddamn those fucks!" The general was red in the face. He looked like a street fighter seeking someone to slug. He picked up the desk phone, held it aloft for a second, then set it roughly back in its cradle.

"I'll follow up on this," he said, nodding vigorously. "This will not be the end of it."

Riggleman wasn't so sure that that was a smart idea, but couldn't think of a diplomatic way to say so.

"Yes, sir."

"Where were we?"

"My next stop was at Creech, to speak with Cole's old buddies, his former CO, his sensor."

And here, as far as Riggleman was concerned, was where things had again felt strange, the same way he'd felt when the official transcripts of the court-martial had landed on his desk so speedily, yet with an artfully concealed gap of twenty-two missing pages.

At Creech he'd expected to run the usual gauntlet of PAOs and legal officers. Instead, an MP escorted him straightaway to an empty staff room reserved for his interview sessions. It was equipped with a tape recorder, a legal pad and pencils, a full thermos of hot coffee, a basket of sweet rolls from the officers' mess, and a printed timetable of all scheduled visitors—everyone he'd requested, plus two volunteers. Each of them obediently trooped in to see him, right on schedule, most of them with smiles on their faces. And there was none of the usual checking of watches or interruptions by impatient COs to say, as was often their custom, "Son, I hope you're about to wrap this up, 'cause we've got a war to fight."

Maybe Hagan had smoothed the way. Maybe someone else had. And maybe he was foolish to regard this as a problem instead of a blessing. But there it was, all the same. Doors were being opened before he even knocked, and he had yet to find out why.

Earlier that morning, Riggleman had debated whether to mention these suspicions. Now, in studying the general's face, he concluded that doing so would be a bad idea. Instead he proceeded straight to his findings.

"No one had any particularly helpful leads when it came to Captain Cole's current whereabouts. But the most interesting of these contacts, sir—in fact, to my mind the only interesting one—was his sensor, Airman Zach Lewis."

"How so?"

"He was very protective, very reluctant to say anything. He was the only one who demonstrated that attitude, the only one who was less than cooperative."

"Well, they were fellow crewmen for almost a year. It's a bond, I'd imagine, like the bond between a pilot and his wingman."

"I'm aware of that sir. This was different."

"Not having been a pilot, I'm not sure you're in position to know that."

Riggleman felt himself flush. So there it was again, the same old class distinction, the same old shit. *You're not really full-blooded Air Force if you've never been a pilot, the stratospheric royalty, the jockocracy.* Well, fuck that. He gripped the sides of his chair and pushed on.

"With all due respect, sir, if you'll let me explain my reasoning."

"Proceed." Hagan leaned back, frowning, skeptical.

"At first he was fairly relaxed. A little adversarial, but nothing out of the ordinary. Everything changed the moment I asked whether he'd had any recent contact with Captain Cole. From that point on, no matter how I phrased the question—personal contact, by phone, by email, by letter—he began employing classic avoidance and evasion techniques. For every denial he would look off at some point over my shoulder, or down at his lap. He was moving his hands awkwardly, blinking rapidly. He was lying, sir. They've been in touch, I'd bet money on it. And if I had to guess, it was contact with a direct bearing on whatever is at the heart of Captain Cole's disappearance."

Hagan leaned forward, interested once again.

"Then pull his phone records. His email."

"I did, sir. Nothing."

"Well, you see?" Hagan frowned and leaned back.

"No, sir. It's not that simple. Airman Lewis had recently erased all contents of the Trash folder in his personal email account."

"Nothing unusual about that. It's good op-sec. I must do that once a week."

"Agreed, sir. But he'd gone to rather extraordinary lengths, sir."

"Explain."

"Well, when most of us empty the Trash folder, it may empty the folder, but it doesn't wipe those emails from the hard drive."

"No?"

"No, sir. So I remotely checked the contents of his hard drive, scanning for whatever it was he'd been so eager to get rid of—on the very morning of our interview, I might add."

"And?"

"Nothing. And while I can't verify this without actual physical possession of the hard drive, from all signs it would appear that he has wiped it clean in a manner suggesting a level of technical knowledge not normally possessed by casual users like Airman Lewis."

"How do you know he's a casual user?"

"His Internet usage profile, sir. Online history, browsing patterns, everything. None of it suggests that he has the expertise to clean those emails from his system. Not without someone else telling him how to do it."

"So you think Cole told him how?"

"Or whoever Cole's working with."

"Bickell?"

"Possibly. Among others. As you'll soon see. In addition, anyone with that level of security consciousness would almost invariably erase his browsing history as a matter of routine as well, but Airman Lewis left his intact."

"I see. Interesting, I'll grant you, but it's not exactly conclusive."

"Agreed, sir. But I would argue that at the very least it makes him worthy of continued scrutiny."

"So go to it, then."

"It's just that, at this point I may need to use some, well, extralegal means."

"Well, hell, not to ask the wrong question, but hasn't that already been the case?"

"Yes, sir. But not to the extent I'm proposing. This would require a tweak that could be effected only by gaining direct physical access to his personal computer, sir. Preferably while he's on shift. And it would leave behind a distinctive programming footprint, possibly traceable by a qualified investigator."

"Let's not sugarcoat it, Captain. You're proposing a B and E?"

"Preferably under some sort of SF cover."

Hagan frowned. He puffed his cheeks and slowly blew out the air. "I hate to complicate matters unnecessarily."

"My sentiments as well, sir."

"Would the Security Forces have to be in the loop on this in any way?"

"Absolutely not, sir."

"Still. It's a delicate affair, doing it this way."

"Yes, sir."

"And because of that, I'm not going to authorize in any way, shape, or form your pursuit of this course of action."

"Yes, sir."

"What I'm going to do instead is to instruct you to use your own best judgment and discretion and proceed in whatever manner you see fit. Understood?"

"Perfectly, sir." All too well, in fact. Hagan was covering his ass, in case he ever had to testify under oath to either a court-martial or a congressional investigation.

"Okay, then. There's more, I hope."

"Yes, sir. One last item. Our best breakthrough to date."

This finally coaxed a smile out of Hagan.

"Proceed."

"The car, sir. The one in the aerial surveillance photo. It's generated some promising leads."

Hagan's eyes lit up.

"I thought there was no tag visible?"

"There wasn't, even with digital enhancement. Not even a partial. But the model was clear, a 2011 Chevy Cruze, silver, standard issue tires, which matched the tread pattern I found at the scene. Four different rental companies serving LVI use that make and model, so I checked every rental of a 2011 Cruze during the three days leading up to and including the date of the photo. There were seventeen in all. Based on footprints I found between his trailer and where the car must have been parked, I focused first on female renters. Only three of the seventeen were women."

"Good."

"But none of them came up as a suitable match. There was a pharmaceutical sales rep from Tulsa, a girls' getaway weekend group from Bakersfield, California, and a great-aunt out of Spokane who'd flown in to see her niece and nephew. None of them even recorded enough total mileage to make the trip out to the trailer and back. That left the fourteen men. Four stood out as possibilities due to occupations alone, but I was able to immediately eliminate two because they turned in their cars at least an hour before the time signature on the surveillance photo."

"Excellent." Hagan looked as pleased as he had all morning.

"That left Wilson Corey, age thirty-one, former Marine and Iraq War veteran now employed as a corporate security officer for Rimbaud Solutions, a developer of data mining software from Palo Alto, California; and Stephen Merritt, age thirty-eight, a freelance journalist with a specialty in national security reporting, from Baltimore, Maryland."

"A reporter? That's worse than a goddamn spy."

"Yes, sir. And I'm afraid he's the one. Corey's business in town checked out as legit. So I focused more on Merritt, and when I ran the Visa card he used to pay for the Chevy Cruze, I got a hit on a second car rental two days later at Logan Airport in Boston. That was only a day before Captain Cole visited Owen Bickell in Moultonborough, New Hampshire."

"I'll be damned. Bingo. So you think they're traveling together?"

"By car, at least. Cole never showed up on any flight manifests, or on any of the security at either LVI or Logan. Meaning they probably linked up somewhere near Boston."

"So where is this reporter fellow now? Can we bring him in?"

"It's not that easy, sir. He has no fixed address at the moment, and he seems to be moving around a lot."

"Well, who's his employer?"

"Up to a year and a half ago it was the *Baltimore Sun*, and he was living in an apartment on Clement Street, South Baltimore. Then he took a buyout, began freelancing. Three months ago he moved out of the Clement Street apartment, but left no forwarding address."

"None? What about family?"

"He's divorced. No children, and no family in the immediate area. His parents are deceased. He has two sisters, one in Chicago, the other in Plano, Texas."

"He must be paying his bills from somewhere."

"He switched to electronic banking at the time of his move, so he can pay from anywhere."

"Well, hell. Maybe *he's* the spy."

"I contacted his ex-wife, living in Takoma Park, Maryland. She hung up on me. I got in touch with some former colleagues at *The Sun*. No one seemed to know where he was living, but all of them believed he was still around. One thought he might have shacked up with another *Sun* reporter who'd taken a more recent buyout, at about the same time he vacated the Clement Street address. Her name's Barbara Holtzman, age thirty-nine. She also covers national security issues, and as recently as last year she was accredited to cover coalition forces in Afghanistan."

"*Two* of 'em. Jesus Christ." Hagan shook his head.

"She owns a house in the Middle River area just east of Baltimore, but as of two days ago she'd placed an order to have her phone and electricity disconnected. Neither the power company nor the phone company had a forwarding address."

"Fuck. A step ahead of us. You think they know you're on to them?"

"Doubtful. I've kept a very low profile. I used a cover for the calls to their colleagues, and only made contact in the past day and a half, and by then she'd already put in the orders to shut off her utilities."

"So where does that leave us?"

"I ran their vehicle records. Merritt owns a 2001 Honda Civic, Holtzman a 2006 Toyota Prius. Both are registered in Maryland, and both are associated with E-ZPass accounts with the Maryland DOT. Yesterday afternoon at"—he paused to check his notes—"at five eighteen p.m., both cars were recorded making E-ZPass payments at the toll plaza for the Chesapeake Bay Bridge, heading east."

"Away from Baltimore."

"Yes, sir. My assumption is that they're still somewhere on the Maryland Eastern Shore, although they also could have gone north from there, toward Delaware, or south into Tidewater Virginia. The latter location is where Captain Cole grew up, although his parents are deceased and he no longer has relatives living in the vicinity. They also could have returned undetected to Baltimore, since there is no toll plaza for the westbound crossing. But I do know that, as of an hour ago, neither car had recorded a further hit on the E-ZPass network, which means that unless they've changed their means of transportation, they're probably within a relatively short drive of where they crossed yesterday."

"Good. But do you think Cole is still with them?"

"There is always the chance that they've parted ways. But the coincidence of Merritt's location with rental cars in both locations where Cole was present suggests that he is likely to be continuing to provide transportation for him. I think it's a safe bet they're still traveling in tandem."

"But for what purpose?"

"Some sort of journalistic exposé would be my guess."

"Mine, too, and that's a serious problem. Most of Cole's work—hell, pretty much all of it—was classified. If he's telling all, then he's become a danger to national security."

"Yes, sir."

"That means we need more than what we've got, and we need it now. You've done good work, Captain, but it's not sufficient."

"I agree, sir. And that prompts me to inquire about the possible availability of another tool."

"Yes?"

"UAVs, sir."

"In civilian air space? Over Maryland?"

"It's already done routinely, sir, especially on the Eastern Shore. Training flights from Air Force bases and the like. We'd just be expanding our range a bit. As long as we notified local Civil Air authorities I doubt it would be a problem, or would even attract much notice. And our cover would be easy—a training exercise."

"The notification alone would attract unwanted attention."

"Possibly, sir. But not nearly as much as that Global Hawk drone that crashed near Salisbury, Maryland, just a few months ago. That was also a training flight. Or that was the official version, anyway."

"Are you doubting the official version, Captain?"

"No, sir."

"Too risky. Even if we got approval, we'd be looking for what, a needle in a haystack?"

"You'd be surprised what sort of filtering and ID capabilities you can wring out of state-of-the-art cameras and the newest image recognition software, especially if you can program in image data for a car's specific make, model, and color. These are the same tools scientists are using to pick out endangered seals from all the other black dots on the Arctic ice cap, sir."

This at least made Hagan pause. But only for a second or two. Then he shook his head.

"No. I'm not ready to go there. Especially when we're not even sure they're still on the Eastern Shore."

"Yes, sir. Although one other piece of evidence suggests that they are still there, sir."

"Yes?"

"It concerns Steve Merritt. In searching various records and databases I uncovered a tenuous connection to the DOD contractor Intel-Pro. Probably a little unconventional, for a journalist, but I guess it wasn't all that surprising because he's done several past stories referencing them, or some of their people, one of them as recently as six months ago. But it was intriguing to me for two reasons."

Hagan didn't look particularly pleased, but he remained silent, so Riggleman kept going.

"For one thing, the company's training facility is on the Maryland Eastern Shore. They sometimes host journalists for various dog and pony shows, so that could be a potential destination, at least for the journalists. Find them, and we probably find Cole. Secondly, as I'm sure you're already aware, sir, IntelPro has connections to several aspects of the Air Force UAV program, particularly in overseas theaters. That would be another reason that Captain Cole might seek them out."

"That's a dead end."

"Excuse me, sir?" Had Riggleman heard him correctly?

"I said that's a dead end. It's not worth pursuing." Hagan looked down at his desk, pushing some stray papers into a pile. "I'm . . ." He paused, searching for a word. "I'm acquainted with some of their people. Or with some of their methods, to put it more accurately. And if Captain Cole or, well, *anyone* from the Air Force attempted to establish any sort of unauthorized contact with them, they'd let us know. Immediately. So you can consider that base covered."

"Yes, sir. But if he's using an alias—"

"Besides, Captain. You already have an additional tool at your disposal. The one I gave you last time."

Riggleman was pretty sure he knew what the general was referring to, but it wasn't a topic he was eager to pursue, especially not when he was already feeling rattled. Never before had Hagan told him that an avenue of inquiry was off-limits. It was yet another first for this strange investigation, and now he was about to be asked to telephone a source who, try as he might, he knew virtually nothing about.

Riggleman had spent two hours the previous day searching for any information at all about the name and number that the general had given him at their initial consultation. He had come up empty. Completely. That, too, had never happened before, and he was not at all comfortable with the idea of seeking help from someone who was practically invisible.

"Well, come on, Captain, surely you know what I'm talking about?"

"Harry Walsh, you mean."

"No need to say the name aloud. We're both aware of it. But I believe the time has come to put his services to use."

"Unless—"

"Unless what, Captain?"

"Well, I do have a few other possibilities. A couple of eggs I've been sitting on that are just about due to hatch."

Actually, he had nothing of the sort. He'd briefed the general on everything he'd learned and every stratagem he'd employed to find out more. But maybe with a little extra time he could come up with a new lead. Anything seemed preferable to seeking help by calling into a void, an abyss, a deep shadow in which almost anything might be hiding.

Hagan thought it over for a second, folding his hands on the desk. Then he nodded.

"All right then. I'll give you the weekend, Captain. But you'd better have some results for me by first thing Monday morning, preferably conclusive results. Otherwise, you'd better have already contacted the source we, uh, previously discussed. And I don't want you waiting until the last minute before you see me to do so. Understood?"

"Yes, sir."

"Get moving, then."

"Yes, sir."

He left, feeling more pressure than ever.

CHAPTER TWENTY-THREE

WITH THE RETURN of sobriety, Cole had begun dreaming every night—vivid replays of the world he'd inhabited before the crack-up. Carol and the kids were there. So were Zach and Sturdy. The reenactments seemed to last for hours, and were so uncannily accurate that he was exhausted upon awakening, as if he had begun living two lives at once.

The dreams' only variance from archival accuracy was the regular appearance of the girl with one arm, although for whatever reason, the sleeping Cole was never the least bit surprised to see her. The dream version of the girl wore Western clothes and a placid demeanor, unbloody and very much alive in her various poses—watching from the corner of the ground control station while Zach and he piloted a Predator, peeking over the shoulders of Danny and Karen as they hammered away at PlayStation consoles, sitting at the kitchen table while Carol chatted on the phone.

Once she nodded to him from the doorway of a convenience store while Cole pumped gas into his truck before driving out to Creech. She was drinking from a can of Coke. He nodded back. It all felt comfortably routine, almost conspiratorial, as if they were cooking up some plan together. She always turned up in places where she wasn't supposed to be, and each time it made him wonder later, after he woke up, why she had been in that house at Sandar Khosh. It, too, was the wrong place for her, although he still didn't know how he knew this.

That night in the pool house his dreams revisited a moment from the aftermath of the missile attack which had occurred about eight hours after he'd arrived home in Summerlin. The dream began with Cole seated in a vinyl lawn chair, his mind a blank. A voice called out to him urgently.

"Darwin! *Darwin!* Did you see it?"

Cole clenched his fist to throw a punch, then realized the voice was Carol's, not Wade Castle's.

"What?" he croaked. "See what?"

"You *missed* it? Oh, Darwin. Karen *scored*. Her first goal ever!"

Cole stood slowly. Looking around he found himself at the edge of a soccer field, surrounded by other parents in similar poses. Everything smelled of mown grass, sprinkler water, and sweating children. A sunny day in a green schoolyard. He felt like an old grump trying to awaken from a twelve-hour snooze, knees creaky, butt sore. To get into the spirit of the moment, he clapped. His hands tingled as if they'd gone numb, and something foreign and unwelcome rose up in the back of his throat. He coughed and spat, landing the gob between his feet. Looking down, he was mildly surprised to see he no longer wore military boots or a green flight suit. Nikes and blue jeans. Now when had that happened?

He looked up just in time to see Carol shaking her head, then he turned back toward the field, where Karen was being mobbed by her teammates near the mouth of the goal, a squirming bundle of nine-year-old girls in white shorts and bright red jerseys, all smiles and screams and ponytails.

"Atta girl, Karen!"

His voice felt tender, barely used, the tone of command gone now that he was out in the open, standing in his own bright afternoon beneath a watchful sky. Then his glance snagged on a kid standing in profile on the opposite sideline. She wore the colors of the opposing team, but then he saw that she had only one arm, and he knew.

"Why bother?" Carol said.

"What?" Cole looked away from the girl.

"If you can't even watch, why not just stay home and get the burgers going?"

He glanced back across the field, but the girl was now dressed in jeans and a white T-shirt, heading for the concession stand. On the field, Karen's team was back in action, the speckled ball pinging as someone kicked it toward the opposite end. He clapped again.

"Let's go, Karen!"

"Darwin, she's out of the game. Score and you sub out, remember?"

"Right. League rule."

Danny, his youngest, banged into his right thigh and tugged at his trousers.

"Can I get a Coke, Dad?"

"Sure, Dan-O." Cole fumbled for his wallet.

"No, Danny," Carol said. "You know better, not before dinner."

"Sorry, sport. Your mom's right."

He caught the last of Carol's frown—an expression of worry, not disapproval. He knew the look well. She'd be on the phone tonight for at least an hour with Deirdre in Michigan, the key words leaking from the bedroom as he watched a ballgame down the hall. *Distant. Remote. Preoccupied.*

The dream stuttered forward in time to later that night, three in the morning. He was sitting up in bed, suddenly awake in the dark. Carol was also up, sitting with her knees pulled up to her chin.

"What's wrong?" he said.

"It's Deirdre. They're broke. The bank's after them and Mark lost his job."

Pretty much the life of half their neighbors. The signs of economic calamity were everywhere: lawns going brown for lack of watering, empty windows without curtains, auction placards on signposts.

"What about you?" she asked. "What's keeping you up?"

"We killed some children today. With a missile."

She looked up abruptly, rustling the sheets.

"Oh, Darwin. That's horrible." She eased closer and stroked his face with her hand. Over her shoulder, Cole saw the one-armed girl in pajamas, standing in the deep shadows by the window. "And here I am talking about money."

"We didn't see them until it was too late. The girl was not much older than Karen. She lost an arm." He looked over at the girl, but she didn't move a muscle.

"You can *see* all that? Oh my God."

Cole had said too much. Carol's eyes glittered in the dark. Maybe she'd already been crying.

"You can't tell anyone. Not even Deirdre."

"Okay," in a small voice. "I won't."

They held their positions on the bed, as if each was waiting for the other to speak, and after a few seconds he sensed she was making an effort not to sigh. She slid her knees down and rolled onto her side, and soon afterward he knew from her breathing that she was asleep. The girl sat between them now, her back turned to Cole as she appeared to make some sort of comforting gesture toward Carol. He looked away, staring toward the window.

Then he jolted awake, sitting up in bed in the pool house after hearing what had sounded like the cry of a child. Now, only silence. He blinked, sweating heavily. The darkness was so overwhelming that he sought refuge in the bathroom beneath the buzzing fluorescent tube above the sink, his feet icy on the linoleum. He heard the cry again. Not a child, though. A cat.

Returning to the bedroom he heard the brush of a branch against the window, followed by another cry, weaker this time. He pulled back the blinds and saw Cheryl, slumped against the panes, balanced precariously on the sill, her fur matted and bleeding.

Cole opened the door and called her name. Nothing. He walked barefoot around the corner on the frosted grass and found her still huddled on the sill, too broken and weary even to drop to the ground. He gently picked her up, worried she'd lash out, but she was docile and quivering, a mess.

"Easy, girl. Easy. What've you been tangling with, a fox? A possum? Did an owl come after you?"

There were plenty of critters who would overmatch her out here, and as he carried her inside he thought of the tale of the city mouse and the country mouse. Poor Cheryl, not ready for all the challenges out here. An owl hooted twice as he shut the door.

In the light he saw that her blood was already smeared on his T-shirt. He cleaned her off in the bathroom as best he could, but it was soon clear he needed more supplies than the pool house offered, so he slipped on his pants, shoes, and a jacket and carried her toward the main house by the light of the moon and stars, hearing the wind hiss in the pines.

Halfway there he stopped, something chilly touching his spine. It wasn't a noise, exactly. More of a presence, a sense of movement off in the deeper shadows of the trees to his left. The cat stiffened in his arms, sensing it as well, or maybe just reacting to him. Cole turned slowly and scanned the line of trees, half expecting to see a pair of luminous eyes, some animal preparing to pounce. Cheryl fidgeted and nearly squirmed free, so he held on tight and set out for the front door. The house was dark and locked, but he had his key. He locked the door behind him, still holding the cat, unable to shake the strong sense that something was still out there, observing in silence, lying in wait.

Cheryl gave an aggrieved yowl. He stroked her neck and whispered back.

"You and me both, girl. Let's get you fixed up and get me a drink."

There was a medicine chest in the powder room off the kitchen hallway. He put a folded towel on the lid of the toilet and laid the cat on top. Then he got a tube of antiseptic cream and a roll of gauze. He had never been a cat lover, but the animal's vulnerability reminded him of long ago nights when he'd tended to his children after they awoke with a fever or a cough. He sighed. He was homesick, lonely.

"Easy now." He squeezed out some ointment. "This might sting."

The cat took it in stride, eyeing him with what looked like trust.

There was a footfall on the stairs. Barb, probably, their resident prowler. But the voice from the hallway was Keira's.

"Oh, no," she whispered. "What happened?"

"Got in a fight, by the look of it."

She wore a flannel robe, emanating warmth and slumber.

"Can I do something?"

"Maybe hold her? I was going to wrap this gauze on her leg. Otherwise she'll probably just lick all the goop off."

Cheryl purred at Keira's touch. No doubt about who she belonged to, no matter who'd taken her in.

"There's a vet on the Oxford Road," Keira said. "I could take her there tomorrow."

"This'll do for now."

"You're sweet to take care of her."

He let the remark hang in the air, liking its judgment, and he felt himself relax. He realized that he'd been on edge all week, still in a mode of audition, of proving his worth, as exhausting as his first days back at the Air Force Academy, or in flight school.

"I'll make some tea. Herbal, so it won't keep you up."

So much for that drink he wanted, but tea was probably a smarter idea.

He laid the cat on the counter while Keira put the water on to boil. She lifted the kettle just as it began to whistle, then poured steaming water into a pair of mugs.

"Let's take these to the pool house, so we can talk without waking everybody up. I'll bring the cat."

Cole picked up the mugs and followed, wondering if he should say anything about the eerie sense of an intruder he'd picked up a few minutes ago. But now the idea seemed alarmist, especially with steam rising from the mugs with a hint of cinnamon. He watched the shadows all the same, and listened closely. No movement. No noise out of the ordinary. Yet he was palpably relieved when they shut the pool house door behind them.

"Did you hear that owl?" Keira said. "Sounded kind of upset. Wonder if that's what went after Cheryl."

"I doubt she would have survived if it was. Those talons can crack a cat's skull like an eggshell."

"Ouch."

"Sorry. Didn't mean to be so graphic."

Keira laughed. "I don't mind. That's something I've always loved about this place. It's so elemental. Just you and nature and whatever boat happens to be drifting by. It makes matters of life and death seem like things that don't have to be forced, or even endured. They just happen, the way they're meant to."

"Yeah, well, I'm not sure Cheryl feels that way right now."

"No. Maybe not."

The cat curled up on the foot of the bed. Keira took a seat by the pillows, leaning against the headboard as the mug steamed into her face. Cole remained standing, transfixed as she tucked her bare legs beneath her, a gesture of coziness that also happened to clear a space for him on the bed, if he wanted it.

Under other circumstances he would have happily seized the opportunity, and probably would have then pursued the customary male ritual of touch and advance, testing his way toward an embrace, ready to keep going as far as she'd let him. But that was exactly what Steve and Barb would expect from him—the randy, uncultured pilot, forever on the prowl—so he sat down in the armchair catty-corner to the bed.

Keira sipped her tea, and he couldn't help but watch her. Her skin was ambered by the glow of the bedside lamp, an attractive woman on his bed wearing a flannel robe and God knows what underneath. Maybe nothing. And now she was talking, and not a word of it had registered.

"I'm sorry. I zoned out. What was that?"

"I said, why don't you come over here? You look so forlorn, like a lost boy who got left at school."

He did as she asked. And she was the one who began touching. Her hand on his ankle, then his thigh. Touch and advance. A brush of her fingers across his cheek, a caress. He moved closer and she leaned forward, the bed creaking, the heat of her skin warm on his own. She was kissing him almost before he knew it.

"Is this all right with you?" she said.

"I was about to ask the same thing."

"Don't ask anything. Just act." Her voice went straight down his throat. He again did as she asked, and it was better than in any dream. They moved softly, slowly, and then gave way to urgency. Cole couldn't stop looking at her face, his eyes open until the very end, when he finally vanished from the world into the briefest oblivion. When he emerged on the other side he was gasping and alive. Keira smiled, then buried her face against his neck, her heartbeat fluttering on his breastbone.

A minute or so later she stirred.

"The cat," she said, with a note of worry. But Cheryl was still curled on the spread at the foot of the bed, sleeping off her ordeal, ignoring them. Keira sank back into his arms. He was speechless. Happy, yes, but uncertain what to say next, about her or anything. A few more moments passed in silence, and she spoke first.

"So tell me about your wife, your family."

Cole was so taken aback that he didn't know what to say.

"Don't worry. I'm not being judgmental. You needed this. I did, too. And now is probably the time when you'd be the most open-minded about your thoughts, and about your wife."

"Or the guiltiest."

"No. Really, that wasn't what I intended."

He studied her, the sincerity plain on her face.

"You're very different."

"Maybe so. But don't take that to mean that I've got everything figured out. My life's probably as fucked up as yours."

"Well, thanks for the vote of confidence."

"Oh, c'mon. That place you were living? The state you were in? You can't leave all that behind in a matter of days."

"No. That's true."

"So your wife, then. Now that you're back in civilization, don't you find yourself thinking of her more?"

"I've been dreaming about her. Nothing that's, well, erotic or anything." He couldn't believe he was telling her this. Keira's powers in full force, he supposed. "Just daily life, stuff we used to do around the house, or with the kids. The good and the bad."

"That's a start."

"Towards what?"

"Getting back to them?"

He shook his head. "That's over. My fault, but over."

"You'd be surprised how forgiving people can be. Especially when something matters to them."

"That sounds like the voice of experience."

She shrugged, lowered her eyes. "Sometimes the people who could forgive you are no longer around to do it."

"Barb said something about a guy you were with, a photographer."

"He was married. I'm sure she mentioned that part, too."

"Yeah, she did."

Keira sighed, then eased away from him just enough that he wished he hadn't mentioned it.

"That's the problem with the three of us living together," she said. "We've become too interested in identifying each other's weak spots. Sometimes I think Barb's building a dossier on all of us, you included."

"Sorry. I shouldn't have brought it up."

"It's all right. I'm nosy enough myself. He was killed in a plane crash. He was on his way to Paris to see me. I talked him into it. A weekend getaway. *Guilted* him into it, really. And helped him cook up a story idea he could tell his wife for cover. Then he was gone, like a big gust of karma had come along and blown his plane right into the Channel. And when his wife found out I was the one who ID'd his remains . . ."

She looked away, staring at the window.

"I can go back to the house, if you'd like," she said. "I probably should anyway, before the others wake up."

"Not yet."

She nodded, then reached across him to switch off the lamp. Darkness. Outside he could hear the trees in motion, windblown, the night forest still full of presences that Cole could only imagine. But now, with this strangely frank woman folded in his arms—warm and alive, yet alone with her regrets—he felt that they were both shielded, protected. He sank into sleep.

CHAPTER TWENTY-FOUR

"SOMETHING'S OUT THERE."

Keira whispered it as she stood by the window with the shades pulled back, peering into the dark. The wind was down, the owl silent. Cheryl stood next to her, back arched, fur raised, a sight that was somehow as alarming as anything Cole had seen all day.

He sat up in bed.

"What did you hear?"

She shook her head, held a finger to her lips. She was naked, skin a silvery blue in the starlight. By now the moon was below the horizon, drowned in the waters of the Bay. The moment felt especially eerie because he'd just been dreaming of something he would have preferred to forget, another replay. Bad vibes then, goose bumps now, with both moments feeling related.

"I thought I heard somebody moving around, but maybe it was an animal. Too big for a fox, though. And too steady and regular for a deer, or that's what I thought. It sounded like someone measuring his steps, being careful."

"Deer can act that way. Sometimes."

Cole could still see the afterimage of his dream, a view from an infrared camera in which six men were bright green blobs moving toward a huddle of prone bodies in the wake of a firefight, their weapons still aglow from recent use. It was his last mission before he fell off the edge.

He eased out from beneath the sheets and moved to the window. The cat leaned against his ankle, purring now, becalmed. He felt the rub of her bandage. Keira sat down on the bed and pulled up the blanket around herself. She stared at the window as if it were a campfire that might warm them. He sat beside her, and Cheryl hopped up to join them.

Keira studied his face. "You look like you've seen a ghost."

"How do you do that? How do you always know?"

She shrugged, unimpressed with herself.

"I was dreaming about my last mission."

"In the Predator?"

"A recon. A real screwup. I thought I'd erased most of it from my memory, but now it's clearer than ever. Like one of the video archives I asked Zach to send me."

"Have you heard from him?"

"He said he'd try, but that it might take a while. I should probably check back."

"Was that the mission mentioned in your court-martial?"

"It was more complicated than they said. A lot freakier. It happened my first day back after Sandar Khosh, right after we watched those kids running out of the house, the one we blew up."

"They were killed?"

"The two boys were. We saw their bodies. One right behind the other. The girl lost an arm. She was about the same age as my daughter. I don't know if she lived or not, but I've never stopped thinking about her."

"How horrible." The same words Carol had used. It sent a tremor up his backbone.

"Yeah. Pretty much. The next time out we drew recon duty. We were supposed to escort a Special Ops outfit into position for a raid, their eye in the sky. They were going to hit some insurgent hideout. The intelligence said the bad guys were only active late at night, so the plan was to close in just after dark, preferably while the bad guys were preparing dinner."

"Sounds important."

"It was the one part of the job I kinda liked, taking care of units in the field. Shepherds, watching o'er their flocks by night. Sometimes we just hung around to watch 'em sleep, securing their perimeter. Kind of like being in your kid's room when he's gone to bed. You just stand guard, make sure no one comes to harm."

There was a godlike aspect, too, like Barb had said. But Cole never liked admitting that. He enjoyed being a benevolent presence in the sky, but with the power to protect also came the power to smite, should the need arise.

"The whole op was supposed to take ten or twelve hours. Normally Zach and I would've handed off to another crew before the raid even took place, but about eight hours in we got a readout from our bird of impending engine failure. We'd gotten similar warnings before which never amounted to anything, and we figured that would probably be the case this time. But there was no way we were going to hand off now."

"Why not?"

"It's a hot potato. It's just not done."

"Why not call in another Predator?"

"It was too late. They're so damn slow. Wouldn't have made it in time. So we went overtime, in it for the long haul. The sun went down and we switched to infrared. There were maybe a dozen guys in the unit, deployed just to the east of a small forest of pines. The bogeys were in a house on the opposite side, by a stream. We'd reconned the house and everything was quiet. There were lights in the windows, men inside. Then Zach spotted something up in the woods. Three bodies on the move and some optic clutter."

With the dream still fresh in his head, Cole remembered the rest with ease, recalling that he immediately got on the radio to Gray Goose, the call sign for the commander of the ops unit. His own call sign was Redbird.

"Gray Goose, this is Redbird. We've got three possible bogeys in the trees, northwest quadrant. Do you copy?"

"We copy, Redbird."

"Taking her down to eight thousand for a closer look. They appear to be headed away from you, up toward a path on the northern edge of the woods. Zoom it as we go, Zach. I'll angle east so we won't be looking through the trees."

As the infrared image sharpened, Cole realized something that almost made him shudder.

"Looks like children," he said. Zach said nothing.

And three of them, too. How appropriate. In the green tint of the infrared image their eyes were cool dark spots on luminous faces, ghostlike—their victims from the previous day, out on a haunt as they tended a small flock of goats.

"Jeebus," Zach whispered.

"Creepy, isn't it."

"What's that, Redbird? I don't copy."

"Just kids, Gray Goose, and they're moving off. You fellas can stand down."

Now he saw the goats emerging from the woods, just ahead of the children.

"Looks like they're taking some animals home for the night. Out kinda late, but nobody's armed."

"Glad to hear it, guys. Keep me posted."

Zach spoke up, off mike.

"Should I move on?"

"What?"

"Back to our stakeout disposition?"

"In a minute."

Cole wanted a better look at the children, some sign of recognition that they really were flesh and blood. Or was he hoping against hope that they would be the trio from Sandar Khosh, miraculously resurrected in a far valley, miles from home? Who was watching out for them? he wondered. Who would protect them from land mines and ambush at this advanced hour? Where were their parents, their elders?

Zach obliged his whim. Or maybe he, too, was in the same frame of mind. It was a distraction, no doubt, but after nine hours in the saddle at the end of a long and terrible week, they'd earned the indulgence.

Gray Goose shouted into his headset.

"Gunfire! We got gunfire, Redbird! Where the hell are you?"

Shit!

"Looking for your bogeys, Gray Goose. What's the vector on that firing?"

"What the fuck?" Zach asked frantically. "I can't find 'em!"

The camera moved jerkily, too fast. In panning back toward the unit

Zach overshot the position and was having to adjust, all while battling against the usual two-second delay.

"Calm down, Zach. Scan her slowly." Now Cole could hear the gunfire, probably on the pickup from Gray Goose's headset.

"Have you got that directional yet, Gray Goose?" He hoped to hell no one had been hit. "You there?"

"Sorry, Redbird. Just taking cover. It's coming out of the west. Where the fuck were you?"

Cole felt his face redden, but he responded calmly.

"Got distracted, Gray Goose. My bad, but the cavalry is here."

"Got 'em!" Zach announced.

"We have your bogeys in sight, Gray Goose. Four figures, still on the move but maybe two hundred yards west-northwest of your position." The attackers were crouched, so their shapes were barely human. "They're out of the trees. No cover, far as I can tell."

He heard more shots on his headset. The muzzles flashed bright white on the infrared.

"So you've got a fix?"

"Affirmative, locked in. What's your pleasure, Gray Goose?"

"Throw down the God light."

"Consider it done."

He nodded to Zach, who made the necessary command to activate the infrared beam. Two seconds later the four crouching figures were lit up like dancers on a spotlit stage, even though to their own eyes they were still cloaked in darkness. On the ops unit's night vision goggles, the attackers would now be easy targets.

Zach panned back for a wider field of vision. A stream of gunfire poured out from the ops unit, blazing across the screen. Cole heard shouting in his headset, and the sharp report of the weapons. Someone in the ops unit shouted in Pashto, probably telling the attackers to surrender. Three of the four were already hit, and two of those were deathly still. The fourth stood straight up and dropped his weapon, hands in the air. Three Americans surged forward. It was over within seconds.

Cole wondered if the gunfire had alerted the hideout to what was coming. He doubted it. The hut was over a small rise, and the sound of gunfire was hardly uncommon in this part of the world. Zach checked the house, just in case, but there was no sign of new activity. The windows were still lit, and the heat signature of smoke pouring from the chimney glowed on the screen.

But Cole was shaken. His hands trembled. If the attackers had been more patient and a little smarter, they might have killed several of the Americans before Zach and he even knew what was up. They had failed. Check that—*he* had failed, needlessly preoccupied with the three children as they followed goats down a mountain path.

"You okay, man?" Zach asked, off mike.

"Not really. You?"

"That whole thing with the kids gave me the heebie-jeebies. They even glowed funny on the IR."

And for whatever amalgamation of reasons, that mission had proven to be Cole's tipping point. A haunting vision, followed by an error in judgment. Plenty of other pilots had endured far more harrowing moments and had emerged emotionally unscathed, or so it seemed. But Cole had collapsed. Crumpled. He hadn't been up to the challenge.

"You're too hard on yourself," Keira said, bringing him back to the present. God knows what he must have been mumbling.

"Maybe."

"Besides. It was the whole week that got to you. The children who died. That would get to anyone."

"I guess. Wade Castle's mission. And that guy Lancer, whoever he was."

Then Cole's memory seized on another moment from that final mission. Had he dreamed it tonight, or had it really taken place? It was real. He recalled it clearly now, a brief exchange of chat dialogue long after the firefight occurred.

"What is it?" Keira asked. "What did you just think of?"

"That call name. Lancer. He turned up on the recon, too. Later, right after the raid. He had some questions or something for one of the ops commanders."

"What kind of questions?"

"I don't know. I can't remember. But I know his name came up, in the chat. And it wasn't the CO he was talking to. It was the second in command. It was kind of hinky, really. I remember feeling that even then."

"How so?"

"The way the ops guy talked. The language he used when he spoke with me by radio. The second in command, I mean. It was enough to make me wonder if these guys were some kind of hybrid unit. Maybe with an Agency component, or even privateers. Like the stuff Bickell was talking about. I guess I'd blotted all of this out."

He wondered if flying those toy drones this afternoon had stirred up these memories. Watching the images on the goggles had been a little bit like being back in the trailer, sitting in front of the pile of video screens with a stick and rudder at his side.

"You should sleep now. This is wearing you out."

He said nothing. He tried to remember more about that day, the dialogue, the players. Then Keira moved suddenly on the bed, startling the cat.

"Shit!" she said.

"What?"

"The house. Look out the window."

Lights were on.

"Barb's room. Downstairs, too. Fuck. And I left my door open, so she'll know I'm gone. I should go now."

"Take Cheryl with you, show her the bandages. Maybe then she'll—"

"She'll know. She always knows."

"Then we'll just have to live with it."

"Yeah. We will." She kissed him, but in a hurry, like a wife trying to get out the door for work. Then she pulled on her robe, belting it as she eased toward the door.

"See you at breakfast?" she asked.

"Yeah, sure. Might as well take the heat with you."

She smiled and shut the door behind her, leaving Cole alone and uncertain, already wondering what to make of the whole episode. Across the room, the cat yowled, a low strange cry that was almost a growl, and when Cole turned he saw Cheryl arching her back like some Halloween cutout. Eerie.

"Wrong holiday, girl. You're supposed to know it's almost Christmas."

Then he checked the time, which threw him further off balance.

It was exactly 3:50 a.m.

CHAPTER TWENTY-FIVE

ANY CHANCES FOR an awkward scene at the breakfast table evaporated with the sudden arrival of Nelson Hayley Sharpe, who awakened the entire household at first light by knocking loudly at the door.

Cole, hearing the commotion from the pool house, threw on some clothes just in time to witness the initial exchange of pleasantries.

"Who the fuck are you?" a bleary-eyed Steve asked from the open doorway.

"Nelson Hayley Sharpe, and I'm here to save your bacon."

Steve seemed on the verge of either laughing or hitting him, then opted to simply shake his head and step back, gesturing like a doorman for Sharpe to enter. Cole got there before the door closed behind him, and Steve gave him a wry look.

"Get a handle on this guy before I wring his neck, how 'bout it. And maybe make some coffee while you're at it." Then a slight pause, followed by: "Lover boy." He didn't say it whimsically.

Barb was already up. Keira was presumably still in bed. Cole could hardly believe that she'd been in his own bed the night before. Now he wished he'd showered. His scent alone was probably damning. He slunk off toward the kitchen to brew a pot, deciding he'd better just follow orders for a while. Wait for the storm to pass. Same way they handled these things in the Air Force. He heard Sharpe's voice over the gurgle of the water as it filled the pot.

"If you'll lend me a hand, I'll start unloading my gear."

"Gear?" Steve said. "Who says you're staying?"

"You'll be saying it once you've seen what I've got to offer."

"Does Cole know you were planning this?"

"I asked him to let me reveal it. He'll assist me. We need a third pair of hands for the setup, but first I'll need a look at the lay of the land."

Cole heard the door slam just as the pot finished brewing. He carried full mugs out to the living room to Steve and Barb, who were still marveling at Sharpe's little floor show.

"What the hell's he up to?" Steve asked.

"Did you just invite him down here without asking?" Barb asked. "Tell him he could do whatever he wants?"

"You should've at least cleared it with Keira," Steve said. "Or maybe you did. Not that she'd say no to you."

"And why would I want to?"

Keira, coming down the stairs. Same sweet tone as ever, but a set expression on her face. She was showered and fresh, which made Cole feel even staler and crustier.

"I need coffee," Cole said. "Then I'll go see what he's up to."

He retreated to the kitchen. He considered pouring a mug for Keira, then decided he didn't want everyone watching him hand it to her. Their voices were rising in anger as he returned. Fine. Let them tear each other to shreds. It was Keira's house. If she wanted Sharpe gone, then Cole would ask him to leave, but only then. At this hour of the day he had no stomach for the sniping, the jealousy, so he headed straight outdoors, away from Sharpe and toward the water.

Steve surprised him by joining him a minute or so later. They gazed out at the Bay for a few seconds. The sun was just coming up. They walked around to the sheltered side of the house without speaking a word, and spotted Sharpe a few hundred yards up the driveway. He was down on one knee at the edge of the cornfield. He stood and looked up at the sky, moving his hands as if plotting vectors and angles, an engineer with some grand calculation playing out in his head.

"He's a piece of work," Steve said.

"He's that."

"Any idea what he's up to?"

"I'll let him explain. He's right, though. You'll like it."

A pause. A swallow of coffee. Then, without turning to face him, Steve said, "About Keira and you. I'm not going to judge. Hell, I'd have probably done the same thing, given the opportunity. But I won't let you fuck up this arrangement. We've been working together for months, a nice balance among the three of us. If you start wrecking things then you're gone."

"It's her house. Maybe she can decide what works and what doesn't."

Steve exhaled through his nostrils, blowing steam into the cold like a cartoon bull.

"Fine. Explain that to Barb while you're at it. She's already worried enough about Keira's loyalty and motivations." Steve turned toward Sharpe. "I'm gonna go see what this wild-ass is up to. Look at him. Like he owns the place."

Cole held his tongue. Most of the man's anger was probably envy, a guy thing. Barb, on the other hand—well, maybe she was just in the habit of begrudging other people's happiness. Cole sipped his coffee, letting the caffeine kick him up a notch as he braced against the morning chill. The air smelled good. So did the pines, swaying in the fresh breeze off the water.

It looked like Steve was asking questions. Sharpe seemed to be responding with reasonable civility. Based on their body language— upright, face-to-face, maybe five yards apart, arms akimbo—they were feeling each other out. Cole walked out to see what was up, arriving within earshot just as things began to heat up.

"You're going to build a fucking drone? Here?"

"For the use and benefit of your reporting. And it's already built. Fully engineered. Some assembly is required, that's all. Like your dad on Christmas morning, batteries not included. A few hours of careful labor, most of it mine, and it will be operational."

"And if we don't particularly want a drone, or have any need for one?"

"That's a discussion that should wait until you've seen its capabilities. Captain Cole will help me demonstrate. If a greater ability to gather information isn't to your liking, then I'll pack up and go. But until then . . ." He shrugged and tilted his head, a magician waiting for his audience to give the go-ahead for the next bag of tricks.

"Is this how you always operate? Just show up with your stuff and expect everybody to go along with it?"

"I'm not orthodox, Mr. Merritt."

"Steve."

"Steve, then. I can be a little gonzo. And I don't like arguing if that means losing ground to an inferior position. I'm a stubborn man for good reason, namely, that I never fight for a point of view until I'm assured that I'm right. So if I say I'm going to do things a certain way, then you may register your dissent, but it won't have the least bearing on my behavior. Understood?"

"Your way or the highway, in other words."

"Those are the very words."

"I see why they fired you."

"No. You see why I quit. Too many years of bucking the idiocy of people on the take, of generals preoccupied with inflating their budgets, of so-called engineers too worried about how many bells and whistles they could cram into every single project until it was too fucked up to succeed for anyone except the contractors who built the bells and whistles. You're no general, so if you fuck around with me then I'll just go my own way. But I do know how to function as part of a team. We never could have accomplished what we did any other way. I was just fortunate enough to be surrounded, at least for a while, by the most competent people in the field."

Steve smiled, seemingly impressed, if only by Sharpe's chutzpah. He waved toward the stubbly cornfield.

"Have at it, then." He passed Cole on his way back to the house, "Quite a colony of eccentrics we're building here."

He had that right. Cole kept walking, out to where Sharpe had dropped back down to his hands and knees. Sharpe dug a hand into the frosty soil at the edge of the driveway and crumbled the earth in his fingers. He nodded approvingly.

"With a little raking it should be fine."

"As a runway?"

"Yes." Sharpe stood and wiped the dirt from his hands. "Who knows you're out here, besides the three of them?"

"Some of their colleagues and friends, maybe. Keira's parents. But they're in Europe or something."

"Then I hope your pals won't mind if I crash here while I get everything up and running."

"They might. But the final say will be up to Keira."

He looked closely at Cole, studying his face.

"Fucking her?"

Cole flushed and looked down at his feet. It was all the answer Sharpe needed.

"So that explains the weird dynamic. The tension. Except in your case. You look rejuvenated. A couch will do for me, as long as it's not someplace where I'll have to hear your bedsprings creaking all night."

"Finished?"

"Oh, I'm just getting started." Sharpe grinned wolfishly. "Relax. The setup is perfect for our needs. And the beauty of it is that no one knows I'm here. I haven't enjoyed an advantage like this in quite a while. Okay, then." He slapped his hands on his thighs. "Let's start putting this thing together."

Sharpe had arrived in a white panel van with Pennsylvania tags. Painted on the side was a big blue monkey wrench with the name "Anderson Plumbing," along with a phone number with a 215 area code.

"So now you're a plumber from Philly?"

"A contribution from a concerned friend. There are more of us than you'd think."

He opened up the back and began unloading crates and boxes, which presumably contained the pieces of the contraption he was about to assemble. He also got out two toolboxes. One last box, a Styrofoam cube with sides roughly four feet long, remained in the back of the van. Sharpe left it there and locked the rear door.

"What's in the white box?" Cole asked.

Sharpe grinned.

"The fear of God. Use only if necessary."

Cole wasn't sure he wanted to know anything more. Besides, as Sharpe began prying open the various boxes and crates it soon became clear that there was plenty of work to be done.

However uneasy the journalists were about this venture, the noise and spectacle of Sharpe's project soon got the better of their curiosity. Within an hour all three reporters were pitching in. Steve and Cole uncrated the wings and fuselage. Sharpe wouldn't let them near the smaller parts, like the chip packages, or the cameras.

Barb and Keira handed him tools as he worked, standing to either side like nurses flanking a surgeon.

"Socket wrench, six millimeter."

"Epoxy."

"Allen wrench, that L-shaped thing over there."

It was nearly four o'clock by the time the drone finally looked like an honest-to-goodness aircraft. Keira glanced at her watch and gasped.

"I'm late," she said. "Sorry, but I have to leave for an appointment."

Barb and Steve exchanged knowing glances.

"Your super-secret government source who lives out here?" Barb asked.

"Yes, if you really have to know."

"You'll miss the test flight," Sharpe said, his first attempt at actual conversation for more than an hour.

"It's ready?" Steve asked. He looked excited. Christmas morning indeed, now that the toy was assembled.

"As soon as I tighten the landing gear, make another adjustment or two. We should have enough light left for a shakedown cruise. But let's let Keira clear the area first. We don't want to risk flying through her windshield as she heads up the drive."

Sharpe continued to work while the others watched Keira depart. The dust from her Nissan trailed off into the woods as the sound of her engine faded into the distance. A few minutes later, Sharpe was done. He tested the wind, then Cole and he positioned the plane for takeoff. Cole stepped back, and Sharpe started the engine by punching commands onto his iPad. Cole put on the headset. The image was even clearer than on Bert's, and with a better configuration of controls and commands. There was also a stick-and-rudder contraption for him to use, a pretty admirable setup. The headset and goggles were even comfortable, as if they'd been built just for him.

"I was guessing at your head size when I fitted them up last night," Sharpe said, a hint of pride in his voice.

"They're perfect."

The old excitement again, creeping into his veins like before a Viper mission, and even sometimes during Predator flights, if the assignment was interesting enough. He had the cockpit view now, peering down the barrel of the driveway, which Sharpe had already raked and swept. The wind was right, and Sharpe was ready.

"Okay," he said to Sharpe. "Take her up."

A whirring noise as the engine amped up, surprisingly quiet for all its oomph. No louder than, say, a weed whacker with an electric motor. Sharpe had built quite a machine, fast and stealthy, and with an intrusive set of eyes. Cole watched from his virtual cockpit as Sharpe handled the takeoff by autopilot, and he got that familiar flutter in his stomach as it lifted off, gained altitude, and then turned gracefully up and across the cornfield. The tree line loomed a few hundred yards away, but they would clear it with ease.

"Okay," Sharpe said. "Switching her to your control on three. Take her wherever you feel like. Maybe up to seven, eight hundred feet before you try anything fancy."

"Hey, I've got an idea," Barb said. "Sort of a test mission."

"Let's hear it," Cole said, "I'm open to anything." And he meant it. This felt good, even this faux brand of flying with two feet on the ground and people's voices in his ear.

"Find Keira. Get a bead on her car."

Steve laughed nervously.

"Well, it *would* give you some practice in tracking a moving object," he said, warming to the idea.

Then Barb.

"Absolutely. And if Captain Cole's half the pilot I think he is, he'll track her down in seconds flat."

"So there you go," Steve said, like they were a tag team now.

"Then we'll find out who she's really meeting with."

Cole's heart sank. Exactly the kind of mission he didn't want. Not something for the cause, just a random act of intrusion. Give them the power, and right away they abused it. Or maybe he was reacting on Keira's behalf. Would he have felt the same way yesterday, before last night? Had Keira counted that into the equation, perhaps, seeking his loyalty? Now he was the one being calculating. Leave the pettiness and scheming to them. But of course Barb and Steve would now be *expecting* him to resist, and that made him want to just go ahead and do it, let them see that it was no big deal. He would prove Keira innocent of their brand of duplicity. Clear the air and actually make things better.

"Okay," he said, "if that's what you want. This bird's certainly got the speed for it, so we'll do it. We'll go spy on your friend and colleague." He was wearing the goggles, watching the treetops zip past below him, so he couldn't see their expressions. But they didn't answer, so maybe at least he'd shamed them a little.

Cole easily found her car, heading north on the road toward Easton.

"Are you too low?" Barb asked. "Won't she see you?"

"Wouldn't that make it more fun for you?"

"C'mon, Cole," Steve said. "If you're going to do this, do it right."

"If *we're* going to do this, you mean. Relax, I'm at eight hundred feet. As quiet as this thing is she'd have to be looking for it, and we're directly overhead now. It's a six-foot wingspan, painted white against an overcast sky, a nonreflective finish so it won't even shine too much if the sun comes out."

Cole slowed down, keeping pace. Keira was doing about fifty-five. It was flat country, wide open, and there was barely a breath of wind, which made the flying ridiculously easy. This thing handled like a dream. Cole heard footsteps shuffling toward him on the driveway. Sharpe, probably.

"Kick out the stops, man!" Sharpe said. "See what she'll do!"

"Later. Aren't you watching my monitor? They've got me following Keira."

"Oh, for Chrissakes!"

"All hope's not lost. Show them what your other eye can do. The main spycam. I'll take her up a little and start circling the target as it moves. I'm a little worried about airspace, though. We're closing in on the Easton Airport. Just a bunch of little private aircraft, but still."

"I've checked the charts," Sharpe said, still sounding grumpy. "We're fine."

"The noise suppression's pretty impressive. How much did that set you back?"

"Let me worry about the budget."

It made him wonder how Sharpe had managed to bankroll all this.

Maybe Castle wasn't the only one working for someone other than who he was supposed to be. He wished he could take off these goggles and look him in the eye. Or maybe mistrust was contagious, and he'd picked up the bug from Steve and Barb. The whole idea made him weary, a little depressed. You got the power, you abused it. Human nature. And he certainly wasn't immune.

Keira had turned onto the Easton bypass and moved through a few stoplights as she negotiated a stretch of road through a series of strip-mall developments—fast food joints and big box stores. Cole did a barrel roll and even a loop, half to try it out and half to test their patience, but no one complained, which made him figure Sharpe was doing an okay job of keeping the second camera trained on their quarry.

"I'm putting her into a circling pattern at eight hundred feet and switching back to auto," Cole announced.

"Fine," Sharpe said. He sounded preoccupied. "That'll be another nice test, see how well she holds her patterns. I'm locked in on, uh, the subject."

He sure was. When Cole took off the headset he saw Keira's car in startling clarity as it pulled in to a small parking lot outside a red clapboard café, on the bypass near Route 50. Steve and Barb were practically draped over his back, enraptured by the view on his iPad. Sharpe glanced back at him, eyes dark with suppressed fury.

"There, she's getting out," Steve said.

"Look," Barb said. "Someone's getting out of that other car. The BMW. They're waving. A woman."

"Must have been waiting on her."

Keira met the woman in front of the café entrance, where they hugged briefly before heading inside.

"Seems to know her well. Can you zoom on the tags of the BMW?" Barb asked. "Do we still have enough light? Do you think we can get a number?"

"Easily," Sharpe said, downcast.

And there it was, clear as life despite the low angle of the setting sun, Barb with her notebook out, writing it down. She fairly sprinted into the house for her laptop and was back in a flash, already with the right webpage up, searching the numbers.

"I knew it," she said. "Knew it. It's Felicity Barrow, her agent. That's her 'government source.' Her fucking *agent*."

"How long have we been airborne?" Cole asked, wanting to talk about anything but what they were watching.

"Almost twenty minutes," Sharpe said.

"How's the fuel holding up?"

"Plenty left. Not an issue." A monotone. Going through the motions but nothing more.

Cole looked at Steve, who seemed a little torn. A glint of triumph, perhaps, having proved his worst suspicions, but there was gloom, too.

The women emerged from the café after only twenty minutes. No more than coffee and a snack, perhaps. And if they'd talked business, then the chat must have been decisive, straight to the point. There was a brief exchange of papers in the parking lot, Keira taking a small pile of them from Felicity and then getting into her car.

"Omigod!" Barb exclaimed. "Ten to one it's a contract."

"A book deal?" Steve said.

"A book, a film, maybe both. Looked like enough for anything and everything. Oh. My. God." She sounded giddy. Cole couldn't bear to look at her, so he kept watching the screen.

For a moment Keira seemed to glance upward, and Cole flinched, wondering if she'd spotted their drone, their eye, gazing back at her. But she was just tossing hair out of her eyes. She hadn't seen a thing. She climbed back into her car. Her agent's BMW was already pulling out of the lot.

"I better take over if we want to have her landed by the time she gets back," Cole said. He slipped the goggles back on.

"Okay," Sharpe said. "Back under your power now. Are we done with surveillance for the moment?"

"Yes," Cole said, answering for Barb and Steve, who were now muttering to each other, walking back toward the house. Hatching a plot, no doubt. Dreaming up the best and most dramatic way to confront her when she returned. *And why not?* he supposed. It certainly looked bad, even to him. And it threw everything into a new light, including all of last night.

Cole landed the plane with ease. Sharpe thanked him and went immediately to his plane to inspect it for damage. Cole joined him as he was crouched on one knee. It was a relief to be away from the others, although he was already dreading the moment when Keira would come wheeling around the curve from the trees.

"Now you see exactly what I was talking about. The hazards of getting involved with journalists," Sharpe said, still looking at his plane and not at Cole.

"This isn't about journalism. This is about them. And about this thing you brought us."

Sharpe shook his head.

"Goddamn idiots. They'll carve each other to pieces before they ever get the story."

"Your bird look okay?"

"She looks fine. You did well. *I* did well. But what exactly have we accomplished here, other than fuck things up in this group of yours?"

"Like you said. The genie's out of the bottle."

"They don't know the half of it," Sharpe said, scowling toward Barb and Steve. "But they'll learn soon enough. I can at least see to that."

"What's that mean?"

"Whatever I want it to."

He walked away, still in a sulk, then checked the rear door on his trailer, making sure it was locked. He turned and grinned at Cole as if daring him to figure it all out. More dramatics, the last thing he wanted now, so he walked away without a further word. He went into the house for water, maybe a snack. He expected to find Barb and Steve in a celebratory mood, perhaps cocktails, the clinking of glasses. Instead they were drinking coffee, seated at the kitchen table with somber expressions.

"Unbelievable," Barb said. "You were absolutely right."

"I'm not so sure." For the first time Steve sounded uncertain.

"What do you mean, not sure? She said it was her source, and look who it was. It has to be some kind of side deal."

"We don't know what those papers were."

"A contract, like you said. A deal that cuts us out."

"We don't *know* that. There might be a perfectly good explanation."

"C'mon, Steve."

"*You* c'mon. We've all worked on stories where we thought we had the goods, everyone dead to rights, then it turned out we had it wrong, or had misinterpreted something. And Keira's a good person at heart. The more I think about it, the less I think she'd do something like this."

Barb stared in disbelief.

"We just *saw* her do it."

"I don't like what I saw, either. I'm just not convinced she'd do it that way."

"Well, she's done it. And this is professional. It has nothing to do with her personal side."

"It has everything to do with it. And with what we just did, too, spying on her. Maybe you can separate the two, but I don't think she does, and I know I don't."

Barb held her hands out in abeyance.

"Easy. I didn't mean it that way."

"Then how did you mean it?"

She sighed.

"Okay. We'll wait to hear her side. It's not like we can kick her off the property. But if she's making an outside deal, she has to cut us in on it. And if she won't, then that's the last she gets from us."

"I'm on board with that. But then what? What if she says no?"

"We go back to my house and double down on our own sources, starting Monday. We go our way and she goes hers."

"What about me?" Cole said. "And Sharpe, with his drone?"

Barb turned around. It was obvious by her reaction that she hadn't heard him enter. Her expression looked more sad than disapproving.

"We'd be happy for any help you can still give us," Barb said.

"He's chosen sides," Steve said. "Or have you forgotten?"

"That's personal, too," Barb said, "and probably none of our damn business."

"But you said—"

"I *know* what I said. I don't have to like it, and neither do you. But I'm not going to start telling people who they can sleep with."

"Relax," Cole said. "I doubt anyone would willingly sleep with anybody who just followed her down six miles of highway with a spycam.

Don't you think?" He looked at Steve. "Or had that already occurred to you?"

Steve shook his head but said nothing.

It was dark now. They expected Keira to come wheeling up the drive any minute. But half an hour passed, then an hour. Had she seen the drone after all? If so, maybe she had pointed her car west and kept on going, leaving them behind for good. But this was her family's place. She would at least come back long enough to pack her things and kick them out.

A second hour passed, then a third. They scraped together some pasta, a wilted salad, and the dregs of a cheap Cabernet and ate together in silence. Steve was the first of them to express concern.

"You think she's okay?"

"Call her cell if you're suddenly so damn worried," Barb said.

No one made a move, although Steve did check online updates from the county and state police. Cole went outside and found Sharpe tinkering with the engine by the glare of a flashlight, fine-tuning the settings. He asked if he could help. Sharpe put down his screwdriver and looked up at the sky.

"What I'd really hoped to do today was make an initial run over toward IntelPro. Start getting the lay of the land. But I guess the True Confessions crowd had other ideas."

"Couldn't we go in the dark? Don't you have infrared?"

"Yes. But not for our maiden over there. We need a wider margin for error until we get a better feel for the place, don't you think?"

"Maybe so."

They heard a car engine in the distance, which made them look up. A few seconds later, Keira's Nissan emerged into the clearing.

"Well, this should be interesting," Sharpe said.

"I better go see how it goes."

Sharpe said nothing. He nodded and went back to work on his drone.

CHAPTER TWENTY-SIX

COLE WALKED INTO the house just as it was beginning.

"Great," Keira said cheerily. "I'm glad you're all here." She unknotted her scarf and tossed her coat on a chair. "I got some great stuff."

"You look empty-handed to me," Barb said.

And it was true. No notebook. No envelope. No documents. Presumably the stuff she'd gotten from her agent was locked in the car, or maybe somewhere else altogether. Signed, dated, copied, and already returned, for all they knew. Fully enacted, with a check on the way.

"No, seriously. You wouldn't believe what's going on."

It was then that Keira, usually so well attuned to everyone's moods and signals, finally realized something was amiss. Steve was slouched in a chair with his arms folded. Barb sat catty-corner, legs crossed, lips sealed. Cole lingered by the door, hoping she wouldn't look him in the eye.

"What's going on?" she asked. "What's happened?"

"You were seen," Barb said.

"Seen?"

"With your so-called source. Caught in the act."

"By who?"

"Does it matter?"

"There was no one there to watch us. There's never *anybody* there on Sundays. It's why we meet there."

"So this wasn't the first time?"

"I told you. It's a good source."

"*She*, you mean."

A pause, just enough to slow her down, make her think about it.

"Yes, she."

Keira looked at each of them in turn, puzzled, but maybe starting to get it.

"What do you mean, 'You were seen'?"

"Keira, for fuck's sake! We know it was Felicity Barrow. We know you've been meeting your agent. Stop trying to act like it didn't happen!"

"It was me," Cole said.

He blurted it out before she could ask another question and dig herself—or them—any deeper.

"It was all of us, really, but my doing. We followed your car with the drone and we saw you there. A high-res image, sharp enough to read the tag numbers on both cars and to see you take the documents from her in the parking lot, or whatever it was she put in the envelope."

"A book contract, right?" Barb said. "And I'm betting your name is the only one on it."

Keira looked back and forth between Barb and Steve.

"I'm sorry," Cole said, disconcerted that she hadn't yet turned around. "I know it doesn't matter now, but I'm sorry. I shouldn't have done it, but I did."

He didn't know which was worse, her silence or the way she continued to look at the others as if he wasn't even there. Without a word, she turned and went past him, right out the door, not even a glance. They heard a car door slam and waited for the sound of the engine. Instead, she came rushing back in, the door banging open behind her. She was red in the face, and walked briskly to the coffee table in front of Steve and tossed the manila envelope—the one they'd seen—onto the tabletop. It landed spinning, then hissed to a stop.

"There. Take a lot at my 'book contract' and big movie deal."

No one moved.

"Well, go on, goddammit! Open it up and see! Then tell your spaceman Mr. Science fly guy Nelson Sharpe to come have a look, too, because he'll probably be as excited as anybody. I'll be upstairs when you're done. Packing." She headed for the steps, then stopped. "Or not packing. Actually I don't know what the hell I'll be doing. Calling Felicity, maybe, so I really *can* get a book deal. Fuck you guys. *All* of you."

They listened to the force of her footsteps, first as they ascended the stairs, then as they crossed the floor above them and came to a halt at her bed, which heaved and went silent. Barb sighed loudly.

"God. We handled that with real tact and finesse, don't you think?"

Steve stood. "I'm going up there."

"To do what?"

"Try and sort it out. Take the blame, like I should've done from the beginning. Tell her it was my idea."

"Why?"

"Because it was?"

"It was all of us, Steve. That's the whole problem. *We're* the whole problem. How many times have you seen a double-bylined story with my name in it? Once? Never? And there's a good reason for that. I don't play well with others. And you—well, anytime you try to deal with a woman professionally you let your dick do most of the thinking, if thinking's even the right word for it. That's been clear for years."

"That's bullshit."

"It's not bullshit. It's half the reason you're going up there now."

Enough, Cole thought. They could go on like this all night.

"Maybe we should look in the envelope first," he said.

They turned and stared at him. Barb offered a pained smile.

"Leave it to the pilot to make the first germane point of the afternoon."

Steve was closest, so he sat back down, undid the little clasp, and shook out the contents. Folded papers, different sizes, but a lot of them. He furrowed his brow as he spread them on the table.

"Holy shit."

"What is it?" Barb asked.

"Property plats. And some kind of design plans. There's a landscape blueprint, a building permit. All of it's from the county planning office."

Barb walked over and started sorting through the pile. Cole followed, looking over her shoulder at the blueprint. He was shocked by what he saw, but held his tongue. A footfall on the stairs made them turn around. It was Keira, shaking her head in disbelief.

"Some book contract, huh?"

Barb lowered her head, saying nothing.

"So do you want to hear what all of that means or not?" Then, to Cole: "Go and get Sharpe. If I'm going to keep working with a bunch of people I can't trust, then one of them might as well know what he's doing. He'll be all over this."

Cole left the house without a word. He found Sharpe putting away his tools.

"There's some stuff in there you'll want to see," he said. Then, when Sharpe merely grunted, exhibiting little enthusiasm: "Fits neatly with all your theories."

This perked him up. He wiped his hands on a rag and followed Cole into the house, where Keira had gathered up the loose papers and was facing Barb and Steve across the coffee table. Sharpe plopped down in an empty armchair. Cole remained standing, taking up a position at the end of the couch. It felt as if they were gathered for the reading of a will.

Barb motioned with a hand, seeking permission to speak.

"Keira, I'm—"

"Save it, okay? First things first. Yes, my source down here is Felicity Barrow, but not for any of the reasons you think. She can't be identified as the provider of this material because there are other people she's protecting. Is that understood?"

Cole and the reporters nodded. Sharpe, new to this side of things, took his cue from the others and nodded belatedly.

"She's had a place down here for thirty years, long enough to be pretty plugged in. For a while now she's been a big opponent of development, so she's got all kinds of sources in the planning and zoning offices. When IntelPro moved in ten years ago she was all over it. At first she liked the idea. Setting aside all that acreage for training pretty much guaranteed it would never be bulldozed for condos or a golf course. But she's always been curious about their intentions for future use.

"I told her a while back about this piece we were working on, and said there might be a tenuous connection, given that IntelPro was how two of us got onto this story. She said she'd keep her ear to the ground for anything useful. That's how I first heard about the two ex-CIA trainers, Barb, the ones you're supposed to meet with."

"Thanks."

Keira ignored it.

"A couple months ago, strange stuff started to happen out there, enough to make her nose twitch. Construction crews were coming and going. Cement trucks, backhoes, lots of heavy equipment. She checked for permits but the county said everything had been sealed, and they wouldn't tell her why. She filed about a dozen Freedom of Information requests and they still haven't answered. Last week one of the suppliers for IntelPro's mess facility and commissary began filling weekly orders for some new facility out there. Separate invoice. Low volume, but different enough from the usual profile of institutional foods to make it interesting. Neighbors of the place claimed that a handful of Latinos had moved to the premises. A family of groundskeepers, that was the working theory. Then one of her sources at the courthouse gave her this stuff—building permits, blueprints, a landscaping plan, everything you were just looking at."

"It's a landing strip." Cole said. "That's part of it, anyway."

Sharpe practically sprang up out of his armchair.

"May I see the item in question?"

Keira handed him a blueprint, which he spread open on the coffee table.

"Exactly what I expected," he said, smiling now. "And these outbuildings, three of them. Little hangars, probably, places to park all their new hardware, out of the elements and out of sight, except when they're using it. Even when they start flying, they've got enough acreage to take anything up to a higher altitude, well beyond view, before they ever leave the premises. And look." He jabbed a bony forefinger at the plans. "Here's the location in relation to the rest of the property, the exact coordinates. Perfect."

"Think you can fly over for a better look?" Keira asked.

"I can program the location right into the flight plan. Once we're there, Captain Cole can make any adjustments we'll need. My cameras will easily do the rest. This is a gold mine. No wonder they're suppressing it."

"But how can the county keep this a secret?" Barb asked.

"With federal permission, of course," Sharpe said. "With the right kind of contract this installation would have semiofficial status, which would mean that the contract itself could be classified. Or any sort of plans filed with the county."

"And you think it's for drone development?" Cole asked. "Testing new technologies, for private sector applications?"

"And for domestic applications as well. Has to be."

"Yeah, well," Steve said. "This is all great stuff, a helluva story. But it's not *our* story."

"How do you figure that?" Barb asked.

"Well, what does any of this have to do with Wade Castle?"

"Who says it has to? We take a week, maybe two, to work the hell out of this one. Then we write it and sell it. If anything, we buy ourselves a few more months for the Castle piece."

"Meanwhile burning half our sources, to the point they'll never help us again."

"Your source, maybe. An IntelPro guy who hasn't contributed anything for a month now, except to piss all over some of our best material."

"That's not true."

Cole watched Keira. This would usually be the point where she would intervene for one side or another, or to advocate for cooler heads and greater civility. This time she looked on with a blank expression, seemingly content to let them fight it out to the death. And that left it to Sharpe, of all people, to bring matters back into focus in his typically blunt manner.

"Shut the fuck up, both of you, and hear me out. This *is* a Wade Castle story. He's half the reason IntelPro has all these new toys, or at least the means to make them and use them. He's the key to their whole R and D program." He hammered the blueprint with his fist. "No matter what he did before, no matter how many fuckups there have been along the way, in my opinion *this* has been the intended endpoint, and if you'll just pursue the facts at hand to their logical conclusion, I'm sure that's what you'll discover to be true."

"Who asked you?" Steve said. "An interloper, brought in by another interloper, brought in completely against my advice, and all of it has been a mistake."

"That's unfair, Steve." It was Keira, finally speaking up.

"Of course you'd think so. You're the one sleeping with the inter-loper. That's how far off the rails we've gone around here, and now we're sitting around talking about doing illegal shit like flying a drone over half the Eastern Shore to snoop on a bunch of people who could really fuck with our lives if they wanted, when what we ought to be doing is some actual journalism, using the sources we've got while con-tinuing to develop more."

"Too passive," said Sharpe. "Too damn passive, especially when you have this great new tool at your disposal. I thought you existed to gather information. Well, that's what these damn things do, and very efficiently."

"And it's *illegal*, and could land us in deep shit. We could pay hack-ers to help us, too, like Murdoch's people in the UK. Hell, we could even tap some phone lines if we hired the right people. Another great tool."

Barb, who had been on Sharpe's side, now looked uncertain for the first time. Keira, stung by Steve's latest attack, again held her tongue.

"Maybe you're right," Barb finally said. "But we should at least sleep on it."

"I'm good with that," Steve said. "With a full night's sleep maybe everyone will come to their senses."

Sharpe hissed like a snake that had been stepped on and headed straight for the door. Cole, weary of the discord, followed, grabbing Steve's car keys from a table by the door as he left the house.

"Hey, could you at least ask?" Steve said.

But Cole kept going, letting the door shut behind him. He found Sharpe fuming at the edge of the driveway, headed toward his van.

"We're doing this," Sharpe told him. "Be ready at sunup."

"They don't sound so sure about that."

"Oh, they will be."

Cole thought he had a pretty good idea of why Sharpe was so certain.

"Are you sure about this?" he asked.

"About tomorrow?"

"About tonight."

Sharpe, for the first time since Cole had met him, looked taken aback. "So you know?"

"I do now, I think. By that look on your face. This is about what's in that other box, isn't it?"

Sharpe broke into a grin, but Cole didn't share his sense of fun and had no intention of hanging around for the follow-up. He held aloft Steve's keys and headed for the Honda. Sharpe called out to him.

"You're welcome to join me. You might even learn something."

"I already know way too much about the fear of God," Cole said.

Then he kept right on walking.

CHAPTER TWENTY-SEVEN

COLE DROVE FAR too fast up the dirt lane, throwing gravel against the undercarriage like a hailstorm from below. He didn't slow down until he reached the narrowest stretch, where branches raked the Honda's sides like the claws of a raptor, screeching and groaning against the metal.

"Shit. Sorry, Steve."

He let up on the gas and exhaled deeply. It would be highly uncharitable to ruin the man's car, even though he was exasperated with all of them. He drove the ten miles into Easton and stopped at the first booze store he could find, where he gazed longingly at the amber rows of bourbon before proceeding to the glass refrigerator cases in the back. He picked up a six of Bud, paid in cash, and cracked open the first one while seated behind the wheel in the darkness of the parking lot, facing a sign on the wall of the store that said no drinking on premises.

A long, deep swallow and he felt better. Then a second. Better still. Although if a cop came along he was toast. One check of his fake ID and the whole operation would crash and burn. Or his part of it, anyway. Big fucking deal.

Christmas lights flashing from the eaves bathed him in a continuous cycle of red and green, making him look full of fury one moment, queasy the next.

Some Christmas.

Better than last year's, though, out there alone in the chilly trailer where there was no Star of Bethlehem hanging among the firmament in a massive sky. No beasts at the manger, either. Just a couple of coyotes rummaging through the trash.

Then he leaped back another year, to the one before his collapse. Carol's family had trooped out to Summerlin for the holidays, and they'd enjoyed themselves immensely. Golf on Christmas Eve, tennis every afternoon. An hour after dinner on the big day, everyone piled into the van to drive over to the Strip, where they watched the water show from the fountains at the Bellagio, booming cascades swaying to a soundtrack of Sinatra. Carol's dad had won two hundred bucks on the blackjack table at Harrah's, then treated everyone to steaks at Vic & Anthony's in the Golden Nugget. The in-laws adapted to the idea of a Vegas Christmas quicker than he had, although Cole had gotten a kick out of seeing holiday lights strung from palms and cacti, not to mention the weirdness of Christmas tree lots sharing corners with pawnbrokers and nickel slots.

But that was ancient history. The kids were two years older now and living in another house, decorating someone else's tree. Santa was some guy in a mall in Michigan. Cole didn't even know what their school looked like, who their teachers were, or what kind of haircuts they had. If he were to burst through the door uninvited, would they even know him?

He asked himself why was he bothering with all of this shit. Why had he even come here, an awkward appendage to a trio of journalists, writers who probably saw the world in a completely different light from the way he did, and now with an oddball engineer thrown into the mix. He could leave this instant, he supposed. Drive away, either back to the desert beyond Vegas or, hell, maybe even take a wild chance by heading up to Saginaw. Arrive clean and sober and contrite, begging for forgiveness and throwing himself at the mercy of the in-laws. A Christmas miracle fit for the Hallmark Channel.

Wasn't that his real goal in this, once you got to the bottom of all the baggage? Purge all his ghosts by figuring out what had really gone wrong, maybe while getting some payback along the way. Then he could finally move forward, an inch at a time, toward something that might resemble a workable future.

Saginaw. Cold and unwelcoming this time of year, and probably at least six hundred miles away.

He could drive Steve's car to a bus station, mail him the keys. And then what? Phone Sharpe and the journalists later, from out on the road? Ask them what they'd found out, to see if there were yet any answers? Because he would definitely want to know.

So there it was, then. He still wanted—*needed*—answers. Without them, he would never move forward. And some degree of retribution was still necessary, just as it was for Sharpe, for Barb, maybe for all of them. Meaning there was work yet to be done, and his role was vital. It would be his most important mission in ages, perhaps ever. Is that what was scaring him?

"Fuck," he said.

The beer was empty. So was a second one, and a third. He'd been sitting here drinking for more than an hour, maybe two. A wonder he hadn't been arrested.

He crumpled the empties and stuffed them into the bag atop the rest of the six-pack. Then he opened the car door and set the package on the pavement, a gift to whoever pulled in next. He started the engine and pulled out of the lot, heading back in the direction he'd come from, toward Keira's place.

Unfinished business was calling.

The main house was dark, and he parked by the pool house so the noise of the car wouldn't wake anyone. Stepping into the night, he looked up through the trees at the stars. Now he wished he'd kept the rest of the beer, because he didn't yet feel like sleeping. Maybe a walk would help. Down the lane and back, a two-mile round trip, or perhaps that was a stupid idea out here in the cold and the dark.

He was still trying to decide when he heard the first scream, a woman's cry of terror emanating from the house.

Cole broke into a run, covering the ground in seconds, only to find the door locked. There was another scream, and a light went on upstairs, illuminating the porch as Cole fumbled for the key. He heard Steve now, or some strung-out version of Steve.

"What the hell is happening?"

The fear of God, indeed. What was Sharpe doing to them, and where was he?

Cole unlocked the door and stepped inside. The first thing he heard was buzzing—thrumming, to be more precise, like the sound hummingbirds make as they dart and weave among themselves, competing for nectar. He reached for a light switch as Steve came lunging toward him from the kitchen doorway, a chef's knife in his hand.

"It's me!" Cole shouted.

Steve stopped in the sudden glare, barefoot and waving the knife at something as it buzzed past his head. Barb was coming down the stairs two at a time, flapping her hands around her head as if plagued by a cloud of gnats. A second buzzing object, then a third, did a quick revolution around her before whizzing down the stairs ahead of her. They joined the one that had harassed Steve, and then, like a squadron of UFOs in some demented sci-fi movie, they flew in formation toward the living room, where three more were already hovering. Barb, Steve, and Cole eased through the doorway and watched in stunned silence as the six tiny craft formed into a V, the way geese did in migration. Steve raised the knife and went for them like a madman, shouting as he hacked at the air. But they were too nimble for him, dispersing in all directions and then re-forming along the back of the couch before making a beeline toward the fireplace on the far side of the room. They cleared the top of the screen, then disappeared one after the other up the black tunnel of the chimney.

Keira had now joined them, wearing only a T-shirt, hair in disarray, her eyes like full moons. They all looked at each other. Steve gently laid the knife on a side table and exhaled, muttering under his breath. None of them seemed to believe what had just happened.

The front door opened. It was Sharpe, his bony head in profile against the depth of the night. He stepped into the light of the foyer, grinning, holding an iPad in one hand and one of the dainty little drones in the other.

Steve opened his mouth to shout something, but Cole silenced him with an upraised hand. Barb just shook her head. Sharpe, holding the floor, began his remarks with the air of an orator addressing the well of the Senate. It was a snatch of seasonal poetry, a famed bit of verse, and as Sharpe declaimed he raised the little drone on high.

"To the top of the porch! To the top of the wall! Now dash away, dash away, dash away all!"

Then, in a quieter voice, and with an admiring gaze at the little drone, he concluded: "And away they all flew, like the down of a thistle."

Barb was the first to recover from the shock of it.

"Merry Christmas, asshole. Was this really your idea of a sales job?"

"That was just the sound and light show," Sharpe said. "The warm-up act. The sales job is just beginning."

"Fuck you," Steve said. "You're done here."

Sharpe looked toward Keira as if appealing the verdict. When she spoke, her voice was hoarse but steady.

"What is it you want to show us?"

"All of the reasons you can't possibly quit now."

Sharpe's tone was now deeply earnest, almost humble. The change seemed to have an effect. Keira nodded and backed away, as if to clear room for his approach. Barb looked at Steve, who shook his head but surrendered, at least for the moment, although there was still fury in his eyes. Cole followed them to the couch, where they continued to stand while Sharpe set his iPad on the coffee table and activated a video.

It was shot in infrared and appeared on three split screens at once, starring all of them in their respective bedrooms, green blobs sleeping beneath the sheets. Keira reached for the tablet, and Sharpe had to snatch it away.

"We'll take your word for it that you caught us all unawares. I thought you had a point to make. But if voyeurism is your whole message, then we get it."

"Actually, you don't," Sharpe said. "Not yet. The video's just for show, sort of like the buzz job by my tidy little armada."

He set down the drone on the coffee table, and they couldn't help but stare at it. Smaller than a butterfly, or even a hummingbird. Like one of those Matchbox toys Cole had played with as a kid, except more delicate and insectlike. The wings looked as if they folded in on themselves. There were two tiny rotors on top, and an even smaller one on the front. The whole thing was no more than two inches long.

"My own design," Sharpe said. "Not theirs." Presumably he meant the Pentagon. And maybe also IntelPro, or private industry in general. "But it will be theirs soon enough, in one form or another, which is why we have to pursue every tool at our disposal, before these things proliferate beyond our control, or at least without public knowledge."

"Big fucking deal," Steve said. "So you flew a bunch of robotic bumblebees down our chimney, which, I might add, you were only able to do by opening the damper when no one was looking. Then you shot some video and scared us out of our fucking wits."

"I also did this."

Sharpe reached into his pants pocket and pulled out three thumb drives. He scattered them on the table.

"Those six drones you saw were only the second wave. The first group, which I'm not even going to show you, because that's how proprietary I feel about their capabilities, were able to insert these thumb drives into your personal laptops."

"And stole our shit?" Barb asked.

"Copied it. While you slept. Then returned the copies to me, which I'm now returning to you. As a courtesy, of course. A gesture of trust. I haven't even had time to inspect the contents, and don't wish to. I'm only interested in finding out what's over there." He nodded vaguely toward the west, and IntelPro. "Seven miles as the crow flies."

"My point still stands," Steve said. "You don't really know *how* they'll react if they find out what we're up to. And all this shit you want to do—and did already, right here in this house—is probably damned illegal. And we could all go to jail for it."

Sharpe stepped around the coffee table and got right up into Steve's face.

"Legality is no longer the point. The point, in case you haven't been paying attention, is that Captain Cole and I will do this whether it happens from here or from some other empty field within range of their facility. And once we've acquired God knows what sort of richness of material from our work, you'll want access to our findings. Except then we'll just be sources, and you won't have to trouble your delicate sensibilities over how we acquired our information. That, I believe, is the point here. We're doing it, and you'll want the results. The only remaining question, then, is whether you'll actually be here to watch us do our work."

"So you're saying there are no rules anymore?"

"Not in this field of endeavor. Not when everyone's airspace is wide open. And not on a single page of the PATRIOT Act. The advantages for your profession, and for this particular project of yours, would seem to be painfully obvious. Information. It's there for the taking, and we're going to go and get it. And we'll do it just as we did it tonight, without leaving a single fingerprint—yours, mine, or anyone else's. So shall I help you, or shall I go? Because if you ask me to leave, whatever I learn will go to some other more deserving party in the Fourth Estate."

Steve sagged, defeated. Then he looked over at Barb, as if deferring to her judgment.

Her expression was somber but resolute.

"How soon were you hoping to get started?" she asked.

"Sunrise. Catch them while they're sleeping, figuratively speaking."

Barb then looked at Keira, who nodded.

It was unanimous. It was done.

Cole, watching from behind an armchair, said nothing. But if he was going to be piloting this thing, then he'd better get some sleep. He headed for the door without saying a word.

Hours later, but still well before sunrise, Cole awakened.

A noise had done it. A gunshot, or that's what it had sounded like. But now it was dark and quiet, probably the middle of the night. So maybe it was something else. Sharpe again? Another goddamn demonstration of his powers, of his almighty ego? Surely he wasn't that stupid. And this noise had been too loud for any of his stealthy handiwork.

Cole lay on his back for several seconds more, blinking into the darkness, seeing nothing, hearing nothing. Just as he was beginning to wonder if he'd dreamed the whole thing, there it was again, unmistakable this time—a gunshot, sharp and loud, and echoing through the trees.

Had it come from the woods, or from the house?

He stood to dress, heart beating fast. Pants, a shirt. He picked up his socks, then tossed them aside and pulled on his shoes, not bothering to lace them. Before bolting out the door, he turned just long enough to glance at the bedside clock, which froze him in place with its message.

It was 3:50 a.m. The hour of death.

CHAPTER TWENTY-EIGHT

MUCH EARLIER THE DAY BEFORE, on a bright and warm Sunday morning, Trip Riggleman was on the verge of admitting defeat. Everyone else he knew was out Christmas shopping, or at some holiday party, on base or off. He was still working, and still getting nowhere. The allotted weekend was nearly gone, and he was no closer to finding Captain Darwin Cole.

He had done his best, he thought. He was particularly proud of the extra care he'd taken in handling the break-in at Airman Zach Lewis's apartment. The installation of the necessary software on Lewis's home computer had gone off without a hitch, ensuring that any emails the airman sent from then on would copy to a new and secret account of Riggleman's. Even the required "borrowing" of a Security Forces uniform and gear, designed to reassure any nosy neighbors that his entry to the Lewis apartment was authorized, had been accomplished with the utmost discretion. Although he wasn't looking forward to making good on the promised bribe—a bottle of liquor, plus the hacking of an SF sergeant's ex-girlfriend's email account.

But in the hours since then, Lewis hadn't sent a single email, much less any messages to his old buddy, Captain Cole. Nor had Riggleman made progress on any other front. So here he was, mustering his resolve for what General Hagan had mandated would be his last resort—a telephone call to the mysterious outside source known only as Harry Walsh, occupation and affiliation unknown, and, as far as Riggleman had been able to determine, unknowable.

He picked up his cell phone, a virgin model he'd acquired specifically for this call. Then he set it down. He did this twice more before standing and pacing the floor of his office. The entire building was empty except for a few bored security people. Riggleman tried to come up with a valid reason for postponing the call further, but came up empty. General Hagan's instructions were quite clear: Don't report back to me on Monday morning without success unless you've first contacted he-who-shall-remain-nameless, i.e., Walsh. And don't wait until the last minute to do it.

Yet Riggleman remained wary, and with good reason. The moment you sought outside help was the moment you began losing control of an investigation. Maybe Hagan didn't realize that, but Riggleman sure as hell did. Privileged information, once you set it loose, inevitably wandered off to all sorts of unlikely places, some of them hazardous to your employability, or even to your health and well-being.

Also troubling was that he still hadn't been able to find out a damn thing about Walsh or the phone number. Zilch. Blank slate, top to bottom. Anyone who could pull off such a thorough erasure of personal and professional data was a little daunting. As for the number itself, the area code was for Alaska, but there was no known match for the rest of it.

Yet Walsh was the only way forward. So he again picked up the phone and quickly punched in the number.

Someone picked up on the first ring, but no one said a word.

"Uh, Harry Walsh, please?"

"Whoa now. Are you calling from a secure phone?"

"Well, mostly. A virgin phone, anyway."

"Your current location?"

"Nellis Air Force Base, outskirts of Vegas."

"No. Definitely not secure, so let's keep this short."

"Sure."

"Who's calling? Name and rank, please, assuming you're not a civvie."

Riggleman hesitated.

"Now, or I hang up."

"Okay, okay. This is Air Force Captain Trip Riggleman." He then stated his unit, all the while chafing at the idea that he had to give his particulars but Walsh didn't. Already he had placed himself at a disadvantage.

"Who gave you my name and number?"

"Uh . . ." He was about to mention General Hagan's name but didn't feel comfortable doing so. "I'd, uh, rather not say."

"Then this conversation is over."

"What?"

"Name?"

"Well, given the position you've put me in—"

"You're in Hagan's shop, right?"

"Right."

"Operating under his orders?"

"His chain of command. That's all I can say for now."

"Clear enough. But why me?"

"I was ordered—asked, rather—to contact you if I reached a certain point in my work. I'm now at that point."

"Are you in some kind of jam regarding Air Force personnel of a certain security clearance?"

"A jam?"

"Are you looking for something, or somebody?"

"Yes, exactly."

Riggleman sensed a relaxing of tension after his answer, or maybe he was just breathing easier now that they seemed to be getting somewhere.

"Which is it, then?"

"Somebody. An ex-pilot from Creech. Flew Predators until about a year and a half ago. A Captain Darwin Cole. The best I can determine—"

"Whoa, whoa, whoa. Stop right there. Hagan's after this?"

"Look, let's not—"

"Yes or no."

He was in too deep not to keep going. "Yes."

A long sigh, of either bewilderment or anger.

"This pursuit of yours ends now. Immediately. Understand?"

"I'm afraid that's not my decision to make."

"This is nonnegotiable, Captain. I can't make it any clearer for you.

You tell that to your general, and you do it today even if you have to yank him off the fifteenth green, or out of his whore's honey hole. Understand?"

"I, uh, yeah. I think I do."

"But first you erase my name and number from your memory, and from all your records and databases, along with any record of this phone call. Better still, destroy the phone. The taxpayer probably owes you a new one, anyway."

"I don't think that—"

Then Riggleman stopped talking, midsentence. No use. Walsh had ended the call.

His first impulse was to call Hagan. He had the general's home number, though he had never dared to use it. But what would he say? *"Walsh told us to get fucked."* Not much of a plan. Now he was in a worse spot than before. No progress, and spurned by his last resort.

He considered walking over to the officers' club, although it was not yet eleven. He could have brunch, a beer, maybe two. Sit there among the Christmas lights and tinsel garlands while he regrouped. Think things out. At best, he'd come up with an idea. At worst, the beers would offer solace. But with his luck the only other patrons would be fighter jocks coming off some ungodly shift, and he couldn't bear the thought of elbowing between them and their shots of Weed just to order a Bud Light.

Riggleman walked over to his window and stared out at the other drab buildings on the base. A high of eighty degrees was predicted for later that day, and here it was nine days before Christmas. Happy fucking holidays.

From across the room on his desk, his laptop emitted two sharp beeps, and he perked up right away. It was the signal he'd set up to notify him whenever Zach Lewis sent an email. *Probably nothing*, he told himself, hurrying over. A quick shout-out to a friend, or a reply to something from weeks ago.

When Riggleman opened the email his whole outlook changed. The recipient was an unknown Gmail address, and Lewis had sent several attachments. Each was a video file, taking up a pretty hefty chunk of megabytes. But for the moment the best part was the message itself:

Monkey,

Sorry for the delay. Waited for the weekend so there wouldn't be many people around. Got everything you wanted plus an extra on the Lancer dude, but this'll have to be it for a while. Some pencil pusher is nosing around, asking everybody and his brother about your "possible where-abouts." Worst part is that Sturdy and the whole chain of command is pressing us to tell all. Brass, huh? So keep laying low. Later, your bro Zach

Merry fucking Christmas, after all.

So he'd been right all along. Lewis *had* known something, and his hunch had paid off big-time. But who was this "Lancer dude," and why was the name so familiar? He remembered now. Lancer had been mentioned in the censored part of the deposition taken from Cole's CO, Sturdivant, during Cole's court-martial proceedings. That told him that the brass—maybe Hagan, maybe someone higher—hadn't wanted him poking into any corners where Lancer might be lurking, whoever he was. He filed away that item, mentally adding it to his collection of leads.

Armed with the new Gmail address, he easily hacked his way into Cole's account. He then identified the Internet Protocol address for the computer that had been used to set up the account and send its only two emails—one to Zach Lewis, another to some computer in Northern Virginia, an address he set aside for checking later. He then began tracking down the most recent online activity for Cole's computer, as well as for the various servers and wireless networks the computer had been using. This led him first to Barb Holtzman, a journalist whose name and details he already had. Evidently Cole was using her machine.

The last known server that she or Cole had used was a wireless network operating for a Comcast subscriber named Edward C. Lyttle, with a billing address on Nightingale Road in Oxford, Maryland. The address would be easy enough to pinpoint, but what was Edward Lyttle's connection to Cole? He Googled the name, only to find that Edward Lyttle was some sort of agribusiness executive, with a full-time residence in upstate New York. Maybe the Oxford address was a vacation home. Had Cole simply broken in, taking squatter's rights?

Riggleman checked the location on Google Earth. Huge spread, lots of waterfront. Farm fields, a forest, and hardly a neighbor within sight. Not a bad place to hide out. But all that space made it an easy place to infiltrate and surveil, too. Riggleman was already contemplating his next move.

He searched for any overlap between the names Lyttle and Darwin Cole, and he scored right away with a *Boston Globe* profile of Cole from several years earlier, datelined in Italy and written by Keira Lyttle. From there he quickly established that Keira Lyttle was Edward Lyttle's daughter.

So there was a third journalist, then. The guy, Steve Merritt, plus Barb Holtzman, who was letting Cole use her computer, and now Lyttle. All three of them wrote about military affairs and national security issues, and he was betting that all three were now holed up together and plotting to do God knows what from that big waterfront property owned by Lyttle's father on the Maryland Eastern Shore.

Riggleman checked his watch. Not yet noon. With some quick footwork online he could arrange an afternoon flight to Baltimore or Washington that would put him in the area by nine or ten. Well after dark, but for what he had in mind, darkness was desirable. The more darkness, the better, in fact, especially if he was able to procure some night vision equipment. It would be a recon job, plain and simple, and the location seemed to offer ideal space and cover. With any luck Riggleman would be able to secure a positive ID of Cole and the exact coordinates of his whereabouts by the time General Hagan arrived at the office tomorrow morning for his first cup of coffee.

He immediately began setting up the logistics to put his plan in motion. Flight reservations and the rental car were a snap. So was the motel, a motor court out on Route 50 near the Easton bypass. He reserved it for two nights, just in case, then made a list of items to pick up on the base, and then at home, on his way to the airport: Boots, for clomping around in mud and underbrush. A camouflage uniform? Might as well. Plus some greasepaint for glare. Or would that be over-kill? He'd take some and decide later. A sidearm, because you just never knew. Fortunately he still had a Beretta M9 in his possession as part of the borrowed SF gear. The SF Taser might also come in handy, so he put that on the list.

Within half an hour he was ready to roll. The last thing he did before heading to the airport was to shoot an email to Hagan, to let the general know about his plans. Immediately he wondered if it was a bad move. Hagan, not exactly the kind of guy who stayed plugged in at all hours, probably wouldn't see it until Riggleman had completed the job. But what if, for whatever reason, he saw the message sooner and ordered a halt to Riggleman's op? After all the hinky stuff that had cropped up already, it certainly wouldn't be out of the question.

Or, worse, what if Harry Walsh, or whoever he was, spent the rest of his Sunday contacting his connections and otherwise moving heaven and earth to stop him. *Get this fucker off the case, now!* And if Hagan had Walsh's private number, there was a decent chance Walsh had Hagan's.

So Riggleman shut down his laptop, shut down his smart phone, and even shut down his new cell phone, the one he had used only once. But he didn't destroy it as Walsh had demanded. Something told him he might yet need a record of that call, if only for his own legal protection.

For the next twelve hours at least, he was going to be officially out of touch.

He locked his office door and set out for the parking lot. It was time to go operational. Time to get Cole in his sights and shoot him down. Figuratively speaking, of course.

CHAPTER TWENTY-NINE

COLE, ON FULL ALERT NOW, pulled back the blinds and checked outside. Lights were again on in the main house. One downstairs, two upstairs. Either the gunman was inside, lording it over them with blood on the floor, or everyone was awake for the same reason he was. Sharpe's van was silent and dark, all locked up.

He stepped reluctantly into the night and the cold, walking quietly but briskly toward the house. Halfway there he stopped, overcome by the same creeping sense of another presence that he'd experienced the night before—someone, or something, watching from the trees. Or maybe even from above. He imagined himself as a green blob on an infrared display.

He moved behind a pine and peered at the dark line marking the edge of the woods. Nothing, as far as he could tell, although he knew this observation was meaningless. If someone back there wanted to drop him, it probably would have happened by now. He stepped out from behind the tree and made his way to the door, pausing on the porch to listen for sounds from inside. Muffled voices, no sense of panic, a few footfalls at an easy pace. He pushed on through. Three of them—Barb, Steve, and Sharpe—were gathered in the living room, just beyond the foyer. They looked up in unison, eyes a bit wide.

Sharpe looked at Cole and grimly shook his head as if to say, "Not my doing. Not this time."

"Where's Keira?" Cole asked.

"In the kitchen," Barb said. "She called the cops. They're keeping her on the line."

"Some deputy named Tony," Steve said. "She seems to know him."

"And you're surprised?" Barb said.

"Probably a friend of the family's," Cole said. It was too early for their usual bullshit. Keira emerged from the hallway, cell phone pressed to her ear.

"There's a police cruiser now at the upper end of the drive," she said. "They're looking around, but they're thinking it might be hunters."

"At this hour?" Steve said.

"Spotlight hunters," Cole said. "I knew guys back home who did that shit."

"Spotlight?"

"For deer. Blind 'em and shoot 'em. Illegal. It's why they do it in the middle of the night."

"Tony said some of the neighbors heard cars coming and going. I don't think we were the only ones who called."

"Cars?" Barb said. "In the plural? Jesus, how many people are out there?"

"Is there a coffeemaker handy?" These were Sharpe's first words since Cole had come through the door, and it was clear he didn't give a shit about what the others were saying. He looked detached from them, as though thinking this was their fight, not his. Cole saw his sleeping bag, unrolled on the living room carpet. Couldn't they have at least offered him a bed? Maybe this had been his punishment for the stunt with the minidrones. Or maybe Sharpe had preferred it this way, with easier access to his boxful of toys out in the van.

A voice squawked on Keira's cell phone. She pressed it to her ear while everyone watched. Her mouth flew open, but for a moment no words emerged. She turned away from them and spoke in a low voice, the words inaudible. A few seconds later she turned back around, shaking her head, holding the phone at her side.

"What is it?" Barb asked. "What's happened?"

"They found a body. On the property, up in the woods. Shot."

"Hunting accident?" Barb asked hopefully, almost desperately.

"Shot twice," Keira answered. "The two shots we heard."

"No accident, then," Steve said. He was already reaching for his coat. "One to knock him down, then a second to make sure. We need to get a look at the scene before they've had time to clean it up. Some-body bring a notebook."

Barb had already produced one from somewhere—did she sleep with a supply?—and she held a pencil in her right hand. Steve paused at the door.

"You coming, Keira? It would probably help to have you out there, since you know the cops."

"Sure," she said, barely a whisper. She turned slowly, took her coat from the closet, and got Barb's out as well. They trooped out the door together, a team again, at least for now, pursuing their story. Cole's first impulse was to join them, but something made him hesitate. Maybe he didn't belong, not this time. After the door shut, the room was enveloped in silence. Then Sharpe spoke up.

"Any theories?" He looked somber, but not particularly surprised.

"No idea. It's the hour of death."

"What?"

"Nothing. I should go out there. See what's up."

"Suit yourself. I'm going to find a room upstairs where I can get some sleep. We're flying at first light, provided the cops have cleared out. We need to make the most of every opportunity now, because it's pretty obvious someone is trying to shut us down."

"Maybe they got shut down instead."

"By whom? It's not like the woods are crawling with our allies."

"True. Doesn't make much sense, does it?"

"None at all."

Cole paused, looked around, as if wondering if there was anything he should take with him. "Okay, then. I'm off."

Steve led the journalists toward the murder scene, which was lit up by the headlights of two Talbot County police cars parked at angles facing the body from the driveway. The body lay about ten feet into the trees. The victim had fallen perhaps a hundred yards from the house, about seventy from the pool house. Even from a distance you could tell it was a man. He wore a camouflage uniform and some sort of floppy jungle hat. Off to one side was a rifle with a sighting scope. He was either a hunter who'd come to the wrong place or some sort of freelance commando. But on what sort of mission? To watch them, or to bring them down? And if either was the case, then who had brought him down, and why?

Steve watched Keira for her reaction as they reached the scene. He'd already been feeling guilty about the drone thing and the way they'd accused her, and now there was a murder on her family's property, with God knows what sort of ramifications. She'd grown up with this place, a haven of peace and safety, and now she'd probably never feel the same way about it again. They'd ruined it for her, and a man was dead. She was probably scared, too. He knew he was, out here in the wild with shooters on the loose and all their secrets up for grabs, now that the police were involved.

Two cops were at work. One was unspooling yellow crime scene tape around a framework of trees in a tight perimeter around the body. The second was down on one knee, examining but not touching the rifle. The first cop looked up as he heard them approach.

"Hey! Get back! Get away from here!"

"No!" the second one said. "Hold your ground, damn it, before you track any more footprints onto the scene. Right there. Hold those positions until I give the word. And we're going to have to get a look at the soles of your shoes now, all three of you."

"Oh, for fuck's sake," the first one said. "Here comes another one."

Steve turned and saw Cole coming toward them through the trees.

"You! Hold it there. And take your shoes off."

"Take 'em off?" Barb complained. "It's twenty fucking degrees."

"Don't worry, little lady," the first one said. "Only need to remove 'em long enough to get a look at the bottom. Then you can slip 'em back on. But, like he said, don't move. Calbert's a stickler on this stuff." He lowered his voice and smiled. "Been watching too much *CSI*."

"I do it cause its protocol, damn it. You know that, Earl."

"Hey, man. Just doing my best for community relations, Calbert," the cop named Earl said. He winked at Barb. Steve suppressed a laugh. But Keira was still pale and silent, her face looking drained in the glare of the headlights. Cole had halted some fifteen feet behind them. The look on his face made him seem forlorn back there in the shadows, as if he was aching to join them. Aching to join Keira, more likely.

The whole episode from the other night still rankled, although what had they really expected? Bring in a military guy who probably hadn't been laid for more than a year, and stick him out in his own little cabin—his own idea, Steve reminded himself—on a property belonging to an attractive woman who hadn't been quite the same since her married boyfriend went down in flames over the English Channel, like in some war movie. Squeeze that much needfulness into a small space and something reckless was bound to happen. Besides, he had detected a spark between them almost from the beginning, and he grudgingly conceded that there was a redeeming hint of sweetness about it.

Was he envious? Well, yes, but why not let them have their fling? The four of them could probably keep working together as long as Barb was okay with it. Why, then, had he been so eager to follow Keira's car down the highway with the drone? Spite, probably, a realization that shamed him. Or maybe Barb was right. He'd been thinking with his dick.

"Hey," he whispered to Keira. "You okay?"

She nodded but said nothing. Hadn't said a word since they walked out here.

"Have you called your mom and dad?" Barb asked.

She shook her head.

"I'll do it in the morning. After everything's calmed down."

They stood in the cold while the cops did this and that, taking photos of the soles of their shoes and of footprints here and there. After another twenty minutes a third car arrived. Some sort of crime scene tech emerged, pulling on a white smock over a sweat suit and donning a plastic white hat and latex gloves. He got out a kit for making casts of footprints, then took a handful of plastic bags from the car along with a pair of tweezers.

"Who are the idiots, Earl?" he asked.

"From the house. Don't worry, Calbert froze 'em in their tracks. I got shots of their treads."

The tech guy shook his head, then got down to business in the small area around the body. Steve figured the county probably didn't have a huge staff for handling this kind of event, but he didn't know enough about crime scene work to judge if they were handling it well or not.

After another twenty minutes or so the cold and the lateness of the hour began to seep into his bones. He was damn tired. He yawned.

"Earl?" It was Calbert, motioning the other cop toward him. The two cops leaned their heads together, whispering.

Steve distinctly heard Earl mutter "No shit?" but Calbert kept his voice down and continued for a while longer while Earl kept nodding.

When they finished, Calbert turned toward them and said, "Okay, you folks can move freely again. But go on back to the house and stay out of our hair. We'll be down there later to ask some questions. Just sit tight and let us do our jobs."

"You got an ID on the victim yet?" Barb asked. Steve perked up, eager.

"Maybe we do, maybe we don't," Earl said.

"Goddammit, Earl!"

"Keep your shirt on, Calbert. I ain't telling 'em nothing more." Then, to Barb: "We'll be releasing all that later, after the proper notifications have been made."

"Maybe," Calbert said.

Their punishment for having tromped across the crime scene, probably.

The tech was now down on his knees with a flashlight and tweezers and another of his plastic bags. He had placed little metal sticks with orange DayGlo flags at spots where there must be footprints. Steve made a mental note of where the flags were in relation to the body, the driveway, and certain trees, in case all this stuff was cleared away when they came out later. He turned and joined the others.

Cole waited for them to pass, then dropped into step behind them. They reached the driveway single file, then walked four abreast back to the house. Twenty yards later Barb brought them to a halt, holding up her hand like a patrol leader in a combat film.

"Listen. You hear that?"

A rumble of engines, from the upper end of the drive. They turned and saw more headlight beams working their way down toward the scene.

"You people get moving, you hear?" Calbert called out. He stepped out into the driveway as if to make sure. "Don't make me come arrest you, now."

"Must be somebody they don't want us to see," Barb said.

"The feds?" Steve asked.

"Maybe. But which ones?"

"I said move it. Right now!" Good lord, he'd actually drawn his sidearm.

"Relax," Steve said. "We're going."

And they were, although slowly, and while glancing over their shoulders. Steve thought he could see the outline of a big dark SUV of some sort. A Chevy Suburban, or maybe that was just wishful thinking, since he knew Suburbans were often the choice of federal law enforcement. No tags were even close to being visible from this far off, and pretty soon they were too far down the driveway to see much of anything except the glow of lights.

They were just arriving at the house when Steve's cell phone rang.

He pulled it from his pocket and checked the display, but the incoming number was blocked—which gave him a clue as to who it might be. And that surprised him a bit, shocked him even. It was 4:43 a.m., and the grapevine was already lighting up to spread the word. The cops must have notified someone very early based on something they'd found at the scene.

"Hello," he answered. The reply was the voice he expected.

"Sounds like an eventful night down your way."

"Figured I might hear from you, but not this soon. What do you know about this?"

The other three had stopped to listen.

"Very little, Old Pro. Probably less than you. But what I do know is significant, and I'm calling to say that you can stand down. The quarry has not only been treed, it has been brought down."

It took Steve a second to add it up.

"Fort1? The body is Wade Castle's?"

The other three watched him closely. His mind was in a whirl, but he knew he needed to take care not to make some sort of slipup that would compromise the Source's identity.

"Please, Old Pro. No blurting of names, not on this line."

"Sorry. But is it him?"

"The one and only."

"Why? And who would've done it?"

"Good questions. Wish I had the answers."

"What *do* you know?"

"Nothing I can talk about now. Maybe never, which is why I'm going to hang up. Loose lips and all that, Old Pro."

"Our work's not finished."

"But your story is. That's what happens when you no longer have a living, breathing subject. It passes into history. And we're surely finished as well. Thanks for the drinks, though."

"You can't do this, asshole!"

But the asshole had already done it, hanging up and vanishing into the ether. And as the other three stared at him questioningly, Steve was left to wonder whether any of his efforts, with all their tricky compromises, had ever been worth it.

CHAPTER THIRTY

BY SUNRISE THE BODY WAS GONE. Cole walked out there and saw tire tracks and footprints, pressed into the mud like fossils, but there were no more orange flags or webs of yellow tape. The grass was flattened where the body had been, with a stiff circular bloodstain that made it look like the scene of a sacrificial rite. He was surprised to find Sharpe kneeling at the fringes like some monk in solemn meditation.

"You're the last one I expected to find here."

"The ghoul patrol has already paid its respects. By the time they got back to the house they were already arguing. Woke me up, so I had to go *somewhere*. Ready to fly?"

"Doubt we'll have much of an audience."

"Fuck 'em. Long as they don't try to stop me. I'm just worried the police will be back. Wouldn't want them to see what I'm up to. So we should get started early."

"I need coffee first."

"Have at it. They're probably at full volume by now. I'll be setting up in the peace of the great outdoors."

Cole turned to go.

"Tell me something," Sharpe said.

He turned back around. Sharpe looked troubled.

"Yeah?"

"I get why Castle came. Everyone here's been poking around in his business. But the gun? And the idea of someone stalking him, trying to kill him? That should've happened long ago or not at all. Doing it now makes no sense."

"Maybe he'd done something new. Pissed off the wrong people."

"And exactly who are the *right* people in this mess?"

"Good question."

Sharpe nodded, still frowning. "I'm having trouble getting used to the idea that someone died here. All these years of designing shit to kill people, but I've never been around something like this. There's even a smell to it."

"I know. It's freaky."

"You, too? Weren't you around combat way before the drone shit? Didn't you even have an air-to-air kill?"

"That was a ball of flame, way off in the distance. I didn't even get a good look at it. Like you said, this is right in your face, with its own texture."

"Maybe it's good for us. Not to get all cosmic, but we both *knew* the man, for God's sake."

"Hard to see how something like this is good for anybody."

When Cole reached the house, the others were deep in subdued conversation. He poured a mug of coffee and stood in the kitchen door while they traded theories and ideas.

"What I'd really like to know," Steve said, "is why Castle had a sniper rifle."

Barb frowned.

"Who said it was a sniper rifle?"

"Well, it had a damn scope. And I don't think it was for deer."

"He has to have known we were after him," Keira said.

"Meaning what?" Barb said. "That he was going to plug us?"

"But why shoot *him*?"

None of them had answers, but Barb had a follow-up question.

"So, whoever did this, do you think it's safe to surmise they're on our side? Or at least that they're not against us?"

No one had an answer for that, either.

"Well, one thing I know. It sure as hell doesn't kill our story. If that's what your source thinks, Steve, then he's out of his mind."

"I was about to tell him that when he hung up."

"First there was Castle. Now there's the cover-up, and this is part of it. It makes it even bigger. The cover-up always does."

Keira's cell phone rang. She went into the hallway for privacy. They heard her speaking in a low voice, and she was back in a few minutes.

"That was Tony, my cop source. They've made an arrest."

"Shit, already?"

"Then it sure as hell wasn't the feds," Steve said. "They clean up their messes and get the hell out."

"Not always, I guess," Keira said.

"It *was* the feds?"

"Depends on your definition." She turned toward Cole. The others turned with her. "It's some guy from the Air Force. Based at Nellis."

Cole almost dropped his coffee.

"Got a name?"

She checked her notebook

"Captain Trip Riggleman. Had his Nellis ID with him. Also had a Beretta M9 pistol, camouflage, a rough map of the property—*this* property—night vision goggles, and a bunch of printouts with our names on them, the names of everybody in this room except Sharpe. But most of his notes had to do with a missing former Air Force pilot, Captain Darwin Cole."

"Shit," Barb said. "Shit, shit, shit! How do you spell his name?"

Keira told her. Barb flipped open her laptop and began clicking away, already looking for more. Steve and Keira gazed at Cole, as if he might have some answers. And he did.

"I think I've *met* the guy. That aggressors unit, the one I told you about with the Infowar stuff? He practically ran it. He's the nerdy guy who cleaned our clocks. Gave his presentation like he owned us. By the time we left everybody hated his ass. But a killer? An *assassin*?" Cole put his mug on the table. The idea refused to sink in. "There's just no way. He's a clipboard guy, he just isn't the type."

"Or wasn't," Steve said. "He had all the right gear. Maybe they trained him up?"

"Maybe so." The ramifications began to sink in. "Damn. So I guess if he knew where I was, then the whole Air Force must know by now."

"He works for General Hagan," Barb said, clicking feverishly. "Out at Nellis, the next guy up the ladder at Creech in your old chain of command. I was researching Hagan's financials just the other day. Found some weird stuff, too. Why would he want you dead, Cole?"

"Whoa. Who says he did?"

"Okay, maybe not dead. But I doubt he was here to make nice. Then he ends up in some kind of firefight with Castle, and his plans go down the toilet."

"Or maybe they were working together," Keira said, "and something went wrong. An accident, even."

"Let's think this through from our end," Steve said. "We need to marshal our resources and jump on it before the trail goes cold."

"I'll try to get more from the cops," Keira said. "Maybe I can get a look at all the stuff he had with him."

"Good. I've got some federal law enforcement sources. If this guy has a history of going rogue, they might have some leads."

"I'll keep running the financial stuff," Barb said. "Maybe there's a connection."

Then they all looked at Cole.

"Now's your time to shine, big guy," Steve said. "These are your people."

"You're forgetting something. To them, I'm discharged and AWOL. Persona non grata."

"What about your wingman, the guy you emailed?" Barb said.

"Zach? I don't even know if he's answered."

She made a few clicks and turned around her laptop.

"Then maybe it's time to check."

Cole signed on to his Gmail account while the others watched.

"Shit. He replied yesterday, and there's an attachment. Five of them. Video files, they're huge. And they're dated."

"Transcripts?"

"Looks like it. Everything I asked for, plus one more. A Lancer reference, from the recon we fucked up. He must have remembered it, too."

"So Tangora's on there?" Barb asked with an edge to her voice, almost like she was afraid to hear the answer.

"Yeah. It is. You can watch it with me, if you want."

She considered it a second, then shook her head.

"Maybe later, some other time. Or maybe never. But definitely not today. I need to stay on top of my game right now."

"How 'bout I just send you a copy?"

"Thanks. I think."

"Is all this mission stuff still relevant?" Steve asked.

"I think it is. Or might be. Even with Castle dead, Mansur's still floating around somewhere. All those fuckups with Magic Dimes, plus everything Barb saw. There still has to be a reason for it."

"A reason good enough to come down here to kill Wade Castle?"

"Maybe."

"Leave him to it," Barb said. "It could even explain why they sent this guy Riggleman. And for all we know your friend Zach could be in the stockade by now."

Cole hadn't thought of that, but she was probably right, and it pained him. He looked again at Zach's message, with its reference to a "pencil pusher" out at Creech, asking about Cole and making everyone uneasy. Riggleman, maybe. He should have checked his emails earlier.

The house was in full motion now. Keira already had her car keys and was ready to go. Steve was on the phone, talking loudly and gesturing with his free hand as he walked toward the kitchen. Barb was off and running, having borrowed Keira's laptop, apparently content to let Cole use hers to review his new trove of information. He needed a quiet place to work, so he picked up the laptop and headed for the living room. That's when Sharpe came bursting through the front door.

"What's got this beehive all stirred up?"

Cole told him about the arrest.

"Air Force? Doesn't sound like their style."

"I agree. But it is what it is. I've got news, too. My sensor sent me the video record of our missions at Sandar Khosh, both the recon and the attack, plus three others. So it looks like the flying's going to have to wait while I go through everything."

"Five missions? That could take hours. Days, even."

"I can skip over most of it. I know when the relevant shit happened. But, yeah, today's probably a washout."

Sharpe looked put out, perhaps on the verge of an outburst. Then he sagged, as if the inevitability of it sank in. For once, he wasn't in position to call the shots, and he knew it.

"Then I might as well watch with you. But let me put away the bird first, in case the cops come back."

"I'll get everything ready to roll. You bring the popcorn."

Sharpe didn't smile.

"You joke about it, but are you ready for this? I've watched these things before. They're damn vivid. It'll be like flying those missions all over again."

"What do you think I've been doing for more than a year now, up in my head? This'll just fill in some blanks."

"Fair enough. Give me fifteen minutes."

CHAPTER THIRTY-ONE

SHARPE WAS CORRECT. From almost the moment the images of the first mission began unspooling, Cole felt he had gone right back into active duty. The video from the Predator played on three quarters of the screen. The simultaneous chat scrolled on a narrow margin to the right. Radio traffic played on the speaker, everything happening just as it had happened on that day. Eerie. And the first transcript wasn't even from one of his own missions. It was from Rod and Billy's attack on Tangora, from the day when Barb had been present, visiting the local warlord Engineer Haider, the very day she'd snapped the photos of those frightened boys.

By clicking on the bottom of the screen Cole was able to make a timeline pop up, the same way it did on some YouTube videos, or on streaming replays of televised sports events. It showed him where he could find the attack and other key moments. But for the moment he was content to let things play out chronologically, if only to give himself time to grow accustomed to the whole idea.

Captain Rodney Newell spoke up.

"There's our target compound, gentlemen. All hands receiving a clear image?"

"Clear as she goes," a voice replied. It was Lieutenant Colonel Sturdivant, their CO.

Four other replies popped up on the chat screen in quick succession. The first two were from Langley AFB and the combined air ops center at Al Udeid. The next was from Wade Castle, under his chat handle of Fort1:

(FORT1) All clear.

The next one was a revelation.

(LANCER) All clear.

So there they were, peas in a pod. Fort1 had presumably been in Afghanistan or Pakistan, since he wound up flying to the site later by helicopter, with Barb seeing him land. But where had Lancer been? More to the point, who was he, and who had he been working for?

Sharpe settled onto the couch beside Cole. He smelled like the outdoors.

"My God," he said. "Such a clear picture. It's almost like being in the ground control station."

"Pretty much exactly. I've already had a Lancer sighting. Him and Castle, chiming in one after the other on the chat."

"I can save us some time, if you want."

"How so?"

"I know how to search for their later exchanges. A way to bookmark all of them, if you want."

"How the hell do you know how to do that?"

"Who do you think designed half this shit? The things that work well, anyway, none of the cumbersome fucked-up stuff."

"Have at it."

Cole slid the laptop toward Sharpe on the coffee table so he could enter the necessary clicks and commands.

"There. Fort1's on here dozens of times, maybe forty or fifty in all."

"Figures, he was the J-TAC."

"Lancer's pretty quiet. Only four more showings."

"Let's watch 'em all in order, for both of them. And we'll check in on Barb's appearance. I think it's indexed on the timeline. See where it mentions the arrival of a Nissan truck?"

"Got it. Okay, Captain Cole. Strap in."

An hour passed before the first notable event: the arrival at the scene of Mansur Amir Khan, the keeper of Castle's homing beacons, or magic dimes. He rolled up to the compound in his white Toyota truck with orange stripes across the hood. It gave Cole an odd feeling to see it again, knowing what would become of it at Sandar Khosh a month and a half later.

"Funny little fucker, isn't he?" Sharpe said. "Moves like a jockey."

The truck rolled through the gate into the main compound, and you could see Mansur helping two other men unload boxes from the back.

"He's a smuggler," Cole said. "That's how he got all his contacts. I'm guessing the beacon is in one of the boxes."

A large man in a turban walked out to hug Mansur.

"I'm guessing that's Engineer Haider, the warlord killed in the strike."

Not long after Mansur drove away, Lancer popped up for his second appearance. This time he chatted back and forth with Castle.

(LANCER) Beacon placed.

(FORT1) You still vouch for status and ID of HVT?

(LANCER) Affirmative.

(FORT1) Onward gentlemen.

"Why the fuck did they even need a beacon?" Sharpe asked. "Hell, Haider's right there, plain as day."

"Maybe they sent Mansur to verify Haider's presence. Activating the beacon would've been his signal of a positive ID. Still testing out their system, maybe."

"Still seems like overkill."

The battered brown Nissan pickup carrying Barb and her fixer arrived an hour later in a cloud of dust. Two people got out of the truck and were escorted to a building outside the compound. Cole recognized Barb from her posture, her walk, without having to see her face. Then two boys scampered across the grounds toward the same building. It sent a shiver up his back.

The explosion, once the attack came, was huge, destroying the main house inside the walls of the compound and leaving two bodies prone on the grounds outside—the old couple who had been standing near Barb. Sharpe clicked ahead to the next exchange between Lancer and Fort1, which came about eighty minutes after the attack.

(FORT1) Getting new reports. Not liking this.

(LANCER) Not liking how?

(FORT1) Wrong man maybe.

Then, fifteen minutes later:

(FORT1) Definitely a misfire. Theories?

(LANCER) Bad intel. Overton?

"He's blaming Overton Security?" Cole asked.

"That's what it sounds like to me."

"But Barb said that's who Haider worked for. He was one of Overton's damn sources. Why would they want him rubbed out?"

"Maybe he burned them?"

"Maybe. Either way, somebody got duped."

"Lancer?"

"Or both of them. Another fuckup, any way you look at it."

"But Castle must not have thought Mansur was to blame, or why would he have kept working with him? You said they used one of his beacons at Sandar Khosh, right?"

"That's what Bickell told me."

"Shit. None of this adds up."

"Maybe we still don't know what we're looking for."

An hour later, Castle landed in the Pave Hawk helicopter. The screen showed him hopping out of the chopper and heading for the outbuilding where Barb must have still been waiting. That's when the mission ended.

"Here's a theory," Sharpe said. "Lancer knew all along it was the wrong guy, because he was working for IntelPro, Overton's rival."

"So he duped Castle, and maybe Mansur as well, just to rub out some of his competition?"

"Exactly."

"Could be. And Lancer uses this mission to establish contact with Mansur, then starts outbidding Castle on where to place the next beacons."

"It fits."

"But how could Castle have known so quickly it was a fuckup?"

"You'd have to ask him, I guess."

"Fat chance of that now."

They moved on to the second transcript, Cole and Zach's recon mission of the town of Mandi Bahar, which he now knew was Mansur's home village.

To his surprise, he recognized the village immediately, and was struck by the similarity of the setting to Sandar Khosh, even though the two places were miles apart and in different provinces. Each was a small huddle of less than a dozen houses clustered along a dirt road. Each sat next to a small rocky stream, bordering a small grove of gnarled, stunted trees. Shepherd boys took their flocks to and from nearby hills. A child walked out of the trees with a bundle of sticks on his back. A pastoral life, with few signs of warfare or weaponry. They were about to click forward by a few hours when the sight of a figure bursting from a doorway made Cole shout loudly and put a hand on Sharpe's arm.

"Wait!"

It was the girl, the one in the red shawl, white pants, and blue scarf. She ran into sunlight, and then two small boys followed in quick succession. They disappeared from the frame.

"Back it up. Run that again."

"Why. What did you see?"

"It's them. The same three children we saw at Sandar Khosh. The ones we killed."

Sharpe said nothing, and did as he was told. There they were again, bursting out the doorway.

"Freeze that, then see if you can enlarge it."

The resolution wasn't clear enough to see their faces, but it was unmistakably the same three children. No ghosts this time. The real thing, but in the wrong place. And then it hit him.

"Yes! That's it!"

"What is?"

"I've had a feeling from the moment it happened that those kids weren't supposed to be at that house, the one in Sandar Khosh. I could never say why, because I knew I'd seen them before, in our recon. But it wasn't the Sandar Khosh recon. It was this one."

"What does that mean?"

"Keep moving it forward."

The children moved in and out of the frame several more times during the next five minutes. Then the camera seemed to follow them as they headed back toward the house—or that's what he thought was happening until he saw the real reason for Zach's camera work. The sensor's attention had been drawn by the arrival of a white Toyota truck with orange stripes across the hood. The truck stopped, a door opened, and out stepped a little man who was unmistakably Mansur Amir Khan. So this was his house. And these were his children, the very ones he and Zach would kill with a missile strike five weeks later.

But there must be other members of Mansur's family, too, ones that remained alive. Why else would he have still been so concerned about their welfare during their conversation at the row house on Pickard Street? What was it he'd said? "Away. My family is away."

Away where? Did he mean "dead"? Possibly. But now he at least thought he knew why Mansur had moved his family to Sandar Khosh.

"He must've been scared Castle would come after him," Cole said. "After the whole double-cross over the homing beacons. The fuckups and the confusion. So he moved, to get away either from Castle or from Lancer. Then a month later we go and blow up his new house."

"Except Mansur wasn't there."

"But his children were. Most of his family, probably."

"Then why was it a beacon job?"

"Maybe Bickell was wrong."

"Let's look at your recon of Sandar Khosh. It's the next one in line, a week later."

Sharpe got it rolling. There were children in this video, too—playing cricket, running errands, tending sheep. But none was the girl or her two brothers. The house, the one they would target a month later, was under construction, but nearly finished. Sharpe skipped around a little while they watched for anything significant.

"Castle never turned up in this one?"

"No. But Lancer did. I only remembered it when Bickell brought up his name."

"I'll search it."

A pause, maybe ten seconds, before Sharpe got a hit.

"Here he is. One exchange only, in the chat transcript, right at the end."

(LANCER) Need another shot of house under construction, all angles.

Cole's reply was on the audio:

"Coming right up."

Zach moved the camera onto the house and zoomed it while Cole slowly circled their Predator to allow for a prime view of all sides, a task that took about ten minutes.

"Got all you need?"

(LANCER) Yes thx.

Not long afterward the screen went blank. Mission completed.

Cole knew what came next, but he said nothing while Sharpe tapped at the keyboard and made a few clicks.

"Your mission with the missile strike is next. Ready?"

"Let's skip ahead to the other recon job, the one Zach and I almost fucked up. I'm pretty sure Lancer's on it. Might as well get all we can on him first."

"Or maybe you just want to avoid the attack as long as possible."

Cole shrugged.

"That's my business. What time is it?"

"Almost three o'clock. I've gotta pee. And we could both use some water. Unless you want to break for lunch."

"Let's keep going."

"Think we'll finish today?"

"Don't see why not."

"I have to say, it's been fascinating watching you. During these missions, I mean. The way your face changes, the look in your eye. Almost like you're back up there in the sky with it, even now."

Cole shrugged again, uncomfortable with the drift of the conversation, but Sharpe didn't take the hint.

"What does it do to you, flying these things, day after day? Up here, I mean." He tapped a forefinger against his bony head. "I know you fell off the edge for a while. From all the deaths, I figured. But even before that, how were you handling it—the sense of power, of being God, choosing when to bless and when to damn? You'd watch all those lives up close for hours at a time, and then manage their fates for them. It has to fuck with your mind, even when things are going splendidly."

"What about for you, designing the damn things?" Cole's voice had an edge. "Making them better and better, a little more godlike every time they roll out of the hangar? Or down somebody's chimney, six at a time?"

"You don't have to get angry about it."

"I'd just like to hear you take some ownership. You act like it's all our doing, the damn pilots. Or the Agency, the Air Force, the so-called powers that be."

"They're the ones abusing the power."

"And you're the one who gave it to them."

"Fair enough. But if I hadn't—"

"Yeah, yeah. If you hadn't, then someone else would've. I could've said the same thing after Sandar Khosh, but it wouldn't have made me sleep one bit better. So who let you off the hook? Or do you just never think about it?"

"Why do you think I'm out here, ready to take action, fighting fire with fire?"

"Guilt?"

"Or just plain old foolhardiness."

"For thinking you really *can* put it back in the bottle?"

"Or at least rub my own lamp. How 'bout if I go pee now."

"No one's stopping you."

Cole waited, staring at the blank screen. He heard the toilet flush down the hall, then the running of water from the tap. Sharpe brought him a full glass of water, which he downed in seconds. He felt depleted, wrung out, the same way he used to feel after about six hours in the saddle at Creech. It would be a relief to get this over with, but they were making progress, moving closer, even though he still couldn't make sense of an end.

"The transcript says this was a recon of Charwala," Sharpe said.

"That was the nearest village. The house with the bogeys was pretty much in the middle of nowhere, and most of our recon was to secure the perimeter for an ops team setting up for a raid. Zach and I lost our focus and almost missed some other bogeys who came into the area. A firefight started before we could get our shit together. Then we put an IR beacon down on them and the whole thing was over pretty fast."

"The God light?"

"Yeah."

"Love that name."

"I'm not surprised."

"Any particular place you want to begin?"

"Toward the end. End of the firefight, not the raid. I want to hear some of the audio. I was in touch with the unit by voice pretty much throughout. The ops CO seemed like regular Army, all the usual protocols and radio behavior. Very correct. His call sign was Gray Goose. Mine was Redbird. Then his second in command took over for a while, and I remember it feeling kind of skeevy. His handle was something like Duckhead, but it was more a matter of style. Like some dude who was used to things being a little more relaxed. I'm not a tight-ass so I let it go, but it was still odd. That's also when Lancer chimed in, I think. I just can't remember what he said."

"Here we go, then."

They sat through the tail end of the firefight like they were watching a movie. Shaky infrared images and bright green streams of gunfire. There was a cacophony of voices, picked up by the CO's headset, and Cole called out a command from time to time.

"*Redbird, I'm going to recon the area immediately forward of our position, up where my guys are securing the prisoners and collecting the wounded. So for the time being I'm shifting radio control to my second, Duckhead.*"

"*Affirmative, Gray Goose. Standing by for further contact from Duckhead.*"

A few minutes later a new voice came onto the air.

"*How we looking up there?*"

"*Still clear. Is this Duckhead?*"

"*You got it.*"

"*Quiet in all directions on your perimeter.*"

"*Cool. How's the, uh, house looking? This place we're hitting?*"

"*All quiet there as well, Duckhead. Lights remain on, no sign of movement.*"

"In there watching Leno and Letterman, huh?"

"Sure thing."

"Dude, it was a joke."

"I figured as much, Duckhead."

"Gotcha."

Lancer then popped up on the chat screen.

(LANCER) Is that Chuck on audio?

"Uh, Duckhead, we have a chat correspondent Lancer who asks if you happen to be Chuck?"

"What's Lancer's real name?"

(LANCER) all i needed. thanx. tell him its all tight.

"Uh, Lancer says it's all tight, Duckhead. No further ID forthcoming, though."

(Laughter). "Got it, man. I know who it is. Keep it tight."

That was the last transmission from either Duckhead or Lancer.

"I see what you mean," Sharpe said, as the video played on in silence. "You get a decent look at any of the ops guys?"

"Nothing up close. Once they started their raid we were too busy watching for squirters, and threats on the perimeter. Why?"

"Those irregular units can look pretty unorthodox. Beards, nonregulation uniforms. Hats and bandanas when they're supposed to wear helmets. Personal shit all over their flak vests."

"Bickell said there were a lot of those types, half official or completely unofficial. Green badgers, sheep-dipped, he had all kinds of names for 'em."

Sharpe shook his head.

"So who were the guys you helped them whack?"

"They were supposedly insurgency guys. Taliban types, I guess."

"Because if Lancer was willing to rub out an Overton source, and this time Wade Castle wasn't even involved, then it might have been just about anyone, don't you think?"

"I suppose. Yeah."

"And with you guys providing an eye in the sky for them, with the full backing of your unit CO."

"And his CO."

"All the way up to Hagan and beyond. Pretty good taxpayer-financed backup to have in your hip pocket, especially if this turns out to be some little episode of private enterprise."

Silence, while they let that sink in.

"Okay, then," Sharpe said. "Nothing left but the final act. Let's finish it."

Cole nodded, already bracing himself.

"Ready when you are."

CHAPTER THIRTY-TWO

WITHOUT ASKING, SHARPE MOVED the playline up to only a few minutes before the missile strike. It was an act of mercy. Cole wasn't sure he would have been able to bear a long buildup. Even with only a few minutes to endure, he had to force himself to hold his gaze. Everything on the screen looked as fresh to him as if it had taken place the day before.

And then there it was—the white Toyota truck—arriving on the dirt road that led into the village, the cue for all the action that followed.

"Fuck. Freeze it!"

"Why?"

"Just fucking freeze it!"

Sharpe obliged him.

"Look at the markings. Mansur's truck, the one we saw earlier. It was white with orange stripes down the hood. *Two* of them. Look at this one."

"One stripe."

"It's not him."

"Then who is it?"

"Could be anybody. An old man and his wife. More women and children, even. We couldn't see them unload. One fucking stripe."

"Shouldn't Castle have noticed that?"

"Maybe, but I can see where he might have missed it. The last time he'd seen the truck, at least on one of our missions, was a full six weeks earlier. Besides, this was a beacon operation, or that's what Bickell thought. One of the magic dimes had been activated."

"Then who was supposed to be in the house, waiting to meet him? Or who did Castle think was there?"

"No idea, but it turned out to be mostly women and children. And whoever was in that truck, we know for sure it wasn't Mansur."

"Then who placed the beacon, if there was one? Mansur wouldn't have activated it inside his own damn house."

"Another excellent question."

The timeline was creeping ever closer to the moment of truth. Cole knew by his own words on the audio, plus the dialogue on chat, that the firing of the missile was only seconds away. Sharpe could probably tell as well. The tension in everyone's voices was evident. Everything had the unmistakable feel of a lethal mission building to its climax.

"You don't have to watch the rest of this, you know," Sharpe said.

"I know."

But he watched anyway, and listened as the voice of Zach, his old friend and wingman, the very fellow who'd sent him these transcripts, spoke up in an excited tone.

"The dart is away! Fifty-five seconds to impact."

Sharpe reached toward the laptop to click the video to a halt, but Cole placed a hand on Sharpe's arm. Still leaning forward, they waited while fifty seconds passed. The black crosshairs quivered on the rooftop. Zach began his countdown.

And then out the door they came.

First the girl.

Then the boys.

"What the fuck! Can you—?"

"Too late."

The house exploded. A flash of white turning to orange. Boiling smoke. Falling debris. Bodies on the ground. The two boys, limp and still. The girl trying to rise on her elbow, the severed arm only a foot or so away. Exactly as he'd seen it in his memory, hundreds of times before.

The time signature read 3:50.

"Okay," Cole said. "Turn it off."

The screen went blank. Sharpe eased back on the couch with a long sigh and placed a comforting hand on Cole's shoulder.

"It wasn't you."

"You're right. It was all of us. You included. Might as well get used to that."

Sharpe nodded, either too tired to respond or unwilling to upset him further.

"I should eat," Sharpe said finally. "You should, too. Christ almighty, it's practically dark out. I guess flying's out of the question."

"My heart wouldn't be in it, anyway. Not today."

Sharped stood, stretched with a groan, and walked to a window.

"Here comes a car. Your woman's back. In a damn hurry about something, too."

They heard a car door slam, then the door of the house, followed by an outburst of excited voices ending with a shout from Steve.

"Guys! You need to get in here!"

Cole rose to his feet and followed Sharpe to the kitchen, where Keira was taking glossy photos from her satchel.

"The FBI's taken over the case," she said. "Or somebody at a federal level, not sure what they're calling themselves. The local cops won't let me anywhere near them, but I saw three vehicles with government tags pulling into the lot. The good news is that the state medical examiner's office is so pissed off at the way Washington has horned in on everything that they were pretty chatty. Cause of death was two gunshot wounds. One to the chest from maybe twenty, thirty yards, another to the head from up close. Probably to make sure. Two hollow-point 175-grain rounds, most likely from an M24 sniper rifle, or something comparable."

"See?" Steve said.

"What do you mean, 'See'?" Barb said. "This was the killer's gun, not Castle's."

"Whatever."

Keira, ignoring them, continued.

"Castle wasn't carrying any identification—"

"Typical," Steve said. "For an Agency guy, I mean."

"Apparently they can't even get the feds to cooperate on a positive ID, so when I told them that you"—she nodded at Cole—"had worked with him before, they gave me a couple of photos in hopes you could verify it."

"Sharpe knows him, too—or *knew* him, I mean. So, yeah, we could do that."

"Here you go."

She turned the photos around.

A quick glance was all he needed before turning to Sharpe, who was already shaking his big bony head.

"You want to tell them, Captain Cole?"

"Tell us what?" Barb said. The room was silent.

"It's not Wade Castle. Not even close."

"Then who is it?"

Cole looked back over at Sharpe, who again shook his head.

"No idea."

"Me, neither," Cole said. "Never seen him."

"What the hell?" Steve said, looking irritable and betrayed.

"Your goddamn source," Barb said. "Good to the last drop."

"One other thing," Keira said. "This Air Force guy, Riggleman. His weapon was all wrong for it, and none of the other forensics matched—footprints, fingerprints, none of it. They questioned him all night, but they've got nothing on him but maybe a trespassing rap, or an illegal weapons charge, so they're letting him go. It's probably going to end up as an Air Force matter."

"Meaning they still don't know who did it?" Barb said.

"Correct," Keira said. "The shooter, whoever he is, is still at large."

"Wonderful."

"The county guys said they'd post a car at the head of the drive for us overnight."

"Andy and Barney," Steve said. "That'll make me feel safe."

"Maybe we should decamp to some other location for a while," Barb said. "Somewhere a little less vulnerable."

"Not a chance," Sharpe said. "Not for me, anyway. Or for you, either, Captain Cole. We're flying tomorrow."

Cole nodded. In for a penny, in for a pound.

Besides, with the Air Force probably alerted by now to his whereabouts, he might not have long before another Riggleman came after him, and with two cops posted at the head of the driveway, inept or not, he might at least get a few minutes' warning.

"Then I guess I'm in, too," Steve said.

"Me, three." Keira added.

Barb shrugged.

"Majority rules. But I'm moving my bed away from the window."

They stood there looking at one another, wondering what to do next.

CHAPTER THIRTY-THREE

TRIP RIGGLEMAN'S SENSE OF relief lasted about five minutes. He walked into the amber sunlight of dusk, breathed in the fresh air of freedom, then slumped back into his worries. Did he still have a job, his rank, his status? And if General Hagan wouldn't take his phone call last night, in his hour of greatest need, would he take one now, or ever?

He was still hurt and disappointed by the way the Air Force had deserted him in the wake of his arrest, although he supposed he should have known better. Hagan had explicitly warned him that this would happen. It was like in the movies, the ones patterned after that old TV show *Mission Impossible*, where they ran the tape that said, "Should you be caught or killed, we will disavow any knowledge of your actions." Or something like that. Which he supposed should make him feel like a big-time operative but instead made him feel like a chump, a fool in over his head—out in the woods on a cold night in December, miles from home, in completely unfamiliar territory. And stupid enough to be carrying a sidearm that he wasn't even supposed to have.

Damn idiot.

The worst part was that the whole experience had scared the shit out of him, convincing him that he wasn't cut out for any sort of work in covert ops. Do the digging? You bet. Man of action? Only if the action was online.

But in the end maybe Hagan had somehow found a way to save him, because here he was back on the street, his bail paid by an unknown benefactor even though there were still a few charges pending. A weapons charge, that was the big one. Trespassing? A joke. Although the Talbot County cops had actually been pretty cooperative toward the end, and the desk officer who handed him his wallet upon release advised him that, bail or not, the smartest thing might be for him to get out of town for a few days, given all the federal interest in the case. They even brought his rental car up from the impoundment lot to help smooth his departure. Maybe now he should call a lawyer.

He saw right away that the car hadn't exactly been handled with kid gloves. It had been searched thoroughly, even roughly. The glove compartment was still open, and a door panel was loose. Muddy footprints covered the backseat, and someone had dusted the dash and the steering wheel for fingerprints. Hertz would probably charge extra for cleanup, and it now seemed unlikely that Hagan would let him expense this little adventure.

But he was alive, and after what he'd seen the night before, that was no small accomplishment. As he started the car and headed back toward the motel—would he still have his room?—he replayed the events in his head, a dark memory that he figured would haunt him for quite a while.

At first he'd enjoyed it. It was thrilling to climb out of the car in boots and camouflage, a holstered gun, a pair of binoculars. His senses were on full alert, just like when he was a kid roaming the suburbs after dark. Every noise made him flinch. The cold air prickled on his cheeks. *So this was how the big boys felt after they'd been air-dropped into the wilderness of some hostile environment like Afghanistan.* He walked slowly and carefully down the shoulder of the gravel driveway, poised to duck into the trees at the first sign of approaching traffic, the wind seeming to whisper his name.

Finally the house came into view, windows dark, like a ghost ship afloat on a night sea. He moved behind a pine and used his binoculars, scanning slowly from end to end. That's when he noticed the small pool house off to the side. It, too, was dark and silent. Okay, now what? He checked for cars. Three were parked by the house along with a plumber's white panel van. The van was a surprise. Had Cole rented it, or did he and the journalists have another friend staying with them? The idea of some sort of antimilitary conspiracy seemed quite real to him at that moment. The make and model of the cars matched what he'd expected, although he wasn't yet close enough to read the numbers on the tags. He decided to move closer, but just as he was about to step forward a stick snapped in the trees off to his left, and the blood rushed straight to his head. Someone, or something, was moving over in that direction. Too large for a fox or a possum, and not deliberate enough for a deer. Coming after him, perhaps? He sank into a crouch and slowly pulled the gun from its holster. The air was colder than ever. He strained his ears to listen.

That's when he belatedly remembered the night vision goggles, which were still in his shoulder bag. As quietly as possible he holstered the gun, opened the bag, and put on the goggles. The world took on an eerie glow. For the moment, all was silent. Nothing moved. Maybe he'd imagined the noise. Then a large, luminous green body moved out from behind a tree, no more than thirty yards to his left. Fuck! Coming toward him? No. Heading toward the house. Slowly, but in a slight crouch, and with a seeming sense of purpose.

Riggleman was short of breath, his heart drumming. He sank to his knees but kept watching through the goggles. Then, to his alarm, a second person moved into his field of vision from the left. There were two of them! At first he thought it might be a team, some tactical unit preparing to take the sort of decisive action that he could only dream about. But then the second man stopped and raised a rifle into position, taking aim. Riggleman was on the verge of shouting a warning, but the cry caught in his throat as a gunshot banged sharply through the trees. The flash from the muzzle was almost blinding through the goggles. He turned and saw the first man crumple to the ground with a low moan. Riggleman sank to his knees, feeling weak and needing to pee. This wasn't his game, his style. Why the fuck was he even there? He pulled out his cell phone, thinking maybe he should call 9-1-1, or Hagan—anybody—then worried that the light from the phone would attract attention, so he quickly put it away and tried to make himself as small as possible.

When he looked up again the second man had reached the first and was pointing the barrel of the rifle down at his head from only a few feet away. A second shot cracked into the night. The first blob convulsed and then lay still, a horrible moment. Riggleman again grasped his sidearm, wondering how much noise it would make to unholster it. The shooter was back on the move again, but thank God he was retracing his steps, heading away from the house and away from him. It was all Riggleman could do to maintain his balance on his knees as he watched the man depart, even as his butt and his toes began to tingle. His entire lower body was going numb. He wondered if he would even be able to stand.

The shooter gradually disappeared from sight. Riggleman then counted to thirty before painfully rising from his crouch, gripping a tree to steady himself as blood rushed back into his legs with a prickly surge. When he looked back toward the dead man he was sickened to see that his green glow was already fading, as if his very life was draining from him. He had no interest in a closer inspection, and to call 9-1-1 now would be pure folly, given the manner in which he was armed and dressed. Better instead to get the hell out of there, because the shots had been damned loud. Fuck! A light was on in the house. Then another. To hell with stealth. Riggleman heaved a sigh of great effort and began lumbering back toward his rental car as fast as his numb legs would carry him.

Hours later, after he finally drifted into a restless sleep back at his motel, the police burst into his room, guns drawn, shining a bright light into his face. Rough handling and humiliation, plus the sinking realization of his own laxness and stupidity as he saw the cluttered room the way they must have seen it—the camouflage uniform tossed on a chair, the holstered gun on the bedside table, the night vision goggles over by the television, and, worst of all, those reams of paper with their incriminating names and addresses. And him, caught red-handed, the homicidal paramilitary loon with a death wish.

But now, back in the car and turning onto Route 50, Riggleman felt certain he had survived the worst of it. To his relief, the key card still worked in the door to his room. To his further relief, his suitcase was still on the floor. The housekeeper had even made the bed and left fresh towels. Maybe the police had phoned the manager to let him know that everything was okay. Yes, he was going to be fine, which called for a private celebration, courtesy of the minibar.

Riggleman stooped to open the door of the small refrigerator and surveyed his choices. He was about to grab a cold beer when a forearm locked around his neck from behind and a gun barrel poked into his back.

"Don't make a move! Call out and I shoot."

"Okay."

"Drop your hands to your side and lay down on your stomach."

"Okay." Meekly, sadly. Was this guy going to shoot him? Was it the guy from last night?

"Hurry up!"

"Okay." It was the only word he felt capable of speaking.

Riggleman moved slowly, not wanting to alarm the guy. He didn't dare turn and glance, didn't dare do anything other than what he'd been told to do, or keep saying "Okay." He'd never felt more helpless in his life. He stretched out, just as ordered, and pressed his forehead to the motel carpet, which smelled like cigarettes and cleaning fluid.

"Slowly put your hands behind your back. *Slowly.*"

Riggleman did so and felt plastic handcuffs slip around his wrists and tighten. The toe of a boot dug into the right side of his rib cage, nudging hard enough to roll him onto his back. He felt like an over-turned beetle waiting to be smushed. A fairly tall man, mid-forties, black commando sweater and blue jeans, stared down at him. Arctic blue eyes, a five o'clock shadow.

"You owe me for the bail money, but we'll work that out later."

These were the most comforting words Riggleman had ever heard. Not only had this man delivered him from the legal system, he was now speaking of some indeterminate future in which Riggleman was expected to play a role. Even the suggestion of a future seemed won-derful right now.

"Sure. Be happy to." It felt like a big improvement from "Okay."

"Shut up until I ask you to speak."

"Okay."

The man seemed to relax then. Riggleman was pleasantly surprised to realize that he must have been tense as well. The man then put his gun down on the table next to the minibar. Riggleman was beginning to get an inkling of how soldiers must deal with the fears of combat from day to day. It wasn't courage so much as a matter of becoming inured to it, of moving on from one moment to the next as a matter of instinct. Once you gave yourself over to fate, you could breathe again and be yourself. The realization freed him to speak his mind, come what may, and he said the first thing that popped into his head.

"You're the guy from the woods last night, aren't you."

"So you *were* there. Just to the west of me, right?"

"Yes. You passed within thirty yards of me coming and going."

"Damn. I'm slipping."

"I almost peed my pants."

"Shut up for a second."

And that's when it hit him. Not only had he seen this man before, he had also spoken to him on the phone. He even knew his name. Or the name he worked under, anyway. And at that instant he realized, with feelings of deepest gratitude, that General Hagan hadn't abandoned him after all. The general must have seen his email late Sunday. And then, through whatever channels and whatever means, he had worked nimbly and quickly to ensure that someone else had been there to watch over him. This fellow had saved his life.

"You're him, aren't you?" Riggleman said. "I should've guessed it before now. Your voice sounds a little different, but you've probably got some kind of special software installed on your phone to disguise what you really sound like."

"What the fuck are you talking about?"

"Harry Walsh," Riggleman said, smiling now. "Your code name."

The guy actually laughed at him.

"You stupid ass. You saw Harry, all right. But he's dead. He's the other guy."

Riggleman immediately thought of that dimming blob of light. The twitching body, the stillness. Protoplasm gradually losing its heat while he watched.

"Then who the hell are you?"

"That's not important."

"But if—?"

"Shut up and listen. We've got work to do."

"Okay."

CHAPTER THIRTY-FOUR

DEATHS IN A FOREIGN LAND had drawn them all to this story. And now a death in their own backyard had reenergized them. The reporters got back on their phones and laptops, working as night fell. Cole and Sharpe set about planning their flight for the following morning.

A few hours later they were finally overtaken by hunger. They decided to eat well for a change, as if to fortify themselves for a final, decisive push. Keira headed into town for fish and vegetables. Steve drove to a dockside vendor for oysters. Sharpe retrieved a case of beer from his van and filled the bottom shelf of the refrigerator.

They fried the fish, shucked the oysters, popped the caps from the beers, and ate and drank greedily for an hour in the dining room, with its grand view of the darkened bay, a string of lights twinkling on the far shore.

"So," Steve said. "Four hours of darkness and we're still alive."

"I was going to take a walk up to the end of the drive," Cole said. "Make sure somebody's out there."

"I'll go with you," Keira said. "I need to stretch my legs."

Barb looked as if she was about to say something, but Steve warned her off with a frown.

"You children sleep tight," Sharpe said. "Before I turn in I'm going to do a little more tinkering. Looks like a front might be moving in tomorrow, which could reduce our flying hours. Might as well try and reduce our margin of error."

"Nice meal, guys," Steve said. "Barb and I will clean up."

This time Barb made the face, but she stood and began clearing the dishes. Cole grabbed his coat and waited by the door.

The night was chilly, but it felt as if Sharpe was right about new weather being on the way. The air smelled briny and wet, although there were no clouds. The Milky Way spread out overhead, spilling all the way to the horizon. He heard the crunch of gravel and saw Keira approaching.

"You spend much time here when you were growing up?"

"Most of my summers. Our very own family camp, pretty much. My dad would drive out from D.C. on the weekends."

"What did he do?"

"Lobbyist. Agribusiness stuff. Back when everybody thought that was a good thing."

"Well, at least it paid off. Half my neighbors were probably buying his company's products. Corn and soybeans mostly, where I grew up."

"Was your dad a farmer?"

"School principal. Mom was a teacher, until I was born. Office romance."

"And their son had his head in the clouds."

"Literally. And for most of my life. Until all the clouds ended up being on a video screen."

They walked in silence awhile. A doe stirred from cover and receded into the trees. A hundred yards farther along, a fox sprinted across the drive and disappeared.

"We get a bald eagle that nests here sometimes. You should see this place in the spring."

Was that an invitation? Cole wasn't sure, so he let it rest without a reply.

"Looks like they kept their word," she said.

A police cruiser was parked just beyond the gate, facing outward so the officers could switch on their headlights to alert any approaching traffic.

"So I guess we're covered," she said.

"Unless somebody decides to come by boat."

"Or on foot, through the woods."

A policeman stepped out from the passenger side, the one named Earl from the night before. Presumably his partner, Calbert, was again behind the wheel.

"Hi, y'all. Learned some new stuff about the other night."

"Like a name, maybe?"

"Heard it wasn't that CIA man, like Keira thought. Dispatcher said you called that in to the medical examiner a few hours ago. Some strange shit." He shook his head. "But we found an unclaimed car at the Willards' place, right up the lane."

"I thought they were out of town for the season?"

"That's what tipped us off. Shouldn't have been anything there but a boat trailer and a riding mower. Dark blue Chevy sedan, 2012. Maryland tags but a Bethesda registration, D.C. area, parked way up in their carport. Probably belonged to the victim. Must have walked in from there."

"Get a name on that registration?" Cole asked.

Earl smiled, his teeth visible in the starlight.

"Not allowed to say. But from what I heard, they seem to think it's a fake, anyway."

"Figures."

"The funny part was what they did with the car. Feds brought in a big ol' truck, backed it right up the drive, threw down a tailgate ramp, and rolled her right in. Packed that Chevy away where you couldn't see it and drove off, clean as you please. Probably in some secret lab by now."

"That figures, too."

"You ex-military?"

"Not allowed to say."

The teeth glowed again.

"Good one. But this case does get a little funkier all the time."

"And you still don't have a lead on the shooter?" Keira asked.

"Not that me and Calbert have heard. The FBI's pretty much taken this thing over, so maybe you should ask them. Doubt you'll have any more trouble around here, though. Not tonight, anyway." He smiled again. "Me and Calbert will be here straight on through to sunrise, so you people can rest easy."

"Thanks," Keira said. "Can we bring you anything?"

He shook his head, then patted his holster.

"Got all we need right here." Cole heard a chuckle from inside the car. Calbert must've liked that one.

"See you in the morning, then," Keira said.

They turned to leave. Cole waited until they were out of earshot, then said, "Well, there you go. An unbreakable cordon of security. I know I'll sleep sounder."

"Don't be so hard on Talbot County's finest."

He shook his head. "They've got no idea what they're up against."

"Neither do we. But that won't stop us from flying that little toy of yours in the morning."

"It's no toy, that's for damn sure."

"Kind of hard to believe we can even do this, legal or not. Just go zooming over there and poke around, looking at anything we want. Can you imagine if the paparazzi ever get ahold of these things?"

"How do you know they haven't?"

She stopped, pivoted toward him, and moved to within a foot of his face. He could feel the warmth coming off her, and even in the dark he saw the intensity of her eyes.

"Look at me."

"That's pretty unavoidable."

"Answer me truthfully. When you followed me, and they were egging you on and you were piloting that drone right down the road after me, what was that like? I mean, I know you didn't feel good about it, but still. Even for all that it must have been kind of, I don't know, thrilling, maybe, just to know that you could. I mean, you'd just slept with me and everything, and then there you are, looking right over my shoulder without me even knowing it. Waiting for my secrets to open up to you. You read Felicity's license tag, you even saw the papers changing hands, and I never knew a thing until you guys told me. That's quite a drug, knowing you can have that anytime you want."

"Your friends sure seemed to like it. And pretty soon everybody will want a dose. But nobody will want anyone else to use it against them."

"Same with every weapon ever made, I guess. But once you let a few people have it, how do you stop all the others? It'll be just like guns. A few years and they'll be everywhere."

"Now you're sounding like Sharpe."

"He's against this?"

"So he says."

She shook her head. "I don't believe him. That's like a pusher saying he's for the war on drugs."

"You should tell him. He'd like that."

"Wouldn't want to give him the pleasure."

They started walking again. Cole was about to head off toward the pool house when Keira said, "Why don't you come back to the main house for a while. Have another beer and relax while you can."

"The calm before the storm?"

"Something like that."

"I'll lock up out here, just in case."

"Even with all that police protection?"

Cole chuckled as they headed toward the pool house, threading through the boxwoods.

He'd scarcely put his hand on the doorknob when a harsh light beamed straight into their faces and a gun barrel poked into his back.

"Don't shout and don't move," a gruff voice said from behind.

Cole swung around, hands in motion, a roundhouse toward the light. Halfway into his punch someone kicked his feet out from under him and he slammed roughly to the ground. A knee jammed into his lower back before he could even try to scramble to his feet. Then someone swiftly bound his hands behind him with a pair of plastic handcuffs, cinching them until they cut into his wrists and leaving him unable to do anything but squirm sideways, just enough to see that Keira, although still standing, had her arms pinned and cuffed behind her as well, by a second man. So this time there were at least two of them, working together, and for all he knew there might be others in the main house, tying up Barb and Steve. Or worse. He wondered if Sharpe might have gotten away through the woods if he'd been outside at the time. So much for the extra protection.

"Call out and you're dead," the voice said, and it sounded like he meant it. "Any noise at all and you're dead. Both of you."

Whoever had slung him to the ground now pulled him up to his knees, then helped him stand. The flashlight beam came back in his eyes, but he could see both men now, dressed in black and wearing gloves and dark ski masks. Each carried a sidearm.

"Where are the others?" the first guy asked him.

Cole said nothing.

"If you want to live, I need an answer."

The man spoke in low tones, but something about his voice was familiar.

"In the house," Keira said. She sounded upset, out of breath.

"The old guy's in there, too," the second man said. "Saw him go in a few minutes ago."

"Good. We'll get them all at once. Tie these two together, back to back to this tree."

He caught Keira's eye as the second man positioned them on either side of a pine, the bark chafing against his coat. She looked terrified. If these guys were going to kill them, he hoped they did it swiftly, and soon. The rope was around them in seconds. One knot, then another. The second guy was about to secure it further when the first one spoke.

"They're not Houdini. We just need to hold 'em long enough to secure the house. You stay here. If I need help, you'll hear me. If I don't call for you within two minutes, then come anyway, but use all those precautions I taught you."

Taught him? One pro and one amateur, Cole figured, which only baffled him more. But presumably the lesser guy had some training or he wouldn't be armed.

"Keep 'em quiet while I'm gone. If they start making noise, shoot 'em."

Keira whimpered, but Cole wasn't convinced. The eyes of the second guy looked as scared as Keira's. The only one in command of his emotions was the first one, although he was indeed a cool customer. He headed off toward the house. They heard the door creak open, then not much else. A minute passed. Cole could tell the other guy was getting antsy. He bounced on the balls of his feet and kept glancing at his watch, a big model that looked like one a soldier would wear.

The door of the house creaked again, and a man's voice called out just loud enough for them to hear.

"All set. Bring 'em in."

The second guy awkwardly untied them, muttering beneath his breath as he struggled with the knots. He unlooped the rope and followed them to the house. Cole's hands were already numb from the tightness of the plastic bands around his wrists.

As they entered the house in single file, Cole saw an ashen Barb and

Steve standing by the far wall of the living room, bunched between the windows alongside a grumpy-looking Sharpe. All three had their hands cuffed behind them. His mind flashed on an image of their five bodies arranged facedown on the carpet, all in a row in front of the couch, hair in disarray, blood everywhere, the whole house silent except for the wind in the trees.

"Stand over by the others."

He followed Keira. They stood next to Sharpe, in front of the window to the right, then turned to face their assailants.

"Now," the first man said, "the moment you've been waiting for."

The men pulled off their ski masks. Sharpe was the first of the five captives to speak.

"I'll be damned. Hell of a way to get reacquainted, Wade."

"Nelson. Long time. You, too, Captain Cole."

"Wade fucking Castle," Barb said, almost hissing it. "We've met before, too."

Castle narrowed his eyes for a full, frowning appraisal before the light of recognition dawned. "Tangora, wasn't it?"

She nodded.

"Surprised you can remember anything," he said. "You were completely freaked."

"That tends to happen when you've just seen chunks of flesh landing all over the lot."

"And you're Riggleman," Cole said to the second man. "So you're a captain now. General Hagan must like you."

"Likes me so much he forgot to bail me out."

"Enough with the reunion chitchat," Castle said. "Let's get down to our first important announcement. We're not here to kill you or harm you. We're here to work with you. Because, trust me—and I'm afraid that's something you'll *have* to do, if this arrangement is going to work—after the last few days of watching you I think I know what you guys are after, and I'm after exactly the same thing."

The whole room exhaled. Not that Cole had really felt threatened once the masks came off. Maybe he was being naïve, but he even believed the man. To a point, at least.

"Regrettably, there's an awkward bit of housekeeping to attend to.

As it happens, I'm not willing to welcome *all* of you into this arrangement. First, we have to deal with a traitor in your midst."

All five of them looked at each other. For a second Cole even worried that Castle was talking about him—triggered by something from his Air Force file, maybe, or the court-martial. His worries then turned to Keira, if only because she was the one whose loyalty the others had always questioned. Or maybe it was Sharpe, the one with all the shadowy friends giving him whatever he needed.

Castle raised his gun and pointed it across the room at Steve.

"Step forward, Mr. Merritt, to face the charges." Then, turning to Riggleman: "Tell the others what you told me, Captain."

Cole studied the emotions registering in Steve's features. Shock. Outrage. Indignation. A little fear as well, as his eyes flicked back and forth to the gun in Castle's hand. But there was something else, too: Guilt.

Steve stepped forward.

CHAPTER THIRTY-FIVE

RIGGLEMAN WOVE A BRIEF but complicated tale of circuitous financial dealings that began with IntelPro and ended with a fellowship grant for $100,000 that Steve had won several months ago, right about the time he began pursuing his journalistic investigation of Wade Castle, aka Fort1. The account, which reminded Cole of the way the young officer had undressed his entire fighter squadron for its security lapses, led them deftly down a trail of sham corporations, silent partners, and finally to a seemingly beneficent organization known as the Melville Center for Reporting on Strategic and Military Affairs.

"I was told it was legit," Steve protested. "And why the hell would IntelPro go to the trouble of setting up a whole network of bullshit companies just to give me an amount of money that to them is chump change?"

Riggleman, unruffled, was about to answer when Barb interrupted.

"Because you were a secondary recipient, an afterthought." Everyone turned toward her. Her eyes were lit by the thrill of discovery. "Because all those damn companies he just mentioned—the Lane Corporation, the Melville Center, and every last one of their silent partners—has turned up in one way or another in the investment portfolios—the *very lucrative* investment portfolios—of all the officers in Captain Cole's chain of command for Predator ops at Creech. Including your boss, Captain Riggleman—General Hagan. He's right there in the IntelPro cesspool, too. The only link I couldn't find was this Comstock Group you just mentioned. But that's the one that ties everything together. And it ties in this Melville reporting foundation. Which sinks you, Steve."

"I had no idea," Steve said.

"Steve!" Barb admonished.

"*None!*"

"*Steve!* He has you dead to rights! And at some point they *had* to have told you. Otherwise it was pointless for them to do it. They wanted you to know who was paying the freight. It's clear as can be. So give it up, okay?"

He opened his mouth to protest further, then stopped and slowly shook his head. Everyone realized without a further word that it was over. The fight went out of his eyes, and he slumped against the wall. Barb was probably the only one who was no longer watching him. Cole could tell by the distracted look on her face that she was still adding all these new pieces to the intricate edifice she'd constructed in the course of her research.

"Comstock," she muttered again, looking at Riggleman. "That's the keystone, the entity that binds it all. Damn good work."

He nodded back, a bit pridefully, seeming gratified to at last be appreciated.

"Christ," Sharpe exclaimed, the first words he'd spoken since Castle's arrival. "You two should get married or something."

The remark broke the ice, and the dynamic shifted. Even Castle smiled. Everyone did except Steve, who was now the outcast, the interloper. Cole's old role. Castle went from person to person, cutting loose their plastic handcuffs. Then he turned back toward Steve.

"I'd appreciate if you'd hand over your cell phone for the duration," he said. "And you won't be leaving the premises until our work is done."

This brought Steve momentarily back to life.

"What, I'm your prisoner now?"

"Let's say it's voluntary. But how 'bout handing over your phone all the same."

Castle held out a hand. He didn't brandish a gun, but everyone knew he still had one. Cole then voiced the conclusion that he figured everyone else was already thinking.

"You killed the guy in the woods the other night, didn't you, Wade."

"Had to. He was here to kill me." Castle hadn't taken his eyes off Steve. "Hand it over."

Steve gave in. Who wouldn't have, considering what they'd just heard?

"Smart man," Castle said, pocketing the phone. He was about to say more when Steve made a last stand of sorts, a final argument before sentencing.

"IntelPro had a story to tell," he said. "They thought I'd be interested. They also knew what kind of shape I was in. Financially, I mean. Rent, alimony, credit cards, everything overdue and maxed out. Three different magazines stiffing me on checks. So they told me about this new fellowship, said they'd put in a word for me at the foundation. Yeah, the foundation they'd just set up. I found out that part later. At the time it wasn't exactly in my interest to ask too many questions. And when you don't have a rich family, or a place like this to fall back on . . ." He glanced pointedly at Keira.

"This isn't about me, Steve," Keira said.

"I know that. And I know what I've done. But the only agreement I ever made was to keep them posted about what you guys were coming up with, and only in the most general terms. They just didn't want to be blindsided. Otherwise I was fully independent to pursue any angle, and that's what we were doing. I kept thinking, all the way up to the end, that I could find a way to make it work. For all of us."

"Like with that worthless source of yours?"

"He wasn't worthless. He *knew* shit."

"Shit that always steered us away from IntelPro. And so did you. No wonder you fought so hard against using the drone. Mr. Ethics, supposedly. You must have felt like their last line of defense."

"You're wrong. If I'd wanted to stop it, all I had to do was call them."

"How do we know you didn't?" Sharpe asked.

"Stay the fuck out of this. It wasn't like that at all. I still wanted—*want*—to get the story."

"As long as it wasn't a story with any angle that might make them ask you to give the grant money back," Barb said.

Steve shook his head, but said nothing more. Barb stared him down, livid, until he lowered his head in apparent shame. Keira just looked sad. Cole felt bad for all of them.

Castle turned toward Cole, ready to move on.

"Riggleman says you got some sort of email from your old wingman the other day with archives galore. Learn anything?"

Now how the hell did he know that? Unless . . .

"You hacked the account?" he asked Riggleman.

The little captain allowed himself a smile. Victorious again on the cyberfront.

"It's how he found you," Castle said. "But that's old news. The archives. Anything good?"

"First you owe us some answers," Cole said. "Who's the dead guy?"

"I'm sure you were already acquainted with him at some level. Harry Walsh."

"Never heard of him."

"Code name Lancer."

That stopped him. He looked over at Sharpe, who stared back, mouth open. They shook their heads.

"Lancer?" Barb said. "The name Bickell mentioned?"

"He turned up on three of those missions on the transcripts. He was there on the ground, poking around for somebody, maybe even running the show."

"The Tangora raid," Castle said. "The one that blasted Engineer Haider to smithereens. He led me by the nose. His baby, start to finish."

"Then why were you the one who showed up?" Barb said.

"Belated attempt at damage control. That's when I started to realize that my own beacons—the whole Magic Dimes op—were being used against me. Or against competing private interests. IntelPro, sabotaging its competition. So I went on the warpath and off the reservation."

"Couldn't have gone too far off it. You were still in business for Sandar Khosh."

"It's complicated, and Bickell may have muddled some stuff in translation. You only know half the picture. I'd like to see what Lancer was up to on some of those transcripts."

"Fine," Cole said. "We can do that."

"I've got questions, too," Sharpe said. "About how much technology you Agency guys were sharing. I've been told you were giving away the store."

"Not my doing, but, yeah, they made off with plenty. I just happened to be the most convenient person to blame. And now you're planning to do what, go in there tomorrow with your own drone and sniff out what they've done with all their new toys?"

"Something like that."

"Good. I've got a wish list of my own for some sites over there. But first we should compare notes."

"Speaking of notes," Riggleman said, "should we be letting her do that?"

He nodded toward Barb, who was scribbling at the speed of light. Cole couldn't help but admire her. Even though she probably hadn't yet added things up, she knew that every stray piece was important and was gathering them up while she had the chance.

"Take all the damn notes you want," Castle said. "Those fuckers at IntelPro have been smearing my name for months, to the point where even half the Agency believes it. The truth, as the slogan says, will set me free. Scribble away."

"Give her something decent, then," Cole said, "starting with Lancer. Who the hell was he?"

"Not Harry Walsh. That was another code name. Kevin Wardlow. A freelance jack-of-all-trades. Ex-Agency, so he still had some friends in our shop, which he knew how to use. In Afghanistan, IntelPro was paying him to be their middleman with all the locals. He's the guy who fixed it with Mansur to fuck up my beacons op, the whole Magic Dimes thing. Which wasn't too damn hard for him to do. Mansur meant well, but couldn't keep track of all the players. To him one American was just like another. So it became a matter of Lancer trying to keep Mansur out of contact with me and run him for his own uses. By any means necessary. That firefight on your recon mission near Charwala?"

"The recon that Zach and I fucked up?"

"Those were Lancer's boys you were covering for. Your CO and your whole chain of command were in on it. U.S. air support for a gang of privateers."

"Who'd they kill?"

"My guys. Locals, more privateers, but at least they were actually working for Uncle Sam."

"And at the house? The one they raided?"

"Some low-value targets. IntelPro trying to make a name for itself. They'd have gone off half cocked after Osama himself, without a word to anybody official, if they'd had half a clue as to where he was hiding. Anything for a few scalps to pump up their value with the right people in Washington."

Barb was writing so intently now that she was poking her tongue between her lips, as determined as Michael Jordan going in for a slam. Even Steve was paying attention, unable to turn off his journalistic curiosity, or perhaps his growing sense of horror as he realized what he'd been helping to hide and protect. Sharpe, too, was rapt, arms folded. Keira had a notebook out as well. So Cole kept pushing, trying to pry loose everything he could while Castle was in the mood.

"Sandar Khosh, what happened there?"

"I was trying to put an end to everything. Snuff out Mansur and the last of his beacons before he and Lancer did any more damage. I thought I had him when the truck arrived."

"And the kids?"

"Knew they were his the second I saw them. It only confirmed for me that we had the right place. I didn't like it that his family was there, but still . . ."

"Just collateral damage, huh?"

"Worth it if we stopped him. They had their own hit list, with only their own interests in mind. Mansur wasn't evil, just an idiot. But idiots can fuck things up as much as anybody."

"But it wasn't even him. It was the wrong truck."

"I saw that, but too late. I realized it as soon as we started looking through the wreckage."

"One stripe, not two."

"Exactly."

"Then why did you have us keep poking around the wreckage? It was like you were obsessed."

"I was looking for Mansur, for one thing. Still hoping against hope. But the beacon—I was looking for that, too. That was the weirdest part of the whole thing. About half an hour before the strike, I started getting a signal from the house. So afterward I was looking for it."

"Talk about a needle in a haystack."

"I know, but I was desperate. It was on chat, not voice, so you never would have known, but I was pulling my hair out, because the damn signal was still going, even after the strike. And, to make it weirder, it had changed locations slightly, just seconds before impact. From inside to outside. It only hit me later what must have happened."

It hit Cole at that very moment.

"The girl," he said. "Or one of her brothers. They must have been carrying it, or had it in their pocket."

"She had it in her hand. The arm she lost. Later I went back again over the whole transcript, the whole damn video, and you can see it, just barely. Or maybe it's just wishful thinking, but when you look closely there's the slightest shine of something in her hand. This small piece of metal. She must have found it, thought it was some kind of coin, or trinket."

"A toy," Cole said, remembering now the odd words that Mansur had spoken among the jumble of his broken ramblings the other night on Pickard Street: *"My children make toy. They make toy and it is ruin! Ruin!"*

Keira had put a hand to her mouth, as if she'd just witnessed a terrible accident. Steve looked horrified. The only sound was the scratching of Barb's pencil as she captured the last of Castle's words for posterity.

Cole stepped over to a chair and sat down, letting the whole awful story settle around him like a mist. He knew he should keep asking questions, but for the moment he was stalled, unable to move forward. So Barb took over.

"So why did IntelPro move him? Mansur, I mean."

"It was the only way to keep him away from me. After Sandar Khosh I put the word out that I wanted him alive, because I wanted to burn them. Find out everything he knew. They decided to burn me instead, by moving the evidence. Then they started pushing their cover story, to Steve, to guys like you. I was the fuckup, the bad apple, the disease that had to be exposed and then wiped out. And you bought it, all of you."

"Why not just kill him?"

"Lancer wanted him alive. Figured his connections were too valuable, and they could use them later. So they brought him here. Trained him up for a while, right over at the facility, to make him more useful. The plan was to send him back overseas once they got me out of the way. But they couldn't track me down, and once they got word I was stateside they must have decided to just use him as bait, lure me in, because they knew I still wanted him. It's why they left him so out in the open in Baltimore. Then you guys blew his cover, so they brought him here and started working on Plan B."

"Which was?"

"Bring in their freelance asset Lancer. Wait for me to come looking for you guys, then have him take me out."

And they all knew how that had ended.

"What about you?" Cole asked. "Are you freelance now?"

"Not really. But I'm not Agency anymore. For the moment I've been reassigned."

"FBI?" Barb asked. "Homeland Security?"

"An element of the national security apparatus that shall remain nameless. But it's legal."

"To a point that includes murder?"

"Self-defense isn't murder. What's important right now is that I think I know where they're keeping Mansur in their thousand-acre wood. And with that drone of yours we can find him." He turned to Sharpe. "Think you can squeeze me into your flight plan?"

"Absolutely."

"Then let's put our heads together, because in eight more hours we're going to war."

CHAPTER THIRTY-SIX

CASTLE AND SHARPE SPREAD their maps and plats on the dining room table and studied them like generals. Cole edged up behind them, feeling that his moment to shine had finally arrived. It was an hour before dawn, and he hadn't been this pumped for a mission since Kosovo, back when he still flew Vipers.

The reporters, as if realizing their own role had been diminished to that of observers, stayed well out of the way and were mostly silent. Barb, as always, had her notebook out to record the proceedings, while Keira seemed to be studying each of the participants in turn, as if gauging how well they would react once events were in motion.

Steve had an air of banishment, a man under house arrest. He slumped in a chair in the corner, sipping lukewarm coffee and reading a day-old newspaper, although even he couldn't resist an occasional peek toward Castle, Sharpe, and Cole as they pointed in growing enthusiasm toward points on the maps.

Castle showed them satellite photos of the area he wanted to surveil, a small compound with two buildings inside a fenced perimeter, tucked in an isolated corner of the woods. He said he'd infiltrated the training grounds twice already during the past week, but not deeply enough to scout out the compound.

"They've secured it pretty well. For them, anyway. Most of their people generally suck at what they do. It's the best-kept secret of these contract outfits—gross incompetence. Signing them up to track your HVT is like hiring an overnight security guard to find a mass murderer. But they've positioned a lot of personnel near the compound. If it *is* Mansur, then he's not going anywhere without some help."

"Keira said the locals think some kind of foreign family has moved in," Cole said. "Groundskeepers, that was the theory. A Latino family, that was their other guess."

"Probably the cover story IntelPro floated. Or maybe the neighbors just saw beards and skin tone and filled in the blanks. Family, though— that part fits."

"How many of his people did they bring over?" Sharpe asked.

"Never heard an exact number. His wife and kids didn't survive, as you saw." Cole flinched. "So this must be extended family, the usual Afghan village lineup. It's a good way to keep him settled and quiet. Cousins, aunts and uncles, maybe a brother or sister. I really don't know. He's the only one that matters."

Sharpe had already briefed Castle on what he hoped to find in their recon of the new airstrip—evidence that IntelPro was working to cash in on its high-level access to cutting-edge drone technology, and its most sophisticated applications.

"Hell, what's to learn?" Castle said. "This shit's everywhere now, isn't it? They'll be delivering pizzas with these things before long."

"True enough. But the stuff they'll have is top shelf, and then some. Super-advanced. The stuff money can't buy. Not yet, anyway. But when it does go up for sale, they'll have it ready to offer, fully applied and field-tested. And all because your people gave away the store."

"Yours, too," Cole said. "And mine, judging by the arrangements Barb uncovered."

"Guilty as charged, all of them," Sharpe said.

Adding to their sense of urgency was the approaching winter storm. As the first gray light of dawn lit the eastern sky, the gray talons of its leading edge curled from the far horizon, reaching westward across the Bay.

Sharpe frowned as he looked out the window.

"We should get set up," he said. "We'll have enough light for our first approach in about half an hour."

"Won't you need better light for video and photos?" Castle asked.

"By the time we're at altitude and within range, we'll have it. This thing's fast for a drone, but it's not exactly hypersonic."

Keira edged up to Cole's shoulder.

"How are you planning to approach it?"

"On first pass we'll make an overall assessment," he told her. "Find our two targets, design our approaches. With everything that's been going on around here the last few days they're likely to be a little jumpy, with heightened security, so we'll probably recon the airstrip first. We'll get whatever video we can, then take it from there. And hope we're not pursued."

"Pursued?"

"By any of their drones. Sharpe figures there's liable to be some pretty hot stuff over there. Hotter than what we've got."

"So just like a real mission, then?"

"Hey, this is as real as it gets."

He fleetingly remembered the last time that thought had crossed his mind, at a moment when he was watching black crosshairs hover on a mud rooftop, seconds before impact.

"You okay?"

"I will be."

"Ghosts?"

"A few."

"You'll handle it."

A hand on his shoulder, a light squeeze. Then she backed away, leaving him to his work.

"Into the fray, Captain Cole!"

Sharpe was beaming, eager. Cole followed him and Castle out into the cold, where the drone was already perched at the head of its makeshift runway, freshly raked. The long slender wings cast low shadows across the gravel. The wind stirred in the pines.

"Two hours, tops, before conditions go all to hell." Sharpe held a finger to the breeze. "You'll need to do some actual piloting as this shit closes in. The Bay's already whitecapping."

"I won't lose her," Cole said.

They strolled to their places. The reporters followed, tentative at first, but ready for the show. Even Steve was with them. Hell, what else was he going to do?

The engine powered up, loud enough to stir birds from the trees. Cole wondered if the cops were still at their post at the end of the driveway, and if so, what they'd make of the commotion? He put on the goggles and snugged them up. The image flashed on. He held the controls in his hand, then watched with a lift to his stomach as their bird took flight.

"Passing her over to you on three!" Sharpe called out. Cole knew the others would be gathered around Sharpe by now, watching the proceedings on his iPad from the view of the second camera.

"One . . . two . . . three. She's all yours!"

The wind was tricky, bouncing the drone like a balsa glider. It took some getting used to, but he easily cleared the tree line at the end of the drive and soared her up to a few hundred feet. He swung around for a view of the upper end of the property. The police car was gone. So that was one potential problem out of the way.

"Set me that course on the GPS," he called out to Sharpe. "I'll keep a hand in because of the wind, but we might as well let the chips do the initial navigation."

"As you wish."

He could see the leading edge of storm better now, because they were flying straight toward it. Icy fingerlings of moisture and turbulence. The drone was out over the water, on a beeline toward Intel-Pro's real estate, a few peninsulas over. Below, spray was blowing off the whitecaps.

"Pretty stiff breeze already," he said.

"Fourteen knots, gusting to twenty. But you're doing fine. And she's built for it."

He gradually took it up to a thousand feet, and after fifteen minutes the whole training area, all two thousand acres, loomed just ahead. Most of it was wooded, but as they moved closer he spotted clearings here and there. Gun ranges and parade grounds, or whatever they were. He then saw the biggest open area, which, as they already knew from their plats and architectural plans, was the freshly paved airstrip with its brand-new hangars and outbuildings.

The real surprise was parked on a taxiway to one side. The morning sunlight glinted and gleamed on what appeared to be an entire row of aircraft.

"Do you see that?" Cole said, his excitement building.

"My God!" Sharpe said. "Take her closer. Take her down now!"

The sight took his breath away. There must have been two dozen aircraft in all, and they were of all shapes and sizes. Short wings, long wings, no wings at all. There was a silver craft with a delta shape and a sawtooth back edge that resembled an undersized stealth bomber. An odd six-rotor model looked a little bit like the hobbyist quadcopters, but it was three times as large. Straight wings and backswept wings, and eerily designed craft that, for all their sleekness, hardly looked flyable. And, for whatever reason, everything was out on full display.

"It's got to be almost everything they have," Cole said.

"Washing day," Castle said. "Look, see those two guys with steam hoses, cleaning equipment? Christ, it's their fucking *washing day*. Unbelievable."

"Or maybe they do this every morning."

Sharpe was exultant.

"It's like Pearl Harbor, when the Japs caught all our shit out on the runway, wing to wing. It's their whole damn arsenal, just waiting for its close-up."

"What a goddamn toy store," Castle said.

"All that's missing are the minis. They probably test those indoors, anyway. In that big hangar down at the end, if I had to guess. A micro-aviary, like the one at Wright-Patterson in Ohio. And if you think the ones I flew down your chimney the other night were hot stuff, well they've probably got a few not much bigger than a Florida mosquito. Swarms of them."

"In theory," Cole said.

"No. In practice. I've seen them. Hey, look at that big one, off at the far end of the runway? Approximately the same wingspan as an Avenger, I'm guessing. Sixty-six feet. Can fly up to fifty thousand feet, top speed of four sixty. A match for the fastest drone the Air Force has right now. But no match for that smaller one two slots down, with the red wingtips. Looks just like our X90 prototype. Air speed of eight hundred, if you can believe it."

"Hot shit," Cole said.

"And it can outfight anything comparable. A true combat drone. Armed with two small missiles and a rapid-fire cannon. A sight to behold. Fire away, Captain Cole! Keep making passes and I'll keep shooting it. Video, stills, the works!"

"Will do. By the way, there's radar. I've seen at least two dishes already."

"Saw those as well."

"Think they've picked us up?"

"Maybe. Although I did employ into the design a little, well . . ."

"Stealth technology?"

"A touch or two. Nothing too elaborate."

"Jesus. How much did this thing cost?"

"Enough that you'd better watch yourself on those treetops. We want her close, but not a catastrophe."

"I don't plan on going in low enough for them to eyeball us. Besides, this wind's a bitch."

"Fine. But at some point we'll just have to say damn the security and go straight in. This opportunity's too good to miss."

"Look!" Steve said. "Over to the left!" Even he was caught up in the enthusiasm. "There's a bunch of guys running. They're pointing up at us."

"How's that possible?" Sharpe said

"I guess better radar tech can be stolen, too," Cole said.

"Good guess. Yes, that's probably it exactly."

Cole swung his camera to port so that the men came into view on his own screen. Two of them were pushing one of the parked aircraft onto the runway, and they were moving fast. The others had dropped their cleaning equipment.

"Looks like they're scrambling one to intercept you," Castle said.

"I see it. When it's airborne I'll head upwind and into the sun."

"Fighter tactics," Sharpe said.

"Won't mean shit if this stuff's half as hot as you say."

"I doubt they'd risk one of their better models. From the looks of that one, it might even be a trainer. But that also means they won't just be trying to follow you, or take your picture. They'll be out for blood."

"Looking for a collision?"

"Whatever it takes."

Sharpe said it with relish. He was enjoying this. Cole was, too. The idea of having an actual air-to-air opponent was certainly a thrilling change from his Predator missions, when the biggest danger apart from equipment failures and the elements was the occasional clumsy potshot fired by mujahideen with rocket-propelled grenade launchers, and even that had only occurred twice, and at very low altitudes.

Besides, the craft he was piloting now was much faster and more maneuverable. It was nimble, fun to fly. And with the full-surround view offered by the headset he practically had to stamp his feet on solid ground to remind himself that he wasn't actually airborne.

Cole spent the next few minutes making passes over the airstrip so Sharpe could collect as many images as possible, and from every conceivable angle. All the while he remained aware of the craft being readied for takeoff, which flashed into view on each pass.

"We're good on the imaging!" Sharpe called out after the fourth pass. "And they're airborne now, so watch yourself."

"Keep him in view on your iPad. I'm blind to him right now."

"He's coming up on your starboard side, already up past the tree line and banking around on a course to intercept you."

"We'll see about that."

Cole throttled down, trying to gauge the capabilities of the rival drone. Banking slowly, he headed straight into the sun and out over the water.

"The winds are trickier above the Bay. Let's see what he's got."

"I'm watching him," Sharpe said. "Nothing fancy yet, unless he's holding back. Maneuverability looks pretty average."

"Is he armed?"

"Hadn't even thought of that. But, no, I don't think so, unless there's some kind of hidden weapons system. Here he comes. Giving it everything he's got, if I'm not mistaken."

Cole banked into a 180-degree turn out over the water, the screen wobbling from the turbulence in a way that made his stomach jump. The pursuing aircraft came back into view. It was maybe three quarters of a mile away and closing fast, glinting in the sunlight as it made a beeline for him.

"Whoever's flying it isn't particularly sophisticated," he said. And it was clear to him that his rival definitely hadn't studied the principles of superpilot John Boyd, who, besides designing the F-16 Viper, had revolutionized pilot training forever with his Energy-Maneuverability Theory of aerial combat.

"Nah. This guy doesn't know shit. Watch this."

From what he'd seen so far, Cole concluded that the other craft was at best only a shade faster than his, and marginally less nimble. Cole veered away from it with ease and came in off the water just above the treetops. He banked down into a second and smaller clearing, the one that looked like part of a firing range.

"He's coming after you. Right on your tail and closing."

Cole banked sharply to starboard and jammed the stick into an immediate climb, straight up into the sun once again—temporarily blinding unless you knew exactly where you were and where you were going. The pursuing plane banked to the right as well but, when faced by the glare, waited for a fraction of a second before ascending. Cole hurtled up over the tree line with no more than twenty feet to spare as he came up out of the clearing. He couldn't see how his opponent fared, but Sharpe, moving his own camera independently, must have, along with the others. All six of them give out a sharp cry of triumph, like the crowd in a football stadium when the linebacker smashes the ball carrier to the turf.

"Whoa, baby! He's gone with the wind!" Steve exclaimed giddily before going silent, as if suddenly reminded that he still had no reason to celebrate.

"Crashed in the trees!" Sharpe announced. "Captain Cole, you're free and clear to pursue our final target. Let's go find Mansur."

CHAPTER THIRTY-SEVEN

COLE TOOK THE DRONE back down to treetop level so he wouldn't be so easy to spot from the airstrip. With IntelPro's eye in the sky out of action, their enemies might believe, at least for a while, that he'd crashed as well, and now he was almost certainly flying too low to show up on their radar.

From Castle's direction Cole heard the rustle of charts and satellite photos.

"You need to head due southeast," Castle said. "You'll be there in no time. It's a small clearing and will come up fast. I think you've already got the coordinates."

"I do, and I think I see it, just ahead. Wow, they really *are* isolated. The clearing's too small for me to get in. I'm taking her up a little, for better visibility. Don't want to get knocked into the trees by a gust."

The view came into focus, offering far more detail and dimension than the satellite had picked up. There were two buildings. The larger one seemed to be a house of spartan design. Painted cinderblock construction with three small windows on each floor across the front and back, but none on the sides. Peaked roof, black shingles. Its half-acre lot was enclosed by a high fence topped with razor wire. The surrounding clearing, maybe five acres in all, was enclosed by similar fencing, with some sort of guardhouse by the gated driveway entrance.

Armed men in military uniforms patrolled the grounds, one on each side of the compound. Presumably, more were on duty inside the blockhouse. Another stood in a watchtower in a far corner, opposite the blockhouse.

"Like a prison," Castle said.

"Look!" It was Keira.

The front door of the house opened, and an armed man in uniform emerged. Trailing him was a small fellow in civilian clothes who, even from three hundred feet up, was recognizable right away to anyone who'd met him.

"Mansur," Cole said.

"Well, that was easy," Sharpe said.

"Plenty left to do."

"I'm getting good images. Stay on this side of the house."

"Have to make a turn here. You might lose him for a second."

Cole banked up and around to the rear side of the house. When the front came back into view they saw that four more people were walking single file behind Mansur. They seemed to be following the guard toward a gate. Two more people stepped from the house as they watched.

"They must have flown in half his aunts and uncles," Castle said.

"Getting busy down there," Sharpe said. "We've stirred up the hornets' nest, and something's afoot. Look out by the main gate, coming in from the woods."

An open-top jeep and a military-style cargo truck with a canvas cover pulled up to the gate, which opened to let them enter. A second jeep followed the truck. All three vehicles entered the compound.

"Back at the house!" Keira said. "Cole, you have to see this."

He tilted the angle of his camera, and there, stepping into the sunlight, was a girl in Afghan peasant clothes and blocky shoes. She was skipping more than walking, the only playful pose in the bunch, but her gait was slightly out of balance because she had only one arm.

Cole opened his mouth, but no words emerged. He drew a deep breath, unable to swallow. For a moment he forgot all about flying, even as she disappeared from his view and he passed back above the forest. When he finally managed a few words, his voice quivered.

"It's her. Fourteen months and seven thousand miles, and my God, there she is." No one else spoke, and with the headset on he couldn't see their faces. For a fleeting moment he wondered if he might have imagined it. "Everybody else saw her, right? With one arm?"

"*The* girl," Keira said. "Yes. Just like you described her."

"I've lost the shot," Sharpe said, sounding irritated. "Pay some damn attention to your flying and swing her back around. Something's happening down there."

When the clearing came back into view, the truck's tailgate was down and a canvas flap was open in the back.

"They're loading them up, taking them somewhere," Castle said. "God knows where, but we've sure as hell spooked them."

"Any bogeys?" Cole asked. "Sharpe, give a lookout."

"Checking now. Nothing yet, but that's subject to change. These guys will have been on the horn by now to the main base. We're flying too low to miss."

"Look out," Castle said. "A couple guards look like they're about to open fire."

For a harrowing second or two, Cole thought he meant the guards were about to shoot Mansur and his relatives, the girl as well. Then he realized he meant they were taking aim at the drone—at *him*.

"No way they'll hit us, not with those weapons. But I'll take her up to six hundred, just in case."

Everyone from the house was now loaded in the truck, along with an armed guard. The tailgate went up, the flap down, and the vehicles began to move. The procession drove out of the compound onto a narrow gravel road through the woods. Another armed man rode shotgun in the lead jeep. They appeared to be moving at top speed.

"Don't lose them!"

"I'm on it."

The convoy proceeded along the road through several curves. The pine forest was dense, but not enough to make them hard to follow, and Cole now realized where they must be headed.

"There's a gate up ahead on a road that leads out to Route 50. They're heading for the highway. How are we doing for fuel? What's our range from here?"

"Another fifteen miles, maybe, before we reach the point of no return."

"Shit. They could do that in less than half an hour. Keira, call your buddies with the county cops. Get some pursuit scrambled, westbound on 50."

"Doing it now."

"Tell 'em to send an ambulance, too."

"Why an ambulance?" Sharpe said.

"Just fucking do it!"

"They can't possibly escape," Barb said. "If worse comes to worst the State Police could block them at the Bay Bridge."

"You're assuming the State Police will cooperate," Sharpe said. "IntelPro might already have this wired."

"Or maybe they have some closer destination in mind," Castle said.

"Like what?" Barb asked.

"A place for hiding them. Killing them, even."

"But we'll see it."

"We hope. Just stay on 'em."

Keira had already reached a policeman, who put her through to the dispatcher while he stayed on the line. The convoy had traveled several miles down Route 50 already. They were going at least eighty miles an hour, and Cole was losing ground.

"Fuck!" he said. "They keep this up and they're gone."

"Looks like they're turning onto Hardcastle Road," Keira said. "There's not a damn thing down that way."

"They've got another facility out there," Castle said. "It's on one of my sat photos, some property they picked up a few years ago, for expansion."

"Why head there now?" Sharpe asked.

"No idea."

"Wait! I know this place." It was Steve, the last person Cole expected to get any help from. "I've been there, even."

"Likely story," Barb said.

"No. They gave me a tour, the whole facility, and this was part of it. They, well . . ."—he faltered a second, as if realizing he was about to destroy the last of his credibility—"they had me out there right after I got the fellowship."

Barb didn't answer. Cole imagined she was probably shaking her head. But Castle leaped at the opportunity.

"Make yourself useful, then. What's out there? Why would they be going there?"

"A lot of it's underground," he said. "Some kind of big storage area, acres of it. I remember they were proud of that because the water table's so high and it was a bear to build."

"Acres?"

"Yeah, with an entry portal you can drive a truck through. They didn't take me inside, but I did see that."

"What the hell's it for?" Cole asked.

"They didn't say. Like I said, they didn't take me inside. Just toured me around the entrance, the perimeter."

"Well, if they drive in, it's the last we'll ever see of them," Castle said. "They can kill everybody in the truck and no one will ever know. Incinerate the whole damn load, completely out of sight."

Cole felt desperate, his opportunity slipping away, the girl receding, fading, on the verge of disappearing forever. He would fail her again.

"Keira, where are the police?" Cole asked. "How close are they?"

"On their way. A cruiser and an ambulance. They know it's Hardcastle Road."

"They're not going to make it in time."

Cole had caught back up to the convoy after the turnoff. He watched the vehicles proceed through an open gate. The leading jeep, already twenty yards out in front of the truck, now accelerated away. Cole could see where the road ended, maybe half a mile farther, at the mouth of a ramp that appeared to lead down to a steel door built into a grassy mound.

"There's your underground vault," Sharpe said. "In two more minutes, tops, they'll be inside. Then we've lost them."

"There's a keypad entrance," Steve said. "They'll have to stop to open it. The jeep must be running ahead to take care of it."

"Gone," Sharpe said, the voice of doom.

"Shut the fuck up," Cole said. "We can do this."

"Crash it if you have to," Castle said. "Right at the mouth. Take him out when he's at the entrance."

"Then we lose our eyes," Cole said, "and they'll know it. They'll just walk everybody in past the wreckage and finish them off."

"Dammit, then *do* something."

"That's the plan." Cole was back in command. He felt it keenly, and it emerged in his voice. The cool Virginia baritone, steady. Hand on the stick, steady. Every thought for what he needed to do, lined up in perfect order. Flying again, what he was trained for.

"They're just about there. You're too damn low!"

"I'm on it. Keep shooting your pictures. Steady as she goes."

Their drone was no more than thirty feet off the ground now, barreling toward the jeep as it began braking for the ramp that led down to the entrance to the underground bunker. Everyone was silent, watching.

"Keira, what's the word?"

"They're almost to Hardcastle, going full tilt."

"So are we. Hold on."

Cole gave it all the juice he had, overtaking the jeep just as it reached the top of the ramp. On his screen he saw the driver and armed guard leaning down, putting their hands up over their heads to protect themselves from what they must have thought was an imminent crash, and in doing so they lost control of the jeep. Cole pulled up sharply, not yet certain whether his move had done the trick.

"Get us back into view!" Sharpe shouted.

"Doing it." Calm as ever, the airline pilot asking everyone to please fasten their seatbelts. "Coming around for you now."

The jeep was jammed against the side wall of the ramp and the metal gate itself, which looked crumpled and was still shut. Smoke and steam poured from the hood. The driver was pinned at the wheel, and the armed passenger staggered as he climbed out. He wasn't carrying his gun.

"Fuckin' A!" Castle exulted. "You did it! They'll never get it open now!"

"We're not done yet," Cole said. "Not nearly."

The truck had stopped maybe twenty yards short of the ramp. There was a burst of movement in the back. The flap went up and the tailgate down. Then a man ran out, a fast but awkward gait. Mansur, going hell for leather. Then four more adults. They must have somehow overpowered the guard in the back. But where was the girl? Had there already been gunshots? Without sound, he had no idea. Cole swallowed a bubble of panic and banked the drone to come in straight down Hardcastle toward the unfolding scene.

There she was now at last, jumping out into the winter sunlight from the back of the truck in pursuit of the others, her off-balance skip turning into a full run. But the trailing jeep, which had wheeled around the truck to inspect the damage at the gate, was now doubling back toward them, and the armed guard on the passenger side was standing from his seat, rifle in hand, like a sniper rising from cover.

"Here come the cops," Barb said.

They must have seen the police arriving on Sharpe's camera, because Cole, coming in low and fast, and straight down Hardcastle Road, was focused solely on the man with the rifle, who was now shouldering his weapon.

"No!" Keira said. "He's going to shoot!"

The gunman tilted his head, taking aim. Cole was closing fast, the drone almost at ground level now. Then the man paused, ever so briefly, to wave someone out of his line of fire, but by then his body loomed massively on Cole's screen.

The screen flashed white. Cole wasn't sure if it was from the impact, a gunshot, or both. Then it went blank, everything gone, no signal at all.

"What's happened?" Sharpe yelled. "I've lost everything, what have you done?"

"Crashed it," Cole said. "Took him out. I hope. The cops will have to do the rest."

Sharpe began ranting about his equipment, about waste, about all sorts of incoherent things, but Cole was far from all that. He pulled off his headset, the controls useless now. All he knew for sure was that somewhere out there, maybe fifteen air miles away, Sharpe's fine new aircraft lay in ruins. Perhaps it had even exploded, although there certainly couldn't have been much fuel left in the tank.

But it was the girl he wondered about. The girl and her father, Mansur, and all the others, running for their lives just as the three children had done at Sandar Khosh. At the moment he had no clue whether they were living or dead, although he would certainly remember that last sight of them, running, the girl's stride lopsided as she swung her only arm, pumping it for all the speed she could muster, everyone's mouth open as they panted for breath.

Perhaps he had saved them. Perhaps he had guaranteed their destruction, triggering their ruin with his pursuit. If so, there would be a new hour of death to add to the daily timetable.

He blinked into the sunlight. The others were still staring at Sharpe's blank screen, dumbfounded, except for Keira, who was talking rapidly into her phone.

"Where are the cops?" he asked, hearing his own voice like it was someone else's. "What are they saying?"

"He's down. They say he's down."

"*Who* is? *Who's* down?"

"I don't know yet! Wait." She held up a hand. Everyone was still.

"The shooter. The shooter is down. The drone crashed right into him. The wing hit him, knocked him cold."

"What about the others? Put it on speaker, goddammit!" Cole's voice was hoarse.

"And the others?" she asked.

The answer came back crackly and shrill, and in copspeak, but clear enough for all to hear and understand.

"All parties safe. Six adults and one child, female, accounted for. All hostile parties disarmed and in custody."

Keira beamed at Cole. Now the others turned toward him. They knew his story, and now they knew its conclusion, and they seemed to be awaiting some utterance from him, a summation, especially the journalists, with their usual stock question in this kind of situation already brimming in their eyes: *How does it feel?*

Cole was too moved to speak. Overcome, he dropped to his knees and cried out, half sob and half laugh as a single thought seared his mind like a missile: A crash, yes, yet it was his greatest flight ever. Failure his salvation, with his eye in the sky now blinded and down.

CHAPTER THIRTY-EIGHT

THE POLICE AT THE county sheriff's office didn't know quite what to do with everybody. First they sorted out the rival parties—the IntelPro security guys in one room (except for the one who was out cold, who went to Easton Hospital in an ambulance), the Afghans to another, although no one spoke their language, and even though the little girl who was with them, the one prone to singing and skipping, kept escaping into an adjacent corridor to gawk at the vending machines.

But by the time the crowd from Keira's—an odd mix in its own right—showed up to start asking and then answering questions, pretty much everyone from the other two groups had been moved out of sight.

Cole ended up in a Captain Kerner's office, answering bemused questions about his role in the whole affair.

"So you were the one in control of the, uh, the *aircraft* in question?"

"Correct."

Kerner shook his head. "Well, from what I've been able to piece together from the officers on the scene, your, uh, *plane* crashed into some fellow from that security outfit, one of the, uh, kidnappers, for lack of a better word, although that's federal stuff and not for me to decide."

"Should I be hiring a lawyer?"

"Well, I guess you can if you want. Pay phone's in the hall, unless you've got a cell. But frankly I'm kind of at a loss as to what we might even charge you with, if we were to charge you at all. Bad piloting? Maybe, but that's probably some kind of FAA thing. Assault with a deadly weapon? Possibly. Although from the descriptions I've heard from the other officers at the, uh, the *event* in question, a crash is pretty much a crash any way you look at it."

"Pretty much. Like I said, my screen went blank there toward the end, so I've got no idea what really happened. If it hit somebody, obviously that's not a good thing. But by then I'd lost control of her. We were kind of out at the limit of our range, anyway. Maybe Mr. Sharpe could take you through some of the possibilities of mechanical failure. It's pretty much like I said earlier. We were in pursuit only as a matter of observation, as interested citizens. Which is why we phoned you guys to take care of it."

"Yeah. Well . . ." Kerner shook his head, as if uncertain what to say next.

"So am I free to go?"

"Just promise me one thing, how 'bout it."

"What's that?"

"No more playing with these toys of yours in county airspace. At least not until you fellows get the kinks worked out."

"I don't think I'll have any trouble keeping that promise."

Kerner sighed deeply and ran a hand through his thinning hair. "I gotta say, this is one time when we'll be happy to let the feds horn in to sort things out."

"Have they asked you to detain anyone?"

"Truthfully?"

"Sure."

"They haven't asked for shit. Hell, they can't even decide among themselves who they're sending down here, or from how many different agencies. I do know the Bureau's on the way, maybe because they always get involved. But the rest? After that shooting the other day they had so many guys down here with strange IDs that I kinda lost track."

"Then I'll be on my way."

"Okay, then."

Cole headed down the hallway toward the waiting room. Some good-byes would soon be in order, but he had already made up his mind about his next destination. He had decided to catch a bus to Saginaw. If his family turned him away, so be it, but he doubted they would. At some point fairly soon, he supposed, he would also have to make

amends with the Air Force about his whereabouts and living arrangements. But he had already received some pretty sound advice on that
front, from Riggleman, of all people.

He stepped into the waiting room to find Sharpe, seated alone.

"Where are all the others?"

"The scribblers took off. Looking for the Afghans, I think, or doing
whatever it is they do in these situations, making a goddamn nuisance
of themselves. They were already talking big about a book deal. For
two of them, anyway. I suppose that Steve fellow will just have to go
corporate. The little Air Force captain—"

"Riggleman?"

"Yes. He was trying to reach his general and wondering if he still
had a job. Good luck with *that*, I told him."

"Castle?"

"Disappeared. Not long after we got here. Back into the shadows
where he belongs."

Cole supposed that that should bother him. He still had more questions for the man, but doubted now that he'd ever get a chance to ask
them. Somehow it all seemed okay, mostly because he was still gliding on a powerful updraft of exhausted elation. For the moment he
was happy for any of the others to proceed and prosper however they
pleased, even Steve.

"You look done in," Sharpe said.

"In a good way. Mission fatigue."

"Dehydration, more likely." Sharpe nodded toward a bank of vending machines across the room and handed him a crumpled dollar bill.
"Here. Get yourself something to drink. I've got a ride coming. We'll
drive you back if you like."

"Sure, that would be nice."

Cole crossed the room slowly. He slid the dollar bill into the machine,
watched it roll back out, then finally got it to stay. He punched in his
selection and then listened to the can as it rumbled its way toward
the bottom. A long and sugary swallow, then Cole smiled to himself.
Behind him he heard a door opening, voices in greeting, laughter, a
slap on the back.

When he turned around, the fellow named Derek from the DIY
Drones meet-up was standing there in his ugly leather jacket, smiling

at Sharpe, who was smiling right back. The soft drink can began to feel a whole lot colder.

Derek caught his eye, nodded, and crossed the room. "Heard that was quite a neat bit of flying you did this morning. And with a twenty-knot wind, too. You did us proud."

"Us?"

He reached inside the leather jacket and handed Cole a red and white business card.

DEREK LESTER

VICE PRESIDENT FOR OPERATIONS

TRICORN ASSOCIATES

MCLEAN, VA

"We could use a man of your talents. For testing, mostly. No rush, though. Give me a call whenever you think you're ready."

Cole looked at Sharpe, who shrugged and smiled, perhaps a bit sheepishly, and then walked over and whispered something into Derek's ear. Derek nodded with an air of understanding before departing without a further word.

An awkward silence, which Sharpe finally broke.

"It's the one outfit that lets me operate pretty much as I please." Then, when Cole said nothing in reply, "Hey, it's pick your poison or lose your livelihood. The Pentagon made sure that was my only recourse. All my other clients cut and ran."

"So you went with Tricorn. What's the matter, IntelPro and Overton weren't hiring? And now they get everything you know, everything you develop. Their property, not yours."

"As if they all won't have it eventually, anyway. Hey, you got what you wanted."

"So did Derek."

"Which means all three of us come away from the table satisfied. So did the scribblers. And I'm sure certain members of Congress with an ax to grind will reap their own rewards once this fiasco begins coming to light. Isn't that the way the marketplace is supposed to work? Either way, I thought we made a pretty good team."

Sharpe held out his right hand, a gesture of either reconciliation or farewell. Cole stared at the hand but made no move to take it. He didn't even want to look again at Sharpe's face, although he supposed that at any moment now the man would be smiling, the joke on Cole, the rules having been changed yet again while he wasn't paying attention.

Cole turned and headed for the nearest door and entered a long hallway, not even knowing where he was going. Halfway down it he stopped to collect himself, breathing quickly, feeling the blood rush to his fingertips. Too much damn stimulation for one day.

A door clicked open behind him. He wheeled quickly, angrily, ready to lash out with both fists, only to see that it was a girl—*the* girl—staring up at him with an expression of abiding curiosity. Her eyes gazed without blinking, huge and brown, exactly as he had pictured them in so many dreams and nightmares, in so many waking moments back at his trailer in the desert.

Two women in Afghan clothing stepped into the hallway behind her, with a police officer bringing up the rear. The women said something to the girl in a language Cole didn't understand, but she did not turn to follow them toward the waiting room.

She just kept staring at the man who was staring at her.

"C'mon, sweetie," the policeman said. "Time to go."

The girl raised her arm, waved shyly—once only—and then turned. She broke into a trot to catch up with the two women, who were already heading out the door.

"Good-bye," Cole said hoarsely.

The word seemed to hang in the air for seconds after she departed.

ACKNOWLEDGMENTS

I would like to express my gratitude to several people from the 432nd Wing "Hunters" at Creech Air Force Base in Nevada, who assisted me during my research for this book by allowing me to see firsthand the way such missions operate. Thank you to Public Affairs Staff Sergeant Alice Moore for arranging access and showing me around the base; to Captain Gary Ford for a fascinating interview, to Lieutenant Colonel Lance "Sky" King for an interesting lecture, and, most of all, to the pilot-sensor team of Captain Nicholas "Hammer" Helms and Airman T. J. Masters, whose candid accounts and descriptions helped me gain a deeper understanding of the special pressures and demands of Predator missions. They also offered a valuable window onto the lifestyle of those soldiers who, for lack of better terminology, now serve their country as "commuter warriors" from locations based far from the field of combat.

For offering valuable updated advice on certain scenarios in Afghanistan, I thank journalists Nir Rosen and Dexter Filkins. I'd also like to thank the incomparable aircraft designer Pierre Sprey for his insights on the workings of the Pentagon with regard to the development of aircraft and weapons systems.